APOCALYPSE, *SOON!*

Mama G sat on a chair in the middle of the room . . . her dress was soaking wet and a blanket had been draped around her shoulders.

"What's wrong, Mama Grande?" I asked softly.

She shook her head. "I had to tell," she moaned. "The magic . . . Lenora . . . I had to tell her . . . They made me tell . . ."

"They?" I echoed. I knelt down in front of Mama G, tried to catch her eye. "Who are 'they', Mama Grande? Were they thieves? Burglars? Did gangers attack you?"

Mama G stood up suddenly and looked wildly around her. Her attention became riveted on the floor, although it was clear she was looking right past the objects that littered it. "The hole! The hole in the earth. It's the end. The end of the world! Oh blessed Virgin, the end!"

SHADOWRUN

BLOOD SPORT

Lisa Smedman

A ROC BOOK

ROC
Published by the Penguin Group
Penguin Putnam Inc., 375 Hudson Street,
New York, New York 10014, U.S.A.
Penguin Books Ltd, 27 Wrights Lane,
London W8 5TZ, England
Penguin Books Australia Ltd,
Ringwood, Victoria, Australia
Penguin Books Canada Ltd, 10 Alcorn Avenue,
Toronto, Ontario, Canada M4V 3B2
Penguin Books (N.Z.) Ltd, 182–190 Wairau Road,
Auckland 10, New Zealand

Penguin Books Ltd, Registered Offices:
Harmondsworth, Middlesex, England

First published by Roc, an imprint of Dutton Signet,
a member of Penguin Putnam Inc.

First Printing, January, 1998
10 9 8 7 6 5 4 3 2 1

Series Editor: Donna Ippolito

 REGISTERED TRADEMARK—MARCA REGISTRADA

ACKNOWLEDGMENTS

Thanks again to B.C. Science Fiction Association writers' workshop members who helped to critique this novel. Thanks also to Toni, for answering my various "trivia questions" on Catholicism, and to Luis for his help with the Spanish.

NORTH

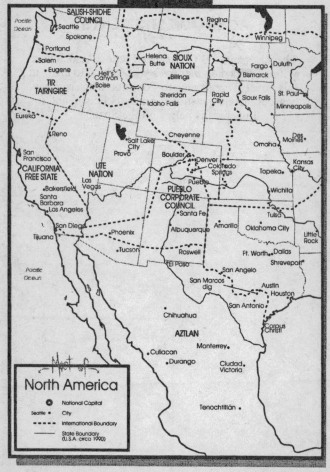

AMERICA

CIRCA 2057

QUÉBEC

Thunder Bay

Lake Superior

Sault Ste. Marie

Lake Huron

Lake Michigan

Milwaukee

Lansing

Detroit

L. Erie

Cleveland

Chicago   Gary

Springfield   Indianapolis

East St. Louis

Cincinnati

Louisville

Charleston

Memphis   Nashville   Knoxville

Jackson   Montgomery   Atlanta

Baton Rouge   Mobile   Albany

Birmingham

Gulf of Mexico

Quebec   Fredericton   Charlottetown

Montreal   Halifax

Ottawa   Montpelier   Augusta

Sudbury   Kingston   Concord   Boston

Toronto   L. Ontario   Albany

Buffalo   Hartford   Newark   Manhattan

Philadelphia

FDC

Roanoke   Richmond   Norfolk

Durham   Raleigh

Charlotte   Wilmington

Columbia

Charleston

Savannah

Jacksonville

Orlando

Tampa   West Palm Beach

Miami

Atlantic Ocean

UNITED CANADIAN AND AMERICAN STATES (U.C.A.S.)

CONFEDERATE AMERICAN STATES (C.A.S.)

YUCATAN PENINSULA

Progreso   Tizim   Puerto Azut

Mérida   Izamal

Campeche   YUCATAN

Tepich

CAMPECHE   QUINTANA ROO

Chetumal

GULF OF MEXICO

GUATEMALA

CARIBBEAN SEA

1

I knew it was going to be a bad day when I saw the dead snake on my doorstep that morning. I should have recognized it for the omen that it was. But at the time, it was just another annoyance.

Everything had gone wrong that week. On Monday, my computer caught a case of "Tourette's virus"—a nasty little program that seeded my outgoing reports with four-letter words, causing my clients to think I'd lost it. On Tuesday my car was vandalized and the jerk I hired to fix it tried to rip me off, not realizing that this was one woman who knew as much about bodywork as he did. On Wednesday, I came down with a head cold that settled in my sinuses, making my forehead pound and my thoughts go muzzy. And on Thursday I received a notice from the Internal Revenue Department via telecom, announcing that last year's return was going to be audited. Again. It was clear that the accountant who kept the books for my one-woman detective agency needed to be fired. Or burned at the stake, with my tax returns as fuel for the flames.

Friday . . . well, I still didn't know what more could go wrong, but it was already a bloody miserable day just the same. It had been raining steadily for the entire month of November, and Seattle residents were starting to joke about 2057 being the year when they'd finally need to build their arks. Nobody even looked at the sky any more; it was always the same lead-gray. The constant drizzle combined with the condensation in my basement flat to produce a faint miasma of mold. Not that I could smell it. My sinuses were filled with concrete. At least, that's how it felt.

The snake lay on my doorstep, spine bent at an acute angle just behind the head and its "throat" chewed open. I could guess who the culprit was. Pinkerton, my cat, usually practiced "catch and release." I'd found rats, starlings, moles—even a squirrel one time, although spirits only knew how Pinkerton had wrestled it in through his cat door—hiding under couches or peeking out at me from shelves. But this time, Pinkerton had gone for the kill.

The snake was an odd-looking specimen. Not the usual greenish-brown garter snake so common in the Pacific Northwest (and that Mama Grande always talks to while puttering in the garden), but instead a mottled buff and brown—desert camouflage colors—dotted with tiny flecks of brilliant turquoise. I'd never seen anything like it. Maybe it was one of the multitude of strange new creatures mutated by the magic of the Awakened world.

I picked the snake up by the tail and looked around for a place to put it. I considered burying the corpse, but getting a shovel meant unlocking the tool shed and I didn't want to get my hands muddy by scraping around in the flower bed. So I carried the snake out to the lane and dropped it in a trash can.

If I'd been thinking clearly, I would have been concerned that Mama Grande would see it. Rafael was at work until later that evening, and she'd be the only one to take out the trash before the truck came around in the afternoon. At the very least, I could have hidden the snake under one of the bags. But I just dropped it on top, in plain view.

As I put the lid back on the garbage can, I succumbed to a fit of sneezing. By the time it was over, my eyes were watering and my nose was running. The drizzle of rain had turned into a steady patter and my hair hung limp. So when Mama G opened her window and called to me to come inside, I opted to spend a little time warming up in her kitchen before setting out. Frag the appointment. I could be a little late for it, if I had to.

My self-appointed grandmother and her grandson Rafael live—lived—on the main floor of the rental house that also held my basement doss. It's an older building, dating from the middle of the last century—solidly blue collar, like the rest of the houses in Auburn. Square and boxy, its two-story bulk covered with stained gray stucco, the place has no pretenses. It probably never did.

The back steps leading up to the main floor are riddled

with dry rot. I constantly warned Mama G not to use them, but she just laughed at me and rolled her eyes. I guess when you come from a country that's been torn apart by civil war, a shaky staircase doesn't seem like much to worry about.

I climbed the steps, expecting my foot to go through a weak spot at any moment. With the way my luck had gone lately, a twisted ankle wouldn't have surprised me. But I made it to the top without injury. Miracles, it seemed, still happened.

As I reached the top, Mama G opened the wooden door and pushed open the torn screen door that fronted it. I hadn't heard the click of a lock, and so I scolded her. "Rafael spent a lot of time installing those voice-recognition locks, Mama Grande. You really should use them."

"Eso no los detendrá," she answered.

Some time ago, I'd uploaded the contents of a LinguaSoft into the permanent memory of my headware so that I could understand Aztlaner Spanish. That didn't mean I could always understand Mama G. "That won't stop *who*?" I asked. But she was already off in another world, bustling about the kitchen. I stepped inside, wiping my wet feet on the mat, and closed the door behind me. I activated the security system, even though I knew full well that Mama G would spend the day in the garden tending her plants— rain or no rain—and would probably leave the back door wide open.

I saw that Rafael had plugged up the holes in the door again. A month ago, Mama G had used his drill to bore a series of five-centimeter-wide holes near the bottom of the door. She said it let "the spirits" inside. As far as I could tell, the spirits amounted to nothing more than a cold breeze on the ankles. But to Mama G, they were real—old friends who shouldn't be forced to wait and knock. Hence the holes.

Mama G was following her usual routine, shuffling in a repetitive S-pattern at the center of the kitchen. It was what she always did when she wanted to say something but couldn't find the words, even in Spanish. It gave her time to think.

While she worked out her frustration, I looked around the room to see how the woman I'd come to regard as my grandmother was getting along. The ceiling was festooned with the usual collection of herbs, hung to dry from a series of screw-in hooks. Jesus in his crown of thorns stared mournfully down from a holographic portrait above the doorway; his slightly bulging eyes seemed to be following Mama G's progress around the kitchen. A chrome-legged table was covered with a layer of newspapers that protected it from the oily collection of motorcycle parts that Rafael had been working on. Beside them sat an ashtray filled with stubbed-out cigarettes. But the dishes had been done and none of the stove elements were on—Mama G's short-term memory seemed to be holding, even though her long-term retention was glitched.

I wondered what she wanted. Perhaps she was going to hint, once again, that I should get married. In her opinion, Rafael and I were the perfect match—we'd known each other for three years, ever since my brief stint working as a security guard, just after I left the Star. It didn't matter to Rosalita that we had nothing else in common—or that I wasn't interested in repeating my last disastrous relationship, no matter how aesthetically appealing Rafael's muscular body might be.

Rafael had put in a good word for me with the landlord after the previous tenant of the basement flat had bugged out. He was a good friend, and often came downstairs for a cup of soykaf or invited me up for some home brew. I liked his company—and adored his grandmother. But that was as far as it went. I wasn't going to marry any man who put his motorcycle first and his girlfriend of the week second.

Mama G's shuffling was slowing down. She moistened her lips with her tongue—her other nervous habit—then stopped suddenly and smoothed her white hair with a wrinkled hand. She stood blinking at me, one hand plucking at the fabric of her dress. Its colorful, pleated skirt was set with tiny round mirrors that had been appliquéed onto the cloth as protection against the evil eye. Then the confusion cleared from her eyes as she remembered what she had been about to tell me.

"Lenora." My name rolled off her tongue. Despite the LinguaSoft, I'd never been able to master rolling my Rs like a native Spanish-speaker. For the millionth time, I regretted not paying attention when my mother had tried to teach me

Spanish. But I'd only wanted to fit in, had dreaded the prejudice that she'd faced as an émigré to Seattle. Perhaps that was why I always insisted on being called Leni, and never used my full name, which was a mouthful: Lenora María Antonía de Torrés. But I made allowances for Mama G.

"You have *un resfriado*, a cold," she said. "I'll fix you some tea."

"I don't have time for tea," I protested, thinking Mama G was going to try one of her odd-tasting herbal remedies on me.

"No té, mí hija," she said. *"Magia."*

I was in for it now. Mama G's "magic" could take hours—days, even, when she really got wound up—and was totally bogus. Not one of her "spells" ever worked. At one point, in an effort to persuade her to stop wasting the money Rafael gave her on thaumaturgical supplies, I'd had a mage friend give her the Dumas Test. She hadn't registered any magical talent whatsoever. But that didn't stop her from trying to cure every ailment known to metahumanity with a host of bewildering incantations and homemade charms.

I suppose her lack of magical talent was for the best. At least I didn't have to worry about her accidentally conjuring up a malevolent spirit with all of her mumbo jumbo.

The trouble was, if you didn't humor Mama G and play along with her "magic," she became extremely agitated and upset. And I didn't want to hurt her feelings. I sighed and sat down at the table while she bustled off into the bedroom.

She returned carrying a ceramic pot, which she set on a clear space on the table. The pot was painted with Mayan hieroglyphs and stylized images of humans wearing tall, ornate headdresses. Made from cheap red clay, it had been chipped and smudged to look like an antique but had in fact been mass-produced in Aztlan for export to "collectors" around the world. Rafael had picked it up at a garage sale a few years ago, back when he was in his "discovering my roots" phase. When that ended, he had used it as a storage jar, to hold odds and ends. As far as I knew, the jar was still filled with a miscellaneous collection of bolts and screws.

Mama G took the lid off the jar and rummaged inside. A downy white feather spilled over the edge and drifted down onto the table. The jar must have been filled with them—although feathers weren't the only thing it held. Her eyes sparkling, Mama G lifted out a snake. For a moment, I thought she really had performed magic by resurrecting the creature I'd found dead on my doorstep. It was a twin of the one I'd just put in the trash, a buff and brown snake with turquoise flecks, as long and thin as a chopstick. But as it wound around Mama G's lean brown fingers, I heard rustling inside the feather-lined pot and realized she must have more than one snake inside it. I shuddered and placed the lid back on the jar, then watched with my nose wrinkled as she lifted the snake to her face and brushed her lips against it in a kiss. The tiny serpent flicked its tongue out in response.

"Wouldn't you rather just make me some herbal tea, Mama Grande?" I asked. I glanced hopefully at the battered kettle on the stove and started to rise. Skunky-tasting tea seemed the lesser of two evils.

"Shh." She frowned at me, her eyes darting to get that crazy edge that I knew all too well. "*La serpiente* is telling me his secrets."

The snake had disappeared. I hadn't seen Mama G lower her hand but presumed she'd set the snake down somewhere. Maybe it had curled up in a fold of her skirt. But when she stood and crossed to the sink to fill a bowl with water, nothing fell to the ground. I wondered where the creature had gone. Perhaps it had already slithered onto the floor and away.

Mama G placed the bowl on the table between us, opened a bag of dried corn she'd taken from the cupboard, and began dropping kernels one by one into the water. She studied them intently, muttering to herself. "Ah, it floats," she would say. Or, "It sinks. It has come from the south. The cold brings the sickness, and the cold shall carry it away."

Just as I started getting restless, her hand darted out and caught mine in a tight grip. Before I could protest, she plunged my hand into the water. Strangely, it felt ice cold—already my hand was going numb.

Mama G stared at a point on the wall behind me and began to chant, still holding my hand under the water. I didn't recognize the language—in the year she'd lived with us, I'd never heard her use anything even remotely similar. It certainly wasn't Spanish. It was more glottal, less melodic. Lots of "ah" vowels and "tl" combinations. I'd never heard it before. I thought I recognized the name Quetzalcóatl—the serpent god of the Aztlaner religion—but I couldn't be sure.

I sneezed violently, but Mama G held fast to my wrist. I had to use my left hand to fumble an already soggy tissue out of my pocket and wipe my nose, which had suddenly started to run again. My sinuses felt as if someone were blowing up a balloon behind my forehead—a balloon that was ready to burst. I sniffled, hoping Mama G would finish soon.

No such luck. Now her upper body swayed back and forth in time with her chant. She wet her lips several times and stared unblinkingly past me. Although her eyes were unfocused, her forehead was wrinkled in concentration. I'd never seen her look so intense. It was a bit unnerving, and if I didn't know better I'd swear she really was casting a spell.

She switched suddenly to Spanish: "*La serpiente* says . . . she says . . . the blood. Jesus' blood on the cross . . . the tree . . . the crossroads. Where the priest walks, the ground shakes. Beware the priest whose magic . . . beware the spirits . . . Oh!" She shrieked and leaped to her feet. "His head! They have taken his head!" My hand emerged from the bowl, dripping water all over the table. Mama G gripped it like a drowning woman, so hard it actually hurt. Her whole arm trembled.

I didn't like the sound of this at all. Mama G often mumbled to herself or talked nonsense to her plants while she tended them, but this was something of a different order. She was scaring herself. She was scaring me. "Mama Grande!" I said sharply. "What are you talking about? Nobody's taken anybody's head."

She let out a long, hissing sigh and her shoulders dropped. Her grip relaxed and her eyes refocused. She seemed surprised to find herself standing. I pulled my hand free of hers and warmed it under my opposite armpit.

"It is done," she whispered. "Your cold is gone. I have sent the airs of sickness back to the mountains."

"*Muchas gracias,*" I responded automatically. I sniffled and found I still couldn't breathe through my nose. My sinuses were blocked. But then, I hadn't expected the "spell" to work, anyhow. I peered at Mama G. Her face seemed more care-worn than before, but it may have just been the kitchen's harsh fluorescent lighting. "Are you all right?"

"Muy bien," she answered after a pause. "Just a little tired. Why?"

"You don't remember what you said just now? About the blood of Christ and someone stealing his head?" I glanced up at the religious holo above the door. Aside from the clothes on her back, it was the only personal item she'd brought with her on the long journey from the Yucatán to Seattle. What was Mama G doing with a portrait of Jesus anyhow? I thought Catholicism was banned in Aztlan. The thing was creepy, with its puncture wounds and moving trickles of blood. No wonder it was giving Mama G waking nightmares.

She ignored my questions. She seemed to have no recollection of what had just transpired. "You are going to work today, *sí?*" she said in a perfectly normal tone of voice. "I will make you some *comida* to take with you."

"I really should be going now, Mama Grande. I'm supposed to be meeting a client who wants me to run a financial scan on a potential business partner." I glanced at my watch. "I'm supposed to meet him at . . ."

"That is not the work you were meant to do," Mama G said. "But it will come, soon enough." She had already opened the fridge and was pulling out tortillas and roast chicken. I didn't have the heart to tell her that my second appointment of the day would take place at a restaurant over lunch. Instead, I accepted the food in its wax-paper wrapping and tucked it into the pocket of my jacket.

I fished out the keystick for my car, then paused. I felt torn. Should I stay with Mama G, in case she had another lapse like the one just now? She seemed all right, but it was hard to tell. Lingering guilt gnawed at me. I hadn't been there for my own grandmother, on the night she finally died after lying in a coma for two weeks. I'd been a Lone Star rookie then, putting in twelve-hour days, and had put off my hospital visit until the next morning. I didn't realize that one night was all my grandmother had left.

Back then, work had seemed more important. But after arriving at the hospital and finding only an empty bed, I'd vowed, in future, to always be there for the people I cared about. Even if it meant some inconveniences—like blowing a contract. Besides, Mama G had done a lot for me in the year I'd known her. When I'd been laid low with the flu and fever for a week last winter, lying out in bed like an invalid, she'd sponged my head and fed me hot chocolate. I suspect the cocoa was laced with "medicinal" herbs—it had tasted a little odd. But it had been one of the few things I could choke down, and it was made with love. You can't buy medicine like that.

"Are you sure you're going to be all right, Mama Grande? I could cancel my first meeting . . ."

As Mama G picked up the ceramic jar, shaking her head, I looked warily around for the missing snake. I didn't want to step on it. Bad enough that one of her "serpent friends" lay dead in the trash can; I didn't want to be responsible for injuring another one.

"No, no. *Cuídate, mí hija.*" She tried to usher me out the back door, but I insisted on going out the front way. I still didn't trust the steps, and I wanted to make sure the back door remained locked—at least for a little while.

Thanking Mama G, I stepped out into the drizzle and made sure she shut the door behind me. Traffic hissed past as I descended the steps and pretended to head for the sidewalk. I stole a glance behind me and saw Mama G in the window. I kept thinking she'd let the curtain fall, but she didn't budge. She just stood there with the jar cradled in the crook of her arm, staring at me. There was no way I could sneak around back and remove the body of the snake from the trash can. I turned and headed to where my car was parked—and forgot all about the snake, until much, much later.

As I stepped onto the sidewalk, my attention was briefly caught by a man and a woman who had just gotten out of a parked car and who were glancing up and down the street as if searching for something. Call it an ex-cop's instincts, but they struck me as suspicious. I scanned their faces: tanned skin, dark hair, a slight Amerind cast to their features. They looked Hispanic, like everyone else in this neighborhood. I guessed their age as early twenties.

The woman was pretty, with high cheekbones and long dark hair, but her expression seemed cold, closed. She wore a black skirt cut in a style that was popular a decade ago, a white blouse with a bright yellow flower pattern, and

low-heeled vinyl pumps that looked brand new. The man
was dressed in dark slacks, shoes that were cheap but polished, and a cotton shirt under a summer jacket that was too
light for this damp climate. He looked overly muscular, as if
he had synthetic muscle under that tanned skin. When he
raised his hand to run it through his hair, I could see the
slotted housing where a retractable spur had been implanted.
I wondered if he was intentionally letting me see that he had
bodyware. The pair looked clean-cut, but even so . . .

I stared directly at them, letting them know they'd been
seen, their presence in this neighborhood noted.

The pair's tanned skin and clothing much too light for our
rain-soaked city marked them as out-of-towners. So did their
car—it was brand new, one of the recently introduced two-
seater Mitsubishi Runabouts. I could see a "Rent-a-Runabout"
sticker on the bumper.

I was debating whether to say something to them when the
woman whispered to her partner and stuffed something she'd
been holding in her hand into a leather purse that hung at her
hip. I only caught a glimpse, but I recognized simsense chips
before they disappeared into her bag. I wondered if they
were BTL. I didn't want that drek being dealt in my
neighborhood. I'd seen too many kids messed up by so-
called Better Than Life simsense. Adults too, for that matter.

"Buenos días, señorita," I said, catching her eye and trying to look like an interested customer. "Got any dreams for
sale?"

"Dreams?" She was a good actress. She seemed genuinely
confused.

"Dream chips. Brain strainers. You deal BTL, right?"

"Oh." Recognition dawned in her eyes. "Oh no. These are
religious recordings." She pulled some of the chips from her
bag and offered them to me. They all looked identical, in
plain yellow cases with red lettering over a multi-colored
cross.

"I see you have a chipjack," she said. "Do you live in this
neighborhood? Could I leave one of these with you and call
on you next week to talk about our faith?"

The male edged up on the other side of me. "Do you agree
that the world has become corrupt?" he asked, an earnest

look on his face. "That God has turned his face from us? Would you like to learn how you can survive the apocalypse that is to come?"

The fanatical gleam in their eyes, combined with their squeaky-clean appearance, clinched it: they were missionaries. The type who go door to door saving souls. The last thing I had time for this morning was a religious debate. I waved the chips away, and the woman put them back in her bag.

I mentally slotted the pair in the "no threat" category and muttered an apology for my suspicions. They'd have fun with Mama G, if they knocked on her door. She'd have no use for the simsense chips, but she'd have a wiz time talking religion with them. She'd probably keep them there for hours, arguing that Christ and Quetzalcóatl were one and the same.

"Sorry," I told the earnest young woman. "I only believe in Asphalt, god of parking. I'm going to make an offering to him now, to make sure I find a space where I'm going. Would you care to contribute to the cause? A nuyen in a parking meter is the usual tithe, although Asphalt also occasionally demands blood. That's why there are so many traffic accidents."

The missionaries' eyes widened and they both took a step back from me—as if I were the crazy one. At the time, I enjoyed the reaction—I liked messing with the minds of religions zealots. Only later did I realize that what I'd said had a special meaning to them.

I smiled as I turned toward my car. "Potholes are the work of the devil," I told them with a wink.

As I climbed into my Ford Americar, I realized suddenly that the vice grips had eased their hold on my sinuses and that I could breathe through my nose again. Not only that but the rain had stopped—at least for the moment.

I eyed my hand, which was just starting to return to its normal temperature, wondering . . . then I shook my head. Nah. The fact that my cold had temporarily gone on hold after Mama G's vanishing-serpent trick and hand-dunking was as much coincidence as the rain stopping after I'd crossed my fingers this morning and wished that it would.

There wasn't any real magic involved, I decided as I drove away.

It was the second incorrect assumption I'd made in that many minutes. I should have listened to my instincts, no matter how foolish they seemed. But it wouldn't have mattered. For Mama G, it was already too late.

2

When I returned home that evening, I could tell something was wrong as soon as I saw Rafael's bike. It's a sleek Harley Scorpion with a distinctive gold-on-black paint job and plenty of custom work. Rafael dreams of becoming a pro in the combat biker leagues some day, so he's always modifying the bike, tuning it and tinkering with it. The crowning glory is a flag from last year's conference finals— supposedly the flag the Seattle Timber Wolves used to score the winning goal. The flag is valuable—and easy to boost, since it's clipped to the back of the bike so that it wags in the slipstream like a wolf's tail. Rafael always unclips it before he goes into the house. And he never leaves the bike lying side-down in the middle of the lawn.

I stepped around the Scorpion and took the steps two at a time. The front door was open, and from inside I could hear the sound of Mama G crying. Rafael was in my face as soon as I entered the house.

"What did you do to upset Mama Grande?" he bellowed.

I immediately thought of the dead snake. "I'm sorry," I said. "I didn't mean for her to see the snake. Pinkerton killed it and I couldn't think of where else to put—"

"What the frag are you talking about, Leni? What snake?"

I paused. Rafael's a big guy, topping two meters. Ork, but with an Hispanic cast to his features and sleek, dark hair pulled back in a pony tail. He's bright, but doesn't look it— his ork blood shows in a knobby brow, and his outthrust jaw gives him a belligerent, tough-guy look. It's probably why he has so much trouble getting a job; employers won't take the time to hear him out and realize that his wetware is fully functional. But he's got a good heart. He really cares for his grandmother—even if he gets a little overprotective at times.

"Slow down, Raf," I told him. "Chill. First tell me what's wrong with Mama Grande. What's happened to her—and why do you think I'm to blame?"

"See for yourself," he told me, and turned so that I could squeeze past him. And that was a relief. Rafael's wide as a door and solid as cement—you don't try to push past him unless you want to get squashed flat.

I hurried down the hall to the kitchen. It looked as if someone had trashed it. Herbs had been torn from the ceiling and scattered about, dishes were knocked onto the floor, and the motorcycle parts Rafael had been working on were lying by the door, as if the table had been tipped over and only recently been righted. Mama G sat on a chair in the middle of the room, clutching a piece of the ceramic jar from which she'd drawn the snake earlier. Her dress was soaking wet and a blanket had been draped around her shoulders. Downy white feathers drifted across the floor, but there was no sign of the snakes that the jar had once held. Like the first serpent, they'd done a vanishing act.

I knelt beside Mama G and put an arm around her narrow shoulder. Tears spilled down her face, dripping onto the piece of painted ceramic she held. I saw with relief that her hands were undamaged and that her arms had only minor bruises—if she had trashed her own kitchen, at least she hadn't seriously hurt herself. But at the same time I felt a pang of guilt for having left her alone that day.

"What's wrong, Mama Grande?" I asked softly.

She shook her head. "I had to tell," she moaned. "The magic . . . Lenora . . . I had to tell her . . . She made me . . . I tried to . . . I shouldn't have . . ."

She looked right through me. I shivered. "Mama Grande? It's me, Leni. Lenora. I'm here. Talk to me."

"I had to tell . . ." The rest was a mumble.

Rafael knelt among the debris on the floor and took his grandmother's hands, wrapping them in his own. He glared at me, as if challenging my right to comfort her.

"I found her standing in the front yard," he said. "She didn't seem to know where she was—she thought she was still in the Yucatán. She wouldn't go back into the house— said it was filled with evil and that the spirits had abandoned it. I finally got her inside, but I still can't get her to let go of that broken jar or to change her clothes. She just keeps saying you forced her to tell you something."

His nostrils flared in anger. "You didn't ask her about Az . . . about her homeland, did you?" he rumbled. "You know how upset she gets when anyone mentions the civil war down there. If you stirred up old memories and got her upset . . ."

The threat in his voice was unmistakable. I was glad Rafael and I were friends. He'd have flatlined anyone else without even asking for an explanation. I fought down my own anger at the accusation. It wasn't going to help the situation.

"That's not the way it was," I said. Quickly, I explained what had happened that morning, describing Mama G's "cure" for my sinus cold—a "cure" that was still holding, spirits be thanked, although it was probably nothing more than coincidence. I also described her strange outburst. "She seemed fine when I left. The only thing I can think of that might have upset her was finding the snake in the trash can."

"Don't be *loco*," Rafael shot back. "Mama Grande loves snakes. She isn't afraid of them."

"No, I mean . . . I think it was a pet." I stood and glanced out the back window. The garbage can was exactly where I'd left it, lid in place. If it was the dead snake that had set off Mama G, she'd have started her trail of destruction outside. But the damage was confined to the kitchen. It almost looked as if a struggle had taken place in the room.

"They made me tell . . ." she whispered.

"*Cálmate,* Mama Grande," Rafael urged. He was still trying to pry the broken bit of ceramic out of her hands. "We'll get you dried off, and you can rest in bed . . ."

I picked up on the change in pronouns right away. "They?" I echoed. I knelt down in front of Mama G, tried to catch her eye. "Who are 'they,' Mama Grande? Were they thieves? Burglars? Did gangers attack you?"

Mama G stood up suddenly and looked wildly around her. Her attention became riveted on the floor, although it was clear she was looking right past the objects that littered it.

"The hole! The hole in the earth. It's the end. The end of the world! Oh blessed Virgin, the end!"

"What is she looking at?" Rafael reared to his feet. "What's upsetting her now?" He followed the path of Mama G's wildly staring eyes, then stopped to pick something up. "This?"

It was a chip case. I took it from Rafael and turned it over, holding it by the edges. Even though I didn't have the equipment necessary to lift a print from it, old police habits die hard. It was empty. The simsense chip it had once held was gone.

The case itself was made of cheap, glossy cardboard. The back was blank—it didn't even list the studio where the chip had been recorded—but the front was printed a gaudy yellow with lurid red lettering. There was no title—just a long, rambling message in Spanish that sounded vaguely like a Biblical passage. It was printed over a cross with multi-colored arms of red, black, white, and blue.

Heed the signs! it shouted in bold letters. *The end of the world is at hand! Ravenous beasts, destruction by earthquake, wind, flood and flame. The end of our age and the beginning of the new era. But a few—those who keep the faith—shall reap the riches, even among the ruins. They shall be rewarded. Power and glory shall be theirs and they shall rule heaven and earth, hand in hand with those who shall rise.*

The text seemed to be saying that the coming apocalypse would be a good thing for the faithful—that the righteous would be taken up from the Earth and duly rewarded. A line at the bottom urged the reader to slot the chip and learn how to save his or her soul.

The thing reminded me of a trideo infomercial I'd seen once, put out by one of the oddball Christian faiths. I couldn't remember details, but the message had been similar: good Christians being called by God to experience eternal bliss in heaven. I'd laughed at the images of multitudes rising out of their graves—it was reminiscent of a bad horror trideo I'd once seen. I assumed this chip had contained something similar.

I showed the chip case to Mama G, then pointed to the

debris in the kitchen. "Was it the missionaries who did this?" I asked.

She nodded mutely.

It all fit. The young couple I'd seen earlier that day had probably boosted the religious recordings—and their nice conservative clothes—to use as a ruse to get elderly folk like Mama G to open their doors. I imagined them charming their way into her kitchen, then trashing things in an effort to scare her into telling them where her valuables were hidden. Except that neither she nor Rafael had any. Mama G, in her confused state, was blending the apocalyptic message she'd read on the case with the violence she had just experienced. No wonder she was terrified to the point of being incoherent.

I started to explain this to Rafael, but something gnawed at me. There was one piece that didn't fit. A rental car? Too easy to trace—unless it had been boosted. Most thieves were pretty stupid—I'd heard of one extortionist who sent his ransom demands using the telecom in the office of his parole officer, not realizing that the signature and time at the end of the message were fingering him. But these two hadn't looked stupid, which made the rental car an unlikely choice. Those vehicles had a limited speed and range, and were rigged to send out a signal that told the rental company's computers exactly where the vehicle was at any given moment. The car's electronic brain automatically alerted the company and shut down the electric engine if the vehicle entered any of the city's "no go" areas like Hell's Kitchen.

"I had to tell her," Mama G whispered as Rafael put the blanket back around her shoulders and at last was able to gently pull the ceramic fragment from her hand. "Her magic went inside my head. She made me remember . . . She made me think of it."

"Made you think of what, Mama Grande?" I asked. It sounded as if Mama G had been the victim of a spell. But she didn't seem to hear my question.

Fresh tears poured down her cheeks. "She pulled it out of my head. I didn't want to tell . . . But the spirits wouldn't protect me. They weren't strong enough. They were weak. I was weak . . ."

She looked intently at Rafael, as if noticing him for the

first time. "Eduardo? Where is the baby? You must take him to El Norte, before things get worse. He should grow up somewhere safe. Don't worry about me—nobody will bother with an old woman. You and Luísa must go. I have friends who will help you." She held up one hand, as if stopping a protest. "No, no! I will not hear it. You must go. This week. It is all arranged."

"Who's Eduardo?" I asked Rafael

"She thinks she's talking to my father," he said. "She must think it's the year our family fled from Aztlan. When I was just a baby."

He turned to Mama G. "Grandmother, it's me, Rafael. I'm grown up. You're in Seattle now. This *is* El Norte. Eduardo died crossing the border, but I made it out. And so did *mí madra*. Don't you remember?"

Mama G stared mutely at him, lost in the memories that had, for her, somehow swapped places with the present. She rubbed absently at the scar on her right arm—a legacy of the violence that had gripped her part of Aztlan in recent decades.

I thought back to what Rafael had told me about his family. His parents had never been revolutionaries, but they were forced to flee Aztlan just the same. Shopkeepers with a grocery store in a small town near Mérida, they'd been accused of supplying food to the rebels, and so they ran the risk of being "disappeared" by the government. They sold the store and fled north, into the Confederated American States.

Rafael's father was killed during the border crossing, but his mother made it. She applied for refugee status to the United Canadian American States, came to Seattle, and set up another grocery store, earning enough to raise her son on her own. But then a Stuffer Shack moved in next door, go-gangers began hanging out in its parking lot, and the store began losing business. Luísa died in a car crash when Rafael was still in his teens, and the store went under shortly thereafter.

If Rafael's mother had relatives in the Yucatán, she hadn't kept in touch with them. It wasn't until the Aztlan Freedom League contacted Rafael that he realized he had a grandmother.

Mama G started to shiver. Her tongue darted rapidly in and out, wetting her lips, and she began swaying from side to side. "The demons!" she hissed in a low, urgent voice. "They will come! And with them the end of the world . . ." Then she sagged in Rafael's arms.

Frightened, I grabbed her wrist and felt for a pulse. It was weak—but there. Her eyes were open but she was wincing. "Lenora? Rafael?" she said. "Where am I? My head . . . it hurts."

I brushed a strand of white hair from her eyes and touched her forehead. It felt slightly feverish.

"We'd better get those wet clothes off her and get her to bed," I told Rafael. "I didn't like the look of that shiver. She may be mildly hypothermic."

We got Mama G dried off and tucked in under her electric blanket. I fetched my old police-issue medkit and applied a mild pain killer and tranq patch combo. Her mind seemed to have returned to the present, but her eyes were still wild and fearful. When she at last closed them and drifted off into a troubled sleep, Rafael dragged me back into the kitchen.

"I'm going to grease the fraggers who did this," he said as he exhaled, pointing at the mess on the floor. His hand balled into a huge fist. "I'll make them sorry for what they did to my Mama Grande."

"We don't even know who they are, Raf," I told him quietly.

His eyes bored into mine. "But you could find out," he said urgently. "You know how to track someone down. And you have connections."

"I could . . ." I paused, lost in thought. If I did hunt down the pair of fake missionaries and give their personal data to Rafael, he would ice them for sure. Or frag them up so bad they'd wish they were dead. Rafael had a lot of anger in him. Usually he channeled it into his sports—he played on an amateur Urban Brawl team—or else blew off steam by blasting his motorcycle through the toughest turf he could find. But in defense of his grandmother and his honor, he'd get himself into trouble for sure. And probably into the slam.

And if I gave the data to the Star instead, what would come of it? Nothing had been stolen—the worst charges the missionary pair would face were trespass and vandalism. With Mama G in a confused state, it would be impossible to prove that they had uttered threats, or even that they had been the ones to trash the place. Proving that they had committed magical assault by using a spell on her against her will would be even harder. By the time Lone Star's mages arrived on the scene, any traces that would have been left in the astral would be long gone. So my choices were between Rafael's over-kill vengeance or a judicial slap on the wrist and the pair being back on the streets the day after their preliminary hearing.

Rafael took my hesitation as refusal. His face turned ugly. "I could hire you," he said in a low voice. "If that's what it would take . . . I . . . I could put my bike up as collateral . . ."

"You don't need to do that, Raf," I reassured him. "You're the last person I'd charge for my time. I'm just as angry about this as you are. I want to see justice done, too."

I held up the chip case. "This is one starting point," I told him. "Maybe the pair lived near the church they boosted this from. And the rental car is another. But there's something that tells me this is more than just a home invasion and robbery attempt. The pieces just aren't fitting together."

I thought for a moment. "Do you think the Aztlan Freedom League might be able to tell us anything about this? They only smuggled Mama Grande out a year ago—maybe someone's still looking for her."

Rafael shrugged. "I don't know. Maybe."

"How did they get in touch with you?" Rafael had never given me the details. He'd been deep into the cloak and dagger stuff and had apparently sworn an oath of secrecy—one that even precluded telling his best friend. At the time I'd been busy and just let it ride. But now it might be relevant.

"They said they were the same group who helped my parents—and me—to come north," he said. "I guess they remembered my name, even if I was only a baby at the time. When they couldn't find anyone else to take Mama Grande, they looked me up."

I winced at that one. Finding the right Rafael Ramirez in

all of the nations that lay north of the Aztlan border would have been an impossible task. Instant data overload—unless the searcher already knew to localize the search to the Seattle telecommunications grid. Had Rafael's mother kept in touch with the AFL, letting them know that she'd settled in Seattle, and had the AFL retained this information all these years, until it came time to smuggle Rosalita out? It didn't seem credible. And why hadn't Rafael's mother ever told him he had a grandmother in Aztlan? Didn't she realize that Mama G was still alive? Was staying in contact with someone in Aztlan really that difficult? Maybe the rebel uprising was more disruptive than the Azzie tridcasts admitted.

Or maybe . . . Nah, I was just being paranoid. For one wild moment, I'd wondered if the Freedom League had suckered Rafael into taking in a woman who wasn't really his grandmother. Someone they needed to hide from the Aztlan government. And what better hiding place than with someone who had no real connection to Mama G whatsoever, but who could be tricked into thinking she was a blood relative?

But that was crazy. Mama G was a sweet, harmless, and somewhat *loco* elderly woman who talked to the snakes in her garden, walked around her kitchen in circles, and puttered about with supposed herbal remedies. She was hardly the stuff of which dangerous revolutionaries were made.

"Ramirez is a pretty common last name," I pointed out.

"Yeah," Rafael agreed. "José said he had a hard time finding me. But the AFL didn't want to just dump Mama Grande in Houston. She wasn't able to take care of herself, and needed somewhere to live and someone to take care of her. And so they made a point of tracking me down."

"The guy from the AFL said his name was José?" I said. It was probably the Azzie equivalent of Mr. Johnson. "What was his last name?"

Rafael shook his head. "He never told me. I figured he needed to keep a low profile."

"Could you get in touch with him if you needed to?"

"Don't know," Rafael answered. "Maybe. He told me to post a message to a particular chat group when Mama Grande and I got back to Seattle, to let him know we'd arrived safely. As far as I could see it was just a bunch of people talking about their favorite hot peppers or shooting the breeze with friends. I had strict instructions: log on, thank him for sending me the banana peppers, and say that they had arrived safely. That was the code. The chat group was called the Salsa Connection. I don't even know whether the AFL still monitors it."

He gestured at the mess on the kitchen floor. "You don't think the AFL had anything to do with this, do you? They were the ones who helped Mama Grande."

"They never explained what happened to make her flee the country?" I asked.

Rafael's eyes grew hard. "She's just another refugee," he answered. "A civilian who got in the way—either of the Azzie government or the Yucatán rebels. Her village was destroyed and she had nowhere else to go. She'd seen enough war—all the violence down there made her a little *loco*. She needed someone to take care of her."

"Or so 'José' told you," I muttered under my breath.

I could see from Rafael's eyes that he hadn't entirely believed the story himself. That the possibility had entered his mind that Mama G had deliberately done something—inconceivable though it might seem—to slot the Azzies off. But he needed to believe a simpler story. He'd been a lonely man, an orphan who yearned for a family. That's what the "discovering my roots" phase had been all about. He wanted Mama G to be exactly what "José" said she was. A frail grandmother who needed the support of a strong, protective grandson.

"What did you just say?" he asked me.

"I'll see what I can turn up," I told him. "I'll let you know as soon as I find out anything." My mind was made up. For now, I'd find out who the two fake missionaries were and what they'd wanted with Mama G—then decide what to do about it later.

"What can I do?" Rafael asked.

"Do you ever talk to the neighbors?" I asked.

"Some of them."

"Ask around," I suggested. "See if the 'missionaries' called on anyone else today, or if they just came here. Let me know what you find out."

In hindsight, I should have told Rafael to keep a close watch on Mama G. But I thought that the threat to her had passed. The pair who had messed her up with magic today had gotten what they came for. They'd made her "tell"—whatever that meant. I didn't think they'd come back.

They didn't. But someone else did.

3

I spent most of Saturday trying to follow up the one lead I had on the two missionaries. By the time I questioned the elf working the car-rental desk at SeaTac Airport, I was bagged and discouraged. She was young, maybe seventeen or so, and regarded me skeptically as I finished my story. Willowy and soft-looking, with long blonde hair, but with enough street smarts not to take my bogus story at face value—even if it was coming from a registered private detective.

"The guy's been pestering my client for several days," I told her. "Lurking outside her door, following her as she goes to work each day, waiting there for her when she gets home at night. He's some sort of nutcase, a wannabe boyfriend who won't take no for an answer and who won't even give me his name. It's creeping her out. She wants to know who this guy is. The only clue she was able to give me is that he had a Rent-a-Runabout when he sat parked outside her place all day yesterday."

The elf stared at me, tapping the counter with long fingernails that had been replaced with "mood nails"—motion-sensitive implants that changed color every few seconds. She had expensive tastes for someone who worked at a job like this.

"So?" she said.

I pointed at the black plastic bubble that hid the counter's security camera. "So I'd like to look through your security recordings, starting with yesterday, to see if I recognize the guy. I'll scan through them in fast mode; it shouldn't take more than an hour or so."

She was dressed in a tight black skirt, high heels, and sequin-spangled blouse—hardly the sort of thing you'd wear to a day job. She reminded me more of the hookers you see down on . . . I shook off the thought, not wanting any reminders of the reason I'd left Lone Star.

Since it was Saturday night, it was a safe bet that the girl had already changed out of her work clothes and would be heading out to a club the instant her shift ended. She glanced at the clock behind her. "We're closing in fifteen minutes. You'll have to come back tomorrow."

I sighed. I'd been to six different Rent-A-Runabout agencies already that day, and was getting more than a little bit frustrated. I'd started with those closest to home and worked outward in a spiral from there, without any success. Now that I was here, I didn't want to fight the airport traffic and pay SeaTac's exorbitant parking fees twice. Besides, I had a strong hunch about this one. This time, I was going to listen to my instincts.

The clock read 10:20 p.m.—my guess was that the agency was supposed to be open for another forty minutes but that the biff behind the counter was trying to duck out early. Behind me, a steady trickle of passengers flowed back and forth through the terminal. None were renting cars—most were headed for the taxi stands outside. A constant babble of announcements competed with muzak for my attention, but the counter girl seemed adept at tuning it out.

"How much do you make an hour?" I asked her.

"Why?" She looked at me suspiciously.

I dropped my voice so the security system wouldn't pick it up. "I'll make this worth your while. I'll pay double your hourly rate for as long as it takes me to look through the vids." I pulled a credstick out of my pocket. "First hour paid up front, whether it takes me that long or not. You'll still be out of here early enough to go out clubbing. Come on, it isn't chill to show up before midnight anyway."

The elf's eyes narrowed as she thought about it. "I make fifteen nuyen an hour."

I knew it was a lie. "Fine. Thirty nuyen up front. Deal?"

She smiled. "Deal."

I stepped behind the counter and bent down to look at the closed-circuit video recording system. It was a pretty basic unit, but one that allowed me to fast-forward or reverse through a day's recordings by skipping ahead or back five minutes at a time. I started with yesterday's data, choosing a start time that was half an hour earlier than when I'd spoken with the "missionaries" on the street outside my place. I skipped back through the tape as fast as possible, pausing any time I saw anyone with Hispanic features. There were quite a few possibles, and I had to double check more than once, due to the fuzziness of the playback unit's tiny flatscreen.

After forty-five minutes, the elf was getting restless. There'd been only one customer during that time, and now the counter was officially closed. She sat on the shelf at the back of the booth, swinging her legs and boring holes into my back with her eyes. Nuyen or not, she wanted out of there. It was already 11:05.

I was just about to tell her to chill when I saw what I was looking for. I powered up the sound on the monitor, just to be sure. The screen showed two figures who matched the "missionaries" to a T, standing at the counter and talking to a rental clerk.

"Gotcha," I said. I turned toward the elf and stabbed a finger at the screen. "That's him. He rented a car at—"I glanced back at the monitor's display—"approximately seven a.m. the day before yesterday." I skipped back to the beginning of that segment, when the pair arrived at the counter, slotted a blank chip into the unit, and made a copy of the entire transaction. I'd review it later, in a quieter place.

I looked up at the elf. "Could you access a record for me by time and date?" I asked. "I'd like any data you can provide on this rental. I'd also appreciate it if you could access your computer-monitoring system and tell me where the vehicle is currently located."

The wary look was back in the girl's eye. "I don't know if I should do that," she said. "Customer information is confidential. My boss . . . It's not like you're a cop or anything." She spread her hands, flashing fingernails that had gone a deep crimson.

"I'm a private detective . . ."

It wasn't working.

"Look," I said, tucking the chip away in a jacket pocket. "I'll give you another thirty nuyen for the data. It shouldn't take more than a minute of your time."

"Fifty."

I started to grind my teeth, but it turned it into a smile instead. This was for Mama G. "Fifty, then. Do it."

My time estimate was bang on. It took less than a minute for her to call up the file. The woman had been the one who'd rented the car—which meant that I had to convince the elf that this was probably a close friend of the "stalker" and could lead me to him. The female turned out to be an Aztlan national by the name of Dolores Clemente. She had come to Seattle on a tourist visa, according to the passport she'd used as ID when renting the car. She and her male accomplice were probably both from that country—my guess was that they'd rented the Runabout as soon as they cleared customs. They'd paid in advance for a three-day rental with a certified credstick. They had until six a.m. tomorrow to return the car to any Seattle Rent-a-Runabout agency.

"Can you show me where the car is now?" I asked the elf.

Grudgingly, she touched the icon on the screen that activated the vehicle's log. A pulsing red light and vehicle log summary superimposed on a map indicated that the car had been stationary on Puyallup Avenue for the past two hours. It took me a minute before I recognized the location: Charles Royer Station, a transportation hub that included a heliport and bullet train platforms. It looked as though the pair had bugged out of Seattle without returning their rental car. But just in case they were still waiting for a train, I decided to swing past the station. I didn't have any clear idea of what I'd do if I found them there, and puzzled over what I'd say or do if I met them face to face.

I should have saved myself the skull sweat.

It took me longer than I expected to drive out to the station. Traffic was heavy, even for a Saturday night, and the rain had changed from its usual drizzle to a full-fledged deluge. Maybe the gods really did want to send another flood. My wipers were beating a steady tattoo when I pulled into the vast parking lot that surrounded the station.

That's when the fun began. I circled for the better part of half an hour, trying to pick out the rental Runabout by the light of a single headlight. With the amount of rain falling, I didn't feel like getting out and banging on the hood—a trick that usually turns my car from a Cyclops back into a normal vehicle again. I should have purchased a newer vehicle, especially in my line of work. But the Americar was ex-Star, like me, with its police logos painted over and its flashers and siren removed. I was kind of sentimental about it. Especially about the bullet-stopping armor plates built into its bodywork.

I finally found the vehicle I was looking for in a distant corner of the lot. I paused, listening to my wipers slapping back and forth and peering out through the windshield. The rental sticker on the back of the Runabout was the only identifying mark distinguishing it from the dozens of similar models I'd passed in the lot. The car appeared to be empty, but I'd learned, back on the beat, never to take chances. So before getting out to take a closer look, I slipped a hand inside my jacket and drew the Beretta from my shoulder holster. It was a lightweight pistol, sleek and easy to conceal. I flicked its safety and cracked the door of my car.

Back when I was with Lone Star, I'd had my left ear replaced with a cybernetic prosthesis. The police radio it contained was no longer useful—the Star changed the encryption on its signal every month and I had yet to find a cybertronics technician wiz enough to crack the code and get my receiver back on-line. But the ear's frequency-extension units were still functional, as were its amplification system and noise filters. It took a few seconds of concentration to tune out the pounding of the rain and a couple more to cycle through the range of frequencies. But after that I was satisfied. There was nothing moving—nothing breathing even—inside the Mitsubishi runabout.

I stepped out of my car into the rain. It pelted down, soaking my hair in seconds. I jogged over to the Runabout, Beretta still in my hand even though I really didn't expect to find anything. I put my hand on the handle of the driver's door and opened it even as I peered inside.

Big mistake.

A body sagged out onto the pavement, pushing the door open as it fell. I jumped back in alarm as the door swung wide, and at the same time squeezed the trigger of my gun by mistake. It fired, sending a round ricocheting across the rainslick pavement.

"Drek!" I cursed and mentally chastised myself for being an idiot as I slid the safety back on. I'd seen enough corpses as a member of Lone Star's homicide division. It wasn't like I was some greenie, unused to the sight of a stiff.

I'd just never seen one in this condition before.

The corpse was the female "missionary," Dolores— although the only way I could ID her was by the flower pattern on the scrap of blouse that still clung to one wrist. Otherwise, the body was naked. Her face and scalp were gone, and the rest of her wasn't any prettier. The skin had been entirely stripped from her body, except for her feet and hands, exposing the raw, red muscle underneath.

I pulled out a flashlight and shone it inside the car. Her partner—the male "missionary"—had met the same grisly fate. His body lay slumped in a heap in the passenger's seat, down low where I hadn't been able to see it. It too was minus its skin.

The sharp tang of blood filled the car. I knew I had to work quickly, in case someone had heard the gunshot. I shone the flashlight around, looking at the stains on the seats and doors. I'm not as experienced as the men and women who work in forensics, but I knew a thing or two about bloodstains. There weren't any of the splatters associated with a struggle, or with a weapon being used inside the car. Besides, there just wasn't enough room to flay the bodies inside the cramped interior of the Runabout. The pair had obviously been killed elsewhere and then placed back inside their vehicle while their corpses were still fresh enough for their flayed skin to leak blood.

There were no obvious fatal wounds—no bullet holes, broken bones, or deep cuts—and no signs of major physical trauma caused by a magical spell. During my time with the Star, I'd seen corpses that had been burned by fireballs, punctured clean through by bolts of energy, or crushed to a pulp by what witnesses later said was an invisible wall of force. I didn't see any indicators of that kind of magic here. This pair had either been flayed alive—or had been killed first with a spell that left no obvious physical traces.

I was starting to get nervous about staying. And not just because my own skin was starting to crawl. Even if the rain had covered the sound of my gunshot, I wasn't keen on being

found at the scene of a homicide. Not after the way I'd left the
Star. There were still people there who didn't exactly like
me—and who could make my life miserable if they wanted to.

But I wanted to be thorough, so I forced myself to do a
quick check of the Runabout's interior. I used a slim metal
probe, which I routinely carried in my pocket, to pry open
the glove box and ashtray. Nada. Both were empty, and there
was nothing under the seats. I yanked the keystick from the
ignition and opened the trunk. It too was clean. Empty.

It didn't feel right, somehow, to leave the female missionary slumped out of the driver's door. I used my probe to
lift her upright, then pushed her gently back onto her seat. As
I did so, I noticed an oddity in the pattern of bloodstains on
the floor at her feet.

Several small, square objects—about the size of the simsense chips she had offered me earlier—had obviously lain
there. They'd cast a series of "shadows" in the form of
blood-free squares. And now those objects were gone. And
recently, too. The drying blood had peeled back as the chip
cases had been lifted from the floor, indicating that they'd
been removed an hour or two after the flayed corpses had
been placed in the car and had leaked the last of their blood.

Someone had been here just before me. If it was the killer
returning to the scene of the crime for a last clean-up of evidence, he or she might be watching from the shadows even
now, debating whether I knew too much.

I turned and sprinted for my car. I was shivering, and not
just from the rain that had started to soak through my jacket.
This case had suddenly gotten high risk.

4

Ever have the gut feeling that something has gone horribly, horribly wrong and there's nothing you can do about it? That's the way I felt driving home from Charles Royer Station. I flattened the gas pedal, running lights and dodging in and out of traffic that had been slowed by the rain. I cursed the whole way, wishing my car had a siren and lights, wishing it still had the ability to part traffic. All the while, dread settled in my stomach like a cold, tight knot.

My fears were confirmed when I rounded the corner of our block. Three Lone Star cruisers and two unmarked cars were parked outside my house with their red and blues still flashing. A cluster of curious neighbors had gathered on the sidewalk and were staring up at our house, where uniformed officers were taping off a crime scene.

I stamped on the brake and brought the Americar to a shuddering halt. The wheels bumped against the curb, jarring me forward. I felt as if I was going to throw up. I fumbled blindly for the handle of the door. Then I was out of the car, walking like an automaton toward the house. It took everything I had to lift my leaden feet and climb the front steps.

One of the uniforms stopped me before I'd gone half way. He was a black man in his early twenties, with polished boots and a jacket so new I could still smell the leather. Probably a recent graduate of the academy.

"This is a crime scene, ma'am. I can't allow you to go any further." He paused and took in the look on my face. "Do you live here? Do you know the residents of this house?"

"What happened?" I asked numbly. My gut knew the answer already.

"There's been a death, ma'am," the officer told me. He

took my arm, as if afraid I'd fall down the stairs if I wasn't supported. He might have been right.

"Who was the victim?" I asked. "Was it one of the residents?"

The officer gave me an odd look. I guess it wasn't the sort of question a civilian would ask.

As I waited for his reply, I hoped that Rafael might have taken someone out—that it might be someone I didn't know who was about to be bagged for the medical examiner. But the young officer soon squashed that faint hope.

"Are you a resident here, ma'am?" he asked again.

I nodded. "I live downstairs."

"Do you know a woman by the name of Rosalita Ramirez?"

I nodded again. I didn't trust my voice. Somehow I managed to choke out a question. "Dead?"

"You'd better speak to one of the investigating officers."

Dead.

"What about Rafael, her grandson?"

"He's O.K." The officer seemed relieved to be able to give me good news. "He's being questioned by the detectives."

"Who's on duty?" I asked. "Armitage? Neufeld? Uppal?"

"Uppal," he answered. Then he looked quizzically at me. "How do you know Detective Uppal? Are you a friend of hers?"

"I'm ex Star," I told him. "I worked homicide for four years." I tugged my arm free of his grip. "Let me go inside. I know the drill. I won't disturb anything."

"You sure you can handle it?"

"I'm . . . sure." I gritted my teeth. Climbing those last few steps would be the hardest thing I'd ever done.

I stopped just inside the door and grabbed the frame for support when I saw the living room. Two detectives— Parminder Uppal and some rookie I'd never seen before— were studying a trail of blood that started near the doorway where I stood and led around a corner into the hall. A large puddle of blood lay at my feet, and the smears and hand prints along the floor told the story of the victim's final, painful crawl away from the attacker. Just at the bend of the hall, I could see a foot peeking around the corner. I recognized Mama G's slipper immediately.

A wave of dizziness hit me. The next thing I knew, Parminder was in my face.

"Leni! Whatever are you doing here? I'd heard that you'd set up a private detective practice. Are you here on a case?"

"I live here." I'd moved since quitting the Star. Twice. I hadn't bothered to send my former partner an invitation to either of the house-warmings.

Parminder Uppal was an attractive East Indian elf with a cultured English accent. She wore skin-tight black jeans embroidered with red runes and a Zoé jacket of fringed red leather shot through with subtle gold threads. Her long dark hair was pulled back in a silver clip embossed with the elemental symbol of fire. She was one of the Star's best mage detectives, and smart as they come. Smart enough to find the one piece of evidence that could have cracked open the last case we'd worked together at the Star. Smart enough to know that her best interests lay in letting that evidence be buried.

"Did you know Ms. Ramirez?" she asked. "Was she your landlady?"

"She was my grandmother. Or at least, that's how I thought of her. She . . ." My eyes were stinging. "I need to see her."

Parminder hesitated, then nodded. "Be careful where you place your feet," she cautioned. "The . . . ah . . . blood . . . We haven't finished videoing and assensing the evidence yet and forensics still has to have a go at it."

Part of my brain was working on autopilot. From force of habit I clasped my hands behind my back—standard procedure at a crime scene, so you don't inadvertently touch and disturb evidence—and let her lead me around the smear of blood on the floor and toward the body. I mentally braced myself as I turned the corner and the rest of Mama G came into view. She lay face down, arms extended as if she'd still been trying to crawl when she died. Her hands and the outside of her forearms were covered with defensive wounds and her neck had been slashed open from the side. Her white hair was stained with blood, and more wounds marked her back. From the angle and depth of the cuts, I could tell that the fragger who had done this had sliced at her from above and behind—had cut her while she was down and trying feebly to escape. It looked as though the killer had held back, inflicting wounds to cause pain, rather than to kill, until the final blow to the neck. It had been a slow, painful death.

I managed to choke out a question: "When did it happen?"

"A witness places the death between approximately ten p.m. and midnight," Parminder said. "And that fits with the condition of the victim," Parminder said. She bent down and lifted Mama G's head slightly. "As you can see, there's no postmortem lividity showing yet. The skin is unmottled. And the body is still quite warm." She lowered Mama G's head and used a metal probe to lift a torn flap of the blood-soaked dress, exposing one of the ugly wounds on her back. "The weapon was a most unusual one. It left a series of jagged cuts, arranged in more or less straight lines . . ."

I lost it. I stumbled past Parminder and ran for the bathroom. Slamming the door behind me, I leaned over the toilet and was sick. When the trembling had finally loosened its hold on my limbs, I grabbed the counter and hauled myself up. I ran some cold water and splashed it on my face. Then I pressed my forehead against the hard, cool glass of the bathroom mirror.

Frag. I'd seen murder victims before. Lots of them. All as gruesome as this—or more so. I'd remained calm and professional and watched the victims' relatives and friends go white with shock as they heard the news. Now I was the one on the receiving end.

I heard a knock on the door.

"Leni? May I come in?"

I shut off the tap. "All right."

Parminder entered the bathroom and handed me a towel from the rack to dry my face. When I was done, she said, "I'm sorry, Leni, but I'm going to have to ask you a few questions. About the . . . your 'grandmother.' Whether she had any enemies, whether anyone would have cause to, ah . . . do her harm. The interview will be recorded, of course. For the record. And I'll be using a standard detection spell to tell fact from . . . fiction."

I just stared at Parminder for a moment, debating what to say. Was there anything I should keep to myself? I couldn't think straight—my head felt as thick and heavy as when I'd had the sinus cold. The cold that Mama G had "cured" only yesterday morning. Too much had happened, too fast.

If I told Parminder about the pair of fake missionaries and their visit to Mama G, maybe she could turn up something. She had all of the resources of the Star at her fingertips. Maybe forensics would find something I'd missed.

At the same time, I didn't trust my former partner. She'd fragged me over once before—and forced me to have to leave the Star as a result. Back when we were partners together in Lone Star's homicide division, I'd honestly believed that she cared as much as I did about bringing the killer of a teenage prostitute to justice. The kid needed someone to stick up for her after her death. Nobody had during her life.

And maybe Parminder had cared. But not enough to risk losing her job by fingering the son of one of Lone Star's board of directors as a possible killer. And so she stood by as hours of investigative work and evidence were buried under a gigapulse of superfluous data. Before I twigged to what was happening, "glitches" and "viruses" had completely corrupted our original files.

Parminder had said she'd back me when I confronted my superiors at the Star, but instead she'd done a quick fade. I was left twisting in the wind with an angry precinct officer at my throat. What I was suggesting—that the very heart of the Lone Star corporations itself was corrupt—was as blasphemous as telling a Catholic that the pope was a troll. And so things got very, very uncomfortable for me in those final months. Eventually I quit. I didn't want to work for an organization that only gave lip service to justice when its own members—or their nearest and dearest—were the perpetrators.

Despite all that, I couldn't see a reason to keep Lone Star homicide in the dark. I decided to tell Parminder everything I knew. Lighting didn't strike the same spot twice, did it?

"You'll want to start by checking out another homicide that occurred tonight," I said. "You'll find the bodies in a rental car in the southeast parking lot at Charles Royer Station. An Azzie national by the name of Dolores Clemente and an unidentified male . . ."

It took me the better part of three hours before the Star

finished questioning me. All that time, they wouldn't let me see Rafael. Standard police procedure: keep the witnesses separate until they've had a chance to tell their stories, just to see if those stories match up.

By that time Mama G's body had been removed for autopsy. But forensics was still at work, scanning for prints, taking blood samples from the smears on the floor, combing the carpet for evidence, and performing astral scans. I decided to take Rafael downstairs to my place. I nuked some water, made cocoa, and laced the steaming cup with a shot of sambucca. Then I handed it to Rafael.

He looked like hell. His eyes were bloodshot from crying and his hands trembled slightly from shock. His normally olive skin had gone ghostly pale.

I glanced at the clock above my stove—it was already past four a.m.—and then at the detectives who were searching the yard outside by the light of portable halogen lamps. The rain had started again, and was probably washing away any evidence they might have found.

I sat down beside Rafael on the couch. "What happened, Raf?"

He took a sip of cocoa and winced as it burned his lips. I thought of offering him cream to cool it down, but I didn't want to miss what he had to say.

"I went out to buy a Growlie bar down at the corner. I locked the doors. Mama Grande was sleeping when I left."

"That was around ten p.m.?"

Rafael shrugged. "I think so."

"And when did you get back?"

He stared at the cup in his hands, a guilty look on his face. "Around midnight," he muttered.

I nodded. He'd probably gone down to the corner and spent the two hours sweet-talking Consuela, the pretty elf cashier, when he should have been at home watching over Mama G. But I didn't point that out. Rafael felt guilty enough already. And I hadn't seen this coming, either. Not in time.

"When I came back, Mama Grande was . . ." The cup of cocoa trembled more violently in his hands. I had to take it from him and put it on the coffee table. "I couldn't even touch her, Leni. Not even to check for a pulse. She just looked so . . . so helpless." His voice rose to a howl of agony. "Oh, sweet Jesus, why did I leave her alone?"

I grabbed Rafael and held on tight. My own cheeks were wet with tears. We clung together for a while, each lost in our own grief. Then Rafael angrily brushed away his tears.

"It was those fraggers who messed with Mama Grande yesterday, wasn't it?" he asked. "Those spineless, candy-assed little *mocosos* came back to take out their frustrations on an old woman, didn't they?" He leapt to his feet and paced through my doss, big hands clenching and unclenching. Then he turned to me and said in a voice as cold as death: "They're meat, Leni. Nothing but meat. I'll kill them."

"You're too late, Rafael," I told him quietly. "Someone else already did."

I gave him the scan on what had gone down that evening. When I was done, he stood utterly still for a moment, then exploded into violence.

"Frag!" he screamed. His booted foot lashed out, and my coffee table did a somersault and crashed against the wall. Coca went everywhere.

I knew better than to try to stop Rafael—he'd make good the damage later. So I let him take out his anger on my furniture. Better that than on some poor slot who happened to get in his way. His foot lashed out a second time, knocking over an armchair. Again and again he kicked it, until the cushion tore and the stuffing exploded out. At last he subsided and stood, panting, fists clenched.

"Here's the way it had to be, Leni," he said in a low, dangerous voice. "I've thought it through, and nothing else makes sense. Mama Grande saw something while she was living in the Yucatán—something she wasn't meant to see. And then, because she's a bit . . . *loco*, she blabbed it to someone. That's why the Aztlan Freedom League smuggled her up here—for her own protection.

"The fake missionaries came to find out what she'd seen. They had to use magic to get it out of her head. When they did, somebody dusted them. And then, to make sure the secret stayed that way, they . . . killed Mama Grande, too."

I nodded. "I think you're right, Raf. The question is who. Drug lords? The Aztlan government? The rebels? Who?"

"That's what we're going to find out. Right, Leni?" His eyes dared me to say no.

"Right, Raf."

"And when we do . . ."

If looks could kill, Rafael could have scragged an army. Little did we know we'd be taking on just that.

5

It was now Wednesday, four days since Mama G was killed, and I still hadn't heard anything from Parminder. I'd phoned her several times to see how the investigation was going, and gotten the equivalent of "no comment." She said only that they were "busy running down the data" on both homicides. Yeah, right, like there was any data to process. There had been no witnesses to either killing, and from what I had seen, squat in the way of evidence at either crime scene for forensics to work with. The only data they had was what I'd given them: the name and passport number of the female "missionary."

I'd tried running that data myself, and had come up with next to zilch on Dolores Clemente. She and her partner, who was listed in the Air Montezuma passenger list as Gabriel Montoya, had boarded a flight from Mérida to Tenochtitlán, and from there taken a midnight flight for Seattle just prior to renting the car. They had tickets for a return flight that left two weeks later, and thus had no reason for going to the train station—unless something had spooked them and they'd decided they needed to leave town in a hurry.

It was a wonder the two had been granted permission to leave Aztlan. The Azzies were notoriously tight-hooped about letting their nationals go abroad, and it was an open secret that heavy bribes were needed to grease the wheels.

I considered approaching the Aztlan consulate, but realized that the Azzie officials would never provide information on one of their nationals to an ordinary person like me—someone who was no longer affiliated with a police force or security firm. To crack that data, I'd need a wiz-hot decker to take on the black ice that was certain to surround anything

Azzie. And I wasn't sure that even my friend Angie was up to it.

Normally, a name and passport number would have been the magic key to a treasure trove of data, all of it available through perfectly legitimate means. But I kept turning up blanks. In the short time that Dolores Clemente had been in Seattle, she hadn't made any purchases, hadn't booked a hotel—hadn't even used a public telecom. She and Montoya had flown in, rented a car, and driven straight to our neighborhood the next day. Which told me that they knew exactly where they were going. Rafael had already confirmed that the pair hadn't called on any of the neighbors. They'd gone directly to our house.

And that was odd. Why so elaborate a ruse—just to get in the door? Why not just muscle your way inside? If the pair were going to pose as missionaries, why not choose a simpler scam? It would have been easy enough to boost a bible from a hotel and pose as garden-variety Christians. Why use simsense chips from some weird, apocalyptic fringe group? I doubted that they'd had time to boost the chips locally, which meant they had brought them all the way from Aztlan.

And that was the other part that didn't scan. The Catholic faith was banned in Aztlan. Carrying religious recordings out of that country was on a par with taking a loaded weapon or pound of heroin through customs. Unless the recordings weren't Catholic, of course . . . But then why was there a cross on the cover?

I fished out of my pocket the chip case that Rafael had found on the floor of the kitchen. I'd uploaded its apocalyptic message to a number of religious bulletin boards, asking if anyone had ever encountered a similar product. Nada. Or at least, nothing conclusive There were lots of guesses, but none of the suggestions panned out. None of the religious recording studios I was directed to had produced the chip. But they were all keen to sell me other recordings that they promised would be both uplifting and inspirational . . .

This time, I scanned in the cover of the chip, isolated the multi-colored cross itself, and posted just that to the religious bulletin boards with a query as to what faith it came from. I flagged the file as urgent. While I was waiting for a reply, I brewed myself a soykaf and stared out at the rain. It was pounding down on Mama G's garden, bending and muddying the plants. I could imagine the state they'd be in after a few months without her to tend them, and I blinked back tears. We'd had her body cremated and then scattered her ashes in her garden. I'd made a silent promise then and there to my adopted grandmother that I would tend the plants as best I could. But I didn't have her green thumb. A part of me knew that the garden would soon return to the weed-choked state it had been in when Mama G arrived. It would be as if she had never lived here. Her efforts would be gone, erased. Just as she had been.

I turned back to the telecom. It was chiming softly, indicating that I already had a response. I scanned the reply, and wasn't surprised by what I found. According to the professor of Native American Studies in the Sioux Nation who had answered my query, the graphic on the cover of the chip case wasn't a cross at all—it was the ancient Mesoamerican "tree of life," with the four colors representing the four directions. So the religious chip wasn't Christian at all, but Aztlaner.

That made me sit back and think. Maybe I was coming at the rest of the puzzle from the wrong direction, as well. Maybe the chips weren't just a cover, but the real thing. Honest to gods religious propaganda. Suppose Clemente and Montoya really were missionaries—they'd certainly had a genuine-looking gleam in their eyes when they talked about the coming apocalypse . . .

On a hunch, I turned back to my telecom and called up the Seattle religious directory for the two-week period bracketed by the two Air Montezuma flights. I used the keyword "apocalypse" and immediately found what I was after—a day-long conference at Seattle University, sponsored by the Unitarian Church, entitled "Religious Interpretations of the Apocalypse: A Cross-Cultural Perspective." And there, on the list of attendees, were the names Dolores Clemente and Gabriel Montoya.

The conference had been held on Monday and Dolores and Gabriel were no-shows, both at the conference itself and at the home of the people who were going to billet them. No surprise—the pair had been in the police morgue for more than twenty-four hours by the time of the convention. Unless resurrection really was possible, they weren't going to be around for any apocalypse, either.

The conference must have been the official reason the two had used to get permission to leave Aztlan. Probably the country was glad to get rid of its religious lunatic fringe, if only for a little while.

I contacted the seminar organizers, but they weren't able to give me much on the pair—just a Matrix address in Mérida. Clemente and Montoya had signed up for the conference just three weeks ago, and had somehow managed to make all of their travel plans and visa arrangements in that short period of time. They were attendees, rather than speakers, and so hadn't been asked to send any biographical data. They'd made only one inquiry: whether it was possible to distribute religious educational material at the conference. The simsense chips, obviously. Which explained why they had so many of them, all the same.

Okay, so religious fanatics were interested in Mama G. They'd used the conference as an excuse to come all the way from Aztlan to Seattle. They'd really come here to quiz Mama G about something, and then used magic to pull that something out of her head. They'd used the simsense chips to . . . to . . .

I thought I had the answer, but needed confirmation. So I called Parminder for the third time that day. As soon as she recognized my voice, she began to protest that she didn't have anything new for me, and to reassure me that the Star was still working diligently on the case. I apologized for bugging her again and quickly came to the point.

"I need your expert opinion, Parminder. I have a question regarding a case I'm working on." I deliberately didn't say which case it was, but she'd probably guess.

"Suppose you were using one of your mind-reading spells to question a witness who wasn't able to remember an event—maybe who didn't want to remember it," I began.

"The spell probes the mind—it doesn't read it," she corrected me. "And I wouldn't do that. Use of a mind probe without the prior consent of a witness is subject to—"

"Yeah, I know it's illegal," I said, cutting her off. "But suppose you *were* using the spell on someone whose memory was fragged. How would you get the witness to think about what you wanted to know?"

"It's possible to go deep enough to sift through the conscious and unconscious," Parminder said. "But that can sometimes damage the mind. It also takes a lot out of the mage working the spell. The end result might be paranoid delusions or permanent memory loss. And that would destroy a witness' credibility later, when he or she was called to testify in court. It isn't worth the risk."

"Suppose the witness was already . . . crazy?" I hated to apply that term to the woman I thought of as my grandmother. I'd always preferred to think of her as amusingly eccentric. "Suppose their long-term memory was already damaged?"

"Maybe hypnosis would work," Parminder ventured. "If the witness were capable of being hypnotized, he or she could be regressed back to the event that they had witnessed. The memories might be recovered that way."

"Is it possible to hypnotize somebody who doesn't want to be?"

"An unwilling witness, you mean? Impossible."

"What if you could force them to think back to the event by some other means?" I asked. "Say, by hooking them up with a trode rig so they receive a simsense recording that mimicked it. Would they think about what they had witnessed, then?"

"I don't see how they could help it," Parminder answered. "They'd be forced to relive the event. But the person's mental images would be contaminated by the simsense, and again he'd be useless—legally—as a witness." She paused, then lowered her voice. "You realize that what you're suggesting is completely illegal. That any mage who helped you to do this would be breaking the law and risking imprisonment of not less than—"

"I'm not asking you to do anything of the sort, Parminder," I reassured her. "I think this technique may have been used on a client of mine."

It only took her a moment to guess what I meant. "On Rosalita Ramirez, you mean. By the missionaries."

I paused for a moment. Parminder hadn't put the word

"alleged" in front of missionaries. So she knew they were legit, too. Interesting.

"Yeah," I answered. "That's why the kitchen was trashed. They probably had to . . ." I took a deep breath, imagining the fear Mama G must have felt as the pair held her down and forced her to experience gods only knew what via the simsense. "They probably had to restrain her while they slipped the trode rig over her head. The only thing I can't figure out is why they wanted to show her a simsense of a religious tract. What memories did they hope it would trigger?"

"Hmm."

"Parminder? I know that sound. You're onto something. Tell me what it is."

"I can't."

"Why not? I gave you the tie-in with the double homicide at Charles Royer Station. That ought to be worth something."

"I just can't."

I was getting angry. "This isn't just some joygirl street trash who was murdered, Parminder. This was someone I cared about. Someone I loved. I deserve to know whether or not you're putting any effort into this—to know what's going on. I won't compromise your investigation by blabbing what you tell me around. I'm not some civilian who's going to blow the conviction for you. Not that you need . . ." I paused to regain my composure. I'd almost lost it—had almost been about to tell Parminder that she was perfectly capable of deliberately fragging up a case on her own. I swallowed my hostility and tried a different tack. "The way I see it, you failed to provide backup when I most needed it, and now you owe me one, *partner.*" I placed heavy sarcasm on the last word.

There was a moment's silence. Then the words I'd been hoping for. "Meet me tonight at seven p.m. at Icarus Descending. You know where it is?"

"I know it. I'll see you there." I stabbed the Off icon on the telecom. Icarus Descending was downtown and very trendy.

It was still only the middle of the afternoon. I'd put my other cases on hold for the week—I couldn't concentrate on anything but Mama G's death right now. So I didn't have much to occupy me until seven o'clock. I got up and puttered aimlessly around my flat, stopped to pat Pinkerton, who was lazing in front of the heat vent, the stared out the window at the rain.

I took a sip of the soykaf I'd left on the table and realized it had gone cold while I'd been talking to Parminder. I added the cup to the dishes in the sink and made myself a fresh one, taking time to pour some cream into Pinkerton's bowl before adding the last of the cream to my soykaf. Then I sat down at the telecom.

I'd already run through it several times, but I decided to give the copy of the recording I'd obtained from the security camera at the car rental agency one last scan. So I slotted and ran it, watching on my monitor for anything I'd missed.

The pair had said very little—Dolores had simply answered the clerk's questions and handed over her passport and credstick when asked to do so. As she drew them from her purse, I could just see a hint of yellow inside that must have been the simsense chips. Gabriel Montoya stood behind her, jacket slung over his shoulder, staring warily around at the people passing through the terminal behind them.

Something was tugging at my subconscious, and so I ran the recording through a second time. Then it hit me. There— when Montoya turned to stare at a pretty blond elf in a tight red dress. When she glanced at him, he raised one hand to run the fingers through his hair in an instinctive preening motion. As he did, the sleeve of his short-sleeved shirt lifted just enough to show a round, whitish mark on his right bicep. The first few times through, I'd taken it to be a scar, but now I realized that it was too symmetrical, too perfectly circular. If anything, it reminded me of an embossed design on leather. The mark showed only for a second, and then Montoya dropped his arm and the sleeve hid it again.

I skipped back a few seconds on the recording, then ran it forward again in slo-mo. When the mark was fully exposed, I hit the Pause icon and zoomed in tight on the mark. At the center was a stylized, glaring face—almost skeletal—surrounded by a sun-shaped circle. Additional circles inside the first held a design of some sort, but there wasn't enough detail to make it out.

I knew I'd seen the face-and-sun pattern somewhere before, but couldn't place it. I made a printout of the zoom and sat there, staring at it until my eyes ached. No joy. I knew the information was on file somewhere within my wetware, but frag if I could access it just then.

I was still puzzling over it when I heard Rafael's motorcycle pull into the back yard. I opened the back door and waved him inside.

He'd been out for another long ride and his boots and bike were covered in mud. That's all he'd done the past few days: ride. He had to keep moving, he said, to keep from going crazy. I knew how he felt. But it was my mind that had to be kept busy, rather than my body. I kept my grief at bay by working on the puzzle that surrounded Mama G's death. By doing that I could distance myself, treat it as just another homicide. Except that it wasn't.

Rafael wiped his feet and came inside. His breath smelled like he'd been drinking, but he seemed sober enough. I offered him a soykaf, but he shook his head. Instead he flopped onto the couch. "Cops find anything yet?" he asked. He played with his hands, cracking his knobby knuckles. I noticed that his fingers were scraped and wondered if he'd been punching furniture again—or if he'd picked a fight with someone.

"I'm not sure," I said. "Maybe. I've got a meeting with one of the investigating officers tonight."

"Yeah." He glanced at the telecom. Its screen still held the frozen zoom of the mark on Gabriel's arm.

"Ugly fragger, isn't he?"

"The guy in the picture—Montoya?" The missionary wasn't overly handsome, but I wouldn't have called him ugly.

"Who? No, this guy—the sun god. The face at the center of the calendar stone. The Azzies sure worship some ugly-looking gods."

I crossed the room and picked up the printout I'd made. "You know this design?" I asked Rafael.

He nodded. "Sure. Everyone does. It's from an altar stone that was dug up in the seventeen hundreds in Tenochtitlán. It's massive—the size of this living room. It's carved with the ancient Azzie calendar. I had a gold pendant of it, once, back when I was interested in that sort of thing. But I sold it a couple of years ago, to buy parts for my bike."

That was why the design was so familiar. I'd seen it on museum posters, embossed on leather purses imported from Aztlan, on T-shirts even. It was an almost universal symbol of the ancient Aztecs. I hit the reverse-zoom icon on the telecom to show Rafael the full picture. "So how come our dead missionary had the symbol on his arm? Was he some sort of Azzie patriot?" I asked.

"That's on an arm?" Rafael peered at the telecom screen. "It look like a brand. That fragger must have been into some serious pain."

"Do you know any more about it—about what it might symbolize?"

Rafael shook his head. "I just know what I was told by my buddy Alberto—the guy who sold me the pendant. He's originally from Aztlan, but he's lived in Seattle since he was just a kid. He runs a jewelry business now, and does pretty good for himself. Gold mostly—replicas of ancient Azzie stuff. Alberto doesn't worship the old gods, but his parents are heavy into that drek and he knows about the country's state religion. He could probably tell you all about the calendar stone."

I glanced at the clock. "Would his shop still be open? Could we talk to him?"

"Guess so. I haven't seen him in a couple of years, but we were pretty tight, once."

I grabbed my jacket and headed for the door.

"What, *now*?" Rafael asked.

"You got anything better to do?"

"No." He lumbered to his feet and picked up his helmet. Small and round, it was the type that bikers called a "lid." Its sole purpose was to conform to the helmet laws—it didn't offer any real protection. "Grab your helmet. I'll give you a ride there."

I looked out at the rain, thinking that my Americar would be a whole lot more comfortable. And the streets would be slick and slippery. But Rafael was careful when I was on the back of his bike. He rode recklessly and pulled incredibly risky stunts when he was alone, but when I rode with him he took it smooth—not slow, mind you, but smooth. He always insisted that I wear a full-face helmet and a heavy leather jacket. Although I was an ex-cop with a number of gun fights and high-speed chases under my belt, he was still protective of me. It was kind of sweet, really. Besides, driving me somewhere would keep him out of trouble. And so I said yes.

The ride took about forty minutes, and the rain-washed air did wonders to clear my head. I was thankful for my helmet's visor; the rain must have been stinging Rafael's face as we whipped along. He pulled the bike up in front of a gleaming new glass and cement building, one of the many new skyscrapers that formed Tacoma's bustling downtown.

Rafael's friend had a shop at street level. It appeared to be fronted by windows, behind which were display cases filled with gold bracelets, pendants, and rings, but scrolling message boards at the bottom of each "window" reminded would be smash-and-grab thieves that these were, in fact, huge monitors that fronted solid concrete walls.

As Rafael buzzed the intercom beside the front door, I paused to look at a display of what looked like large golden spools. I'd never seen anything like them. "What are these?" I asked.

"Ear plugs," he answered. "The ancient Azzies pierced their earlobes and stretched them to make those fit. Alberto says they're a fad among Azzie priests. And among gangers. You know how Seattle gangers go for gold chains and knuckle rings? It's ear plugs in Aztlan. The bigger and flashier, the better."

After a security camera scoped us out, the intercom came to life and a voice directed us to enter. We passed through the outer, barred door into a small space like an airlock and found our way blocked by a second door. It was heavy glass, probably bullet-proof. Through it we could see into the shop itself. A dwarf stood behind a counter filled with jewelry display cases. Gold sparkled alluringly on black velvet.

"*Hola,* Alberto." Rafael waved at the dwarf. "Buzz us in."

"I can't, Rafael. Not unless your friend leaves her weapon outside."

I was suddenly aware of the familiar bulge of the Beretta under my arm. The shop entrance must have been fitted with metal detectors or chem sniffers—or a combination of both.

As the outer door clicked shut behind us, I looked up and saw a small round opening beside the surveillance camera. I hoped it held a taser and not something more lethal—and illegal.

"Aw, Alberto. C'mon, chummer. She's my best friend. I'll vouch for her. She's an ex-cop, for frag's sake."

"Well, all right . . . But only if she unloads the weapon first."

"That's fine by me." I was starting to feel claustrophobic in the confined space. I drew the Beretta from my shoulder holster and released the magazine, held it up so the dwarf could see that the chamber was clear, then placed the magazine in a pocket and reholstered my weapon. "Satisfied?"

The dwarf nodded and touched something under the counter. The glass door opened. We entered and took seats on stools at the counter like a couple sitting down to pick out wedding rings. The air was filled with soothing music—native pipes playing a gentle melody.

Rafael made small talk, asking after Alberto's parents. I noticed that he didn't mention Mama G. The two old friends had not seen each other in a couple of years, and so Alberto would never even have met her. The thought made me sad. A person was only alive as long as someone remembered her. To those who had never met Mama G, she might as well never have existed. As far as I knew, only Rafael and I mourned her.

Alberto had rigged a bench behind the counter so he was at eye level with his human customers. He had the dark, long-lashed eyes of a Spaniard and the high cheekbones of an Azzie native. He wore his hair short and his thick beard trimmed to a goatee. He dressed well, in a tailored suit that de-emphasized the boxiness of his broad shoulders.

"What can I do for you?" Alberto asked when the pleasantries were over. "Are you shopping for something specific?"

"I'm shopping for information, actually," I explained. "I'm a private detective, working on a case." I pulled out the printout I'd made of Montoya's branded arm and slid it across the counter toward the dwarf. "Rafael said you might be able to tell me about the calendar stone—what it symbolizes. And why someone would want to brand it on their arm."

Rafael joined in. "Remember the pendant you sold me, Alberto? What was that story your parents told about it? Something about the sun god, wasn't it?"

"It's the legend of the death and rebirth of the sun," Alberto answered. He reached into the display case and pulled out a golden ear plug nearly as wide as his fist. The front was cast with the same face-and-sun design. Peering at it, I could make out more detail. To either side of the sun god's face were two clawed hands, each holding something. Above and below each of the hands was a rectangular panel with a glyph inside it. Next came a circle filled with Aztlaner glyphs, and then another circle studded with the triangular flares that had reminded me of the sun's rays.

Alberto took the ear plug back from me, gave it a quick polish with a cloth, and continued his description. "In the Aztec cosmology, the time period we're living in is known as the Fifth Sun. The calendar stone records the dates on which each of the four previous suns was destroyed and the date when our current age began. The Fourth Sun, for example, was destroyed by water.

"Ties in nicely with the Biblical flood, doesn't it?" he added. "Except that it was supposed to have happened around A.D. 761."

He ran a finger around the circle that enclosed the sun god's face. "These glyphs are the twenty day signs in the ancient calendar. The Aztecs had a calendar of eighteen months that were divided into—"

"I thought a new era started in 2011," Rafael interjected. "With the Awakening. Isn't it the Sixth World already?"

"That's from the Mayan calendar," Alberto said. "According to the Aztec calendar, the true 'awakening' hasn't happened yet."

"I see." I nodded. "So the calendar stone predicts the date that the world will end?"

Alberto shook his head. "No. Even the ancient Aztecs didn't know when the Fifth Sun would be destroyed. But they did know how the world would end—in a cataclysmic earthquake. And when it does, the *tzitzimine*—the 'demons of twilight'—will swarm up out of the earth and devour humanity."

He smiled. "My parents used to frighten me with that one.

The monsters under my bed were always *tzitzimine*, not bogey men."

"Do people still believe this?" I asked. "Is it part of the Aztlaner religion?"

"Not really," Alberto said. "At least, not within the faith my parents practice. There are fringe groups that take it seriously and are preparing for it—just like there are Christian faiths centered around preparing for the apocalypse." He laughed to himself. "The Christians don't know when their apocalypse is coming, either."

We were interrupted, just then, by a customer. The fellow was typical of Tacoma's nouveau riche—smartly dressed in an expensive suit and shoes. He dropped more than five thousand nuyen on a heavy gold ring for himself, and bought delicate gold earrings hung with brilliant turquoise quetzal feathers for his girlfriend.

While he was tending the customer, Alberto let me hold onto the gold ear plug with its calendar stone design. I noticed that he kept one eye on me all the time, though. Despite the fact that I was Rafael's chummer, the dwarf still didn't entirely trust me not to pocket the thing. Compared to the suit buying the ring and earrings, Rafael and I were terribly under-dressed, not at all like the store's usual clientele, I supposed. No wonder Alberto was wary.

I nodded as I turned the ear plug over in my hands. Things were starting to fit together—even if they didn't entirely make sense yet. The missionaries were part of some weird offshoot of the Azzie state religion. Maybe they had been involved in some sort of illegal cult practice that Mama G had witnessed at one point in time. Maybe all three had been killed to hush something up. But what?

Alberto finished with his customer and ushered the man out through the door.

"What's the god holding in his hands?" I asked as he returned to the counter.

"Hearts," the dwarf answered. He took the ear plug back from me, gave it another quick polish, and placed it gently back inside the velvet-lined display case.

"Human hearts," Rafael prompted. "Go on, Alberto. Tell her the gory stuff."

The dwarf looked somewhat embarrassed. "It's not part of the state religion any more."

"So?" Rafael laughed. "It was, once."

"But not any more." Alberto's voice was tight.

"What isn't it part of the religion any more?" But I could guess.

"Human sacrifice," the dwarf said. "The Aztecs believed that the sun god needed blood to sustain him and keep him in motion. And to help the new sun be born. So they sacrificed at the beginning of every year, and at the beginning of every new age."

"Human sacrifice," I echoed. Had Mama G seen someone being sacrificed? Was that why she'd been forced to flee Aztlan? It wouldn't be the first time a witness had been killed to hush up a homicide.

It was a good guess, nice and neat. But as it turned out, the truth was much messier. Human sacrifice wasn't the only thing Mama G had seen.

6

I shook the rain from my umbrella and ducked through the mahogany and brass doors of Icarus Descending. The place specialized in seafood and was one of those restaurants where every other item on the menu had "market price" entered beside it. If you needed to ask, you couldn't afford it. The restaurant catered primarily to elves—there were maybe two or three other humans there, besides myself. Many of the serving staff were Asian elves and were rumored to be part of a Chinese triad. That was a good one. Why wait tables when crime is so much more lucrative? It was more likely that the customers were triad members—they'd be the ones with the nuyen to eat here.

The restaurant didn't have much of a view, but the decor made up for it. Everything was done in an ocean theme. The bases of the tables were crusted with mock barnacles and the walls and floor looked like seaweed-draped rock. The ceiling was a translucent field of pale blue that rippled and flowed like water. At its center was a single, large yellow glow meant to represent the sun. The effect was exactly like being underwater—the programmer even got the sparkles on the ocean's surface right.

I wondered at Parminder's choice of restaurant. According to myth, Icarus flew too close to the sun. His wax-and-feather wings melted, and he plunged into the sea. I wondered if my former partner was using the restaurant as a subtle metaphor that I was close to getting burned. It would be just like her—subtle to the point of being obtuse.

Or maybe she just liked seafood. The restaurant certainly smelled wonderful. Despite being irked at having to drive all the way downtown and being forced to lay out what was sure to be a day's pay to eat here, I was already hooked—pun intended.

I saw Parminder sitting at a table on the lower level of the restaurant. As I started down the stairs, a brilliant purple squid swam past me at chest level, making me jerk back to avoid running into it. Then I realized that it was the result of a hidden holo-projection unit, as were the tiny silver fish that darted around the diners' feet.

I slid into the seat opposite Parminder, trying to look as at ease in the posh environment as she did. We'd both come from working-class roots, but she'd deliberately honed an air of sophistication that I could never match. It helped, her being an elf. I wondered for the millionth time why she'd joined the Star and chosen homicide. Probably for the intellectual puzzle. She'd prod at a case until she cracked it, no matter how much skull sweat and overtime it took. And then, having satisfied her own curiosity, she'd let it be buried. Saving the world didn't interest her the way it did me.

I ordered a vodka and seven—the real stuff—from the menu screen set into the table, Parminder a glass of Chardonnay. We made small talk as we studied the main menu, touch-keying items that looked interesting to call up a holographic projection and detailed description of the dish's ingredients. I ordered grilled salmon and wild mushrooms, and Parminder chose spiced oysters, muscles, and clams served on bread molded to look like a gigantic clam shell.

"So?" I began after a waiter had brought our drinks and slipped away. "How goes the investigation? What have you got so far?" I tried to look chill, but the anxiety I felt was obvious in my voice. I took another sip of my drink.

Parminder looked around, assuring herself that there was no one within listening range. "Lone Star isn't the only agency with an interest in those two missionaries," she said. "The Aztlan security forces had them under observation."

"Oh yeah?" I waited for more.

"They were members of an apocalyptic religious cult. The Aztlaners normally keep a tight lid on fringe groups, but they wanted to learn what this one was up to. And so the government—facilitated—their trip up north, pulling strings behind the scenes to make things as smooth as possible for our two dead friends. They wanted to see who the pair were hooking up with here in Seattle. But Clement and Montoya were murdered before the Aztlaners had a chance to find out."

"And the pair never guessed that Big Brother was watching them?" I found that hard to buy. "I'd be suspicious as hell if I were trying to leave Aztlan and the wheels all seemed pre-greased. Especially if I was part of a fringe group."

Parminder took a sip of her wine. She continued as if I hadn't interrupted. "The religious sect was legal—on the surface. But the Aztlaner security forces believed it to be secretly involved in illegal activities. There were rumors that its members practiced—"

"Human sacrifice," I said, completing the sentence for her. "Cutting out hearts, and other unpleasantries."

That surprised Parminder. "Ah . . . yes. I see you've been doing some digging on your own." She seemed impressed. "We had to get that information from the consulate."

I shared my theory that Mama G had witnessed a sacrifice, and that the cult members had forced her to re-live this experience so that they could lift some detail of it from her memory of the event. "That's what the simsense chips really were," I told Parminder. "A snuff film, dressed up in religious trappings."

My former partner blinked. "Not at all."

Now it was my turn to be puzzled. "What do you mean? How can you be certain what was on the chips?"

Parminder smiled smugly. Back when we were partners, she always looked that way whenever she'd thought of something that I hadn't. The look still irritated me.

"I spoke to one of the customs officers at SeaTac Airport," she said. "He inspected the simsense chips, and even slotted one or two and skipped through them in a random sample of their contents. According to him, they were little more than travelogues. A running narrative of religious dogma about the end of the world and the death of the sun, combined with a walk-through of various archaeological sites in the Yucatán. Hardly even worthy of simsense, unless you enjoy the discomfort of walking around in blistering heat and feeling the sweat trickle down someone else's body."

"So the missionaries were showing her travelogues while they mind-probed her?" I asked.

"It would appear so."

"Then they're looking for a place," I concluded.

"It would seem so, but why?" Parminder gave a delicate shrug. "I must confess I'm at a dead end with this one. I thought perhaps you could provide me with a lead. Some background on the victim—on your 'grandmother'—that would help me to figure out what the missionaries might have been looking for."

"No joy there," I said. "Mama Grande was pretty vague about her past. She lived in the present and seemed to have short-term memory only. I've told you everything I know, even about the AFL smuggling her out of Aztlan."

Parminder sighed. "I see. That's it then."

"What do you mean, 'that's it'?" I didn't like the sound of that one. "Don't you have any more leads?"

There was a lengthy silence. I could tell that Parminder was debating whether or not to tell me something. I was just about to remind her again of the debt she owed me when she reached a decision. "Forensics found something interesting during the autopsy of Rosalita Ramirez," she began carefully. "Tiny fragments of black volcanic glass—obsidian—in the wounds. The murder weapon was tipped with stone that splintered when it struck bone."

I suddenly felt queasy. I mentally grasped for some sort of professional objectivity, and at last found it. "You're telling me that Mama Grande was killed by a weapon from the stone age? Who the frag would use something like that?"

We had to wait a moment while the waiter delivered our food. It looked delicious, but I suddenly wasn't hungry any more.

"An Aztlaner," Parminder answered quietly. "Their priests traditionally carry *macauitls*—obsidian-edged wooden swords. It's a holy weapon, just like a Sikh's *kirpan* dagger. *Macauitls* are also carried by elite Aztechnology security personnel as ceremonial weapons. They look ineffectual, but are deadly killing tools."

She didn't need to remind me. I pushed the image of Mama G's mutilated body from my mind.

"What about the two missionaries?" I asked. "Did forensics find obsidian in their wounds, too?"

"No. The autopsy points to their cause of death as probably

magical in nature—either a death touch or slay spell. But it was definitely an Aztlaner hit. The removal of the skin was a practice sacred to the god Xipe Totec. In ancient times, the flayed skin was worn by priests worshipping the arrival of spring—the renewal of the Earth's 'skin' of vegetation."

"Priests again," I noted.

The whole thing was starting to get to me. Whoever had murdered Mama G and the two missionaries had announced themselves not just as an Aztlaner but specifically as members of that country's priesthood. They'd done the killings with a deliberate signature, using a highly distinctive weapon and method of mutilating the bodies. It was too heavy-handed to be a frame. Instead it smacked of the deliberate arrogance of someone who felt as confident as if they were on their own turf. And that meant that the killer had nothing but contempt for the Lone Star's ability to bring him or her to justice. Or for my own efforts.

"So Aztechnology or the Aztlan priesthood are involved in this?" I asked.

"I can't confirm that," Parminder said hastily. "And you didn't hear any of this from me officially. But I will tell you this. Our primary suspect in both murders is protected by diplomatic immunity. We can't touch him. It's case closed. Just like . . ."

"Just like the last case we worked together," I said softly. "Only for different reasons. And once again, the killer walks." My eyes narrowed. "Who is this suspect and what do you have on him?"

I didn't really expect her to tell me. I was surprised as all frag when she did.

"Domingo Vargas. He's a mage, a priest—and a consular official. Recently appointed to the Seattle consulate, just two weeks ago. I have a witness who places a consular car at the Charles Royer Station at about the time of the homicides, and he's the only one of the Seattle diplomatic staff who has magical ability and who carries a *macauitl* as part of his ceremonial gear. He's likely the one who killed and flayed the victims."

She played with her wine glass, turning it in obvious frustration. "Because of diplomatic immunity we couldn't enter the consulate and question Vargas. Nor could we question him at the airport when he returned to Aztlan on this morning's Tenochtitlán flight, since Aztlan has extra-territorial privileges over the Air Montezuma hub at SeaTac. We had no choice but to simply let him go."

"So why tell me all this?" I asked. I couldn't scan it. The data was too little, too late. The Azland government had pulled rank on the Star, and now the suspect was gone.

Parminder sighed. "Because I owe you one. And because I wanted to let you know how hopeless it was, and what you'd be facing if you continued to investigate this murder. These people play for keeps—and they don't care who knows it. You've hit the wall and there's nowhere else to go with this one."

I hate being told I can't do something. Especially by someone who I knew had already given up once before, rather than fight the good fight. I was grateful to Parminder for letting me know what I was up against, but she could keep her advice.

I thanked her for the information, drained the last of my drink and pushed my untouched meal away. I decided to leave Parminder with the tab. I figured she owed me at least that much.

I left the restaurant even more determined to find out why Mama G had been killed. I swore that I would do whatever I could to bring her murderer to justice—even if that justice wasn't to be found in Seattle.

Only problem was I didn't know where the frag to begin.

7

The desert air was hot, even at midnight. We were somewhere between San Angelo and Austin, a few dozen klicks from the Aztlan-Canadian American States border. Along that border, two armies faced each other across an eight thousand-meter-wide buffer zone. Armed to the teeth and constantly on alert, the Texas Rangers and the Aztlan Border Patrol (a division of Aztechnology Corporate Security) each waited for the other to make the first move.

Ever since the dragon Dunkelzahn's election to the presidency of UCAS, things had been especially tense between Aztlan and the United Canadian American States. The CAS, which lay between them, was growing increasingly fretful about Aztlan using it as a stepping stone in any attack on UCAS. But the Azzies seemed more concerned with protecting their own borders than with expansionism. There were rumors that they had been vigorously searching for something in this area of late. I hoped we wouldn't run into them—that whatever they'd been looking for would prove a distraction.

Like the border patrols, we were waiting for someone else to move first. A smuggler would be making a run into Aztlan some time tonight. When the fireworks began, we'd motor. And pray we made it through in one piece.

Rafael and I sat on one motorcycle, the AFL "coyote" who would be guiding us on another. Both were dirt bikes—Yamaha Sidewinders with knobby tires to grip the sand and lots of juice to pull us through the tight spots that lay ahead. Both had been painted a flat matte black so that their metal would not reflect the glare of a searchlight. We'd killed the engines while we were waiting for the show to begin—no sense providing any more of a heat signature than absolutely necessary. An infrared-sensing surveillance drone could be overhead, even now.

I was still a little leery of our guide. He gave his name as José, although he was a different José than the one who had first put Rafael in touch with his grandmother. He was human and appeared to be in his forties, with graying hair and stubble on his chin. He wore black jeans and a black shirt with a tear in one arm, and a grimy yellow bandanna around his neck that he pulled up over his mouth to keep out the dust when he rode. His cowboy boots were also black, with tinkling spurs that he'd assured me were real silver. He wore a glove on his left hand, but his right was bare so that the vehicle control rig jack in his fingertip could make contact with the input stud on his bike.

"José" had first contacted us two days ago—on the evening following my meeting with Parminder. He'd responded to Rafael's posting on the Salsa Connection, in which Rafael had mentioned that his "banana pepper bush" had died. Rafael had asked if peppers were ever shipped *into* Aztlan, as well as out of it.

My plans were hazy, at best, and fell back upon standard police procedure: track down my chief suspect and question him. I figured that, if I could confront Domingo Vargas face to face, I at least had a chance—albeit a toothpick-skinny one—of confirming whether or not he had been responsible for Mama G's death.

I didn't hold any illusions about the feasibility of my plan. I knew the chances of confronting Vargas on his own turf were slim to nada. But I had to try—had to give it my best shot. I owed Mama G that much.

And assuming I did manage to force a confession from Vargas, then what?

I honestly didn't know.

After my conversation with Parminder, I realized that, no matter how much evidence I gathered against the priest, the UCAS government could never order him extradited back to Seattle to stand trial. He was protected by diplomatic immunity. I had a crazy notion tucked away in the back of my mind that Rafael and I might perform a shadow-style extraction of Vargas ourselves—but assuming we did get him out of Aztlan, what would we do with him? Act as judge and jury ourselves?

I didn't want to think about that one.

At least I could nose around some and learn what Mama G had been a witness to. I needed to know what the cult missionaries and Atzlaner priests had been so interested in learning—and in subsequently covering up. I needed to know why Mama G had died. I needed answers—as much as Rafael need to kick some Azzie hoop. And so we'd made this journey together.

José's reply had come back within five hours of our posting. We'd been informed—equally cryptically—that our "shipment" would cost us at least three thousand nuyen, and that we could find what we were looking for at a talismonger's shop in Houston. And that's where we'd met the AFL contact—not at the store itself, but sitting at a Tex-Mex restaurant across the street. He'd known us by a pre-arranged signal: he'd instructed one of us to wear a T-shirt with Mama G's favorite animal on it.

It hadn't taken us long to figure that one out: snake. I'd scrounged up a T-shirt promoting the Rainforest Reptile Refuge, a kind of SPCA for reptiles that I'd visited once on a trip north to Vancouver. I'd been investigating a case in which a four-meter-long boa had crushed a woman to death. I needed to know more about the habits of snakes so that I could determine if it had been a homicide or an accident. I'd learned that boas are quite docile—if they're well fed. The pair of gentle giants I'd met had let me stroke their smooth chins, had tasted me with a flick of their tongues, and then had merely watched me, deciding I was interesting but not a threat.

Starve a boa, however, and it can get ornery. Mean enough to take on a full grown human, even. The snake in question hadn't been given anything to eat for two months. Hubby had "forgotten" to feed it while his wife was on vacation. He'd also gotten his wife to take out a rather large insurance policy before she went away. And he'd done a bad job of faking remorse when his wife was squeezed to death by her favorite pet.

I was getting morbid again. Mama G's death had done that to me. And now, just a few hours after meeting José, I had placed my welfare—and a good chunk of my savings—in this stranger's hands. I was trusting him to get me into Aztlan.

All I knew about the man was that he liked Corona beer and, like Rafael, was a wannabe combat biker. He was a fervid supporter of the Houston Mustangs—arch rivals of the Seattle Timber Wolves in this year's race for the conference championships. He even had a tattoo of the team's logo—a horse with motorcycle wheels instead of legs, popping a wheelie—on the back of his right hand. The colors were still fresh—the tattoo must have been brand new.

José and Rafael had immediately bonded by going *mano a mano* in a heated but friendly argument over which team would triumph in this year's Biker Bowl conference championships, and had quoted a bewildering mass of sports statistics as evidence to support their case. Then they'd begun talking bikes. Four-stroke this and compression that—I knew enough about engines to coax my Americar back onto the road again when it stalled or blew its rad, but was bored silly by engine specs and performance capabilities. All I cared about was whether the bike I was riding on was going to make it into Aztlan. And that had more to do with the desert terrain and the vigilance of the military forces that lay between us and the border than it did the machine. And with Rafael's skill as a motorcycle rider.

The border was relatively quiet this far out into the desert. The actual line in the sand was marked with a series of barbed wire fences, fitted out with contact sensors, listening arrays, and anti-personnel radar. This "electronic curtain" was said to be sensitive enough to distinguish an individual person, but José assured us that it was unreliable to the extent that half the time it was ignored. Both the Azzies and the rangers had chased after jackrabbits too many times to be bothered with any more false alarms. Larger radar signatures, however, were taken very seriously indeed.

In this stretch of west Texas, the fence itself was in poor repair. Smugglers in T-birds had punched a number of holes in it—holes that were often left unrepaired. All that was required was a distraction of some sort to get the border patrols looking elsewhere, and you could slip right through. Or so José asserted.

He stared out across the desert through a pair of binoculars. "It looks pretty quiet," he said. "I don't see anyth—"

The scream of engines split the night. The noise almost deafened me, even though my cyberear's automatic noise-suppression system cut in almost immediately. Something flashed past overhead, tearing open the skies with a booming thunder that made all three of us duck.

"—frag was that?" Rafael shouted at José.

Our guide grinned. "A Texas Rangers Phantom IV jet." He slipped the binoculars into a saddle bag and pulled his bandanna up over his mouth. "It'll have scrambled in response to some activity nearby. I'd say our smuggler is about to make his run."

I wondered for the millionth time how the Aztlan Freedom League got its information about smugglers, holes in the fence, and border patrol movements—and prayed that all of it was accurate. I guessed that the Phantom was the "air cover" José had been joking about earlier.

As the jet's roar faded into the distance I heard another noise: the distinctive whine of a low-altitude vehicle. The sound was coming from behind and to our left, and approaching fast. My low-frequency boosters also picked out the grumble of heavier engines, somewhere beyond the border that lay ahead of us.

"Something's headed this way," I told José, pointing in the direction of the higher-pitched sound. "It's making for the border."

In another moment, the sound was close enough for the others to hear. "Let's snag that flag," José said, slamming the kick start of his bike with a booted foot.

Rafael laughed at the combat biker expression José had used and reverentially touched the Seattle Timber Wolves flag he'd clipped to his belt "for luck." His huge bulk shifted as he hit his own kick start, and I wrapped my arms around his waist as he settled back on the seat. "Ready to rumble!" he called out.

By the light of the half moon I saw something moving across the desert. Fast and low, maybe a meter or so off the rock-strewn, washboard ground. About the size of a very large automobile, it rode on four thruster jets that left boiling dust in its wake. It was well to our left, a good klick or two away. Already it was almost even with our position.

As the fighter jet screamed past overhead once more, José surged forward on his dirt bike, aiming it at the border. Rafael gunned our bike and sent it roaring after him. We accelerated rapidly, dust spraying out behind us.

I clung fast to Rafael's broad waist and concentrated on keeping my feet on the pegs, which were rattling with each bump and lurch of the bike. I leaned into the turns with Rafael as we zoomed around rocks and other obstructions. I prayed each time we hit a bump and were airborne for a second or two—to which spirit or god, I wasn't sure. But at the same time, I felt exhilarated. The warm wind whipped through my hair and ballooned out the back of my jacket. The smell of desert dust and motorcycle exhaust filled my nostrils. I could sense Rafael's eager joy at the wildness of our ride. It was infectious, and I couldn't help but give in to it. I whooped, and he fed the bike more gas, sending it scrambling up a low rise with a high, throaty engine whine.

José glanced back at us, making sure we were still following, then gunned his bike across the rise and disappeared down the other side of it. As we topped the hill behind him, I looked to the left and saw the T-bird, still screaming straight ahead at full thrust. It was slightly ahead of us now, aiming at the fence like a bullet.

The Phantom IV made one more pass overhead, deafening us with its sonic boom. The jet must have had its radar-controlled weapons systems locked on to the T-bird, but its pilot did not open fire. I guess José was right: the Texas Rangers liked to put on a show of force, but unofficially approved of the smuggling of illegal goods into Aztlan. The shipments messed with the country's economy and morale, even if only slightly.

The Azzies, however, were another matter. With a civil war going on in their country, they took smuggling much more seriously.

Now the T-bird had reached the fence. It plowed through the barbed wire, tearing it open and dragging a tangle of it behind. Metal fence posts bounced and tumbled after the T-bird for several meters, plowing holes in the dirt. Then one snagged on something, and the remains of the fence tore free. As the smuggler raced on into Aztlan territory, the Phantom IV turned in a screaming arc over the buffer zone and disappeared behind us into the night, away from the border and back into CAS air space.

Rafael kept our bike directly in line behind José's, following our AFL guide. Peering around Rafael's shoulder, I could see the fence that lay ahead. A gaping hole had been torn at a point where the fence crossed a natural ravine. A number of tire tracks converged at this point; it looked as though the AFL underground had used the opening repeatedly.

As we bumped down into the washout, I lost sight of the T-bird. But by using my cyberear to filter out the noise of our own vehicles I could hear the Aztlan Border Patrol's response to the T-bird's incursion into their territory. The noise of several heavy engines combined with the *crump* of exploding shells and the rattle of machine-gun fire. I shivered, hoping we weren't due to be on the receiving end of the same thing. And I silently wished the smuggler well. Not for his own sake—for ours. As long as he was up and running and a distraction, we were safe.

As the broken fence flashed past on either side, Rafael slowed suddenly and swerved the bike hard around something. I was jerked to the side, but in the process caught a glimpse of the obstruction: most of a human body, tangled in a loose strand of barbed wire and lying face down in the dirt. It looked as though the corpse's legs had been torn off.

Suddenly the ride wasn't so much fun any more. But that body saved our lives.

We had made it through the border and were inside Aztlan. Now all we needed to do was make a run south to the tiny town of Ciudad Acuña and cross the Rio Grande—the broad river that used to form a natural border between the former United States and Aztlan, or Mexico as it was then known. And from there we'd use our bogus resident alien IDs to make our way to the capital city of Tenochtitlán and . . .

I never heard or felt the explosion. All I remember is that one minute I was sitting on the back of the dirt bike, holding fast to Rafael, and the next I was sailing horizontally through the air. I also remember hitting the ground and doing a perfect one-point landing on my chin. I bounced once, twice, and skidded to a stop, my leather jacket full of dirt. I lay there for a moment, winded, trying to figure out what had happened. Then my chest began to ache and my chin to throb. When I lifted my head, warm blood spilled down my throat from the cut that had torn my chin open.

Only later did I figure out what must have happened. The gap in the fence had been mined with nasty little anti-personnel devices, designed to take off a leg and leave the victim alive but maimed. Kind of a goodbye present from the Azzies to any of their nationals arrogant enough to think that they could escape that nation on foot. The mine had taken out the rear wheel of our dirt bike, throwing the cycle up into the air and sending Rafael and I tumbling end over end. The saddle bags had taken most of the blast, protecting my legs. We'd been going fast enough to avoid being injured by the explosion ourselves, and slow enough, thanks to Rafael having to swerve around the corpse, that we stood a chance of surviving our respective landings.

When I could breathe again, I called out for Rafael. He lay a meter or two ahead, tangled in some cactus. His body was so contorted, so still, that for a terrifying moment I thought he was dead. Then he groaned and sat up.

I rose to my feet and stumbled over to him.

"Raf!" I wheezed.

Then both of us asked, at the same time: "Are you all right?"

Rafael showed his teeth in what was more of a wince than a grin. His right hand cradled his left arm. "I think I've sprained my wrist," he gritted. "And maybe bruised a rib. And . . . ow!" With an angry tug, he yanked a cactus spine out of his cheek. Then his eyes widened in horror. "Leni—your throat! It's . . ."

I quickly felt for damage. My hand came away bloody, but after a frantic moment I reassured myself that the cut was confined to my chin. Face wounds always bled a lot, but from the feel of this one I'd need stitches. I unzipped my jacket, wadded the front of my T-shirt, and lifted it to press the fabric against the cut and slow the bleeding.

Having assured himself that I wasn't going to die on him then and there, Rafael began to walk back to where the remains of the dirt bike lay. At first I just watched him, but then I suddenly realized what had caused the crash.

"Raf, stop! Don't go any further! The ground is mined!"

Raf halted abruptly, one foot dangling above the ground in what would have been a comical pose, had he not been in such danger. Gingerly, he reversed direction and backed away from the bike, carefully placing each foot in the prints he'd already made.

"Whew!" he said. "I owe you one, Leni."

I laughed, releasing my tension. "You can pay me back any time, Raf."

That was when the spotlight clicked on. We both froze like possums caught in vehicle headlights. I heard a whirring noise and raised one arm—slowly—to shield my eyes from the bright glare of halogen light. A few meters away, a surveillance drone hung at about chest height. Rotors held it aloft, their engines muted to the point where they were little more than a whirring whisper. I hadn't even heard it coming—perhaps the explosion had temporarily glitched my cyberear. The thing moved slightly, positioning itself equidistant from Rafael and I. A second spotlight on the drone clicked on—one for each of us.

"Alto!" a voice from the drone said in Spanish. "You are in a restricted area. Please remain in place until security forces arrive. Do not attempt to move, or lethal force will be used against you." The message repeated itself in English.

The automated warning was polite enough, but the gun ports that studded the armored surface of the drone like round black eyes made it clear that there would be no debate.

I glanced at Rafael. His eyes locked with mine and he tipped his head slightly. *Run?* was the unspoken question.

I moved my head a fraction to the left and right. *No.* But I knew we'd be dead if we stood there placidly, like cows waiting for the slaughter, until the Aztlan Border Patrol arrived. We might not be smugglers blasting through the border in a souped-up T-bird, but we were clearly entering the country illegally. The Azzies would know that there had to be some reason why two Seattle residents had chosen to bypass the months of datawork it took to legally obtain an entry visa to Aztlan—and why they were carrying fake resident alien ID. They'd stop at nothing to find what that reason was, and how we'd gotten the ID. Their interrogation methods wouldn't be pretty.

But we couldn't run. We'd be torn to pieces by the drone's automated weapon systems before we took a single step. The familiar bulge of the Beretta, still in its shoulder holster under my arm, was cold comfort. I'd be dead before I could draw it—not to use against the armored drone but against the flesh and blood security personnel whose vehicles I could hear approaching, even now.

Now matter what we did, we were hooped.

And then I heard the familiar drone of a dirt bike. José! In the aftermath of the crash, I'd forgotten all about him. Had I thought about it, I might have concluded that he had abandoned us for dead after the mine exploded. But now I envisioned him as the cavalry, coming to our rescue . . .

No, frag it. Was that the sound of larger vehicles, in pursuit of the bike? I turned my head slightly so that my aural boosters could pick up the sound better. Wonderful though they might be, the cybernetics were limited by the sound-catching ability of my outer, flesh-and-blood ear.

A burst of gunfire confirmed my suspicions. José was in as much drek as we were.

In my peripheral vision, I saw something pass across the face of the half moon. Odd, I thought. I hadn't heard any roar of jet engines. Did the Azzies have ultra-quiet jets, as well as silenced drones?

I didn't get a chance to ponder the question further. The whine of the dirt bike was suddenly very close, and then José came bursting over the top of the ravine a few meters away from us on the left. He landed—hard—nearly dumping his bike, but then recovered at the last moment and put the motorcycle into a tight tun, its rear wheel skidding wide and sending dirt flying.

"José!" Rafael yelled. "Over here—"

A blast of gunfire from the drone drowned out Rafael's call. The bullets kicked up dirt near the bike's back tire. The drone had lifted, turned, sped toward the motorcycle and shot in one smooth motion—and at the same time the spotlights that had been pinning Rafael and I swung away, leaving us temporarily in darkness.

"Run, Raf!" I screamed as I pelted for the side of the ravine opposite where José had appeared. I heard him a step or two behind me. Together we scrambled up the slope.

Behind us, the drone buzzed after José, its logic circuits having chosen him as the greater threat. Had José deliberately drawn it off?

For a second or two, I almost thought we were going to escape. Together, Raf and I reached the top of the washout, scrambling up the last meter to emerge gasping for air at the top. I caught his sleeve, dragging him after me as I ran away from the ravine, moving parallel with the border fence that lay a hundred meters or so to our right. Then I angled toward it, thinking it was best to get back to the relative safety of the Confederated American States. Just a few minutes into Aztlan, and already I'd had enough of the place.

Big mistake. I'd forgotten about all of the detection equipment that lined the border. We must have been triggering dozens of sensors with every step—sensors that were automatically updating our position for the border patrol. I heard the distinctive whine of a low-altitude vehicle ahead of us, saw its spotlight sweeping back and forth as the vehicle's crew tried to pick us out. Red tracers streaked through the darkness as the LAV opened fire, fragmenting a nearby cactus with its first burst. Within seconds, the spotlight would find us and we'd be dead. And we weren't even close to the fence yet. Not that the Azzies would respect the sanctity of us having reached CAS ground, were it possible to reach it.

Just as the LAV began to turn toward us, I heard a rustling noise above. A sudden wind buffeted me from behind. I had just made up my mind to separate from Rafael, to run in a different direction and try to draw the Azzie's fire, when something grabbed me from behind. It felt as though a steel cable had wrapped itself around my chest—more than one cable, actually. I heard Rafael cry out and realized that he must have been snagged, too.

As the searchlight of the LAV swept over us at last, I caught a glimpse of what was wrapped around my chest. A taloned foot? With *feathers*? Then I was jerked off the ground. Tracer fire streaked across the space I had just occupied while the earth fell away below.

I looked over and saw that Rafael was also in the grip of a taloned foot. Then I twisted around—too surprised to care about the aching of my bruised chest—and looked up behind me.

The sight nearly caused my heart to stop.

We were being carried aloft by a dragon—a winged, serpentine creature whose body was covered in feathers. Two enormous eyes above a fang-filled mouth reflected the moonlight in a brilliant turquoise glow, and the rushing sound of beating wings filled my ears. A long, snakelike tail, tipped with feathers, streamed straight out behind the creature as it flew upward into the night.

"Good gods, Raf," I gasped. "What the frag . . . ?"

Even by the low light of the moon, I could tell that Rafael's face was white. He whispered his answer, unwilling to draw the attention of the beast that held us firmly in its grip: "A feathered serpent. A quetzal dragon."

I hadn't really needed the explanation. I'd actually meant to ask "why," not "what." I'd seen dragons on trideo; they were a part of the Awakened world. They owned corporations, headed up armies and underworld organizations and, even though they were normally quite reclusive, took part in normal civil life. Hell, they even ran for the presidency of UCAS—and won.

But they were also carnivores, with a taste for live prey. According to the parabiology holos I'd scanned in school, they liked to swoop down and catch their prey unaware, then carry it off to their lair to feed upon it at leisure.

I wondered if we were going to be the feathered serpent's next meal.

8

I tried not to look down. The ground was very far away—the LAV that had been shooting at us looked bug-sized and the border fence was a hair-thin line of silver in the moonlight. The desert swept past my dangling feet as the feathered serpent flew away from the border and to the southwest.

I've never been particularly afraid of heights or flying, but being carried hundreds of meters above the ground by a creature that might, on a whim, let go of me at any moment was not my idea of fun. I held fast to the lizardlike foot that had clamped around my chest, bracing my arms and trying not to make any sudden movements that might cause the creature to change its grip. The wind whistled past, whipping my hair and causing my pant legs to flutter and my eyes to water. The night air was still warm, but I shivered anyway.

I was glad to see that Rafael had stopped struggling. He stared up at the feathered serpent, his face a mixture of awe and apprehension. Then he looked over in my direction. "Leni," he called to me. "Do you still have your Beretta?"

I almost laughed out loud. But I could feel the answer to Rafael's question. The feathered serpent's grip was squeezing the gun tight against my chest. There was no way I could draw it, even if I wanted to. And I didn't. Not until we were on the ground. Even then, I knew that threatening a creature close to twenty meters long with anything less than a missile launcher would be suicidal. But I wasn't one to go down without a fight. And if it made Rafael feel better . . .

"I've got it," I said. "But there's no point in icing our 'pilot' just yet. Not until we've landed."

"Right." He drew up his legs, holding one foot slightly forward. "I've still got my ordnance."

He was referring to his Streetline Special, a cheap com-

posite gun that he had tucked into the top of one of his heavy
black motorcycle boots. I'd scorned it as touchy and unreliable—Rafael was more likely to blow his own foot off by
"holstering" it than he was to hit anything in a firefight—but
now I was glad of the backup. This dragon's next meal was
going to bite back. But for now, the only thing to do was
wait—and try to enjoy the view.

The feathered serpent seemed oblivious to us. It flew on
through the night, powerful wings beating a steady rhythm.
The feathers that lay sleek against its long, serpentine body
rustled gently in the wind. Occasionally its head turned as
it scanned the ground below and, with a flick of its tail,
changed direction. It seemed to be navigating by the dark
ribbons of river canyon, which it followed for a time, and by
the lights of the towns that we were passing. We crossed a
wide expanse of river that I guessed must be the Rio Grande,
and ahead in the distance I could see a larger smudge of
yellow light framed by mountains, one of them shaped like a
saddle.

As we flew past the lights I recognized the city as Monterrey by its distinctive landmark—a towering slab of concrete, more than twenty stories tall, topped by green lasers
that swung through the night like searchlights. The monu-
ment was ugly as hell and had been built in the last century. I
recognized it from the knowsoft I'd slotted on Aztlan, back
in Seattle. The *Faro del Comercio*—Beacon of Commerce.
A tribute to all that was ugly and crass about big business
and megacorporations.

Every now and then I caught a whiff of the dragon's fetid
breath as it exhaled on a downstroke. The smell was a cross
between ammonia and rotting meat. It burned my nose and
throat and made me cough so hard I almost retched. At first I
thought that my sinuses might have been weakened by my
recent cold, but Rafael seemed equally affected. I began to
wonder if the stories about dragons breathing poisonous
fumes that could knock a person dead in seconds were true.
If so, our weapons would be of little use.

As I finished coughing, Rafael caught my eye. His thoughts
must have been running along similar lines. "I'm sorry, Leni,"
he said. "If I hadn't dumped the bike . . ."

"The mine blew the fragging wheel off, Raf," I told him. "It wasn't your fault that we—"

Silencio! The "voice" of the feathered serpent was a whistling hiss. The words entered my mind directly—the dragon's mouth never even opened. To emphasize its command, it squeezed with the talons that gripped me—just enough to force me to exhale sharply. The squeeze lasted a second or two—long enough for me to get panicky about ever being able to breathe again. Then the grip relaxed enough for me to gasp in a lungful of air.

I glanced over at Rafael, who mirrored my worried frown. The creature's telepathic words had been "spoken" in Spanish. Did it understand English, as well? Frag it—this was an Awakened creature. For all I knew it could read minds.

I didn't have time to ponder that last one. My stomach fell upward into my throat as the feathered serpent folded its wings and dived. The ground rushed toward us and the wind tore at my clothes and hair. I closed my eyes, opened them, and closed them again as the dragon thrust out its wings and we swooped into a steep U-curve. Canyon walls flashed past us on either side as the dragon's flight leveled out a few dozen meters above the bottom of the canyon and I fought to hold down my supper. Then I heard the sound of a chopper engine overhead. Looking past the feathered serpent's narrow torso, I saw a dark shape that must have been an Azzie helicopter gunship. Even though my cyberear seemed to be working again, the dragon had heard the threat a few seconds earlier than I had. Its hearing and night vision must have been sensitive indeed. Sensitive enough for us not to have a hope of escaping the thing.

For the rest of the journey we hugged the ground. I wondered if the creature knew about radar-equipped helicopter gunships. By now we had passed the larger city and entered a rougher, more mountainous region. We were low enough that I could see the remains of a road that hadn't been used in some time—scrubby bushes were growing in the middle of it where the asphalt had cracked. At one point a bridge that once connected two sections of the road had fallen away into the canyon below and now lay in a skeletal heap of concrete flesh and exposed metal bones.

We rounded a bulge of hillside and, ahead in the moonlight, I could see that the road ended in a wide expanse of asphalt that must once have been a parking lot. Derelict buildings with broken windows ringed this area. Behind them, leading at a steep angle up the hillside, was a funicular—a pair of old-fashioned cable cars that were once hauled up a steep pair of tracks by a metal cable. The two cars lay at the bottom of the tracks behind the buildings, the cables tangled and slack against the hillside. At the top of the tracks, behind a pile of loose rock, a dark, jagged hole led into the earth.

It seemed to be our destination. With powerful backstrokes of its feathered wings, the dragon hovered a moment above the flat area at the top of the funicular tracks. Then, when we were still two or three meters above the ground, the dragon released its grip and Rafael and I fell. After so long in the air, my legs were like jelly. I landed on my feet, but immediately collapsed to my knees and had to throw out my hands to stop myself from falling flat on my face. Rafael had also landed hard, but at the same time was scrabbling for the weapon in his boot. Cursing his injured wrist, he at last hauled the Streetline Special from its hiding place. I rolled behind a rock, reaching into my jacket for my Beretta as I did. Drawing it and flicking off the safety, I braced my weapon as the feathered serpent landed and aimed for its eye. I figured I'd only get one shot.

Before my finger could twitch, my adrenaline-fired fear was suddenly gone. In its place I felt a wave of calm sweep over me. The trembling in my arms stopped, my hands relaxed their grip on the Beretta, and I actually smiled, so at ease did I feel. It was like the mellow rush of a tranq patch, hitting with a rush that affected body and mind at once. My muscles felt as relaxed as if I'd just been given an hour-long massage, and my mind had entered the calm you experience just before a sound night's sleep . . .

I tried to summon up some fear, to shake off the effect. A tiny part of me recognized that the dragon was using magic to mess up my emotions, and was angry. But it was a distant voice, shouting a warning from far away. It was all I could do to glance over at Rafael, to see that he too had lowered his weapon. If I hadn't been feeling so good, I would have cried to see my powerful half-ork friend reduced to a complacent piece of prey, just waiting to be eaten.

Then the dragon "spoke" again. *Do not be afraid. The kinswoman Rosalita was a friend. No harm comes to you here. Follow.*

Turning away from us, the feathered serpent folded its wings and scuttled into the hole in the hillside. It moved on two short legs, but at the same time undulated its body like a snake, slithering with a whisper of feathers against stone. As the tip of its plumed tail disappeared into the cave, the spell broke and my heart pounded in my chest.

"Sweet Jesus!" Rafael exclaimed violently. He lurched to his feet. "It knew Mama Grande!"

I stood and shoved my Beretta back into its shoulder holster. A gun wasn't much good when your mind couldn't give your finger the command to pull the trigger. "Come on," I said to Rafael. "Let's find out what it wants."

Telling myself to calm down—that if the dragon wanted to make a meal of us it would have done so by now—I stepped over the rubble that half-blocked the entrance to the cave and clambered inside. Rafael flicked on the silver lighter that his father had given him, years ago, and that he carried everywhere with him still. It illuminated the cave with a fitful yellow light.

A more or less flat path wound its way between fantastic formations of stalagmites and stalactites. Some of the shapes suggested hulking beasts or demonic faces, while others were more benign, reminiscent of mounded ice cream cones. Water dripped from the ceiling in places, *plinking* against the stone below in a steady drip. Above the path, the ceiling of the cave was hung with an electric wire, from which drooped a series of burned out or broken light bulbs. I sharpened the gain on my cyberear and could just hear the slithering whisper of the dragon as it disappeared into a deeper cave. Tipping my head in that direction, I beckoned for Rafael to follow.

The path wound through a series of caves, some still marked with rusted signs that bore such fanciful names as "Chamber of Clouds" or "The Eighth Wonder." I tried to picture this as the tourist attraction it must once have been, with happy families chattering and shooting trid—or whatever they'd used to record holiday memories decades ago. Now the floor was rough underfoot with fallen stone, and the system of caverns was a damp, dark, eerie place. Despite the dragon's words of reassurance, I couldn't help but wonder why it was leading us so far away from the outside world.

Every few steps we had to pause, while Rafael let his lighter cool. The brief moments of absolute darkness were the most unnerving of all. Every drip of water became the scuffle of a monstrous foot, and the faint breeze that whispered through the caverns was the soft laughter of a predator stalking its prey. The air inside the caves was cool—a contrast to the hot desert night.

Rafael cursed as his lighter again became hot enough to burn his thumb. As the tiny light went out, I could see a dim glow ahead. From an inner cave wafted the smell of the feathered serpent's noxious ammonia-and-carrion breath. Feeling my way along cautiously, arms extended and tapping ahead with my foot before I set it down on the path, I rounded a bend and entered yet another cavern. Rafael followed, one hand on my shoulder. He let out a low whistle at the sight that greeted us.

The dragon lay on a wide bench of stone in a cavern that was filled with natural pillars where stalagmites and stalactites had grown together and fused. The feathered serpent itself was the source of the glow I had seen—each of its feathers shone with an unearthly, bioluminescent light. The serpentine creature's body was mostly green, but shaded into a brilliant turquoise closer to the tail and from there into a dull, fire-ember red. The tips of its wings, tail, and the crest of feathers that surrounded its head were a multitude of colors: red, yellow, royal blue, turquoise, and green.

The thing lay coiled like a serpent, wings folded back and legs tucked away somewhere under the coils of its body. Its head was erect and its mouth was closed, but a long, slender tongue darted in and out, tasting the air. As I stood, uncertain whether to approach it, the dragon ruffled its brilliant crest and "spoke" in a hissing whisper that echoed in my mind.

The helicopters are searching for us, it said. *We shall wait here.*

It seemed anachronistic, somehow, for a creature as ancient as a dragon to be speaking of modern helicopter gunships, especially in this setting. I reminded myself that there were dragons that ran corporations and dabbled in the stock market. It shouldn't have surprised me to find a dragon wearing a business suit.

"We're hiding?" I asked.

Yesss.

"Who are you?"

You may call me Soñador.

The word was Spanish for dreamer. I couldn't begin to guess what a dragon would dream about—what its hopes, dreams, or wishes might be.

"How did you know my grandmother?" Rafael's voice was edgy, tense. I was glad to see that the Streetline Special was back in his boot.

Rosalita was one of those who was called by Snake, the feathered serpent answered. *Once, when I suffered wounds, she healed me.*

"Called by Snake?" I repeated. "You mean Mama Grande really was a shaman? She wasn't just eccentric?" I rubbed my nose—my sinuses were still clear. So the ice-water cure hadn't been bogus after all. It was legit. Magic. I wondered how many other things that we'd assumed about Mama G were going to be proved wrong.

The kinswoman Rosalita was a powerful bruja, the dragon said. *But then her thoughts became confused. She lost her memories—and her healing magic.*

"How?" Rafael asked abruptly. "Why? When did it happen?"

The feathered serpent hissed out loud at Rafael in annoyance. Its crest rose to form a bristling halo around its head. *We do not know how or why. Only when: just before she left Aztlan. If you want to satisfy your curiosity, start in Izamal. That's where the* sacerdote *found her, just after it happened.*

I frowned at that one. *Sacerdote?* Mama G had fallen into the hands of the Aztlaner priesthood once before? Then why had Vargas waited until she came to Seattle to question and kill her? I could only suppose that the priesthood hadn't realized who she was at the time.

The dragon cut off my train of thought. *After her mind became confused, Rosalita became a danger to herself—and to those she once helped,* it continued. Its crest had flattened, and its telepathic "voice" had lost the angry, hissing edge. *Those of us on the revolutionary council decided that she should leave Aztlan. And now her kinsman returns in her stead. I owed the human Rosalita a debt of healing, and so I have saved your life, and that of your companion. The debt is paid.*

"The revolutionary council?" Rafael asked incredulously. "My grandmother was a rebel fighter?"

Not a fighter, the dragon said. *Those whom Snake has called seek to heal, not harm. They share the secrets of life, not death.*

"I doubt if Mama Grande was a revolutionary herself, Raf," I told my friend. "But it looks as though she was helping the rebels by healing their wounded. And I'll bet she traveled in some pretty high circles, if she was healing dragons and was known to this 'revolutionary council.' She probably knew the names and faces of the rebel leadership. That would explain why the AFL took such care to get her out of the country and to a hiding place as far from Aztlan as they could manage. The way she rambled on as her memory faded in and out, she might have let some paydata slip that could have led the Azzies straight to the rebel forces."

Rafael frowned. "I wonder if that's why my parents had to leave Aztlan. Because of Mama Grande being linked to the rebels. That would explain why my mother never spoke of her. She'd have been angry, have blamed Mama Grande for my father's death. Wow. That's harsh." He sat heavily on a low mound of rock. "So what do we do now?"

The question had been directed at me, but the dragon answered. *We wait. Soon the helicopters will give up the search. And then I shall leave this place.*

"And what about us?" I asked Soñador. "And our guide, José? Did he make it? Did you see him? Do you know where he is?"

The feathered serpent weaved its head from side to side. *I do not know that human's fate.*

"Couldn't you look for him?" Rafael asked. "He was a good guy, someone I'd be proud to have on my team. Last time we saw José, he had a pack of Azzie nasties on his tail. Are you just going to leave him to fend for himself?"

He is not the one to whom I owed a debt. He merely made

me aware that you were coming. His well-being is not my responsibility.

"Why, you cold-blooded . . ."

"Raf!" I grabbed my friend's arm as he started to rise. "Be chill! That's a dragon you're talking to, for frag's sake. Don't slot it off!"

Rafael grumbled something unintelligible and balled his fists.

I decided to approach things on a more practical level. "Where are we?" I asked Soñador. "How far are we from Tenochtitlán?" The capital was our next stop; I had the name of a "data dealer" in that city who would help us track down information on Mama G's killer. José was supposed to have escorted us there, but now we'd have to make it on our own. At least we had the fake ID he'd prepared for us.

I thought the dragon's eyes narrowed slightly at my question, but couldn't be sure. The light that came from its feathers made it difficult to make out its expression.

You are only a few kilometers from the settlement of Monterrey, it answered. *From there you can arrange for conveyance to Tenochtitlán. All roads lead to that city, and all lead from it. All things begin and end in Tenochtitlán.*

The feathered serpent was probably referring to mundane transportation routes, but its words sounded almost prophetic. I stared at it, wondering what details it was choosing not to reveal to us. How and when had Mama Grande healed it? What magical secrets had the pair shared?

It seemed that I wasn't about to get the chance to even ask. Soñador rose to its feet and headed toward us. I stepped warily aside as it made for the cavern's exit.

We may leave now, it said. *The helicopters have ended their search.*

"But aren't you going to help us to—"

The light from its feathers suddenly went out. The dragon padded away into the darkness, its claws making scraping sounds on the stone floor of the cave.

"Frag!" I felt around for Rafael, bumped into him in the dark. "I hope you still have your lighter, Raf."

He flicked it on, revealing an empty cavern. A single feather, about the length of my forearm, was wedged in a crack of rock near my feet. I bent and picked it up. The spine was white as ivory, the feather itself as stiff and shiny as starched silk.

"Our first souvenir," I joked dryly. I handed it to Rafael. "Welcome to Aztlan."

"Come on," he said. "Let's get out of here while there's still fuel in my lighter. I don't want to get stuck in this place."

I thought then that the feathered serpent would be the weirdest thing we'd see in Aztlan. I didn't realize that even stranger sights were yet to come.

9

We reached Monterrey just before dawn Sunday and spent the day making travel arrangements. I tried to contact José, but without success. My postings on the Salsa Connection went unanswered. Our guide was either in hiding someplace where he couldn't reach a telecom—or dead. It seemed we would have to make our own travel arrangements.

We flew to Tenochtitlán, rather than taking the bus or train. The bus would have been a twelve-hour grind in the company of unwashed farmers and their chickens, while the train was an old-fashioned steel-tracks affair that stopped at every little dirt-water town, making for lots of checks by local *policía* with too much time on their hands. José had assured me that our fake ID would stand up to intense scrutiny by Aztechnology Corporate Security (ACS was under contract to provide policing throughout the country), but I figured that the fewer times we put it to the test, the better. And so we paid for an early-morning commuter flight in peso normas—currency that couldn't leave the country and so we might as well spend it—and joined the crowd of suits at the check-in counter on Monday morning.

Aztlan has some pretty lax weapons laws—even resident aliens can carry handguns without a license. But Air Montezuma doesn't like firefights on its flights, and so my Beretta and Rafael's Streetline Special had to be checked through as luggage. A clerk placed them in foam-lined red plastic boxes that would remain sealed for the duration of the flight, scanned a thumbprint onto the claim tags she slapped on them, and then directed us to our boarding gate.

We'd purchased two small travel bags and some clothes and toiletries in Monterrey to give ourselves the appearance of proper travelers. We'd also been told—at least three

times—to pick up breathers. According to the sales clerk
who sold Rafael his shaving kit, they were a necessity of life
in Tenochtitlán. She'd barely suppressed a bemused smile
when I said we'd already bought two top-of-the-line Fellini-
Med models, noted for their effectiveness against both par-
ticulates and noxious gases. Only when we reached the
capital did I find out why that was so funny.

The AFL had supplied Rafael and I with fake ID datacards.
According to these pocket-sized pieces of data-encoded
plastic, we were Lola and Rico Terrones, a married couple
from Seattle who had been working at Nuevo Laredo's race
track for the past four months. According to our resident alien
data, we had been granted work visas in Aztlan on the basis
of our skill in caring for and training the chemically and
cybernetically boosted greyhounds that ran at the Galgó-
dromo. A bit ironic, really. I've been strictly a cat person ever
since the time when, at the tender age of six, I patted a dog
and got my arm ripped open for the trouble. The sum total of
my knowledge of dogs is which end the bark and bite are
attached to. But Rafael actually followed greyhound racing at
one point in time (what sport *didn't* he watch on trid?) and
could reasonably fake it. The region's lingering code of
machismo would allow me to play the supporting role of less
knowledgeable wife.

As resident aliens, we could travel as we pleased in Aztlan.
We didn't have to provide a detailed itinerary of our every
move, the way tourists visiting on a travel visa did. Nor were
we limited to a maximum of sixty days in the country. Not
that we intended to stay that long. We'd be a maximum of a
week or two.

Or so I thought at the time. As it turned out, one of us
would not be returning at all.

When I'd first decided to press ahead with my investigation of Mama G's death, I'd thought that the warm sunshine
of Aztlan would be a welcome change from the chilling rain
of Seattle. As soon as we reached Tenochtitlán, I realized my
mistake. From the air, all that can be seen of the capital is a
thick brown smog that obscures the ground. The occasional
skyscraper or upper layer of an enormous stepped pyramid
juts through this obscuring haze, but otherwise the sprawling
mass of dun-colored buildings that fill the highland valley

are completely hidden from view. Somewhere below the haze, nearly eighteen million people (closer to twenty-two million, if you count the SINless) eat, sleep, live—and breathe.

Or try to. As soon as we collected our luggage and found our way out of the bustling maze of the Aeropuerto Benito Juárez, the combination of heat and smog hit us. Even with a breather on, I felt as though I had been wrapped in an electric blanket that was set on high and dropped into the smoky haze of a forest fire. My clothing stuck to my sweating skin, I could taste the pollution in the air, and my lungs felt as tight and raw as the first time I'd tried smoking. And this was with the breather on. Pity the peasant who was too poor to afford one. *El humo grande*—the "big smoke"—would lay him low in seconds.

Add to this the fact that the city lies in a mountain valley at nearly twenty-three hundred meters above sea level. The altitude alone was enough to make me dizzy, never mind the oppressive heat and air pollution.

In its will, the great dragon Dunkelzahn had offered twenty million nuyen to the first person or company to develop a plant that would act as a biological filter to clean up the air in Tenochtitlán and other smog-choked cities. I could see now what had inspired this bequest.

We soon found out why the sales clerk had smiled at our Fellini-Med breathers. In the decades before cybereyes had made glasses obsolete, a person could be instantly recognized as a brainwipe by the type of eyeglasses he wore. The worst, my grandmother once told me, was having to wear the squared-off, black plastic frames that were all her struggling family of six could afford. Back when my grandmother was a kid, in the decades that saw the introduction of glam rock and all of its customized accessories, the rage in eyewear was tinted-glass lenses, color-coordinated frames, flamboyantly outré shapes, and flip-up shades. Sixty years later, she still could remember the names the other kids teased her with on account of her glasses.

Rafael and I weren't being called names, but we were getting looks. And it was easy to see why. Suddenly the stories I'd heard of Aztlan go-gangers geeking other kids for their breathers made sense. All around us, the smartly dressed

citizens of Tenochtitlán were wearing breathers that looked as
though they'd come from a jeweler or a custom bodywork
shop. Some were shining chrome or candy-apple red, while
others looked as though they had been laminated with silver—
or even gold. Many were set with precious stones, including
sea-green jade and multicolored opals. A few glittered with
the fiery flash that only comes from a real diamond. Others
were hung with lace or trimmed with embroidered velvet. The
shapes and forms also varied—a number were molded to look
like the masks you see on ancient Aztec and Mayan sculp-
tures, while others bore delicate filigree work that took the
form of stylized feathers, intricate geometric shapes, or deli-
cately tinkling bells. Compared to these, our breathers were
functional and plain in the extreme. They immediately marked
us as fashion-unconscious—and as tourists in Tenochtitlán.

Just as well that José hadn't tried to set up a cover identity
for us as Aztlaner nationals. Between the breathers and the
rubber-necking we did as we rode through the city, we'd
never have pulled it off. As resident aliens visiting the capital for the first time after contracting to work in Aztlan, we
had a better chance of playing our parts.

We hopped a taxi from the airport and directed the driver
to take us to one of the Comfort Inns, a chain of medium-
cost hotels recommended by the datasoft I'd slotted earlier
that day. I'd had trouble making a booking—it seemed like
every hotel in Tenochtitlán was full. I'd finally managed to
snag the last room at a hotel in Iztapalapa, a suburb to the
south of the downtown core. It wasn't the nicest part of the
city, but I figured an ex-cop and a would-be combat biker
could handle it.

The dataguide told me how much to expect to pay for a
taxi—and had offered hints on how to barter the driver down
to the proper amount. It had also warned me against accepting a ride from the throng of "taxi" drivers who cluster outside the arrivals gate. They were the ones whose cars had
non-standard GridGuide software—or worse yet, who fell
back upon their own navigational abilities. According to the
guide I'd slotted, at least once a week one of these *carcachas*
wound up crunched against a divider or smashing head-on
into a vehicle that was going the *right* way down a one-way
street.

Compared to these wrecks, the Volkswagen GoCar we climbed into was a luxury vehicle. I sighed in relief as the doors sealed and the air conditioning kicked in, and removed my breather. Rafael did the same—although the taxi was too small to have the head room his massive frame demanded. He slouched down, one muscular arm lying across the back seat, and fluffed out his sweat-stained shirt to catch the cool breeze from the cab's blowers.

We only got to see a little of the city as we rode to our hotel. For one thing, the smog limited visibility to about a dozen blocks or so. And much of the drive was confined to the city's complex system of elevated autoroutes. But we did dip down to ground level now and then—exiting a ramp at a dizzying speed that made me clutch the edge of my seat— and so we saw a little bit of street-level Tenochtitlán.

The city's been the cultural and political capital of this area since the Aztecs founded it in the thirteen hundreds. It's a dog's breakfast of architectural styles—ultra-modern tinted glass skyscrapers and geodesic domes rub shoulders with heritage buildings constructed shortly after the Spanish conquest (buildings that are patched together with plenty of ferrocrete, and can hardly be called "original" any more). Gleaming luxury hotels alternate with tiny concrete-and-plaster shops that are fronted at street level with corrugated metal roll-up doors painted in vivid primary colors. The culture clash is everywhere—traditionalist Aztlan buildings and taco stands share street space with pagoda-roofed noodle and sushi bars, monumental arches supported by Grecian pillars, New York-style haberdashery shops, a smaller-scale reproduction of the Sydney opera house, dome-topped towers reminiscent of something out of a Russian fairy tale, and streetside cappuccino bars that looked as if they had been lifted, clientele and all (but with fancier breathers, of course) from the rainy streets of Seattle.

Despite the cosmopolitan air, Tenochtitlán is very much an Aztlaner city. A number of the larger buildings are decorated with wall murals and mosaics celebrating the original "Mexico's" liberation from Spain and other historical events such as the changing of the country's name to Aztlan by President Francisco Pavón after the Azatlán Party's victory of 2015. And despite the fact that the average citizen thumbs his nose at "traditionals," tributes to the ancient Aztecs are everywhere.

Our taxi swept around more than one traffic circle—six lanes of cars jostling in and out in a whirlpool of exhaust and honking horns—and passed numerous public squares dotted with pedestalled statues. Some of these were human figures: rifle-toting revolutionaries, top-hatted statesmen, the Aztec king Cuitláhuac in his feather headdress and cape, and a winged "angel of independence." Others were statues of the gods. I couldn't see much as we whizzed past, but I got an overall impression of fearsomely grimacing skeletal monstrosities.

Even though I had Azzie blood flowing in my veins, this country felt totally foreign to me. My mother had severed her ties with her "heathen" relatives in Aztlan when she emigrated north with my father and grandmother. I was born in Seattle and had been raised to be a good Catholic girl by parents who did everything they could to assimilate and fit in. Rendered cultureless by the UCAS melting pot, I had nothing in common with the people I saw on the streets around me. Their clothing, gestures, attitudes—even the pitch of their voices and the way they walked—were completely alien to me. Even the weather didn't feel right.

We stopped at one of the few traffic lights and were immediately swarmed with street vendors who did their best to get us to crack the windows of the air-conditioned cab. Rafael waved to one dwarf kid who had to stand on tiptoe to peer in through the window. She was dressed in ragged track pants and a grubby sweater and held a cardboard tray filled with cigarette packages, candies, home-recorded copies of chips that bore what looked like badly scanned sports team logos, and toy-sized jaguar and serpent figures made from garishly colored plastic.

"*Recuerdos! Cigarros!*" she called out in a piping voice that was muffled somewhat by her breather. "Chee-eeps! *Ollamaliztli* chee-eeps! Souvenirs! Cigarettes!"

Rafael smacked his lips. I could guess that the smog had left the same raw taste in his throat as it had in mine. He pulled some hard cash out of his pocket and began sorting through the unfamiliar metal-coated plastic coins. Before he could finish counting them, however, the driver jammed a fist down on the horn. The street kids jumped back as the traffic suddenly surged into motion again.

"Hey!" Rafael shouted to the driver. "I wanted to buy some candy. Next time don't pull away so fast!"

The driver, a troll who was even more scrunched in the tiny cab than Rafael was, smiled back at us in his rear view mirror, exposing jagged, yellow-stained teeth. "Here," he said, holding up a box of mints. "The stuff the street kids sell tastes like donkey *excremento*. Try one of these."

While Rafael and the driver—whose name turned out to be Hector—made small talk, I stared out the window. We were nearing the heart of Tenochtitlán now, and the downtown core was dotted with what looked like Aztec pyramids. The stories of these gigantic government buildings were stacked layer upon layer like a squared-off wedding cake and seemed to be made of massive sandstone blocks, trimmed with gleaming copper. At street level they had the usual collection of doors and windows, but the higher levels were fronted by gigantic sculpted heads of what I could only assume were ancient Aztec gods or rulers. Goggle-eyed monstrosities alternated with leering serpent heads and skulls decked out in feather headdresses and ear plugs.

In front, on flagpoles, Aztlaner flags hung limp in the smoggy air. The symbol that appeared on them was the same as the crest on the license that adorned the side of the meter that was rapidly ticking away peso normas: an eagle, poised on a cactus and holding a snake in its beak. According to legend, the sun god Huitzilopochtli had prophesied that when the wandering Aztec tribe saw an eagle sitting on a cactus and eating a snake, they would have arrived at their new homeland. The omen came true on the swampy island that was the original core of Tenochtitlán—the name that translated as "płace of the cactus."

The symbol was a source of Aztlaner pride, but it creeped me out. It reminded me of Mama G's death. I thought of the dead snake I had found on our doorstep the day before her murder, and of the way my adopted grandmother's throat had been slashed open by a *macauitl*. The national symbol seemed all too evocative of the death of this innocent healer shaman, carried out by the warrior eagle of the Aztlaner state. It wasn't an image I wanted to dwell upon.

I'd noticed a strong paramilitary presence ever since deplaning in Tenochtitlán—the international airport had been filled with Aztechnology Corporate Security guards, suited up in full combat armor and carrying the latest in personal high-tech weaponry. I was used to seeing guards with SMGs or assault rifles at airports—especially at those with a suborbital hub, a favorite terrorist target. But in Tenochtitlán, it seemed, there was a pair of them on every street corner. Back home, your average Star member carries a heavy pistol and stun baton. In Tenochtitlán, the *policía* on the beat is more heavily armed than a Star SWAT officer. Several of the cops had obvious cybermods, and more than one had odd-looking trinkets hanging from their heavy armor that I guessed must be the spell foci of a combat mage. They looked like hard-hooped fraggers, indeed. The sort of *policía* you'd avoid making eye contact with, rather than turning to for help when you'd been mugged.

I supposed the heavy security was due to the country's ongoing civil war. Only a few news reports had trickled out—and you could bet your hoop that these were all heavily censored by the powers that be. But it sounded like the Azzies had their hands full. In the week before our arrival a priest had been killed when the government VTOL he was traveling in exploded in mid-air on its approach to Tenochtitlán after returning from Mérida, a civil war hot spot. When I heard the news I thought for one wild moment that it might be Vargas, but instead it was a priest of Huitzilopochtli, the Azzie sun god. And three years ago, a car bomb exploded outside of the Aztechnology corporate headquarters itself, killing twelve people. No wonder the country's various security forces kept a nervous watch on the passing traffic. Most of the heat was confined to the Yucatán—but they never knew where or when the rebels might strike next.

Rafael jostled me, breaking my train of thought. As we approached the Cuitláhuac traffic circle the cab driver pointed something out that he called a *tlachtli*. Rafael craned his neck to see it. The building looked like some sort of stadium, a narrow rectangular structure topped with seats on either side and plenty of ornamental stonework. Right next to it was a *teocalli*—one of the many temples of the multi-deity Aztlan state religion.

"You mean you're not in town for the *ollamaliztli* play-offs?" The driver sounded incredulous.

"No," Rafael answered. "But I'd really like to see them. Court ball's a mega-frosty sport."

"I can recommend a good sports bar to you," the troll continued. "It's called Deportista Virtual and it's down on Rio Sena in the Zona Rosa. Not that expensive, though—I'm sure you could afford it. My cousin manages the place. The bar serves the best tequila and *botanas* in town, and every time the Jaguars score there's a free round on the house. Just mention my name, Hector Escalante, and you'll get a booth with a good trid seat. And there's a government betting station right next door."

The troll pulled out a pack of matches bearing the Deportista Virtual name and address and passed them back to us with one hand as he cut across three lanes of traffic and zoomed up yet another autoroute on ramp. He half-turned to continue his sales pitch, then suddenly yanked the wheel hard over, narrowly missing a heavily armored vehicle painted a dull matte black. I had a much closer look than I liked of the Aztechnology Corporate Security logo—a stylized, snarling jaguar face—and then we fell behind the patrol car as Hector jammed on the brakes. Rafael and I were thrown forward against our seatbelts.

"Chingada!" the troll swore explosively. "That's one *poli* I don't want to hit." His face had drained of color and his hand shook slightly as he down-shifted. He reflexively began to cross himself, then jerked his hand away from his chest.

"It's okay," I told him. "My parents were Catholic. I won't tell anyone."

"Ah." He relaxed slightly.

Rafael was still looking at the stadium, which was below us now. "I suppose it's mondo expensive to see the game in the meat," he said, sitting back at last. "Your cousin couldn't get us tickets, could he?"

The taxi driver burst into full-throated laughter. "She," he corrected. "And there's *cero* chance, *carnal*. Even if you had the pesos . . ." Suddenly realizing that he might have embarrassed us by implying that we weren't flush enough, he smiled sheepishly. "That is, you'd have to know someone very well connected. My cousin Eriqueta may be able to put you in touch with—"

"Never mind," I said. I didn't want any entanglements or distractions. "We probably won't have the time."

Rafael seemed choked. "Aw, come on, Le—Leola. It's the nationals. This game is completely intense. These boys take it seriously. In the 2052 finals, the captain of the Tenochti-tlán Jaguars cut his own heart out at the end of the game."

"He what?" I asked. "Why? Did he lose?"

"No, *señora*," the taxi driver chimed in. "Jorge Xochitalco led his team to victory, coming from behind with two goals in the final minute of the game. And then he sacrificed him-self and dedicated his win to Tezcatlipoca, god of the smok-ing mirror. They say he did it to avoid the curse."

"This curse was worse than cutting out your own heart?" I asked incredulously.

"Oh, *sí*. Xochitalco knew he was going to die anyway and be claimed by a rival god. And so he sacrificed himself."

"How do the *policía* know he killed himself? Maybe someone else did it and made it look like he committed sui-cide." Despite myself, I was hooked. Suicide and murder had been my business back when I worked with the Star. There were any number of indicators to tell the difference between the two. Hesitation marks—lesser cuts made while the victim is working up his nerve, the loosening or removal of clothing over the area where the bullet or knife is going to impact, whether the angle and depth of the wound itself corresponds with the handedness of the victim . . .

"He killed himself, all right," Rafael said. "He did it on national trid—millions of people saw it live on the sports-nets. They're still selling chips of it. He shouted out some-thing like, 'For the glory of Tezcatlipoca!' and slashed open his own chest with a snap-blade. Then he reached into the wound and grabbed his own heart and tried to yank it out." He shuddered. "I don't know how he did it. Must have been juiced on drugs. Or pumping mondo mana."

"Xochitalco was a very religious man," Hector said. He kept one eye on the traffic, cutting deftly back and forth across the four lanes that were flowing at breakneck speed along the autoroute, and the other on the rearview mirror as he engaged us in impassioned conversation. "The sportscasts say that he entered a *telpochcalli* when he was just six years old, with dreams of becoming a warrior priest. Then he discovered *ollamaliztli* and dedicated himself to sport, instead. But he still remained faithful to Tezcatlipoca. He kept the novice warrior's lock of hair at the nape of his neck until his team won the nationals in 2051—he considered that the equivalent of taking a prisoner in battle. And he—"

"But why kill himself?" I still didn't get it.

"Tezcatlipoca and Huitzilopochtli are as much rivals as the Jaguars and the Serpents are," our driver explained patiently. "Xochitalco wanted to insult Huitzilopochtli by sacrificing himself to another god in the *tlachtli*—the ball court is dedicated to the sun god and has his temple right next door. And it's a well known fact that Huitzilopochtli would have claimed Xochitalco otherwise. It's the curse, you see."

Hector took a deep breath. He was wound up now, and there would be no stopping him. I settled back and made myself comfortable.

"It started back in 2049, the year the Ensenada Eagles won the nationals. On the way home from the game, Nando Lopez died in a plane crash. He was flying with Aero Mariposa—Butterfly Air. And the butterfly is a sacred symbol of Huitzilopochtli."

I snorted. Curse indeed. I'd put money on it that Lopez wasn't the only one to die in the plane crash. And that those who had perished with him hadn't slotted the sun god off in any way.

"The next year, Gustavo De Brize led the Zempoala Cats to victory and died in Veracruz one month later when he got caught in the middle of a shootout between two go-gangs. One of the gangs called themselves Los Colibrí—the hummingbirds. And that's what warriors who died for Huitzilopochtli were said to have been reincarnated as in ancient times: hummingbirds.

"When the Jaguars won in 2051, Chucho Chamac drowned after falling off the yacht in which the Tenochtitlán team was celebrating its victory. When they found his body, washed up on the shore at Cancún, an eagle was feeding on it."

"Let me guess," I interrupted. "The eagle's a symbol of the sun god, too."

Hector nodded eagerly, gesturing with his cigar while he alternated steering and shifting with one hand. "The curse continued, even after Xochitalco's suicide. In 2053 the captain of the Guadalajara Acóatl had a heart attack the day after the final game and died on the operating table. The next year Ortega, captain of the Eagles, got drunk and fell off a ledge during the awards presentations in the adjoining *teocalli* and broke his neck. And the captain of last year's winning team—the Mérida Mariposas—died in a motorcycle crash two months after the finals. They say he hit a highway sign and was instantly decapitated. The sign, of course, bore the national symbol."

"The eagle of Huitzilopochtli," Rafael said in an awed voice. He was eating this up. "The one on the cactus that's killing the snake."

Then Rafael's eyes caught mine, and I saw the sadness in them. So he'd noticed the connection of the symbol to Mama G's death, too.

Rafael leaned over the seat, frowning. "You left out 2055."

Hector smiled. "Ah, that is the mystery. What happened to team captain Emilio Ibanez of the Tampico Voladores? No one knows, *carnal*. He disappeared from the *tlachtli* on the very night the Flyers won their hard-fought victory. But you can be certain that Huitzilopochtli claimed him, just the same."

We descended yet another off ramp and bulled our way, horn blaring, into the narrow street at the bottom of it. Hector double-parked the taxi in front of a blocky-looking concrete hotel whose street-level windows were all barred. I could see why—the neighborhood was one step up from being a squat, and several steps down from our own neighborhood in Auburn. Tough-looking men lounged on the sidewalk in front of the hotel, idly kicking at trash and giving our vehicle the once-over, and graffiti had all but obliterated what once was a colorful mural on the side of the hotel.

"This is it," Hector said brightly. "The Iztapalapa Comfort Inn." He thumbed an icon on the meter. "That'll be 27,500 pesos."

It had been an expensive trip—the equivalent of 55 nuyen.

I had my suspicions that Hector had taken us on a longish detour that circled through the downtown core and that a more direct route would have been cheaper. But I had to admit that the ride had been entertaining.

I hadn't paid much attention to the team names and playoff dates that Hector had rattled off. To me, they were just another drekload of sports trivia and the "curse" was just superstitious nonsense. But Rafael had committed to memory every word.

At the time, I thought it was all useless information. The usual drekload of statistics, topped off with superstitious nonsense about a curse. But I'd later come to be thankful for Rafael's endless capacity for soaking up sports trivia.

10

Before we left for Aztlan, I had tried to track down information on Domingo Vargas, the consular official who was the Star's primary suspect in Mama G's death. I'm not a shadowrunner myself—I prefer the outside of a detainment facility, thank you very much—but I do have a handful of connections among Seattle's shadow community. You have to, when you're a private detective. I'm good at legwork—at good old-fashioned, face-to-face question and answer interviews. And when I need muscle, Rafael can stand behind me and scowl. But decking's a specialized skill—one I sometimes have to turn to the runner community for.

Angie, my usual contact, had tried to scare up some data. She hadn't gotten much more than I already knew: Domingo Vargas, age forty-seven, consular official with the Aztlan diplomatic corps. Priest of the Path of the Sun—the Aztlaner state religion—who had dedicated himself to Xipe Totec, god of spring and renewal. Currently serving as a *bacab*— some sort of priestly title—at the Temple of the Sun in Tenochtitlán. That temple had not one, but four high priests, a system based on the fact that the ancient Azzies thought of the world as having four directions, each associated with a different color, and each assigned to a different god.

I learned also that Vargas was born and raised in Xpujil— a tiny village in the Yucatán that owes its existence to a nearby temple pyramid that was originally a tourist destination but whose ancient *teocalli* now was an important center of worship. Hermetic mage—he'd received his training at the Ciudad Universitaria in Tenochtitlán. His current address was inside one of the Aztechnology arcologies the Aztlaners jokingly call *castillos*. And "castle" is an appropriate name. Nobody but Tenochtitlán's elite gets inside one of these sprawling complexes, and the security that seals them off from the world at large is said to be more effective than a moat filled with torpedo sharks. If Rafael and I tried going in after Vargas, we'd be eaten alive before we even got a glimpse of the inside of the *castillo*. No, if we were going to confront Vargas, it had to be somewhere outside the arcology.

Aside from his trip to Seattle, Vargas only rarely left this corporate fortress. Although he did travel, some, to conduct religious services. Angie had dug up a documentary tridcast on the Path of the Sun that showed Vargas in his ceremonial gear, conducting a ritual in a small Aztlan town that had been hard hit by drought. The ceremony involved Vargas pricking his hands with a cactus spine and "raining" a few drops of blood on the parched soil. According to the tridcast, it had worked. The rains came the next day.

In the trid, Vargas wore what looked like a gold lamé jumpsuit, skin-tight over his somewhat paunchy frame. The outfit was complete with a close-fitting hood with eye holes that left his lower face bare. "Hands" and "feet" dangled at his wrists and ankles. It harkened back to ancient times and was intended to represent the flayed skin of a sacrificial victim.

After seeing the bodies of the missionaries that Vargas had killed in Seattle, I wondered if he also had other, similar costumes made of actual human skin—maybe a whole collection of them. Just how far did the Aztlaner priests take their religion, anyway?

In the tridcast, Vargas' face was painted red with yellow stripes across it, but Angie had been able to edit this color out. His hair was close-cropped, and judging from the bit of it that showed under the hood, was a solid gray. His face was fleshy with heavy jowls, but still aristocratic, more Spanish than Mesoamerind. His downturned, pouting lips were reminiscent of those on the gigantic stone heads the ancient Olmecs used to carve. His eyes were a dark brown, almost black. Flat and cold as obsidian. I imagined them staring down remorselessly as he struck Mama G again and again with his *macauitl* . . .

And that was all Angie had gotten me. A few scraps of data that were a matter of public record and an image that

haunted my dreams. Nothing on Vargas' current where-
abouts in Aztlan or his future movements. When I'd ex-
pressed my disappointment, she'd actually had the guts to try
a run against the consulate's private telecommunications
grid—and had immediately run into some black ice that sent
the master persona control program in her cyberdeck into
meltdown. Later, shaken, she'd admitted that she'd been
lucky not to get her brains fried as well. She'd had to jack
out—fast—and had suffered a headache for two days as a
result of the dump shock.

Angie had come through, however, with the name of a
"data dealer" in Tenochtitlán—an old friend of hers whose
trustworthiness and discretion she personally guaranteed.
This friend—whom Angie referred to only by the nickname
of Caco—relied upon a network of contacts throughout
Aztlan who gathered hard data, rumor, and gossip the old-
fashioned way—by listening to it with their own ears while
working their day jobs as servants, shopkeepers, and security
guards. Caco paid for this data in peso libres, which had
value outside of Aztlan and thus were coveted by those
planning on leaving the country—as Caco's information-
gatherers often had cause to do. Caco then brokered this
"word on the street" back to Tenochtitlán's shadow community, swapping information for pesos or sometimes just
trading data for data. If anyone could find the skinny on
Domingo Vargas, Angie had assured me, it was Caco.

Although Angie had met Caco in the flesh twice, she
didn't know if the data dealer was male or female. The
description she'd given me of Caco wasn't much help,
either. Average height, average weight. Average features
with no distinguishing marks or obvious cyberware. Collar-
length, slightly wavy brown hair, brown eyes. Skin tone
half way between Euro and Mesoamerind. Neither a flashy
dresser nor scruffy. The kind of person who would blend
into an Aztlaner crowd and never be given a second glance.

Those who were looking to buy information didn't find
Caco—instead Caco found them. The procedure, Angie told
me, was to approach any of the *esquincles*—the street
urchins who sold cigarettes, candy, and trid chips on street
corners throughout Tenochtitlán—and ask for Chiclets, a
brand of gum that had been popular in the previous century.

If the kid gave you a blank look, that meant they didn't know Caco. If the kid smiled and agreed to put you in touch with someone who did sell Chiclets, that meant that they dealt with Caco in person. Or—more likely—knew someone who knew someone who knew someone who . . .

After checking into our hotel, I started my search for Chiclets. I scored on the third *esquincle* I asked. I made the kid repeat the name Angie used on her runs—"Brain-dancer"—until I was convinced that he could pronounce it properly. Then I sent him on his way with two hundred pesos, then killed time in a nearby plaza, watching the Azzie drivers play chicken with each other. Decades ago, in an effort to cut down on pollution, the city council had decreed that each car was banned from driving in the city one day per week. Drivers responded by buying a second car, and the new set of wheels allowed their family members to take to the streets as well. The number of vehicles doubled and the result was the current anarchy that passes for driving. Amazingly, there are relatively few accidents. Ekchuah, god of travelers, must have been a busy deity.

The reply came back in two hours in an actual, honest-to-gods Chiclets container—a tiny, bright yellow cardboard box as scuffed and dirty as the kid who handed it to me. It was empty, but when I at last thought to unfold it, I saw words scrawled on the inside. An address in Iztapalapa. No date or time. A pun, perhaps? No time like the present? I might as well find out.

Rafael, meanwhile, was engaged in an avid discussion with a streetside taco vendor about the relative strengths and weaknesses of the Tenochtitlán Jaguars and the Texcoco Serpents. The first two games in the *ollamaliztli* finals had been held earlier in the week, and each had resulted in a victory for the Jaguars. The whole of Tenochtitlán was celebrating, and the street vendor was happily predicting that the Jaguars would button up the finals by winning the next game—that the final two games would be strictly exhibition matches. He told Rafael that only a fool would bet on the Serpents now—but that the odds were very good, indeed. Rafael listened gravely, nodding between bites of his taco.

I dragged Rafael away and we headed on foot to the address I'd been given. It proved to be a streetside *pulquería*—a cantina that specialized in pulque, a drink made from fermented maguey cactus. The place wasn't much more than a hole in the wall—literally. Just a large, square, concrete-walled space that could be closed off from the street by a roll-down metal door. No windows and no decor, save for battered-looking plastene tables and chairs that looked as though they'd been boosted from a public picnic area. Its floor was covered in coarse sawdust.

There were grocery shops on either side of the *pulquería* and the sidewalk was crowded with produce stands. A number of street vendors worked a nearby intersection. I thought that one of them—an ork kid whose shtick seemed to be washing the hub caps of the cars that were parked on this stretch of street—winked at me as I passed her. But I couldn't be sure.

Inside the *pulquería* itself, a scruffy-looking collection of young street punks—all of them with the sharp cheekbones and dusky skin of their Aztec and Mayan forebears—sat sipping a foamy white beverage through straws that allowed them to drink without removing their breathers. They looked like gangers. They had the lean, hungry, watchful look of the street and wore the heavy gold jewelry that served as their badge of honor, showing they'd made it to the top of their particular drekpile. More than one had earlobes that were distended by heavy gold ear plugs like the ones I'd seen in Alberto's shop. Several had gold-plated breathers.

I saw the bulge of what I guessed was a sawed-off shotgun under one synthleather jacket, and heard the *snick* of razors as one of the few women present—a bleach blonde in a tight pink sweater—flicked her cybernetic implants in a gesture like a cat flexing its claws. From the way she leaned possessively against one of the better-dressed punks, I guessed her to be in the biz and protecting her turf. I did my best to look uninterested in her man, pointedly avoided making eye contact with her, and walked directly to the bar at the back of the *pulquería.*

A barrel-chested human with the battered nose of a boxer and wearing a stained undershirt and jeans served pulque from a large plastic barrel, ladling it out into paper cups. He stood behind a bar that was made from a table placed over two sawhorses. Files rose in a buzzing spiral each time he lifted the barrel lid, and a yeasty-sweet smell filled the air. A very lethal-looking HK227 submachine gun hung on a peg hammered into the wall behind him—a deterrent for anyone who might think about stealing the credslot that was clipped to the bartender's belt or the coins that were piled in a tin cigar box that sat on one end of the bar. A curtain closed off what I guessed must be a doorway leading to a storeroom where other barrels of pulque were stored.

I paid coin for a glass of the stuff and chose a seat near the door with my back to the concrete wall. As I stirred the drink with its straw, I used my cyberear's amplification system to listen in on the conversations of those around me, paying particular attention to the quietest voices. They seemed to be talking about the usual ganger topics: scoring drugs, joyriding in boosted cars, and sex. Some things just don't change from one sprawl to the next.

A minute or so later, Rafael jandered into the *pulquería*. He ordered a drink, then sat on the opposite side of the room. He studiously ignored me, instead winking at the blonde as he settled into his seat. The next time she got up to get a drink, she ran her fingers playfully through Rafael's hair, then laughed and swished away from him as he tried to catch her hand. Her boyfriend bristled and half-rose to his feet in a challenge, but settled down again when the blonde returned to the table and snuggled up beside him again. Rafael grinned viciously behind his breather as she returned his wink behind her boyfriend's back.

I shook my head. The blonde was cheap-looking, not at all pretty. I thought Rafael had better taste than that. But perhaps he was just providing the distraction he'd promised. I just hoped a fight wouldn't break out before Caco arrived.

I took a sip of the pulque, which was milky and slightly fizzy. It had an unpleasant texture, slippery and cloying, like saliva. And a strange, nutty aftertaste. I hoped that Caco would show up soon. I didn't want to drink any more of the stuff than I had to.

I didn't have to wait long. I felt Caco's presence within twenty minutes of sitting down, just as I was wondering how much longer I could make my drink last without raising the bartender's ire. There was just a tickle at the base of the skull, at first. A cat's-paw presence that whispered through my mind and caused the hair on the back of my arms to rise as a shiver slid down my spine. I was being mind-probed— my thoughts were being magically sifted and assensed. I tried to resist, but my feeble efforts to block the spell were swept aside like fragile cobwebs.

I half-rose from my seat, then suddenly found myself unable to move. Sweat trickled down my temples as I fought back against the magical presence that had so easily invaded my mind and that now was not only reading my thoughts, but directing my actions. With a supreme effort I was able to glance over at Rafael, only to see that he was sitting rigidly in place, staring straight ahead with a glassy expression on his face. I knew it wasn't the pulque—the two glasses he'd drunk wouldn't even have given the big guy a buzz yet. He too was a victim of a spell. And that scared me even more. A mage who was able to mind-probe one target and control the actions of another so effectively and completely at once? This was one fragger who could pump mondo mana.

Suddenly my mind was my own again. I shot to my feet, heart pounding and every instinct telling me to bolt for the street. But before I could coordinate my actions, a figure appeared in the seat across the table from me in the blink of an eye, as if an invisibility spell had suddenly been dropped.

"*Hola*," the newcomer said in a husky voice that could have been male or female. "I'm Caco. You're a friend of Braindancer's?"

Just at that moment, Rafael surged to his feet, hauling the Streetline Special from his boot and pointing it at Caco's back. Within a heartbeat, half a dozen gun barrels were pointed back at him. The sawed-off shotgun was out from under the ganger's jacket, the bartender balanced his HK227 in one hand while still holding his dripping ladle in the other, and even the blonde had pulled a slim little Walther pistol from a pocket—although the gods only knew where she concealed it, since her clothing was skin-tight.

Caco half turned and smiled at Rafael, then patted the empty seat at my table. "Why don't you join us, Rafael?"

Rafael's face was purple with anger. For a heartbeat or two, I though that lead was about to fly. Then a kid's voice on the street outside bleated a warning: "*Los polis!* Chill!" And all of the guns disappeared. Rafael had the presence of mind to hide his own gun behind his back and reach for his pulque instead as a heavily armored Aztechnology Corporate Security patrol car rumbled past in the street outside, its surveillance cameras sweeping the street. Then he shrugged and crossed the *pulquería* to sit with Caco and me.

While Rafael composed himself and tucked his gun back in his boot, I took a good long look at Caco. Angie was right—it was hard to tell what gender the data dealer was. Caco's features were angular enough to be male, but there was no hint of stubble or an Adam's apple. The wrists were slim and the hands delicate, but the arms that emerged from the loose-fitting shirt were muscular enough to be those of a man. I couldn't see any hint of breasts, but then I've known a number of athletic women who had equally boyish figures. And the wavy brown hair and long dark lashes are as common among Hispanic men as women.

Caco was dressed in plain jeans and a white shirt that smelled faintly of men's cologne, and so I slotted the data dealer as "him" in my mind. But dress Caco up in a skirt and pumps and I'd just as easily have used the pronoun "her." Either way, the data dealer had the sort of face that would blend into any Aztlaner crowd. Even a trained observer like myself would be hard pressed to provide a description the *policía* could use to pick Caco out in a lineup.

A round of pulque appeared on our table, delivered by the bartender. It seemed to be on the house. I figured I should be polite, and took a sip.

"You wanted to buy some information?" Caco asked.

I hadn't said so—out loud, at any rate—but I nodded. "That's right. We want data on a certain Tenochtitlán resident."

Caco stared at me. I wondered if he was mind-probing me a second time. I was already thinking of the trid image of the Aztlaner priest, but I tried to keep the anger and sorrow I felt out of my mind, tried to suppress the gruesome images of Mama G's murder that came bubbling up unbidden. It was impossible. The most certain way to think about something is to try *not* to think about it. I wondered if my urgent need to see justice done would affect Caco's price.

"Domingo Vargas, *bacab* of Xipe Totec . . ." Caco said quietly. I was relieved that he maintained a low voice. The patrons of the *pulquería* might be Caco's people—but that didn't guarantee that they weren't also working for Aztechnology at the same time.

"What do you want to know about him?" Caco asked.

Rafael leaned over his pulque, speaking in a low voice. "His movements. What he's doing and where he's going in the next few weeks. We need to ..." He stopped, not wanting to say more.

Caco stared at Rafael for just a moment then nodded. "To get close to him," Caco said, supplying the unspoken. "For vengeance, and for honor."

I decided to take the plunge. The mage had already read my mind, after all. If Angie was wrong about us being able to trust Caco, we were as good as dead anyhow.

"We want to confront him," I said. "We want to get to him when he's alone and unprotected by bodyguards. Just to question him—not to take vengeance on him." I shot a meaningful look at Rafael. "We're not going to play judge and jury on this one."

Rafael stared at his cup of pulque, refusing to meet my eyes. He muttered something that sounded like agreement. But then my cyberear caught him adding under his breath: "Not unless we have to."

The data dealer sat back and sipped from the glass of pulque. "I have little to offer at the moment, and it may not be useful to you," Caco said. "So I will charge you only a small *mordida* of 250,000 pesos. For that, I can tell you where the person you are interested in will be making a public appearance. But I must warn you that getting close to him there will be impossible."

I looked at Rafael and raised an eyebrow.

He shrugged. "Better than nothing, I guess."

I nodded and pulled five plastiweave 50,000-peso notes out of my pocket. I figured that Caco would want to avoid leaving an electronic data trail behind.

Caco neatly folded the bills and slipped them into a pocket. "Your target will be making only one public appearance in the next two weeks, when he attends the final game of the *ollamaliztli* finals. He will most likely be chauffeured to it from his *castillo* in a government VTOL, which usually lands directly on the rooftop of the adjoining *teocalli*. There is a private balcony in the temple, overlooking the ball court, from which the priests and their attendants watch the game. A number of *sacerdotes*—priests of the sun—will be there.

"As a priest of Xipe Totec, your target is one of the four *bacabs* who will oversee the sacrifices to the gods that the victors traditionally make in the *teocalli* when the game is over. The other three *bacabs* will include those of the gods Tezcatlipoca, Quetzalcóatl, and Huitzilopochtli. If you require the information, I can give you the names of two of those priests—although they have yet to appoint a successor to replace Guzman, the *bacab* of Huitzilopochtli who was killed in the VTOL explosion last week. That information will cost you more pesos, however . . ."

I declined the offer with a wave. I didn't see how the information could help us. Later, I would wish I'd had more foresight.

"When the victory celebrations have ended, your target will most likely depart via government VTOL, which will take him directly back to his *castillo*. There is a chance that he will enter the *tlachtli* briefly when the playing field is consecrated at the beginning of the game, but only a small one. His god does not traditionally have a part in the blessing of the court."

Rafael's eyes glittered menacingly. "So all we have to do is get tickets to the game, pretend we're going into the temple with the other worshippers and . . ."

Caco smiled and gave a slight head shake. "Tickets to the final? Perhaps. But you will never get close to your target. Security at the ball court and temple—both physical and magical—is airtight. A number of Aztechnology executives will be on hand at the finals, and they're a prime target for the rebels, who are bound to step up their activities in response. Everyone entering the stands will be searched, assensed, probed . . . It's a game you'd lose before ever setting foot on the playing field, *carnal*."

I could sense Rafael bristling with frustration. Like me, he hates to be told he can't do something. But I had the sense to see that Caco was right. I knew enough about the Path of the Sun, thanks to the documentary that Angie had scrounged up, to realize that Aztlaner temples were off-limits to the general public. Only priests—and victorious ball players, I supposed—would be allowed inside the *teocalli* that adjoined the ball court. Just trying to penetrate the security that would be in place at the ball court itself during the national *ollamal-iztli* finals would be hard enough, let alone trying to enter the *teocalli*. Trying to sneak into the temple would be equivalent to lying on an altar and handing the ACS guards the sacrificial blade. Suicidal, without a doubt.

"See what else you can dig up," I told Caco. "We can afford to wait—at least for a little while. There has to be a better approach."

"Perhaps," Caco said. "If I hear anything, I'll send an *esquincle* to your hotel to sell you some Chiclets."

Rafael frowned. "How do you know where we . . ."

Caco winked. "Tenochtitlán has many eyes and ears. Not all of them are as sharp as those of your friend, but they hear what they hear. They—"

I heard the scream at the same time that Caco did. It was a child's voice—the same one that had called out a warning about the ASC patrol car earlier. The kid got out two words— *"Espíritu sangriento!"*—before the voice was choked off in an ugly gurgle. I heard the clatter of a bucket falling to the sidewalk, and then the slow, rolling rattle of a hubcap.

Caco's face went white. *"Es malo,"* he said. Then the seat in front of me was suddenly vacant. Caco had become invisible once more.

I had only a few seconds to wonder what a "bleeding spirit" was before the drek hit the fan.

11

Everyone in the *pulquería* scrambled as the "bleeding spirit" entered. At first I thought it was a freshly killed victim, already brain-dead but still staggering into the bar on automatic pilot like a chicken that continues walking after its head has been cut off. Male, human—but with a face that looked somehow wrong. Flat. Deflated. Expressionless.

Dead.

The corpse was studded with what looked like the quills of a porcupine. Then I realized that they were the broken stubs of arrows—some still with feathers intact. Blood seeped from the wounds like mist, evaporating before it hit the floor. The corpse wore only a weird loincloth to which feathers had been stitched. Its bare feet slapped heavily against the pulque-slippery concrete and it staggered, turning slightly.

That was when I saw the crudely stitched seams that ran up the legs, back, and arms of the corpse. And got a glimpse into its empty head. This was no victim only recently killed, but a walking balloon of skin from which the flesh and bone had been removed. A spirit made entirely of blood encased inside a homunculus made of human flesh.

It was headed straight for me, arms outstretched to wrap me in its foul embrace.

I screamed—adding my voice to the others that rang out around me. The corpse projected a palpable aura of fear that twisted my stomach into icy knots and that made me want to throw my weapon down and run wildly away. I fought the emotion back, my hand shaking almost uncontrollably as I tried to reach into my jacket for the Beretta. I prayed that my legs wouldn't buckle under me.

The gangers must have thrown off the effects of the

magical fear a second or two before I did. In an instant, the room was filled with the echoing roar of gunfire. At last I was able to haul the Beretta out of my shoulder holster. I didn't even bother aiming for a vital spot—just pumped round after round into the balloonlike body of the spirit.

Rafael had his Streetline Special out and was also popping away with it. Somewhere to my left and behind me, the HK227 opened up in a throaty roar. I glanced back at the bartender, making sure I wasn't going to wind up in his line of fire, and saw the curtain behind him flapping shut. Someone was beating a hasty retreat—probably the invisible Caco.

The corpse shuddered under the hail of gunfire but seemed otherwise unaffected by the bullets. Bits of flesh flew away and within seconds it was more shredded than intact. But then it turned to confront the blonde. Her mouth dropped open in surprise as her boyfriend joined the others in scrambling madly away from the thing—perhaps she'd expected him to show some *machismo* by stepping in front of her to protect her—and then she snarled angrily. She got one good slash at the monstrosity with her implanted blades, tearing open its limp face and releasing a misty spray of blood. But this gutsy move put her in our line of fire. Forced to stop shooting, the other gangers could only gape as the spirit clutched her to its chest. For a second or two, the blonde disappeared from view. We still heard her screaming, though— a long, desperate wail that quickly faded into silence. Then her body suddenly became visible again as she thudded to the floor, dead. Her face was as bleached as her hair; it looked as though her body had been drained of its blood.

Scrambling backward to get another table between myself and the blood spirit, I changed the magazine in my weapon and began firing again. The thing was blocking the wide doorway, lunging out at any who tried to escape past it. I made my decision—if Caco had chosen the back door, it had to lead somewhere. Another glance told me that the bartender had already exited the same way.

I fired a few last rounds at the walking corpse before the panicked part of my brain realized that I was wasting my time. Its flesh was all but gone now, and in its place was a misty shape composed of droplets of red, still vaguely humanoid in form. It flowed across the floor of the *pulquería*, its "legs" walking with a smooth sliding motion. It didn't exactly have eyes to turn upon me, but somewhere deep inside I knew that I was its target.

"Come on, Raf!" I screamed. "This way!"

We charged into the back room of the *pulquería*—only to be confronted by a dead end. It was a storeroom, filled with plastic barrels of pulque and without an exit.

"Drek!" Rafael screamed. "We're trapped! There's no way out!"

Then I saw the overturned barrel, still rocking gently back and forth. The wall beside it looked like solid concrete, but one section of blocks was a slightly lighter shade of gray. There was no time to search for the trigger to what must have been a hidden exit. "There!" I pointed at the differently colored patch. "Hit the wall, Raf! The bricks are fake."

After only an instant's hesitation, Rafael ran headlong across the room, throwing his shoulder against the wall. I expected to hear a splintering crash, but instead he just vanished through the bricks as though they weren't even there. I heard him land with a thud somewhere beyond the wall, then roar in pain. He'd probably landed on his injured wrist. And that's when I realized what I was looking at: an illusion. The wall—or at least, that section of it—didn't really exist.

I scrambled in that direction just as the blood-mist spirit ghosted into the storeroom, flowing in around the curtain and then assuming humanoid form once more. Outside in the *pulquería*, all was quiet. The gangers were either dead or had escaped. I heard the wail of a *policía* patrol car, then gunfire, and was thankful I hadn't run out into the street. Assuming I survived my run-in with the blood spirit, the last thing I wanted was to be face to face with an Aztechnology Corporate Security guard, a smoking Beretta in my hand.

I thought I had more time, but the blood spirit was quicker on its "feet" than I was. Just as I leaped over the barrel and through the illusionary wall, its misty hand brushed my shoulder. In that instant, the world fell out of focus around me and I felt an overwhelming weight of despair and hopelessness come crashing down upon me. I heard my voice, as if from a distance, wailing in the same tone the blonde had used seconds before her death. The cut on my chin sprang open and blood poured from it. A ruby-red mist filled my vision, blinding me. I knew I was about to die . . .

And then I heard Caco's voice. He was chanting in a strange guttural language I didn't understand. One moment it sounded as if the words were coming from a great distance, from the bottom of a dark well. The next moment Caco's voice boomed loud in my ears.

Suddenly the fog of despair that had filled my mind lifted— just a little. I felt Rafael's broad hand clamp around my arm, felt his muscles strain as he tugged me to safety. I was heaved up into the air, and as the world came back into focus again, I found myself dangling over his shoulder, bouncing around and trying not to be sick as he ran down a narrow alley. I'd lost my Beretta, but didn't care. I was alive.

Rafael had paid me back for warning him about the mine. With interest.

I couldn't see Caco anywhere. I could only assume he was still invisible, could only hope Caco had gotten away.

We made it away from the *pulquería* somehow. I think Rafael hailed a taxi—I have vague memories of traffic blurring past, of a long ride first on elevated autoroutes and then through narrow, twisting streets in the gathering dusk. We didn't go back to the Comfort Inn, but instead wound up dossing down in what looked like an even less reputable hotel.

If you could call it that. Tucked between the stanchions of an autoroute and so noisy and filled with vibrations that you'd swear the cars were driving through the hallway outside, it was little more than a flophouse in which closet-sized rooms rented for five hundred pesos an hour. Judging by the sweet smell of rotting garbage that hung in the air, it was situated close to the city dump. I hoped Rafael had the presence of mind not to use his lighter—the methane levels might be high enough to cause an explosion.

All the same, it was a place to rest my head. And I desperately needed down time. The blood spirit had taken something from me—something vital—and all I wanted to do was sleep.

Rafael spread a relatively clean blanket over the piece of foam that passed for a mattress and I lay gratefully down on it. Before allowing myself to pass out, I made him promise that he wouldn't do anything stupid. And then I laughed silently at myself. As if I were in a position to issue warnings, after nearly getting us both killed by trusting a runner I didn't even know.

Rafael solemnly nodded his head, promising to behave himself, and closed the door of the room, leaving me in darkness.

I woke up suddenly as the door opened, my hand reaching into my jacket in a reflexive motion. Drek! My shoulder holster was empty! Then I saw Rafael's huge frame silhouetted in the dim light of the hallway and relaxed. He shut the door behind him, palming the sensor that turned on the grimy light bulb that hung above my "bed." Then he squatted on the floor beside me, grinning. I could smell the beer on his breath. He'd been out somewhere, drinking.

It felt like only a few minutes had passed. But when I glanced at my watch I saw that it was already close to seven a.m. "Gods," I said as I sat up. "I've been out nearly eleven hours." I hardly knew where I was for a moment. What day was it? Monday? No, by now it had to be Tuesday.

"I figured I should let you sleep," Rafael said. His oversized canines were still bared in a gleeful grin. He looked tired, though. There were dark circles under his eyes. I guessed that he hadn't slept.

"O.K., give," I said. "What have you been up to?"

He reached into his pocket and pulled out two rectangular pieces of plastiweave. As he waved them triumphantly in his hand, I noticed the holo-logos, emblazoned on either end of the tickets: a leaping jaguar, and a coiling serpent.

"I got them," he said proudly. "Tickets to the fifth game of the *ollamaliztli* finals."

It took a moment for my brain to clear. I'd only just woken up, after all. "Frag it, Raf!" I said petulantly. "Can't you think of anything else but sports? For spirits' sake, we're here to catch Mama Grande's killer, not to watch some fragging *ball game*!"

Rafael's face fell. "But Vargas will be there," he said. "At the game. It may be our only chance to grab him."

All at once, I felt like drek.

"Sorry, Raf," I said, lowering my voice. "You're right. But let's not use those tickets unless we have to. Trying to confront Vargas in such a public, well-guarded place would be a desperation measure only. I still think there must be some other way. There has to be a better time and place other than the *ollamaliztli* finals to catch up with Vargas. Perhaps Caco can come up with something else . . ."

Rafael stuffed the tickets angrily back into his pocket. "Frag Caco and the spell that drekker rode in on. I don't trust that slag. I'll bet he's the one who led the spirit to us. The meet at the *pulquería* was a set-up."

"It couldn't have been," I said. "Caco didn't even know our names before yesterday. It was the first time we met, and we were the ones who initiated the meeting. And when the blood spirit attacked me, Caco was the one who saved me by . . ."

Raf glowered. "Caco was gone by then. I was the one who pulled your hoop out of the fire."

"You didn't hear Caco chanting?" I asked incredulously.

"Nope." Raf snorted.

"Oh." I shook my head and let it slide. The only explanation for our escape was that we'd had magic on our side— Caco's magic. But I could see that I wasn't going to persuade Rafael of that fact.

"I don't like Caco," he continued stubbornly. "The fragger knew stuff about us that—"

"Probably as a result of reading my thoughts," I said, getting exasperated now at my friend's stubbornness. "Besides, Angie recommended Caco. She said he was someone we could trust."

"Well, frag Angie, too."

I held my temper. Just. "You're right about one thing, Raf," I said in as concilliatory a tone as I could manage. "Someone did sell us out. I hate to say it, but it has to have been José."

"Null chance!" Raf snorted angrily. "That chummer was chill all the way. He—"

"Think about it, Raf," I urged. "José knew we were headed for Tenochtitlán. Even if he didn't know why we wanted to sneak into Aztlan, he knew that we wanted to get in without anyone knowing, and that Rosalita Ramirez was your grandmother. If those two facts reached Vargas' ears, he'd put one and one together and realize that we were coming after him. He'd try to eliminate us. And that attack in the *pulquería* stank of the Azzie priesthood. And of Vargas, specifically."

Before leaving Seattle, I had scanned some anthropology on the public databases, reading up on the ways the ancient Aztecs killed their sacrificial victims. They cut out their hearts and tossed them down pyramids by the thousands, tied them to altars and made them fight with useless, feather-tipped weapons against warriors armed with deadly obsidian blades, or tied them to an X-shaped framework and shot them full of arrows. The latter, which seemed to have been the source of the blood spirit that attacked us in the *pulquería,* was reminiscent of the ceremony I'd seen Vargas perform on the trid documentary. The arrows caused the captive to "rain" blood upon the earth, nourishing it and guaranteeing its fertility. It smacked of Vargas' god, Xipe Totec.

But why had Vargas chosen to send a spirit after us? As a priest, he was part of the establishment—a powerful man. Why not just call in the ACS heavies to do the job?

I hated this case, and not just because it was dangerous to my health or because my adopted grandmother was the murder victim. This investigation was making me an expert in the macabre. I had already seen things that magicians north of the border considered to be impossible. The rumors of "blood magic" being practiced in Aztlan were scoffed at by law enforcement officers and thaumaturgical professors alike.

And yet the magic that had animated the walking corpse was unquestionably the blood magic that the dragon Dunkelzahn had spoken of in its will when it offered a bounty on any blood mages captured alive, and a reward for verifiable accounts of blood magic use. And that made me pause and think. If I did follow through on my crazy idea of actually extracting Vargas from Aztlan, we could hand him over to the Dunkelzahn Institute of Magical Research and collect a bounty of one million nuyen.

For a moment or two, my conscience warred with my greed. Whether Vargas was guilty of Mama G's murder or not, we could turn him in and collect a cool million. If we really could extract the priest . . .

I shook my head. I'd make that decision when—and if—that time ever came.

Rafael was still grumbling about how José couldn't possibly have betrayed us. And I must admit, I had a hard time with that one myself. It would have been simpler for the guy to turn us over to the Azzies as soon as we entered the country. Unless something had gone wrong. Like our bike hitting a land mine . . .

All this speculation was making my brain numb. Better to deal with the here and now, instead.

"How'd you get the *ollamaliztli* tickets, Raf?"

He grunted as if he weren't going to answer me. Then vanity got the better of him. He pulled a book of matches from his pocket and tossed them onto the mattress beside me.

"Remember the cab driver?" he asked.

I nodded as I picked up the matchbook.

"His cousin came through. I went to the Deportista Virtual and asked for Hector's cousin Eriqueta. She put me in touch with a scalper named Fede. He lived up to his nickname, too. Ugliest fragger I ever saw. His face was a solid mass of scar tissue, as if it had been burned. Anyway, he scored me the tickets to the fifth game in the *ollamaliztli* finals. Fede was going to charge me five hundred thousand pesos apiece for them, but I bartered him down to half that. It meant giving up my lucky Seattle Timber Wolves flag, but it's worth it if it gets us a shot at Vargas."

I sighed. "And suppose we go to the *ollamaliztli* game, Raf. If we use those tickets, we have to go through the hardest-hooped security on the planet. They're going to make sure we enter that stadium empty-handed and that we stay in our seats and not go wandering off anywhere. But supposing we do manage to sneak away from our seats and corner Vargas somewhere. What do we do then? Take his hand, click our heels three times, and say, 'There's no place like home?' "

The allusion was lost on Rafael. He gave me a blank look. "We'll think of something," he growled. "Besides, Fede says he can help us, if the price is right. He's been around *ollamaliztli* all his life and says he knows the Tenochtitlán ball court inside and out. He knows a way past the security points, and figures he can get us into the *teocalli* itself. He's even willing to help us—"

"Gods and spirits, Rafael—are you *loco*? You told some *scalper* that we're planning to confront a high priest at the *ollamaliztli* finals? Did somebody brainwipe you when I wasn't looking?"

"It's not like I gave him Vargas' name or anything." Rafael chewed his lip petulantly with an oversized canine. Normally I found his contrite expression cute, but I was too angry at him and wasn't entirely sure he was telling the truth. Whether or not he had spilled Vargas' name, the scalper would certainly be able to figure out that a priest was our intended target, given our interest in getting into the *teocalli*. He could have been selling the information to Aztechnology as we spoke.

I'd expected more of Rafael—expected him to use the wetware the gods had given him. Now I knew why his girlfriends loved him for his brawn and not his brain. The latter only seemed to function part of the time.

"We're not going to the game, even just to watch it," I said firmly. "It's not worth the risk. We'll hold off, pray that we aren't being sold out, and wait for another opportun—"

Suddenly the floor wasn't where it used to be. Everything was in motion. I fell to my knees on the mattress and saw Rafael fall sideways and clutch at the wall for support. The air was filled with a low rumbling sound, overlaid with other noises: breaking glass, the groaning of stressed ferrocrete, and something on the floor above falling over with a heavy thud. From the autoroute above the hotel came the sound of squealing tires and the crunch of metal on metal.

I clawed my way back to my feet as the shaking stopped. "What the—"

"Earthquake!" Rafael shouted. He threw open the door. "Let's get the frag out of here, Leni. This place is a death-trap. It's likely to pancake on us."

Visions of the last big earthquake that hit Tenochtitlán immediately filled my mind. In 2029 they'd lost the national palace, what remained of the subway system—and an entire neighborhood of residential apartment buildings that had been a lot sturdier than our hotel. I was right behind Rafael as he ran out of the room and down the corridor. A handful of people—most of them European or Asian males and all of them in various stages of undress—seemed to have the same idea. They jostled past us as we ran down the rickety steps at the far end of the hallway and out the front door.

We emerged onto a sunlit street and a city that was grid-locked in the morning rush hour. All around us horns blared as traffic surged back into motion, weaving its way without stopping around the traffic signs and chunks of masonry that had fallen into the street. Street vendors paused as the earth wobbled under us once more—a less violent tremor than the first one—then went back to calling out their wares.

Above us, a window in the hotel slid open and a woman in heavy makeup leaned out of it and laughed. "Hey, gringo!" she shouted down at an embarrassed-looking Euro who stood beside us in his underwear. "Come back and get what you paid for. Let's see if you can make the earth move for me again, hey, big boy?"

A kid sitting on the hood of a stripped-down car echoed her laughter. He was maybe eight years old, but he already had the street-smart look of a ganger. A nasty-looking snap blade hung on a chain from his belt. His hair was slicked straight back with gel and a dark bruise marked his cheek. He wiped his nose frequently and smelled faintly of solvent. But he seemed steady enough on his feet as he hopped off the car and swaggered over to where we stood.

"*Hola, señor, señorita,*" he said, a wide grin on his face. "You're not from Aztlan, are you? If you were, you'd know that we always get *los temblores* at this time of year. I think you need a guide, *sí*? Someone who knows his way around the *barrios* and can show you around Tenochtitlán."

"Come on, Raf," I said, ignoring the kid. "Let's walk."

We tried to give the kid the brush-off, but he clung to us like the glue he'd probably been sniffing. He dogged our footsteps, following us down the street and repeating his offer to guide us. Raf finally turned and pressed a handful of pesos into the kid's hands.

"Go away, kid," he told the boy. "We're not interested."

The boy continued to follow us.

Now I was really angry. The earthquake had rattled my nerves, as well as shaken my body. "Leave us alone!" I shouted in Spanish at the boy while trying at the same time to wave down one of the battered-looking taxis that were the only rental vehicles brave enough to venture into this area. "We're leaving Tenochtitlán. We don't need a guide."

"Hokay, *señorita,* hokay." Then he cocked his head and grinned. "But the Chiclets lady would like you to know that what happened yesterday wasn't her fault. If she'd wanted to kill you, she could have had the job done, easy." He swung the chain at his belt, and the snap blade sprang open. In one smooth motion he flipped it into his hand, catching it and folding it shut. "She wants you to know she's still working for you."

Then he turned and bolted away, running as fast as his feet could carry him. "Thanks for the pesos, *babosos!*" he yelled back over his shoulder. Before I could recover from my surprise, he'd rounded a corner and disappeared.

The driver of a derelict-looking taxi finally saw me waving. As he ground his gears, putting his vehicle into reverse and backing up to the curb for us, I saw him surreptitiously tucking a string of what looked like rosary beads into his pocket. He'd probably pulled them out to pray when the earthquake struck. The sight reminded me of Hector, the driver who had recommended the sports bar, and his fearful cringe after making the sign of the cross. Catholicism might be officially banned in Aztlan, but it was far from dead.

Rafael looked at me, one eyebrow raised. "Where are we going?" he asked.

I hadn't known until that moment. "To the Yucatán," I told him. "To the town of Izamal. The feathered serpent told us that it was the home of the *sacerdote* who found Mama Grande after she lost her magic and memories. I didn't understand the comment at the time—it didn't make sense that the Aztlaner priests would let a rebel sympathizer like Mama Grande go free again. But I just figured that they didn't know who she was.

"Now that I think about it some more, I realize that there are two types of priests in Aztlan. Those who follow the Path of the Sun, and those who follow a different path: Christianity. If the priest who found her was Catholic, it would explain why Mama Grande brought the holo of Jesus north with her when she fled from Aztlan. Because it meant something to her. It represented hope, rescue—the person who had helped her after her memory became glitched."

Rafael nodded, at last understanding. "The *sacerdote*—the priest who found her. If we can track him down, we might be able to learn more about why Mama Grande was killed. Maybe she hadn't lost all of her memories yet, and was still able to tell the priest whatever it was the cultists were after. If we can find out what it is . . ."

I completed the thought for him. "Whatever Mama Grande knew, Vargas learned it. He wouldn't have killed her, otherwise. And judging by the simsense images the cultists used to trigger Mama Grande's memory, it's a place. It's a safe bet that both they and Vargas were looking for something—and that Vargas will go to that location, now that he knows where it is. If we can figure out where he's headed . . ."

Rafael smiled. "We can get to him."

I paused before opening the door of the cab. As Caco had said, the city had ears. "And the best part of it is," I said in a low voice, "if your scalper or our friend Caco does sell us out, our 'target' will be expecting us to make our move at the *ollamaliztli* finals. We'll have the element of surprise on our side if we strike before then."

I was wrong, of course. We were the ones who were going to be surprised. And more than once.

12

The motorcycle bumped its way along the poorly paved road, its plastic fenders rattling. I sat on the back of the tape-patched seat, my arms around Rafael's waist. We'd been trying to pass a poultry truck for some time now, but its driver was barreling along at *loco* speeds and refusing to let us by. I wondered what his hurry was. The chickens stuffed into the wire cages strapped on the flatbed of the truck smelled terrible and the heavy wheels of the vehicle were churning up dust like crazy every time the driver cut a corner too tightly and veered onto the gravel shoulder of the road. I was glad for my breather, which kept out the worst of the dust and diesel fumes. Wearing it meant not being able to wear the full-face helmet that had come with the bike, but I was more than willing to sacrifice safety in order to breathe filtered air and feel the wind through my hair.

We'd decided to travel to Izamal by motorcycle. The town lay nearly twelve hundred klicks from Mexico City, near the northern end of the Yucatán peninsula, but I didn't want to risk taking a flight into Mérida, the principal airport in the region. The Yucatán peninsula was the flash point of the civil war, and the Aztlan Armed Forces (yet another sub-division of Aztechnology Corporate Security) would be highly suspicious of "tourists" entering what amounted to a low-level war zone. Traveling by motorcycle offered us a lower profile. We could take the back roads and avoid most of the military checkpoints.

We'd picked up the motorcycle for a cheap price in Tenochtitlán on the day the earthquake hit, and set out early the next morning. It was now Friday, and we were in the middle of our third eight-hour day of riding. The bike was a Dodge Sidewinder, painted with a distinctive diamond pattern that mimicked the rattlesnake after which it was named. I'd wanted a bike with a more comfortable seat—I could feel every bump and pothole through the worn padding—but Rafael had considered the bike a lucky find and had insisted that we buy it. It seemed appropriate, somehow, that we were using a bike named for Mama G's totem animal.

We were well into the Yucatán now, on a secondary highway that would take us to Mérida. All around us was flat, sun-baked desert—a vast expanse of scrub-dotted limestone and yellow soil, unbroken by rivers or lakes. The only "hills" in the region were the ruins of ancient cities—bleached mounds of rubble that mark where a building or temple once stood. The other landmarks were of more recent manufacture—power lines, oil rigs, razor-wire fences that marked the edge of civilian no-go zones, and the occasional radar dish or military landing pad, surrounded by security fencing and low bunkers that I guessed held light tanks, troops, or LAVs.

It's hot in the Yucatán—even the air flowing past us as we rode along failed to cool me. The sweat evaporated instantly from my exposed skin, but was pooling under my breasts and against my stomach where my leather jacket trapped it against my body.

We'd already drunk most of our bottled water—liters and liters of it—and only a centimeter or two of bathtub-hot liquid remained. I yanked a plastic container out from under a bungie cord and poured the last of the water it held onto the bandannas that Rafael and I wore around our necks. Most of the liquid slopped onto the bike or ground as we hit a bump, but enough soaked the scarves to cool our necks for a few blissful seconds.

I wondered again how Rafael could ride for so long with a sprained wrist. The vibrations of the bike must have hurt like drek, let alone using his wrist every time he revved the engine or braked. But I'd frequently seen Rafael continue an athletic competition or game regardless of aches, pains, or injuries. I suspected his will to carry on bordered on the abilities of a physical adept—maybe he'd inherited a natural magical talent from Mama Grande. But I'd never mention this to him. Rafael considered himself a "pure" athlete, unsullied by implants, augmentations—or magic.

The wheels of the truck ahead of us threw up yet another cloud of eye-stinging yellow dust, and I could hear Rafael curse. When we hit a straight stretch, he shouted, "Hang on, Leni!" and gunned the motorcycle more fiercely than before. We pulled out to one side of the truck, surged past it—and emerged from its dust cloud only to find the road ahead blocked by an armored personnel carrier, a jeep, and the concrete barriers and striped fencing of a military checkpoint. Rafael jammed on the brakes, sending us into a skid. I gasped and ducked my head behind his broad back, thinking we were about to crash. He kept the bike under control—barely. But by the time we stopped, we'd knocked over a number of bright orange cones that had been set up to direct traffic. I looked up to find that we were dead-center in the checkpoint, only a pace or two away from a very slotted-off looking military officer.

The officer—a fair-skinned elf whose tan uniform was stained with sweat, even though he wore no armor—glared at us. He backed off a step or two, leveling the boxy-looking SCK Model 100 submachine gun that was smartlinked into his wrist, and waved two soldiers in our direction with a flick of his free hand. He didn't look the slightest bit Azzie—I suspected that he was a mercenary.

On the far side of the checkpoint, four soldiers had stopped a dusty Ford Export pickup. A group of five traditionals—four men and one woman—stood beside the truck. All had the distinctive high cheekbones and arched noses of the Maya and were dressed in loose-fitting white shirts with brightly embroidered hems, baggy pants—or a skirt, in the case of the woman—and sandals. Like all of the *campesino* farmers in this region, the men carried machetes in sheaths hung from belts. They watched fearfully as two of the soldiers searched through the bags of corn, jerry cans of kerosene, and boxes of produce that filled the back of the pickup. The other two soldiers kept watch over the farmers, assault rifles at the ready.

The pair of soldiers who had been directed toward us clambered over the barrier and reached our bike as the poultry truck rumbled to a halt behind us, enveloping us in a cloud of dust. They wore heavy armor and helmets that reminded me of the Star's riot gear—but with built-in cooling units, I noticed enviously—and carried high-velocity assault rifles. One moved with the unnatural smoothness of someone whose motor control has been overridden by a move-by-wire implant and the other was targeting us with a needle-thin red laser sight that beamed out of his cybereye. I wondered if all Aztlaner soldiers were augmented and cybered. This pair seemed as cold and professional as their merc officer. And they were just as slotted off at our clumsy intrusion into their checkpoint. I knew we couldn't expect any sympathy.

"Get off the bike and keep your hands away from your body, *por favor*," one of them said in a cold voice.

As a police officer, I'd given similar directives enough times to understand the unspoken subtext. Any move even mildly suggestive of reaching for a weapon—or of bringing a weapon hidden in a cyberlimb to bear—would bring instant retaliation. And given the fact that we were in a war zone and that these were not police officers who needed to justify the use of lethal force, I was extra careful. I did exactly as the soldier directed, sliding off the back of the motorcycle and keeping my hands open and in view.

The dust raised by the poultry continued to swirl around us, even though the driver had shut his vehicle down. I thought I could hear him singing in his cab.

"I'm sorry, officer," Rafael said as he killed the ignition and slowly climbed from the bike. He started to remove his breather, but the two soldiers shifted suddenly, tensing and raising their rifles. Rafael left his hands where they were, up near his face. "I was trying to pass the truck, and couldn't see because of the dust," he explained, waving it away from his face. "We weren't trying to run the checkpoint—we just didn't see it until it was too late. My wife and I rode down from Nuevo Laredo to visit with friends in—"

The whirlwind struck without warning. One minute we were trying to convince the soldiers that we weren't worthy of being shot, and the next we were in the middle of what felt like a tornado or hurricane. A blast of dust-filled air threw me sprawling to the ground. Rafael managed to stay on his feet a second or two longer, then was spun backward against the bike, knocking the Sidewinder over in a clattering heap.

The two soldiers stayed on their feet, but staggered about like drunken men.

Dust stung my eyes and blasted like sandpaper against my face. Feathers from the chickens on the truck whirled past like thick white snowflakes as the birds' frightened clucking filled the air. Then all at once, as one, the birds fell ominously silent. The feathers swirling around me now were tinged with red.

New noises filled the air. I heard screams and the roar of automatic weapons fire from the spot where the pickup truck had been stopped. Realizing that I was in an exposed position, I crawled for the only shelter I could see through my squinting eyes: the underside of the poultry truck. I couldn't see Rafael, but prayed that he too had the sense to keep his head down.

Once I'd reached cover, I used my cyberear to filter out the frequencies that corresponded to the wind—nearly every fragging frequency on the scale—and listened for Rafael's voice. Nada joy.

As I squirmed around, changing my position under the truck, I saw the driver's legs as he stepped down from the cab. He didn't seem affected by the whirlwind at all—his walk was steady and his pant legs weren't even fluttering. I could hear his voice more clearly now—it wasn't singing at all, but more of a chant. It sounded like the strange, glottal language Mama G had used in casting her healing spell.

As the driver moved away from his truck, I could see him clearly. He had the high cheekbones, dusky skin, and arched nose of a traditional, and was dressed, like the farmers, in baggy white clothing. He seemed to be walking in the eye of the storm. Perched on his head, completely unaffected by the wind, was a straw cowboy hat with a brown and white feather shoved into a dusty red bandanna that was tied around the crown of the hat. His arms were flung out wide, fingers fluttering like the wing feathers of a bird. He sang his chant in a melodic tenor voice, shuffling his feet in a rhythmic dance and stamping the earth. Then he threw back his head and let out a shrill, high-pitched cry that sounded like the scream of an eagle.

I heard more gunfire and shouted commands—and also an agonized scream. My cyberear picked up a faint rumble that

I guessed was the APC engine starting up. I couldn't see more than a meter or two in front of me—the dust was that thick. Strangely, it seemed to be filled with tiny swirls, thicker clumps of dust that resembled knots in wood—or eyes. I had the unshakable feeling that the whirlwind was looking at me, weighing me—and then disregarding me.

The thought that I could have been the target of its wrath sent a shiver down my spine. It was obviously an elemental or nature spirit of some sort—probably the latter, since the truck driver's motions suggested those of a shaman communing with a bird totem. For a moment, I wondered if he'd summoned the whirlwind to protect Rafael and me from the soldiers. But that didn't seem to fit with his earlier actions—cutting us off on the highway and being a jerk by not letting us pass. No, something else was going on here.

The dust cleared for a moment and I spotted Rafael. He was hunkered down behind the Sidewinder with his pistol out. He squinted into the wind, either looking for me or for a target. I shouted to him, but he didn't seem to hear me.

And then I saw the soldier that stood a few meters behind Rafael, legs braced against the wind. The targeting laser sight in the soldier's cybereye swung around, moving with steady precision toward Rafael's back. Even as I scrambled out from under the truck and staggered to my feet, the soldier raised the weapon that was smartlinked with his laser sight, matched its aim with that of the laser, and . . .

A machete carved into the soldier's neck, slicing through the armor like butter and sending a spray of blood flying into the wind. The farmer who wielded the blade had appeared from out of nowhere, charging against the whirlwind to strike the blow. Now he raised the machete a second time, and slashed again at the soldier's neck. The assault rifle flared and spat a stream of bullets that punched into the motorcycle's muffler, turning it to Swiss cheese and startling Rafael into sudden awareness of the danger he was in. Then the soldier collapsed onto the ground. The farmer threw his head back, punched a triumphant fist into the air, and whooped—although even with my cyberear I could barely hear his cry against the wind—then turned and ran back to where I'd last seen the pickup truck.

I staggered over to Rafael and hauled him to his feet. He

was still shaking. "Come on, Raf," I yelled into his ear. "Let's get out of here!"

"But the bike . . ." he protested.

"We can come back for it later."

The whirlwind was ebbing slightly, but its noise was still deafening. The shaman who had summoned it stood a few meters away from us, head drooping and chest heaving as he panted like a man who had just run a marathon. His hands hung limp at his sides. Beyond him, the farmers were finishing off the soldiers—slashing with their machetes at the men who lay on the ground. Five of the soldiers were down, and then the female campesino took out the sixth with a brilliant turquoise bolt of energy that blasted out from her fingertips. The officer, however, was nowhere in sight.

That's when I saw the APC's turrets begin to move. The heavily armored vehicle had turned slightly and its engines were revving. It was swinging around, slowly bringing its heavy canon to bear on the farmers, who were too busy finishing off the soldiers to notice. Within seconds it would blast them to pieces.

I told myself that this wasn't my fight. But at the same time I knew that the *campesinos* only had one hope: me. And I knew that the enemy of my enemy is my friend—and it wouldn't hurt to have some friends in these parts.

All of these thoughts went through my mind in a nanosecond as I noticed that the rear hatch of the APC was still open. Then I was running toward it. Whether they meant to or not, the men with the machetes had saved Rafael's life. I owed them one. And like Rafael, I wanted to kick some Azzie butt.

I scrambled in through the hatch just as the elven officer inside the APC let out a low, triumphant chuckle. He was jacked into the APC controls, connected to his vehicle by a smartlink. His eyes were unfocused, staring off into space as he concentrated on the virtual feedback his mind was getting through the link. The APC had stopped its turn, and I heard the soft whine of the cannon as it came to bear. Within a second, it would fire.

But a second was all I needed. I slammed my hands forward, knocking his head into the control panel above the driver's seat and tearing the link from the datajack in his skull. He moaned and tried to rise, but was disoriented by the sudden jack-out. I used the opportunity to punch him in the sternum, thinking to knock the wind from him—and then screamed in pain as my fist struck what felt like a solid metal wall. Drek! The fragger was dermal-plated! I should have expected that when I saw that he wasn't wearing armor.

My agony gave him the second he needed to recover. Snarling, he lunged at me, trying to wrap his hands around my throat. They closed instead on my shoulder as I ducked away—but then I was pinned up against the side of the APC, with nowhere to go in that narrow space. Grinning in victory, the elf squeezed, and I yelped in pain as what proved to be superhumanly powerful, cybernetic hands pinched with agonizing force against the nerves in my shoulder, instantly numbing my arm. Flashes of white light danced in front of my open eyes as I saw him reach with one hand for the pistol that was holstered at his waist . . .

And then I heard the *pop! pop!* of Rafael's Streetline Special. The elf sagged, releasing me, and I blinked the pain-induced tears from my eyes. The elf had caught the bullet in one of his pointy ears. I guess he wasn't dermal-plated there.

"Thanks, Raf!" I called out. "You're one up on me. Now I owe you another one."

I pushed myself upright. My arm was still numb. But even so I had the presence of mind to snag the elf's pistol with my good hand. Rule number one for rookie cops: never leave a perpetrator armed—even when he appears to be down. It was one rule I always stuck to, even though I'd long since left the Star.

The pistol was a Savalette Guardian—a chromed-steel monster of a gun that you don't see much on the streets. It fires high-powered slugs in bursts of three—the elf had probably needed the cyberhands to handle the recoil. It was too heavy a weapon for me, and was certainly too big for my shoulder holster, but I kept it anyway. Beggars can't be choosers. Especially in Aztlan. I shoved it into the inner pocket of my jacket.

Rafael grinned at me through the open hatch. Then he turned around, startled, as the farmers crowded in behind him, slapping him on the back and crying out, "*Muy bien!* Good shooting!"

I heartily agreed. Rafael's Streetline Special wasn't noted for its accuracy. Must have been my lucky day.

One of the men leaned in to offer me his arm as I climbed from the APC. *"Muchas gracias, señorita,"* he said. "We will take it from here."

Another of the farmers climbed into the vehicle, rolling up a shirt sleeve to reveal a datajack on his wrist. He shoved the bleeding corpse of the elven officer out of the way, sat down in the driver's seat, and jacked the APC's link into his wrist.

I looked around at the grinning *campesinos* who surrounded Rafael and I. "You're not farmers, are you?" The question was stupid, but it needed to be asked. "You're rebels—revolutionaries."

"We might be," one of them said coyly. "Or we might just be *bandidos.* An armored personnel carrier is worth *mucho* on the back market—once you get the blood stains out of it."

The others laughed at his joke as they hauled the body of the elf from the APC.

Rafael glanced around at the men. "My *abuela* worked with the rebels," he said. "Her name was Rosalita Ramirez. She was a healer. I came to Aztlan to find someone who can tell me more about her. Did any of you know her?"

The affect was instantaneous. My cyberear picked up murmurs of a *"la serpiente"* and whispered questions about Rosalita's disappearance. The rebels gave Rafael and I sidelong glances, uncertain whether or not to believe that a grandson from El Norte would have turned up suddenly in the Yucatán, just like that. It was just too convenient, they thought. Too much like a trick Aztechnology would pull. We had to be spies . . .

Their looks were suddenly very guarded. I noticed that one of the men was slowly raising the machete that was balanced across his shoulder and was easing around Rafael to get a better angle of attack. The woman had one hand behind her back, and was starting to make a series of slow, complex gestures that looked like the formula for a spell. There was a tense moment in which no one spoke . . .

"And you, *señorita?"* The shaman joined the group. He was still breathing heavily, and sweat trickled down his temples. But he seemed to be very much in charge. The others parted for him, and listened deferentially while he spoke. "What brings you to Aztlan?"

I took the plunge. "Rosalita Ramirez was killed a few days ago, in Seattle. I'm helping my friend Rafael to investigate her murder. It has—connections—with Aztlan."

The shaman had piercing eyes, sharp as those of . . . well, an eagle. Was there a hint of skepticism in them still?

"Would it help you to trust us if I told you that we know a member of your revolutionary council?" I asked. "Someone who uses the name Soñador."

The shaman shrugged but looked skeptical. "If that were true . . ."

"Rafael," I said, "show them your souvenir."

Rafael grinned as he reached into his jacket. The rebel with the raised machete tensed, but then relaxed again as Rafael pulled out the feather we'd found in the cave. The rebels reached out tentatively to touch the beautiful plume, then jerked their fingers away as if it were a religious icon they dared not desecrate.

"It seems that you do know Soñador," the shaman said with a touch of what sounded like awe in his voice. "Or at least, that you have met the feathered serpent. I think there is someone you should talk to. Come."

The rebels seemed more relaxed now. At least they hadn't taken our weapons from us. One of them clambered into the APC and then sealed its hatches. We stepped back as the armored vehicle revved its engines and then pulled away. It disappeared down the road in a cloud of dust. The spirits only knew what the rebels planned to do with it. But the APC packed enough firepower to give the Aztlaner forces a nasty surprise.

The rebels left the bodies of the Azzie soldiers where they lay. They searched them thoroughly but didn't take any of the gear or weapons. They also left the shaman's poultry truck behind. The chickens in the wire cages were all dead, and a thin trickle of blood ran from the back of the truck. I supposed the birds had been buffeted about by the wind. It seemed cruel, to me, that the shaman had left them die.

The rebels insisted we ride with them in their pickup truck. They helped Rafael lift the motorcycle in over the tailgate, then the woman and one of the men climbed up and settled themselves on top of the farm supplies and produce that filled the back of the truck, beckoning Rafael to join them. The shaman insisted I sit up front in the cab with him and the driver. I knew what they were doing—deliberately separating Rafael and me. But we'd decided to trust them, at least for now. I'd had one wildly paranoid moment when I wondered if *they* had set this all up for *us* but then decided that the likelihood was extremely remote. We'd blundered into their civil war—and now we would make the best of this fortuitous meeting. Whoever the rebels were taking us to had probably also known Mama Grande and would be a valuable source of information.

As he climbed into his seat, the rebel who would be driving the pickup tossed his machete onto the dashboard. I noticed that its blade was engraved with the words: "Freedom is the Road to Happiness."

I gestured at the weapon. "Is that a rebel slogan?" I asked. "Or is it some sort of spell focus?"

The driver laughed. He was a portly man with a drooping mustache and pockmarked skin. "No, *señorita*. The blade is quite mundane and the slogan is just an expression. All of the farmers engrave their machetes. It's a local tradition."

The shaman filled in the rest. "A machete's a more valuable weapon against a government soldier than that pistol you pocketed."

As the pickup pulled away from the checkpoint, back in the direction from which it had come, I pulled my jacket shut. I thought the pistol might have been showing, but it wasn't. The shaman must have felt the bulge in my jacket and guessed what its inside pocket held.

"But why machetes?" I asked.

"Government soldiers are protected by spells that provide a barrier to bullets," the shaman said. "Some are even magically protected against blast and fire. They could literally walk across a minefield and not be harmed."

The driver grinned. "But the government didn't think to protect them against the lowly machete."

The shaman's elbow nudged my pocket. "If that pistol is government-issue, I'd suggest you get rid of it," he said. "If the soldiers find it on your person . . ."

I could imagine the rest. But old habits die hard. I was

used to carrying a gun—even though I knew it was little more than a psychological crutch in a situation like this.

"Thanks for the warning, but I'll keep it for now," I told him. "There may be more trouble ahead."

I was right, of course. But it was trouble that a gun wouldn't solve.

13

The blindfold over my eyes was soaked with sweat. It was hot in the cab of the pickup. I was squeezed in between the eagle shaman and the rebel who was driving. The road we were traveling must have been unpaved and full of potholes. Either that or the pickup truck didn't have any shocks left. We bounced and jostled our way along, and I kept one hand on the dash to prevent myself from being flung forward into the windshield.

During the trip, the rebels kept the truck's radio tuned to a live broadcast of the *ollamaliztli* game—the third game of the national finals. They had it cranked up loud so those in the back of the truck could listen, and I could hear Rafael's deep-voiced cheers or groans each time a goal was scored.

Despite my normal antipathy toward sport, I was caught up in the game—having a blindfold over my eyes and not being able to see anything probably helped. I spent most of my time trying to imagine what the game looked like. It sounded something like basketball—the object seemed to be to get a ball through a ring. But the ball could bounce off walls and still be in play, and the game also made use of "end zones." I just couldn't picture it.

The Jaguars were ahead for most of the game. They scored six points to the Serpents' two, and victory looked certain, since seven points was game. Two Jaguars and three Serpents had been knocked out of play—this was a brutal sport in which lethal weapons could be used to take out an opponent—and the Serpents' captain had a broken arm. The announcers described his injury in gory detail, and speculated whether illegal combat drugs were the only thing keeping him going. But then the Serpents came from behind, scoring five goals in a row to win the game.

The driver beside me cheered and shut off the radio, and I heard the rebels in the back avidly discussing whether magic had illegally been used. The Jaguars were rumored to be shamans of that totem animal, while the Serpents were said to be pumping Kamikaze, an illegal combat drug, and masking it after the game with an inhibitor. The female rebel thought magic was fair game—naturally enough, since she was a mage of some sort. Her beef was that only human males were allowed to play at the national level. Why, her sister was every bit as good at *ollamaliztli* as any man and yet she . . .

At last the truck ground to a halt. We were inside something cool—a building, perhaps. And dark, I saw when my blindfold was removed.

The pickup truck had pulled into a room just large enough to accommodate it. Stone walls surrounded us and the entrance was a rough hole in one wall with rubble piled to either side. It looked as though an original doorway had been widened so that the truck could pass through it. Sunlight streamed through the opening and swallows swooped in and out. Other than a jet engine, high overhead, the air was still. We must have been way out in the country, far from any town or road.

The rebels had insisted that Rafael and I wear bandannas tied over our eyes while they drove to their base. As we climbed out of the pickup truck and followed them out of the stone "garage," I saw that we had come to an ancient, ruined city. All around us were stone-walled buildings, multi-leveled edifices that looked like a series of wide, flat blocks, placed one on top of the other with the smallest on top. Regularly spaced, rectangular doorways led into darkened interiors. Wide stone staircases at the center of each level led to the story above.

Most of the buildings' upper stories had collapsed into heaps of rubble and had grasses or trees growing from them. But the architecture was still impressive. Plain, fitted-stone walls were accented with stone that had been carved to form a lattice pattern or with panels that were covered with blocky hieroglyphs or stylized images of ancient rulers and gods. The stones were all a dusky orange-gray, but I could see flecks of paint, here and there, that told me that this must once have been a colorful place.

I was struck with the weight of history that permeated this land. I was used to living in a modern city—Seattle was founded in 1852, but any vestiges of its comparatively short history had long ago been paved over, obliterated by highways, or buried under arcologies. In contrast, this region of the Yucatán was ancient, the bones of its centuries-old cities still visible. As we passed by a ruined building, I trailed my fingers across the pitted surface of its stonework, feeling the outlines of hieroglyphics that had been carved by ancient hands. For the first time, I had an inkling of what had driven Rafael to explore his Azzie heritage. This country had deep roots.

And then I remembered the human sacrifices performed by the ancient Azzies and pulled my hand away from the stone. Those roots were watered with blood.

We wound our way along a trail that traversed the site, at one point passing through a huge, freestanding stone arch. After about fifteen minutes we came to a more or less intact building whose lower stories were devoid of doors. We climbed the wide staircase that led to its uppermost story, which was about fifteen meters above ground level. The building was square, rather than rectangular, and looked a bit like a temple.

The stone steps were weather-worn, narrow and steep. I could only fit the ball of my foot on them, giving me the feeling that I was balancing precariously in space. I leaned forward, one hand touching the steps above to keep my balance. The stairs were so steep that climbing them was more like trying to scale a steep hillside. You didn't stand up straight to do that; lean back a little and you'd topple backward and fall. I noticed that Rafael was doing the same—and concentrating intently on the stonework right in front of him. He was such a daredevil on his motorcycle that it had never occurred to me that he might be afraid of heights. The rebels chuckled to themselves and moved as if they were climbing a normal flight of stairs. But I noticed that they were sweating as much as Rafael and I were. Even for someone used to this heat, the climb was a real workout.

By the time we reached the uppermost story, I was

gulping air. I paused and turned around. The stairs were so steep I couldn't even see them unless I stood right on the edge. It felt as though the balcony we stood on was floating in space.

The building was a good choice for a rebel base—the balcony-like platform that surrounded the upper level provided a clear view over the flat scrub land below. I could see for several kilometers, all the way to a collection of pastel-colored buildings that must have been the nearest town.

We had climbed to the central doorway on the fourth story. On either side of this rectangular opening was a pillar carved in the shape of a snake, with its tail in the air and gaping serpent head at the bottom. The stonework was chipped and broken, but I could make out the manes of feathers that surrounded their faces. Had the people who built this site once met with feathered serpents—perhaps even with Soñador itself—centuries ago?

The shaman, who had introduced himself simply as Águila—Eagle—led us inside the building. The interior consisted of a number of long, narrow rooms, all empty and with floors covered with wind-blown dust and bits of broken stone. At first I wondered why we had come here, but then Águila pulled a magkey out of his pocket and slotted it into what looked like an ordinary crack in the stonework. I heard the hum of an electric motor and stepped back warily as a portion of the floor slid open, revealing a flight of stone steps. Dust trickled into the opening.

The three rebels we had met at the checkpoint disappeared down the steps. After a moment, Águila motioned for us to follow them. Rafael and I exchanged glances, then shrugged. There was no turning back now.

I descended the steps carefully, following them as they turned a sharp corner. The walls were rough stone and the ceiling overhead was shaped like an inverted V, narrow at the top and sloping out to meet the walls. There wasn't much head room—Rafael had to walk with his shoulders hunched to avoid banging his head. The air smelled of dust—and strangely, of plastic—and the temperature dropped steadily as we descended. After the heat of our climb up the steps outside, it was downright chilly. I shivered and zipped up my jacket. Above us, I heard the trap door slide back into place and Águila's footsteps behind Rafael. Even with my cyberear's amplification system I couldn't hear much more than a murmur of voices below as the rebels, who had descended more quickly than us, exchanged greetings with someone. The sound was muffled, as if by a closed door.

Despite its ancient appearance, the stairway was illuminated with lights that had been bolted into the walls. They must have had battery packs; I didn't see any electrical wires. As we rounded a second bend I saw a large niche on my right and paused to peer into it. Inside it was a huge stone sarcophagus, its sides crammed with hieroglyphs and its top depicting the image of a feather-caped noble in a tall, ornate headdress. The lid of the sarcophagus was cracked, and didn't sit properly on its base. I wondered how they'd gotten the thing down the narrow staircase. Maybe they'd constructed the building around it.

The lights from the stairway threw a shadow across the sarcophagus as Rafael crowded in behind me and peered over my shoulder. Águila paused on the steps above.

"It's empty," the shaman said, answering the question I'd been about to ask. "It was carved to hold the body of King Topiltzin—a Toltec ruler of the tenth century. He was famous for refusing to perform human sacrifices—instead he sacrificed animals or butterflies to the gods. So pious was he that people began calling him after the god he held above all others: Quetzalcóatl, the feathered serpent. Or Kukulcán, in the Mayan language."

I wondered why the shaman was giving us the history lesson. But I didn't interrupt.

"Although this sarcophagus was carved for Topiltzin, he was never placed in it," Águila continued. "According to legend he sailed away to the east on a raft of serpents, promising to return in the year *Ce Acatl*—One Reed in the ancient Aztec calendar. Some say he did return, in 2039, to lead the riots in Celestun. Others claim that he will not return until 2091, the next One Reed year."

I was reminded of something I'd scanned in the guide to Aztlan I'd slotted earlier. I hadn't bothered uploading the information to my headware, and had to rely upon old-fashioned wetware memory to dredge up the information.

"Didn't the legend of Queztalcóatl's return correspond

with the arrival of Cortés in 1519?" I asked. "Isn't that why the king of the Aztecs welcomed the Spanish conquistadors into Tenochtitlán—only to find out they weren't gods when they attacked and looted his city?"

"I remember that, too," Rafael rumbled. "Quetzalcóatl was supposed to be a white guy, with a beard. Montezuma was afraid to attack him, and lost his capital city as a result."

Águila nodded. "That is correct. Tenochtitlán will fall once more, when Topiltzin returns to conquer it. And Aztechnology's reign of blood will at last come to an end."

The fervor in the revolutionary's eyes made me pause. It reminded me of the eager gleam I'd seen in the eyes of the missionaries—the ones who had used their memory-probing magic on Mama G. Prophetic reckonings seemed to run deep in the culture of Aztlan. The only difference was that this time, the prophecy called for the Azzie government to be destroyed—not the entire Earth.

"Pardon me," Águila said as he used the extra space provided by the cryptlike niche to squeeze past Rafael and I. We followed him down the remainder of the stairs to a heavy metal door. He slotted the magkey once more and I heard a lock click open. Pushing the door wide, Águila walked through it and held it open as we followed.

As I passed through the doorway, something glitched in my cyberear. Suddenly all I could hear was static. I quickly turned down the volume to almost nil and listened with my meat ear instead. I wondered if the rebels had some sort of jamming device that was scrambling radio signals—I suspected that the now-defunct police radio in my cyberear was somehow affected by it.

The space beyond the door was reminiscent of a military bunker. The walls were of stone, rather than ferrocrete, but the overall feel was the same. Olive green metal shelving along the walls held foodstuffs, medical supplies, and weapons—including a number of sophisticated-looking arrays of tubes that I guessed were anti-tank or anti-armor missile launchers. Military style cots filled alcoves to either side of the main room, and rebels—dressed like *campesino* farmers but moving with the purpose of trained soldiers—bustled back and forth. I heard the hiss of a ventilation unit and guessed that filtered air was being pumped in from somewhere outside.

After the rebels' machete attack at the checkpoint, I'd been thinking of their revolution as a low-tech peasant uprising. I now saw that they had some sophistication and technological know-how, after all.

We followed Águila through two more rooms and into a third. Half a dozen rebels whom we had not yet met stared at us as we went by, interrupting their avid post-game analysis of the *ollamaliztli* game to mutter behind their hands about us. I was starting to get nervous. I thought we'd proven ourselves to be friendly, back at the checkpoint. But it was clear that, should they change their minds again and decide that we were spies after all, we would not walk out of this bunker alive.

We entered a room that was filled with electronic gear. A troll dressed in camouflage pants and shirt and black military boots whose spit-shine was overlaid with a fine layer of orange dust sat with unfocused eyes, mind-deep in the Matrix as she worked the cyberdeck balanced in her lap. Twin cords ran from the deck to datajacks in either temple, at the base of her horns. The horns themselves rose from her head in tight spirals and were ornately carved with what I guessed were Mayan or Aztec hieroglyphs.

I wondered how the rebels were able to access the Matrix from this distant location. My guess was that there must have been some sort of satellite uplink concealed in the ruins above.

Behind the troll stood a tall, thin human. His skin seemed unnaturally white in the artificial lighting of the bunker and was shaded with blue where a tracery of veins lay close to the surface. With his frizzy, bright red hair and full beard, he looked more like a northern Euro than a mestizo. His pants were white and crisp enough to have been bleached and starched, and his shirt bore a richly colored, embroidered design in a complicated geometric pattern reminiscent of feathers or leaves. His fingernails were long and neatly tapered, as if they had been manicured. A neat freak, I decided. And clearly the leader of this rebel group, judging by his air of authority and command. He seemed unsurprised to see us—almost as if he had been expecting us. I could only guess that one of the rebels from the checkpoint had told him we were on our way here. Strangely, he seemed familiar to me—although I would swear a court oath that we had never met before.

"*Hola.* Welcome to my *hacienda*," he said, smiling at his own joke. The bunker was Spartan and strictly functional—anything but a lavish estate.

Rafael and I nodded our hellos.

Águila doffed his cowboy hat and held it in his hands, turning it nervously. "Is there anything else, Kukulcán?"

"Not at the moment," The redhead answered. "Close the door on your way out, Águila."

The shaman looked disappointed at this dismissal, but did as he was told. Now we were alone with the rebel leader. Alone, that is, except for the troll, but she was too deep in the Matrix to acknowledge us.

Rafael broke the silence. "Kukulcán, huh? Is that a code name or do you really think that you're the reincarnation of the Toltec king Topiltzin?"

Kukulcán smiled. "Would you believe me if I told you that my surname was actually Cortés?"

I shrugged. "Anything's possible."

Kukulcán wet his lips with the tip of his tongue. And in that moment, I realized why I'd thought he looked familiar. The gesture was similar to the one Mama G had used—to a snake's tongue flicking out and into its mouth again. But there was still something else about him . . .

"I am told you are looking for information on a kinswoman of yours—your Mama Grande. You are obviously quite determined to succeed in this quest, to have made it this far into Aztlan."

"We're motivated," Rafael answered dryly. "The man who murdered my—"

I dug an elbow into Rafael's muscle-solid stomach. "Did you know Rosalita Ramirez?" I asked.

Kukulcán nodded. "Quite well. Many of my fighters were healed by her."

"We're traveling to Izamal to learn more about her," I told Kukulcán.

"I know," he interrupted. "You wish to speak to the *sacerdote* who helped Rosalita."

Rafael gaped. "How did you know . . ."

Suddenly I knew why Kukulcán seemed so familiar. "We've met before, haven't we?" I asked him. "In a cave near Monterey. But you weren't in human form then."

Rafael turned to look at me. "You mean this is . . ."

The troll using the cyberdeck shifted slightly in her seat. Kukulcán waved a hand for silence. The gesture was sinuous and flowing, like the movement of a serpent.

"The man you are looking for is Father Gustavo Silvio," he said. "To meet with him, go to the church in Izamal. Light a candle in the alcove of the Virgin and then wait in the confessional. He will contact you."

Kukulcán looked at us appreciatively. "I did not think you would make it this far," he added. "Two foreigners, alone in Aztlan . . . You have proven yourselves both resourceful and capable of surviving here."

"Thank you," I said. "But there is one thing we could use help with. Getting out again. When it comes time to leave, we'll need to get out of Aztlan quickly and quietly, and for that we'll need the help of the AFL. I don't want to use our original contact—we think he may have been . . . compromised. Is there some other way to get in touch with the Freedom League?"

Kukulcán nodded at the troll. "We monitor a number of different message boards. When the time comes, leave a message with your location, and we will make sure it is forwarded. My assistant will handle it personally."

He gave me an LTG address, made both Rafael and I repeat it to be sure we had memorized it properly, then nodded.

"Now I must ask that you leave," he said. "I have— business—that I need to attend to. Águila can take you back to the main road, and from there can brief you on the roadblocks and government patrols that lie between here and Izamal. That should make the rest of your journey easier. It will help your fate to unfold as it should."

His smile looked genuine—warm almost. "I wish you well. I would love to see you strike a blow for freedom."

"Thanks," I told the feathered serpent. Its support was starting to make sense. The enemy of my enemy—and all that drek. Whatever steps we took to bring Mama G's murderer to justice, we'd be a thorn in the side of the Azzie government. And that could only be good for the rebel cause.

The fact that Kukulcán—or Soñador, as he also called himself—had let us see his human form made me feel much better. The feathered serpent obviously was confident enough in our abilities to think that we could avoid capture by the Azzies. Or maybe it just didn't matter. Maybe Soñador had a dozen different names and faces.

But what was that comment about our "fate?" I was a firm believer in free will—I didn't even call up my horoscope in the morning tridcast. The Azzies, though, seemed to be big on fate and prophecies.

By the time this was over, I'd change my opinion. For the moment, however, I remained blissfully optimistic—and unaware of what the future would hold.

14

If I'd thought that Aztechnology Security Corporation maintained a heavy presence in Tenochtitlán, compared to Izamal, they'd been discreet.

Izamal is a town of about fifteen thousand people—it used to be larger, but the VITAS epidemic had hit it pretty hard, and it never really recovered. It's smack in the middle of the Yucatán and used to be dependent upon the tourist trade before the rebellion heated up. Now the streets are filled with soldiers, patrolling in jeeps, standing guard outside key buildings, watching everyone who goes by.

We reached Izamal about three hours after our meeting with Soñador, and it was already getting dark. The motorcycle was loud—its muffler was strictly decorative after the confrontation at the checkpoint. Exhaust poured through the bullet holes in it, making it roar like a tank. Soldiers gave us surly looks as we roared past, and I prayed that they wouldn't stop us, just out of spite.

Several of the buildings in Izamal bore telltale pockmarks where bullets had struck their pastel-painted walls. Citizens scurried along the sidewalks, heads down to avoid making eye contact with the patrolling soldiers. In one jeep we passed, a cage in the back held a bird as big as a human, with a nasty-looking beak and lashing tail. I'd never seen a cockatrice before—it looked like an oversized rooster. Magically active, the bird could paralyze with a flick of its tail. I should have guessed that the Azzie troops would be making use of Awakened beings.

We were looking for a hotel or *posada*—somewhere to spend the night. But everyone seemed to be closing up shop. Merchants rolled down and padlocked the corrugated metal doors that fronted their stores, apartment block residents swung heavy wooden doors shut, and windows were being shuttered against the night. Hotels were few and far between, and those we did pass had "Closed" signs hanging in their windows.

As the gloom deepened, a helicopter gunship flew low overhead. A speaker mounted on the belly of it blared a warning down to the streets below. "*Atención! Atención!* Curfew will be in effect in fifteen minutes. Clear the street, *por favor.* Please clear the streets."

I tapped Rafael on the shoulder and shouted in his ear. "We're fragged if we don't find somewhere to doss down soon."

He let the motorcycle glide to a halt at an intersection. The building beside us had been painted a pastel pink with green trim around the doors. Graffiti splashed across it in red paint showed through a patch of whitewash that had been unsuccessful in covering it up. "Cristeros!" it proclaimed. I wondered who Christ's warriors might be.

"Do you want to try and get out of town?" he shouted back over the muffler roar.

"We'd never make it." I glanced over at two soldiers who had pulled up beside us in their jeep. Both were well-armored, and the one in the passenger seat wore night-vision goggles and carried a lethal-looking assault rifle. I made the mistake of flashing him what I'd intended as a reassuring smile. It must have clued him to that fact that I wasn't a local. He sat up straighter in his seat and began to turn the barrel of his rifle toward me . . .

Just at that moment Rafael gunned the motorcycle and sent us roaring around the corner, down a side street. It must have looked like an evasive move. As I clung tight to his waist, I glanced back and saw the jeep's driver frantically turning the wheel to follow us.

"Blast us out of here, Raf!" I shouted. "We've got pursuit!"

Rafael leaned lower over the bike and gave it more gas. Shops and homes flashed past on either side as we picked up speed. We cut one corner tight, pegs scraping the ground and sending up sparks, and zoomed through a red light in an intersection that was empty of traffic. The curfew must have already gone into effect—the streets were bare.

I thought we'd lost the jeep, but then it shot out of a side street directly behind us. I heard the angry, muffled *chuff-chuff-chuff* of an assault rifle and saw a streak of red tracers lance past on the right. I clenched my teeth together and held on tight as the motorcycle took another sharp turn. Any second now, I would take a bullet in the back . . .

We roared into the plaza at the center of the town, circling around the edge of it to give a wide berth to the two tanks that squatted there like black metal bugs. I gulped when I saw them, but they seemed inactive at the moment. Or perhaps their drivers didn't want to waste heavy ordnance on so small a target as us. Or maybe they just wanted to sit back and watch the chase.

The plaza was surrounded by Colonial-style buildings, each of them built on top of low mounds that were all that remained of the Mayan city on which the modern town had been built. On the far side of the plaza, a stone staircase that looked suspiciously like those on the temple pyramids led up to a wide courtyard flanked by curving arches.

"Hang on!" Rafael shouted.

I gasped as we hit the stairs. The bike bucked its way up them like an angry horse, leaving a plume of blue smoke in its wake and nearly shaking me off the back. But somehow I held on. I heard another burst of rifle fire, saw chips fly from the stone steps as we raced past. But we must have been moving too erratically to make an easy target. After what seemed an eternity, we reached the top of the stairs and soared into the air. We seemed to float for one heartbeat, two . . . and then the motorcycle slammed down into the courtyard, rear tire smoking as it fought for a grip on the flagstones.

The rifle fire stopped. The angle of the steps must have cut us off from the soldiers' line of sight. But I knew it wouldn't be long before they radioed for backup.

At the far end of the courtyard stood the looming bulk of the sixteenth-century church that had dominated this town's skyline for centuries. A rusted and bullet-scarred sign we passed identified it as the Santuario de la Virgen de Izamal. This must be the church where the feathered serpent Soñador had said we could contact the priest who'd helped Mama Grande. Sanctuary of the Virgin—the most likely spot to find an alcove of the Virgin. Besides, it was the only church in town that was still standing.

As we circled around to the rear of the church, I could see that its windows had been boarded and its main doors padlocked shut. The statues of saints that had once filled niches in the outer walls had been defaced by having their heads knocked off, and the bell tower had collapsed. Garbage lay in heaps in what had once been a surrounding garden. But even so, the building was an impressive one, with plenty of columns, domes, and arches. I could imagine its glory in former decades.

"Raf!" I shouted. "We're sitting ducks on this bike. Every soldier in town will be looking for it now. Let's hole up in the church. Perhaps the priest will find us before the soldiers do."

Rafael cut the engine of the motorcycle and let it roll silently down one of the weed-choked walkways that led to the church itself. It was almost dark now, and searchlights from the helicopters that circled overhead stabbed down into the town below as the Azzies searched for curfew violators.

We hid the motorcycle in an alcove that sheltered one of the church's side doors—padlocked like the rest and hung with a *No hay paso* sign. From there we crept around to the back of the church, looking for an access point. We found a place where some lumber that looked like smashed pews had been piled in a heap against a wall, underneath a window. The plastiboard that had been nailed over the window was loose and swung back easily.

Rafael gave me a boost and I climbed in through the middle of what had once been a stained glass depiction of Christ on the cross. The center of the window was little more than twisted strands of lead, but the edges of the window were still intact—on either side of me was a nail-pierced, bloody hand.

Rafael clambered in behind me and eased the plastiboard that covered the window back into place. The interior of the church was utterly dark, but I had the sense of cavernous space. I heard the flick of Rafael's lighter, and then a pool of warm yellow light surrounded us.

"What now?" Rafael asked. His low voice echoed against the high ceilings and stone walls.

I looked around at the jumbled, dust-covered mess that

filled the church. The altar had been smashed and lay in pieces, the few pews that remained had been shoved into a heap against one wall, and the carpets that covered the central aisle were filthy and mold-spotted. Murals on the walls and ceilings had been crudely painted over with black paint and the carved wooden statues of saints that had once stood in alcoves had been tossed to the floor and burned where they lay. A sour, damp-charcoal smell hung in the air.

I spotted a confessional booth near the front of the church. An alcove, larger than the others, was set into the wall nearby. In it stood a shadow-shrouded statue. A wrought iron rack for votive candles stood in front of the alcove, but the red glass cups that once held the candles lay on the floor beneath it, broken. The shards glittered with the same hue as freshly spilled blood in the flickering illumination of the lighter. I hoped that wasn't an omen.

"There's the confessional, and the alcove where we're to light a candle," I said in a whisper. Somehow, it didn't seem appropriate to talk out loud. "Let's check it out." I cringed as a helicopter roared past overhead, and only relaxed when its engines had faded into the distance.

We crossed to the alcove for a closer look. It held a wooden statue of a female figure in a blue robe trimmed with gold, cradling an infant in her arms. The faces of both woman and child had been hacked off—only the crisscrossed scars of deep axe cuts remained. And someone had been at her robe with a knife in an effort to scrape off its gilt trim. From the dents and scuffs on the body of the statue, I guessed that it had been tumbled from its base. But someone had lifted it back into place again. Next to the alcove, a marble plaque on the wall commemorated the visit of Pope John Paul II during the Festival of the Virgin in August of 1993.

"Looks like Mary's had a tough time of it," Rafael said.

I nodded. I knew that Catholicism had been banned in Aztlan since 2041, but the mutilated statue of the Virgin Mary brought it home to me. I'd never been one for religion—my mother had to literally drag me to church when I was a kid and then threaten to take my toy laser gun and plastic cop badge to make me behave once I was there. After my parents separated, my father stopped going to Mass, and

I happily returned to playing cops and runners games on Sundays. But I had fond memories of the serene face of a similar Virgin Mary—although in my parents' church, she had been a holo. Mary had always seemed so much more approachable than the stern saints and so much less frightening than the mutilated bodies of the martyrs or the tortured corpse of Christ on the cross.

Programmed by my early upbringing, I started to raise a hand to cross myself. Then I stopped. Religion was just so much bulldrek—window dressing in this modern age. If you wanted a miracle, magic and technology were the answers— not prayers to some non-existent saint or god.

Rafael reached into the pocket of his jacket and pulled out one of the candles we'd purchased at a *tienda* on the way into town. With Catholicism banned in Aztlan, we figured we'd have to bring our own votive candles to the church. I just hoped the Virgin wouldn't take offense at a birthday candle shaped like the number one. Rafael picked up the most intact glass cup from the floor and melted the base of the candle onto it. Then he set the candle on the wrought-iron frame in front of the statue and lit it. "Might as well," he said. "Maybe we'll luck out and the priest will come by tonight."

"Or maybe the Azzie soldiers will find us first," I reminded him. But there was little else we could do. Venturing out into the streets right now would be suicide.

"If you find a hiding place that will give me covering fire, I'll take the first shift in the confessional," I suggested.

Rafael nodded his agreement. While he hid himself among the benches that had once housed the choir at the front of the church, I turned to the confessional and opened its wooden door. It was an old-fashioned style confessional, one in which both penitent and priest had to enter in person—unlike the virtual linkups found in modern churches. The carvings on the outside of the confessional were gouged and the door hung from one hinge, but the seat inside and latticework that separated priest from penitent were still intact. I sat down on the seat, hoping that the closet-like structure wasn't about to become my coffin. And waited. And listened. And despite my jittery nerves, eventually dozed . . .

I sat bolt upright as I heard the click of a door closing. I plunged a hand into my jacket and hauled out the Savalette Guardian I'd taken from the dead elf at the checkpoint. Its high-powered slugs would easily punch through the wood that separated the two sides of the confessional. I flicked its safety, raised it . . .

That's when I came to my senses. If the Azzie soldiers had found me, I'd be dead already. I realized that it must be the priest who sat behind the screen. I decided to go through the routine, so as not to scare him off.

"Bless me, Father, for I have sinned. It has been . . ." I had to think for a moment. "It has been sixteen years since my last confession."

"What are your sins, my child?" a soft male voice asked.

I took a deep breath. Where to start? If the Catholic god did exist, he'd need gigapulses of memory to upload everything I had to say. Since my last confession I must have committed dozens of mortal sins and hundreds of venial sins. I hadn't attended Mass or taken Communion since I was thirteen. Not to mention that I'd gone through a period of trying out different churches in my early twenties—of worshipping "strange gods before thee."

And yet, I didn't figure that any of that really mattered. I considered myself one of the "good guys." I'd been a crusader for justice when I was with Lone Star, and in my private detective work I only took on cases when I honestly believed that the client was in the right. It meant passing up nuyen from time to time—I certainly could have made much more as a shadowrunner working clandestinely for the corps—but it left me with a clean conscience.

But there was one thing I'd done wrong. One big thing. "I . . . I failed to prevent the death of my *abuelita*," I began. "She was murdered. And I could have prevented it."

"How could you have done that?" the soft voice asked.

"I could have realized how much danger she was in. I could have arranged for additional protection for her. I could have—"

"I'm sure you did everything you could."

I sighed. Logically, I knew I'd made all the right moves. But a little voice inside gnawed at me. If I'd only done this. If I'd only realized that . . .

"Is there anything else you'd like to confess?"

"No."

"Even after sixteen years?" The voice sounded slightly bemused.

"Father Gustavo Silvio?" I asked.

There was a pause, as if I'd surprised him by knowing his name. Then, "Yes?"

"I'm a friend of Rosalita Ramirez. Can I speak with you outside the confessional?"

The pause was longer this time. "Very well."

I put the pistol away and stepped out of the big wooden box—only to see Rafael pop up from his hiding place near the altar and aim his Streetline Special as the middle door of the confessional also opened.

"Leni!" he shouted. "Behind you!"

I threw up my hands. "Don't shoot, Raf!" I called back. "It's the priest."

"Where the frag did he come from?" His voice still sounded edgy and tired, but he lowered his pistol. I decided that Rafael must have dozed off, just as I did. We'd both been exhausted.

Father Gustavo Silvio stood beside me, looking back and forth between Rafael and I. He looked young, perhaps in his mid-twenties. That would have put him at maybe ten years old when Catholicism was banned in Aztlan—too young to have been ordained by anything but an underground practitioner of the faith. He wore lay clothes—naturally enough, since he couldn't wear a priest's vestments—and was strikingly handsome—good-looking enough to make me wonder if Catholic priests still practiced celibacy. He had the lean body of an athlete, dark hair that swept back from his face in a series of curls, and eyes that were intense and somehow sorrowful at the same time.

A gold cross that hung on a chain against the smooth skin of his chest gleamed in the light of the candle. He saw me staring at it, and lifted it for me to see.

"The four-branched tree of life," he said with a smile. "Which, conveniently enough, is amazingly similar to the Christian cross and can double as a symbol of our faith." He turned it over to show me the acronym INRI engraved on the back.

The explanation wasn't necessary. I'd already recognized

the cross from the simsense chip case that the missionaries had left behind in Mama G's kitchen.

Rafael crossed the church and stood slightly behind the priest. I noticed he hadn't put his pistol away.

"How do we know this is Father Silvio?" he rumbled suspiciously.

The priest shrugged. "How do I know you're friends of Rosalita Ramirez?"

Rafael's eyes narrowed. "I'm her grandson. I took care of her after the AFL smuggled her north."

"Has she returned to Aztlan?"

I shook my head. "She was the one I told you about in the confessional," I told him. "She's dead. Murdered. We've come to Aztlan to track down her killer."

The priest gasped and the color drained from his face. His eyes blinked rapidly as he fought back tears, and he murmured a brief prayer under his breath. If he was faking his surprise and alarm, he was one of the best actors I'd ever seen.

"I am . . ." He seemed too choked up to get the words out. "I am so sorry to hear that. But why have you come to me?"

I decided to name-drop. I hadn't been told not to, and I wanted to see what the reaction would be.

"One of the rebel leaders—Kukulcán—told us that you helped Rosalita after she lost her magic and memories, Father Silvio," I said. "We thought that you might—"

"*Por favor,*" he said. "Call me Gus." I'd done enough interviews as a police officer to be able to sense an undercurrent of agitation, but the priest covered it well. "I would prefer it if you did not use the term Father when . . ."

He paused, listening. My cyberear had regained its functionality the moment I left Kukulcán's bunker, and I used it now to amplify the sounds of an engine and the squeal of brakes outside. It sounded as if one of the jeeps had stopped outside the doorway where we'd hidden our motorcycle. I heard voices, and then a bright light flashed on, shining through the cracks in the door.

Excited shouts outside confirmed the worst: our motorcycle had been spotted.

Father Silvio scooped up the glass jar that held the candle, raised a cautioning finger to his lips, and beckoned urgently for Rafael and I to follow him.

"Come quickly," he whispered. "We must leave. Hurry!"

Shielding the candle, he turned and ran. As Rafael and I bolted after him, I heard the sound of the padlock chain rattling. I expected it to slow the soldiers down some—enough to let us get out of sight. I was wrong.

An explosion erupted in a flash of light and heat behind us, smashing the heavy wooden door flat against the ground and filling the church with dust. A bright light shone into the church, throwing my shadow ahead of me in stark relief. For the second time that evening my back tensed in anticipation of a bullet. I thought longingly of the armored vest I'd been forced to turn in when I left the Star, and wished I was wearing it now.

The priest was a few steps ahead, beseeching his god in a loud, worried voice. Rafael jogged backward, trying to take aim at the soldiers but squinting and unable to see with the bright light in his eyes. I knew it was futile—they'd cut us down before we ever got the chance to take even one of them out. I grabbed his arm, dragging him after me. I even said a prayer myself—old habits die hard.

When I saw the angel, I knew I'd lost it. I'm not really sure if that's what it was—all I know is that a shimmering appeared in the air above us. The ghostly figure looked like a woman in a long robe, her wings beating languidly and her hands outstretched in the protective gesture you see in biblical illustrations. She was there for the blink of an eye—and then I couldn't see her any more. I kept my head down and ran, telling myself it was only a trick of dust swirling in the light.

I heard shouts and the stamp of running feet as the soldiers poured into the church, but somehow, they didn't see us. Or if they did, for some reason they didn't shoot. Rafael and I piled through the doorway after the priest and pounded down the stairs, around a corner, along a hallway past a number of smaller rooms and eventually into what looked like a dead end—a room walled with bookshelves whose floor was heaped with charred Bibles and hymnals.

"What the frag?" Rafael asked angrily. "We'll be trapped

here!" He spun angrily around, waving his pistol as if looking for a target.

The sound of booted feet reverberated against the ceiling above us. The soldiers must have been searching the main floor of the church. I drew my own pistol. I was determined to go down fighting.

Father Silvio—Gus—seemed oblivious to our plight. He squatted beside the shelves, reaching under one and fiddling with something. My cyberear caught a faint *click* and a small passageway opened. It looked as though there was an escape route from this room, after all.

"This church was built in the 1560s, when the natives outnumbered the colonials by several thousand to one," Gus told us in an urgent whisper. "The early priests built this *refugio,* but to my knowledge never used it. It's almost as if they foresaw the need that future generations of priests would have for it."

He held the tiny door open while Rafael and I crawled inside, then followed us and sealed it shut. Then he led us down a narrow flight of wooden steps that squeaked alarmingly underfoot

We wound up in what must have been the sub-basement of the church. By the fitful light of the candle, I saw that the walls on either side of us were constructed at an odd angle— the upper part of the wall was perpendicular to the floor, but the lower wall sloped down like a ramp. Several of the stones on the upper, vertical portion were carved. Despite the fact that this carving had been defaced, I could tell that it was centuries old. I'd seen enough Mayan glyphs by now to recognize their boxy shape, even if the picture-words they once contained had long since worn away.

I noticed that the priest's hand was dripping blood. He must have cut his palm on the broken rim of the glass cup that held the candle. On top of that he was starting to stumble with fatigue. I supposed he'd been up most of the night.

I made him stop and sit down on a flat, round stone that was set into the floor. It looked like a stone wheel, with a hole in the middle and carvings of skulls and glyphs around its outer edge. Not the most comfortable seat, but the floor was filthy and thus a distant second choice. I took a look at Gus' hand. The cut was deep, but clean. Gus protested fiercely that he was fine, and by the time I'd talked him into letting me apply some pressure to the wound, the bleeding had already stopped.

I glanced at my watch. It was nearly five a.m. "What now?" I asked him. "Do we wait here until the soldiers have gone? When does curfew end?"

"Seven a.m.," Gus answered. "But if we remain here, the soldiers will use magic to track us down. We'll leave in a minute or two, when I've caught my breath."

Rafael looked around. "What is this place?"

"Part of the original town of Izamal," Gus answered. "When the Spaniards conquered this region, they razed the Mayan temples and burned their holy books. Then they built Catholic churches on the foundations of the temples they had destroyed.

"And now the irony is that the government of Aztlan is doing the same thing. The church above us is slated for destruction, and a Mayan temple will be rebuilt on its rubble. It would have been done years ago, but for the rebellion. Every time the government brings in equipment, the Cristeros find a way to sabotage it."

"The Cristeros?" I asked. "Are they part of the revolution?"

Gus shook his head. "Not officially. But they share the rebels' desire for self-determination for the local traditionals and *campesinos*. They took their name from the Cristero Rebellion of the 1920s, when Catholics fought back against government anti-church policies." He shrugged. "The Cristeros of that century had God on their side—they won their fight. I can only pray that the Lord still smiles upon our efforts."

I had to fight the urge to roll my eyes. I couldn't imagine fighting for so abstract a cause as religion. But then I thought about it. As a Lone Star officer, I had put my life on the line countless times. I suppose I was technically doing it again for the equally abstract cause of "justice." But there was always a concrete reason. A life to be saved. A street kid to be rescued. Property to be protected . . .

Then I realized that the Cristeros shared the same thirst for justice. The church above my head was theirs, and was being stolen from them. In Seattle, the enemies of the people had been street criminals and organized crime. Here, the enemy was the government itself. I was starting to understand the rebels' struggle.

Gus turned to Rafael. "Your *abuelita* sheltered here for a time, when the security forces were looking for her. Before she lost her memories. And now you are hiding here. Life does revolve like a wheel, doesn't it? Both for this place, and the people who—"

Suddenly the earth shifted beneath my feet, sending me staggering. Rafael cursed and threw out his arms for balance, trying to stay upright, and Gus gripped the stone he was sitting on and looked with wary eyes up at the ceiling. I heard creaks and groans from the building above, and dust trickled down onto our hair and shoulders.

"Frag," Rafael said in a choked voice, wide eyes staring at the ceiling. "What's going on up there?"

"Earthquake," the priest said. "It's nothing. Just a small one." Then he rose to his feet. "Come. It's time we left. There is a home near here that we can reach if we're careful. Friends of mine live there and will take us in until the curfew ends."

"And you'll tell us about my grandmother?" Rafael asked. The priest nodded.

Gus had answered readily enough, but I thought I detected a note of reluctance in his voice. I was soon to find out why.

15

A second concealed door led up from the sub-basement into the building that used to be the convent. Like the church, it was abandoned and boarded up—a candidate for demolition. We exited onto a street that was still dark, then crept away into the early morning. Behind us, in the direction of the church, the *crak! crak!* of a rifle cut the night. I guessed that the Azzie soldiers were trigger-happy, and shooting at shadows.

The house Gus led us to was an unusual one. It was built in traditional Aztlaner style around a courtyard, but the exterior had been entirely covered in glazed ceramic tiles. Brilliant blue and green Euro designs butted up against vibrant red and yellow Asian motifs. Here and there, a checkerboard pattern of smaller black and white tiles broke the riot of color.

"The house is a point of vanity for its owner," Gus whispered. "In Seattle you might say, 'He'll never amount to much.' In Aztlan, we have a similar saying: 'He'll never have a tile house.' Whenever someone in this country strikes it rich, they build themselves a tile-faced one to show off."

We went around to a side door and huddled in its arch as Gus knocked. After a few tense moments—in which a truckful of soldiers rattled past the front of the house and we all froze—the door opened a crack and a girl in her late teens, dressed in a maid's uniform, peeked out. She'd probably already scanned us via the closed-circuit monitor that was built into the wall beside the door, but even so was being cautious. Then she recognized the priest and opened the door wide.

"Padre!" she whispered, looking with frightened eyes

toward the street as another vehicle approached. "Come inside, quickly!"

She obviously trusted Gus enough to allow Rafael and I—two total strangers—into the house. We passed through a pantry into a kitchen with all of the modern conveniences. Here we paused while the girl—who looked at Gus with obvious admiration—asked in a hurried whisper what he wanted. I noticed a glint of a gold necklace under the collar of her uniform and wondered if she wore the same tree/cross that the priest did. Rafael also stared at the girl—but his eyes were fixed on a spot a few centimeters below the necklace. And for good reason—the girl was stunningly beautiful, with high cheekbones and long dark hair as sleek and glossy as a cat's pelt.

I watched as Rafael straightened his jacket and squared his shoulders. I sighed with annoyance and hoped he wouldn't try flirting with the maid. But it was probably inevitable.

"My friends and I had to go out before curfew ended," Gus explained. "We were on a . . . mission of mercy. But we ran into soldiers. Can we wait here until curfew is over?"

The maid chewed her lip indecisively for a moment. Then she nodded. "You can wait in the courtyard. The family will be taking breakfast there at eight, but you will be gone before then. I will bring you some coffee and rolls."

I silently thanked her and saw that Rafael was grinning. We hadn't eaten since yesterday afternoon. It was a wonder that the rumbling of his stomach hadn't led the soldiers straight to us.

The maid looked at Gus with obvious concern. "Was there trouble up at the *santuario*?" she asked softly.

"*Sí,*" Gus answered. "But it's over now."

I hadn't thought about it before, but now I realized that the word the maid had used had a double meaning: both "sanctuary" and, in slang, "buried treasure." I hoped it would be proved correct—that the priest really did have something of value to offer us.

The maid led us to a courtyard at the center of the house. At first I thought it was open to the sky, but then I realized that it was too bright—and too quiet. Outside, it was still dark, but in here morning "sunlight" was already slanting in among the potted plants and flowering vines that filled the space. I could hear the tinkle of a fountain and see clouds drifting across the sky. The ceiling had to contain a holo—and some infrared heaters, to give the fake sunlight an authentic feel. I guessed that a very solid roof sealed off this place of refuge from the world outside.

The coffee and rolls arrived within minutes—real coffee and real butter, not soykaf and EZ Spread. We sat in lounge chairs in the shadow of a gigantic stone head—a staring face with wide lips and flaring nose that looked more Afro than Azzie. It was pitted and worn enough to be an actual Olmec sculpture—and was probably worth a million nuyen, if not more. When the maid had gone—ignoring Rafael's wink—I took a long, grateful sip of my *café con crema* and then began grilling Gus in my best police interview style.

"Kukulcán said that you were the one who helped Mama Grande—Rosalita Ramirez—after her mind became confused. We want to find out what happened to her and why. Somebody went to great lengths to pull something out of the tangled web that was her memory and then—"

"Momento, por favor," Gus said, holding up a hand. "I want to make certain of something, first. If you truly do know Rosalita, you will know which leg her scar was on."

Rafael leaned forward, setting his coffee cup down angrily. "Are you calling us liars?"

Gus made a conciliatory gesture, patting the air with his hands. "No, no," he said. "It's just that in Aztlan, one cannot be too careful . . ."

"It wasn't on her leg," Rafael answered. "It was on her right arm. Up high, near the shoulder."

"Bueno," Gus said.

He seemed about to say something more, but I cut him off by holding up a finger. Something had yanked at my cop's instincts, just for a moment there. I had a horrible suspicion, but needed it confirmed.

"This scar," I said to Rafael. "How did Mama G get it?"

Rafael shrugged. "Beats me. Got in the way of some Azzie shrapnel, I always figured."

I stared hard at Gus. Something in his posture when he'd asked about the scar told me that he knew the answer to my question. "How *did* she get the scar?" I asked.

After a moment's hesitation, he glanced sidelong at Rafael and then answered. "Your *abuelita* was not always a Christian," he began slowly. "Before she came to our church she followed the Path of the Sun. She belonged to a cult that is very active in these parts—a splinter group that wants to hasten the coming of the apocalypse—what we Christians believe will be the final battle between God and Satan. She . . . did things she later regretted."

I glanced at Rafael to see how he was taking the news. Bright spots of red marked his cheeks and his jaw was clenched, but he seemed to be keeping it together.

As Rafael met my eyes I saw the anguish he was feeling. "That brand," he said. "The one on the arm of the missionary. My Mama Grande was part of that cult?" The tone of his voice made it clear that he didn't want to believe it.

Gus frowned. "You know these people?"

I decided to come clean with him. As succinctly as possible, I told him the circumstances of Mama G's murder. I left out, however, the name Domingo Vargas. It would probably be more informative if Gus drew his own conclusions about who the killer might have been.

The priest's face was pale by the time I finished. His forehead drew into a worried frown and he toyed with his coffee cup, forgetting to drink from it.

"The government—Aztechnology," he said. "They got to her. Despite all of our efforts, they tracked Rosalita down." He shook his head angrily at the memory. "*Pinche policía,*" I heard him say under his breath, but only because of my cyberear.

"You know something," I prompted. "Tell us."

The priest's frown deepened and then he nodded to himself. He looked up at Rafael and I.

"Your *abuelita* first sought to convert to Christianity nearly twenty years ago," he said. "My uncle, who was a *sacerdote* in Izamal before me, refused to perform her baptism. He said the magic she drew from the Snake—the keeper of secrets and the tempter of Eve and Adam—was evil. She sought to prove him wrong. But even after seeing the work she was doing among the people of this region— among the poor, the sick, and the wounded—he refused to allow her to join the church. He was of the old school, a man born before the Awakening. He just didn't understand.

"When I took over as priest, I saw Rosalita's magic in a different light. She had a healing touch like that of Christ himself. I knew it could not truly be evil. And I understood that a person can sometimes make mistakes—could sometimes start down the wrong path and only later find the way back into Christ's embrace. I also am a firm believer that any who seek salvation should be granted the chance to achieve it, no matter what their background might be—Christ, after all, accepted lepers and other outcasts into his first ministry."

The maid returned with more rolls then—a good thing, since Rafael had already scarfed the last of them down. Gus smiled at her, and I saw them exchange a meaningful look. I couldn't read the subtext, however. The maid cleared away the empty plates and left the courtyard as quietly as she had come. She moved with a silent grace—a bit unnerving, when she appeared suddenly like that, but I supposed that being unobtrusive was the hallmark of a good servant.

"And so I baptized Rosalita," the priest continued. "Your *abuelita* was a woman driven by her need to heal people. When I cautioned her, saying that she was destroying her own health in the process, she laughed at me. Then she explained that her healing was the penance she must do for the sins she had committed as a member of the cult. She mentioned those sins to me once, during a confession . . ." He paused and visibly shuddered. "But of course I am bound by my oath and cannot repeat them to you now."

"I can guess what they were," I said, interrupting Gus. "Murder. Human sacrifice." Even as I said the words and knew they must be true, I found them hard to believe. Mama G had always seemed so innocent, so free from malice of any kind. But I'd been wrong about people before. Not often, but it did happen.

"There's something I don't understand," I said. "If Mama Grande left the cult nearly twenty years ago, why were its members still interested in her? If she was going to turn them in to the *policía,* she'd have done so long ago."

Gus laughed out loud. "Turn them in?" he said, shaking his head. "You don't understand this country at all, do you? The government's priests secretly encourage this sort of activity. It's all part of their plan to awaken the ancient gods and help Aztlan to conquer the world."

I just stared at him, one eyebrow raised. Awaken the gods? Conquer the world? This was starting to sound like some sort of paranoid fantasy or late-night B-trid.

Rafael must have been thinking the same thing. "So why would the cultists—and the government—be so interested in my Mama Grande?"

Gus pursed his lips. "Just before she . . . left Aztlan, Rosalita left a note for me. In it she said she had discovered something that could lead to what she called the 'end of the world.' She said that no one must ever learn the secret she had discovered. She was fearful because the cultists had contacted her—they seemed to sense that she knew something of value and was keeping it from them. She said it was only a matter of time before they made her tell."

I winced. The words were all too familiar. On the evening after the missionaries questioned her, Mama Grande had used that same expression: "They made me tell." I shivered, despite the warmth of the infrared heaters.

"But Mama Grande was . . . confused," Rafael protested.

"Not when the cultists first contacted her," Gus said.

"The note Mama Grande left you sounds like a suicide note," I said. "What happened to her? Did she try to take her life? Is that how she wound up"—I searched for a euphemism but couldn't find one—"brain damaged?"

The priest shifted uncomfortably and stared for a long moment at the Olmec sculpture, refusing to meet my eyes. After a moment he turned back to me. "What do you know about magic?"

"A little." I shrugged. "Mostly about spell effects and how they pertain to forensic investigations."

He looked taken aback at that one. I had yet to tell him that I was an ex-cop.

"Have you heard of a fovea?"

"No. It sounds like a Latin word. Is it?"

The priest nodded. "It means 'pit.' I'm not surprised you haven't heard of foveae—they seem to exist only in Aztlan, or at least to be most prevalent here. They're holes in the mana flow. Blank spots where magic won't work. If a magically active individual enters one . . ."

He suppressed a shudder. And that made me start to wonder about him. But he continued before I could put my finger on what exactly had pricked my suspicions.

"A mage or shaman who enters a fovea in astral form dies or is driven mad. It's much the same effect as when someone tries to use magic in space. It is . . . unpleasant, to say the least."

His voice dropped. "Your *abuelita* entered a fovea deliberately, in an effort to kill herself. Her motivation was pure—she believed she was sacrificing herself for the good of others. But what she did was still a sin."

I nodded. Suicide was right up there on the Catholic top ten list of things not to do, if you don't want to slot God off.

Rafael was silent for a moment. His eyes narrowed, as if he were in pain. "She did what she had to do," he said grimly. "That would be like her. She always wanted to help people. She never cared about her own safety. It fits."

But I was still mulling it over. "These holes in the mana flow," I said. "Can a mage or shaman who's jandering about in astral space see them?"

I was only trying to understand—to get a grasp on what these fovea things were. But my question made Gus shift uncomfortably. He sat up as if he were about to get out of his chair, sat back, then squirmed around almost like a suspect being grilled about a major crime. Then he buried his face in his hand and choked out a sob.

"It's my fault," he said. His hands clenched. "I told her about the fovea. I'm to blame. I share her sin and no amount of penance can ever absolve me of it. I told her about the fovea in jest, saying that there were worse things than the end of the world—one could experience the anguish of entering a fovea. I should have known when she started asking me more and more about it. But I didn't realize what she was going to do until it was too late—until she disappeared."

He looked up at us, eyes begging for mercy. The priest had become the pentinent.

"I found her," he said. "Wandering alone in the desert. Confused. Hurt. Suffering. She had not died when she entered the fovea, but she had been driven *loco*. She could no longer perform her healing magic—the gift God gave her was gone. She could no longer care for herself. I was going to take care of her, to take her in. But my friends in the rebel movement insisted she be sent to El Norte. She had family there, they said. She would be safe. But she was murdered, just the same. And now she is dead, and here you are."

Rafael sat with arms crossed and a steely look on his face. If Gus was expecting absolution, he wasn't going to get it from him. I felt sorry for the priest, but there was one last thread we had yet to unravel.

"This secret that Mama Grande discovered was a place," I said slowly. "At least, that's what my investigation has led me to believe. Think, Gus. Did Rosalita ever mention a specific location that the cultists might be interested in—or even hint at one?"

I held my breath, waiting for him to compose himself enough to answer. But my hopes were soon dashed.

"No," Gus answered. "Never. She did not confide in me—even in the confessional. Whatever the secret was, she took it with her to her grave."

He was wrong, of course, but I didn't correct him. At least one person knew Mama G's secret—the man we suspected was her murderer, the Azzie priest Domingo Vargas. He'd hacked it out of her, one painful *macauitl* blow at a time. And we were no closer to capturing him than we had been before.

I looked at Rafael, whose face mirrored my own disappointment. "That's it," I told him. "Dead end."

"The game's not over yet," he answered grimly. "We'll get that fragger—just wait and see."

I sighed. We might—but it would be tough going. We had only one hope—somehow getting to Vargas during the fifth game of the ball court finals.

It was only a slim hope, full of danger. And I didn't like it one bit.

16

We left Izamal on Saturday afternoon. Teresa—the maid who'd sheltered us in her employer's *hacienda* that morning—had been given the rest of that day and Sunday off so she could visit with her family in a tiny village several kilometers south of Izamal. The town was having a *fiesta* that evening and hordes of people would be converging upon it. Even if the soldiers who'd pursued us in the jeep the night before had gotten a good look at us—and I doubted it, since what they mostly saw were our backs—they'd be hard pressed to spot us in the milling crowds at the bus depot. And they'd be looking for two people, not three.

Teresa had been hesitant, at first, to have us accompany her. But despite her obvious misgivings, she let Gus talk her into it. I guessed that she'd do anything for him—it was as if she owed him some big favor and was willing to repay it in any way she could.

We had decided to make our way back to Tenochtitlán, since there didn't seem to be much else we could learn by remaining in Izamal. If the *policía* did stop us to ask questions, the two tickets to the *ollamaliztli* finals in Rafael's pocket were a good reason for us to be headed in that direction. And they fit with our cover story—that we were sports buffs on leave from our jobs at the Nuevo Laredo dog racing track. Although we'd be hard pressed to explain why we were coming to the capital from the opposite direction, from war-torn Yucatán . . .

The bus was crowded—the three of us had to squeeze into a seat designed for two. Rafael sat between Teresa and I, one muscular arm draped across the back of the seat behind her, smiling and bragging for the entire forty-kilometer journey about how he'd be a professional combat biker one day—and boring Teresa silly, I'm sure. I spent my time trying to get comfortable with my hoop hanging half off the seat. I had to take a deep, steadying breath each time we stopped at an Aztlan military checkpoint—especially since I still had the Azzie officer's Savalette Guardian inside my jacket. But the soldiers who squeezed through the press of people on board the bus to scan passengers' ID datacards didn't even pause to listen to my hastily concocted story about us coming to Izamal to visit our "niece" Teresa. They appeared to be looking for someone else.

Teresa seemed to be looking at the soldiers as nervously as I was. I felt guilty for using her as part of our cover story. She was just a teenage girl, after all—one who led a sheltered life as maid to a rich family. Traveling with two strangers who obviously had something to hide was probably scaring her witless.

I had been using my cyberear to listen in on the soldier's conversations, to give us advance warning should they decide to single us out. As our bus pulled away from yet another checkpoint, I heard two men in the back of the bus in whispered conversation. Their voices were hushed enough that even the people in the seat ahead of them wouldn't be able to hear what they were saying, but with my amplified hearing I caught the word *soñador*. I immediately filtered out everything else—the other voices, the bus' engine rumble, the squeaking of the seats and creak of the luggage rack overhead—to listen in.

". . . but if a *dragón* can become president of the UCAS . . ."

"Soñador doesn't have a chance. The Azatlán Party has governed this country since 2015—the elections are all rigged, but nobody can prove it because it's all electronic. All the ORO Corporation has to do is juggle the data from an election and . . ."

"We could vote the old-fashioned way, by ballot."

"It still wouldn't work. The PRI rigged elections in the last century, and they were using paper ballots then. No, Soñador is truly dreaming if it thinks it can have the Yucatán declared a sovereign nation by popular vote. Only the armed revolution can . . ."

I tuned out. The conversation had told me what Soñador's "dream" was—the dragon wanted to follow in the footsteps of Dunkelzahn and govern its own country. But I really wasn't interested in a political debate. I dozed as the bus bumped and rattled its way along the highway, toward Teresa's village.

Rafael nudged me awake when we reached our destination. Night was falling as the bus pulled up at a depot near the town's central plaza. All around our bus, streams of people surged back and forth, laughing and shouting.

As we prepared to get off the bus, something egg-shaped sailed in through the open window next to Teresa and smacked into Rafael's chest. He shouted in alarm and reared back—knocking me off the seat and into the aisle—only to have those around him burst into laughter.

"Don't worry," Teresa shouted over the uproar. "It's only a glitter egg. All part of the *fiesta*."

Grumbling, Rafael brushed a mixture of confetti and glitter from his chest.

We struggled out of the bus with the other departing passengers and waited while Teresa collected her luggage from the men who were tossing bags down from the rack on top of the vehicle. Our connecting bus didn't leave for two hours, and Rafael insisted on walking Teresa to her parents' home. She refused—adamantly at first, shaking off his hand when he tried to take her arm and insisting on carrying her own travel bag. She at last gave in reluctantly when she saw that she wasn't about to get rid of Rafael that easily.

I could see that Rafael's attentions were doomed to failure. I decided to tag along and play chaperone, just to rub it in.

We made our way across the plaza, weaving in and out of the celebrants. Colored lights had been strung from the buildings, painting the night with festive colors. We passed a *mariachi* band of musicians wearing formal black suits studded with silver buttons who were playing trumpets and armadillo-shell guitars. *Cerveza* vendors stood behind tubs filled with ice and beer bottles, doing a brisk business. Music, laughter, and shouts filled the air—it was almost possible to believe that we'd left the civil war behind. But when a string of firecrackers on a tall bamboo scaffold exploded with sharp cracks and flashes, more than one person around us cried out and ducked.

The air was filled with mouth-watering smells. Food stands offered spicy tamales, beef broiled over charcoal and served in strips, *churros* dusted with sugar, and treats from north of the border such as popcorn or cotton candy. I considered stopping to buy something to eat to satisfy my growing hunger, but didn't want to be left behind. Rafael's attention was totally focused on Teresa—it was doubtful that he'd notice my absence.

Crepe paper streamers hung from the trees, and over the heads of the crowd, magical buskers created illusions of fantastic creatures, including dancing skeletons, a *piñata* that exploded to shower illusionary pesos down on the crowd, and even a feathered serpent that wriggled sinuously above the spectators, drawing gasps and excited gestures.

"What are they celebrating?" I asked Teresa as we made our way through the crowd.

"A day they say is holy to one of the ancient gods," she answered. "It used to be a celebration sacred to Francis of Assisi, patron saint of animals, but we're not allowed to celebrate Christian holidays any more. So we hide our observances behind a *fiesta* dedicated to the heathen gods, instead. There will be a service in the *teocalli* later. I avoid the rituals whenever possible, even though we are forced by law to attend. But a number of people really do believe in these false gods and worship them willingly."

I followed her gaze to a knot of people who were clustered around a man who stood on a plastic shipping crate. While they watched, he pierced his tongue with a spine that looked as though it had come from a cactus, then threaded a string through the bleeding hole. Affixed to the lower part of the string were a series of barbs. Slowly, with a look of rapture on his face, he pulled the string through his tongue, sending gouts of blood flowing down over his chin. I gagged and turned away. Suddenly I wasn't quite so hungry any more.

The crowd around us suddenly parted and hushed and I saw ACS personnel in their by-now familiar tan uniforms and *serape* capes striding toward us. They were mean-looking fraggers, cybered to the max with obvious cyber-limbs complete with weapon gyromounts, hard-mounted and smartlinked submachine guns, dermal plating grafted to their skulls, dermal sheathing colorized in a camouflage pattern, eyes that looked like chrome-ringed trideo camera lenses, and medical pumps mounted over veins in their necks that probably held combat drugs. They moved with a jerky, menacing gait and looked as if they were more machine than meat. I wondered if they were the "cyberzombies" we'd heard rumors about when I was back with the Star.

For one panicked moment I thought they were headed toward us. Then Rafael tugged me back into the crowd and I realized that the grotesquely enhanced soldiers were simply passing by. There were four of them in total, moving in tight formation around a man in a sweeping feather cape and a jade-encrusted headdress. Huge gold plugs distended his ears and his otherwise bare chest was covered with a heavy gold pectoral. His loincloth looked like it was made of real fur—jaguar, by its gold hue and pattern of dark spots—and he wore gilded sandals on his feet.

"It's the . . . priest," Teresa whispered in my ear. She seemed loath to call him by that name and her lip curled up in a disdainful sneer as she spoke. "He'll be conducting the ritual at the *teocalli* later. Let's go."

We turned and made our way deeper into the crowd as the priest with his escort of cybered-up soldiers swept haughtily by.

I didn't think that Rafael could be distracted for one nanosecond from Teresa, but I'd forgotten about his obsession with sport. We passed a stall that was selling souvenirs of the *ollamaliztli* finals, and his eye was immediately caught by one of the items on display. He picked up a palm-sized, animated jaguar doll bearing the Tenochtitlán Jaguars logo. It had a face as cute as any kitten and was covered with a fuzz of spotted fur that the vendor assured us grew out of synthetic skin, developed as a spin-off of the medical industry. I didn't have to be a mind-probing mage to tell that Raf intended to buy it for Teresa. In light of what was to come, his choice of gift was a bit ironic. But I didn't know that at the time.

As Rafael bartered for the Jaguar team mascot—allowing himself to get ripped off in his haste of purchase a gift for Teresa—I watched with bemusement as the object of his affections gave him a sidelong look, then slunk away into the crowd. I grinned as she raised a hand to me and mouthed a silent *adiós,* anticipating how slotted off Rafael would be. I figured that he deserved it—he'd pestered her all the way here, then had refused to let her make her own way home.

His bartering complete, Rafael handed the vendor a fistful of coins and then turned to present the stuffed jaguar to Teresa. "Where did she go?" he asked. In that moment, he looked so genuinely crestfallen that I felt sorry for him—and regretted my vindictiveness.

"Let her go, Raf," I said gently. "Teresa's not interested in you. She . . ."

That was odd. When I'd waved goodbye to her, Teresa had been making her way through the crowd, her small travel bag balanced on one shoulder to keep it out of the way. Now the bag—with its distinctive pink-and-white stripes—lay unattended on the base of one of the statues that dotted the plaza. I couldn't imagine that she had just left it there—in Aztlan, despite the heavy *policía* presence, it was prudent to keep one hand on your credstick at all times. I scanned the crowd but couldn't see Teresa anywhere.

Then I spotted her. She was near the edge of the plaza, walking away with a man who kept one arm possessively around her shoulders. He was tall and whip-thin, with a scraggly beard. Ropy muscles showed under the yellow tank top he wore. For a moment, I thought he must be Teresa's brother or some other male relative—but something about the way he was guiding her along didn't scan. Teresa moved with halting, jerky steps like one of the cyberzombies we'd seen earlier. The man with his arm around her jostled her this way and that, as if directing her movements.

Rafael saw where I was staring. He let out a low rumble that sounded amazingly like a growl and squeezed the jaguar doll in his fist. "Drek," he said in a menacing tone. "I stop to buy her a present and she sneaks off with another . . ."

Then his mouth fell open and his face paled. "Leni, look,"

he said in a choked whisper. "The guy's arm. Do you see his shoulder?"

I couldn't be certain, but thought I saw a familiar circular scar. "A cultist?" I asked incredulously. "What's a cultist doing with Teresa?"

"I don't know," Rafael gritted. "But I'm sure as drek going to find out."

He immediately began muscling his way through the crowd, cutting a swath with his shoulders and elbows through protesting revelers. I followed in his wake, trotting to keep up. I eased a hand inside my jacket and wrapped it around the Savalette Guardian. The big gun was slippery in my grip—my hands were sweating. The cultists may not have murdered Mama G, but they had set in motion a chain of events that led to her death. And now they had turned their attention to another innocent . . .

Before we could reach Teresa, they skinny bearded man guided her to a panel van. She stepped into it—apparently willingly, but I could see her stagger and nearly bump her head, as if she were sleepwalking. Then the skinny man slammed the door shut after her, climbed in through the driver's door, and started the engine. The van pulled away, its blaring horn parting the crowd. It found a relatively clear side street and quickly picked up speed, leaving Rafael and I sucking exhaust as we at last burst out of the crowded plaza.

"We've got to follow them, Raf!" I shouted. I looked wildly around us, but this was real life—not the cop trids where a parked car is conveniently waiting for the hero, keystick in the slot. Then I spotted a scooter parked on the sidewalk. Rafael saw it at the same time and we ran over to it—only to curse in disappointment. Its keyslot was empty.

I guess Rafael didn't notice. He leaped onto the scooter and immediately began leaping up and down on the kickstart lever, cranking it for all it was worth. If the circumstances hadn't been so tragic, I might have laughed—the big ork in his biker's leather jacket looked comical in the extreme, frantically trying to start a scooter that was way too small and too brightly colored to ever be ridden by a would-be combat biker. But then the scooter sputtered into life.

"All right, Raf!" I shouted, slapping him on the back. "Let's go!"

I clambered onto the back, perching on the wire basket that hung out over the rear fender. We roared away—the tiny 200cc engine screaming in agony as the scooter popped a wheelie under our combined weight. A trail of blue smoke snaked out after us as we chased the van down the side street.

I didn't really have time to wonder how Rafael had managed to start the scooter without a key. He hadn't jimmied any electronics or even touched the keyslot—he'd seemed to get it going by sheer willpower alone. Instead I concentrated on keeping the van in sight. Although most of the crowd was behind us in the plaza, knots of celebrating *campesinos* staggered through the streets, singing and laughing as children with glitter eggs darted in and out. Even without these obstacles, the scooter was simply too slow to catch up to the larger vehicle. Before much longer the van had pulled out of the town and was rattling its way down a dusty road that led off into the desert. We'd lost our cover.

"Hang back, Raf," I shouted over his shoulder. "We're not going to catch up to the van, and if we're not careful, the cultists are going to see us following them."

In answer, Rafael leaned over the front of the scooter and slammed his fist down onto the top of its headlight. Metal buckled and glass sprayed onto the road as the headlight suddenly went out.

"They won't see us now," he gritted.

The scooter's taillight was burned out, so we were plunged into complete darkness. The van's headlights painted the dirt road ahead of it a dusky yellow, but we had to navigate by guess and feel. Somehow Rafael avoided the worst of the potholes, seeming to instinctively sense the road ahead. I had to admire his skill—maybe he did have a chance at becoming a combat biker, after all.

The road led out into scrub land, well away from any town. Despite Rafael's efforts, we were falling farther and farther behind. Eventually the van disappeared over the crest of a rise. By the time we'd topped the rise ourselves, the van was nowhere to be seen. It had disappeared into a region that was dotted with low hills. I wondered if its driver had spotted us, despite our precautions, and had turned his own headlights off.

I tapped Rafael's shoulder and motioned for him to stop, then climbed down from my uncomfortable perch on the back of the scooter. I used the amplification system in my cyberear, filtering out the noise of the sputtering scooter engine, and turned in a slow circle, listening for the sound of the van. Nothing. But then I stopped. Had that been a scream, off in the distance where the hills were clustered more thickly together? The sound had cut off abruptly—as if the breath had suddenly left the screamer's body. I winced, imagining the worst.

I looked back at Rafael, who was peering out across the surrounding country with a worried frown on his face. His large hands were wrapped around the scooter's hand grips so tightly they were trembling—although maybe it was just the vibration of the engine that was causing them to shake.

"Frag!" he cursed in a pained whisper. "Where did they go, Leni?"

I pointed toward the hills that were dimly illuminated by the thin strip of moon that had risen as we rode. "I heard a—noise—just now," I told Rafael. "From that direction, behind a hill." I squinted, saw the boxy shapes of the "hill" I'd just pointed to. "From those ruins," I corrected myself. "It wouldn't surprise me if the van is parked among them."

Rafael flexed his wrist, revving the scooter's engine. Its high whine cut the still night air. "Let's go then."

"They'll hear us coming," I told him. "I think we should cut the engine and roll as far as we can down this grade. If we go on foot from there, we'll have a better chance at surprising them and . . . rescuing Teresa."

Even as I outlined the plan, I fretted that it might already be too late. I hadn't been able to tell if the scream came from a male or female throat, but it hadn't sounded good. I decided not to dash Rafael's hopes just yet. We should at least try to rescue Teresa—it was what I'd sworn to always do, after my last case with the Star. Keep trying, no matter what, no matter how hopeless things might seem.

I had an inkling that Teresa no longer needed our help. And I was right. But my grim conclusion as to why was completely wrong. Aztlan held yet another surprise for us . . .

17

I heard the sound of chanting voices, just ahead. We paused in the shadow of a pile of tumbled masonry near the top of the ruined building we had been climbing. I motioned for Rafael to keep still while I listened with my cyberear. While several voices kept up a low, droning chant, one rose above the rest.

"We call and bind you, Nezahualpilli, with this offering of *chalchiuatl*. Let this precious water slake your thirst and feed your ravenous hunger. Let it give you strength and help you to manifest before us here tonight. Let it wash you with its energy and sustain you . . ."

I gave Rafael the thumbs-up signal, and together we raised our heads above the rubble to take a look. I heard Rafael's sharp intake of breath as he took in the scene that lay before us.

On top of a ruined pyramid a short distance away stood a group of seven men and three women, dressed in modern clothing but wearing tall feather headdresses that splayed out above their heads like the fanned tails of peacocks. They were grouped in a loose half-circle around a statue—a carved humanoid figure that reclined on its back, balancing a stone bowl on its belly. One of the men—the one whose voice could be heard above the rest—held something above the statue. His back was to us, however, and I couldn't see what it was. A long cape, stitched together from thousands of feathers, covered his back and shoulders.

The skinny fellow in the yellow tank top who had guided Teresa from the plaza was nowhere in sight, but I thought I saw the boxy shape of his van parked around the far side of the pyramid. I guessed that these were all cultists, although their arms were covered, making it impossible to tell whether they bore the cult's brand.

The building on which the cultists stood was an ancient stepped pyramid—a *teocalli* whose sides had crumbled somewhat, blurring and softening the structure's stacked-box shape into more of a rounded mound. The area around the statue on the upper level had been cleared of debris, however, and the rooms that lay behind this area appeared to be intact. Doorways on either side of the area where the cultists stood led into the interior of the building—dark and sinister, like the sockets of an empty skull.

The entire scene was lit by a roadside emergency flare that flickered near the base of the statue. It threw out a sputtering, garish red light, painting everything the color of blood.

Just above the cultists' heads, a whirlpool of what looked like water turned slowly, every now and then brushing against the tips of their headdresses. One spiraling tendril extended down to the bowl on the statue's belly like an umbilical cord. A low moaning sound issued from the swirling whirlpool—a sound like the combination of a man groaning in pain and water gurgling in a deep well. The sound was eerie and chilling—it sent shivers coursing through my body, giving me goose bumps and making the hair on the back of my arms rise. I guessed that this was some form of ritual magic—but I couldn't imagine what its purpose might be.

The man closest to the statue shifted to the other side of it, so that he was facing in our direction. I saw that he had painted his face black, and that his hands and forearms were also a dark color. A glossy black oval decorated one forearm like a miniature shield. He held what I guessed was a wet sponge. Liquid dripped from it onto the statue below, filling the bowl.

"Accept this precious water that falls upon the *chac mool* like life-giving rain," he said, squeezing the sponge so that a fresh trickle of liquid fell from it. "Drink deeply of it, Nezahualpilli, and appear before us now."

His invocation finished, the man dropped the sponge onto a pile near his feet. He motioned to two of the cultists, who entered one of the darkened, rectangular doorways in the upper level of the *teocalli*. They emerged a moment later, their hands on the shoulders of a slender youth who walked between them. I gasped, thinking at first that this might be Teresa. But it was a young boy, dressed in ragged jeans and sandals and a dirty T-shirt that was too small for him. He looked like the street kid we'd encountered in Tenochtitlán—one of the innumerable SINless gutterpunks you find in any big city.

The boy didn't display any of the jerky motions I'd seen in Teresa as she left the plaza, and so I assumed him to be one of the cultists—a participant, rather than a prisoner. I frowned, puzzled, as four of the adults around him took hold of his wrists and ankles and hoisted him into the air, spread-eagled. Was this some sort of initiation rite? Were they going to ritually wash him clean before accepting him into the cult?

Then the cultist with the painted hands reached under his cape and drew a dagger that had a dark obsidian blade. In the frozen instant that he raised it, I knew what was about to happen. But I was too shocked to react quickly enough. The dagger plunged down, slicing open the chest of the boy. The priest forced a hand into the wound, yanked, and pulled out the boy's heart. With a quick stroke he severed the arteries leading to it, spraying those around him with blood, then turned and raised the heart above the statue, letting blood pour down into the bowl. He squeezed the heart like a sponge, causing blood to spurt out and spatter the statue like rain. Then he led the cultists in a chant.

I heard Rafael retching beside me, and choked down my own bile. As a member of Lone Star, I'd seen the gruesome aftermath of murder before, and had been a witness to several shootings, a handful of them fatal. But I'd never seen anyone dispatched with such cold, cruel precision. I knew now that the leader's hands were stained with blood—not painted—and that the objects I assumed were sponges were in fact human hearts. An entire pile of them. I'd just witnessed my first human sacrifice. I didn't want to see another one.

I glanced at Rafael and saw the same horror and revulsion that I felt displayed upon his face.

"We've got to stop them," he said in a choked whisper.

I nodded grimly and raised the oversized pistol in my hand. "We will," I vowed.

"Do you think that Teresa . . ." Rafael couldn't finish the question.

"I don't know," I said. I looked back toward the *teocalli*. Two of the cultists were dragging the lifeless body of the teenager back into its interior. We had no way of knowing how many bodies the temple contained—or how many living captives had yet to fall under the knife. Was Teresa among them?

The teenage boy must have been under the influence of a spell—or drugs. He hadn't struggled or cried out, even as the dagger plunged into his chest. If all of the captives were similarly subdued, then whose scream had I heard earlier?

The two cultists who'd dragged the body inside the *teocalli* still had not emerged. Rafael shifted anxiously beside me, Streetline Special in his hand. I whispered to him to stay chill. "Wait until they bring out their next captive," I told him. "When I give the signal, take out as many as you can. Aim at those farthest from the captive—if it's Teresa, you don't want to gun her down by mistake."

Rafael grumbled a little at this one, but then nodded. He knew that I had the better weapon—and was a better shot. I braced the Savalette Guardian with both hands—the pistol was trembling in my grip—and sighted along it. And waited. And watched. And debated the morality of what we were about to do—then decided that murderers deserved to be punished. With lethal force, if necessary.

The swirling pool of liquid—which I now knew was blood—boiled upward like a thunderhead. I was reminded, for a moment, of the whirlwind that Águila had conjured up. But then the base of the whirlpool parted, forming a fork that resembled legs. A knot at the top of it coalesced into what could pass for a head with swirling, empty eyes, and two tendrils spiraled down to form arms. The spirit—at least that's what I assumed it to be—grew ever more solid and distinct. Now, in the lurid red light of the flare, I could see that it was a human figure, decked out in a cape and headdress like those who had summoned it, and with a face that was haughty and shadowed. I knew in my gut—without understanding why—that the thing was as ancient as it was evil. It let out a low moan that sent a shiver of ice through my very core.

"Nezahualpilli!" the cultists cried as one. "Speaker of prophecies!" They raised their hands skyward in supplication and fell to their knees. Only their leader remained standing.

"Nezahualpilli, you are summoned and bound," the standing cultist intoned in a deep, authoritative voice. "You must prophesy for me. On what date will the Sun of Motion end? When will the new age begin?"

I am a king—not a slave. You shall not speak to me this way.

The voice boomed loud inside my head, echoing against my skull. I winced, and saw that Rafael was also shaking his head and blinking. So he could hear it too. Strangely, although the words were in an ancient language that was utterly foreign to me, I understood them as clearly as if they were "spoken" in English or Spanish.

It had to be the voice of the spirit, projected telepathically into my mind, violently sweeping aside my own inner voice with its power and force. I cringed, wondering what the frag we'd gotten ourselves into. I figured we could handle the cultists—my Savalette Guardian could pump out rounds faster than they could cast spells, and we'd have surprise on our side—but bullets would have no effect at all on the spirit itself. I could only pray that the thing was too far away to read my thoughts.

The cultist leader pointed his bloody obsidian dagger at the spirit. "I am the master here!" he screamed at the thing. "And you shall answer my questions. On what day will the Sun of Motion end?"

I shuddered at his ferocity. If the cultists were this aggressive with a thing as awe-inspiring as a spirit, I could just imagine how rough they must have been with Mama G.

On the day Four Motion. Just as all the other ages have ended on that unlucky number, so too will this one.

Although my head was ringing with the spirit's words, my cyberear still caught the whisper as one of the kneeling cultists spoke to another in a worried voice: "But that's only one day after the final—"

"At what hour must the *itzompan* be filled to bring about this end?" the leader of the cultists shouted.

Itzompan? I had no idea what the word meant. It sounded

like something from the ancient Azzie language. Was it some sort of magical contract, perhaps? But he'd used the Spanish verb for filling a vacant space, rather than filling an obligation. He had to be referring to an object. Or to a place . . .

The itzompan *must be filled when the precious twin rises in the east. At this moment may the motion of the Earth be triggered. The new age shall be ushered in with the blood of the victor.*

The spirit loomed above the cultist leader like an angry thunderhead. *I have answered your questions,* it shouted into our minds. *Now you will release me!*

"One more question," the cultist leader said. "And then I will return you to your rest. Where is the *itzompan*?"

I thought I saw the spirit's face twist into an evil grin, but it was hard to read the expression of a thing whose body was little more than a pool of blood. *You do not need me to tell you that. Ask your blood brother. He knows where it lies hidden.*

"But the other *sacerdote* has . . . He is unavailable to us," the leader protested. "That is why I summoned you without him. We cannot—"

I tire, the spirit said. *Feed me.*

"No. First you must answer—"

Feed me! The voice hit me like a physical blow, leaving the inside of my skull ringing. When I looked up, I saw that the cultists were also cringing. A few were even holding their heads.

The leader of the cultists turned and flicked a hand in the waving gesture that to gringos looks like "go away" but to Azzies means "hurry forward." I saw movement inside the darkened doorway of the *teocalli* and braced my pistol. I gazed down the sight of my gun at the priest, who was addressing the spirit once more.

"You will enjoy this one," he told the spirit. "Her will is strong and her blood pumps fiercely. She—"

Rafael let out a strangled scream of rage as the cultists led Teresa out of the *teocalli*. She was naked, aside from the gold necklace that still hung around her neck. And she looked dazed. She stumbled blindly between the two cultists, nearly falling . . .

In that moment, Rafael opened up with his pistol. I joined

him a split second later, squeezing the trigger of my Savalette Guardian. I was still aiming at the leader of the cultists, but in that split second he'd already reacted, throwing himself to the side in response to Rafael's gunfire and the collapse of the man next to him. In addition, I wasn't used to the recoil of my acquired weapon. It kicked violently as it spit out three slugs in rapid-fire succession, jerking my hands back and throwing off my aim.

Cursing, I braced my weapon more carefully this time. I picked off one cultist, two . . . Then, when I was satisfied that I had the weapon under control, I aimed at the cultists to either side of Teresa. One went down as two bullets of my three-round burst exploded through his gut. The other screamed and dove for the cover of the *teocalli*.

At first I fretted, thinking that Teresa might still be in a dazed state. I worried that she would wander into the line of fire. But then a strange transformation occurred. I only saw it out of the corner of my eye—I was too busy sighting and shooting at the cultists who scrambled every which way, some of them hurling themselves down the steps and tumbling to the base of the pyramid in a flailing jumble of arms and legs.

Teresa dropped to her knees and braced her arms in front of her so that she was in a crouch and shook her long dark hair so that it fanned across her naked back. Then her forearms lengthened and her knees suddenly bent the wrong way. Hair flowed across her body, growing in a shimmering wave of black until it covered her skin in a sleek pelt. At the same time the hair on her head shrank back upon itself and her ears flowed upward, extending into triangular points. A long tail grew from her haunches and began lashing angrily. She threw open her mouth and roared—the sound was amazingly similar to a human scream—and in that instant her face transformed into the fang-filled visage of a jungle cat. In the blood-red glow of the flare, she was a frightening sight indeed. She looked alert, tense. Not dazed at all.

Rafael must have witnessed the transformation as well. His mouth gaped open and his pistol hung forgotten in his hands. In the instant that neither of us was shooting, I heard the roar of an engine, the scraping of gears being shifted too hurriedly, and the spinning of wheels on dirt as a vehicle roared off into the night.

"Frag it, Raf!" I shouted. "They're getting away."

The caped man who had been leading the ritual chose this moment to try to escape down the stairs that fronted the pyramid. Before he had taken two steps, the sleek, all-black jaguar that was Teresa launched itself into the air. The cat sank the claws of its forepaws into his chest, bit savagely at the cultists's neck, and then rode his body down the stairs, lashing out with hind legs and raking his lower body with its rear claws. Feathers from his shredded cape flew everywhere as the pair tumbled, and when they reached the bottom of the pyramid the leader lay in a bloody heap. Teresa sprang away into the night, still in jaguar form.

All this time, the spirit that the cultists had summoned had simply hung above the pyramid with arms crossed, watching events unfold with an aloof expression. But as soon as the leader of the cultists lay still, it collapsed into itself, reverting back to its whirlpool shape. It condensed, drawing into a perfect sphere—and then it exploded with a flash of magical energy that knocked me sprawling. Tiny droplets of blood spattered my body with the force of a stinging rain. I heard the spirit scream a single word: *Free!* and then my brain seemed to go into overload and shut down.

I don't remember what happened next. All I know is that when I came to, something rough and wet was rubbing my cheek and something heavy was pressed into my chest. I opened my eyes—and screamed as I saw a jaguar's face mere centimeters from my own and realized that its heavy paw was upon my chest, holding me down. Then the jaguar backed off and watched me with eyes that reflected green in the moonlight. I noticed the gold cross that hung around its neck from a chain. And I realized who it was.

"Teresa?" I sat up and rubbed my aching temples. I looked around, saw that Rafael was lying beside me, his back propped against a pile of masonry. His eyes opened, and he sat up and shook his head.

"Looks like Teresa didn't need to be rescued, after all," he said with a weak grin. "She's been watching over us, instead."

I sat up, saw the Savalette Guardian lying a meter or two

away, and crawled over to grab it. I holstered the gun, then looked at my watch. I'd been unconscious for more than an hour. And I felt like drek. Every muscle ached and my head was pounding. I felt as bad as I had the night after my own grandmother died in hospital—after my all-day, all-night drinking binge. I even had the foul taste in my mouth. I wiped my mouth—and my hand rubbed away crumbs of dried blood. My lips weren't cut—it must have been the blood from the spirit. Feeling queasy, I spat until my lips were clean again.

Later, Teresa told us what had happened that night. She was a rebel—a courier for the Cristeros—and had traveled to the village carrying a "package" for them inside the false bottom of her travel bag. She was to pass it along to another rebel at the *fiesta,* then make her way back to Izamal the next day. She didn't really have relatives in the village—hence her reluctance to let Rafael walk her "home" or to let him carry her bag, which she had deliberately left on the base of the statue in the plaza for her contact to pick up.

Teresa didn't know why the cultists had singled her out as a sacrificial victim. Perhaps because she looked young, fragile, and alone. Perhaps because they sensed the magic in her and knew it could feed they spirit they were summoning. Or they might just have seen the bag slung over her shoulder and assumed her to be a traveler nobody would miss— especially if they hadn't noticed Rafael and me escorting her earlier. In any case, the skinny cultist with the beard had used a spell to overpower Teresa and force her to accompany him. Then he'd locked her in the back of the van.

When the van stopped and the cultist opened its doors, expecting to find a terrified teenager cringing inside, he was confronted instead by a snarling jaguar. The scream I'd heard when we stopped the scooter had been Teresa's triumphant roar as she launched herself at her captor, tearing open his throat. She'd dragged his body off behind some bushes, quickly licked his blood from her sleek sides, and then changed into human form. She'd been about to put on her clothes and drive away in the van when the other cultists surprised her. Once again, she fell victim to their spells.

Only when my bullet had taken out the cultist who was magically manipulating her had Teresa come back to her senses. Realizing her danger, she transformed into jaguar form to escape. And while she was at it, she took her revenge on the nearest cultist—the leader who was standing right in front of her. She'd then attacked every cultist she could find, finishing off those that Rafael and I had wounded. Bad news, since that left us with no survivors to question.

Once I was able to move around again, I clambered down the mound where we'd hidden, then climbed the steps of the *teocalli*. The stonework was slippery with blood, and bodies lay everywhere—I counted seven cultists in all, including the leader. Three of them must have escaped while Rafael and I lay stunned by the spirit's mental blast.

Unlike the other cultists, the man who'd been leading the blood ritual did not have a calendar stone brand mark on his shoulder. His distended earlobes confirmed him as a priest, even though he wasn't wearing the traditional gold ear plugs. Maybe he hadn't trusted the other cultists enough to want to risk getting them stolen.

The shieldlike object on his forearm turned out to be an oval of obsidian stone, glossy and black, mounted in a leather frame. I didn't know much about Azzie religion, but I did remember one piece of trivia from Rafael's "discovering my roots" phase. The god Tezcatlipoca was said to have a similar "mirror" in which he could read the fate of any human. In a way, it made an odd kind of sense to find a similar object on the arm of a man who had been summoning a prophesying spirit.

Under his robe, the priest was dressed in conventional clothing—cotton pants, shirt, and shoes. The clothing had been shredded and bloodied in Teresa's attack, but the pockets were intact. Inside one, I found something that was all too familiar—a simsense chip, its blood-smeared cardboard case emblazoned with the Aztec tree of life. It was a duplicate of the chip case that I had found inside Mama G's kitchen after the cultist missionaries had roughed her up.

At the time, I didn't think my find was all that significant. The priest was obviously in league with the cultists, after all. Only later would I learn that the priest's blood wasn't the only stain on the chip case.

As I searched the priest, I noticed something peculiar about his body. A catheter had been surgically implanted into his chest, over one of the major veins. Had he been undergoing some sort of medical treatment that required the regular attachment of an IV line? If so, he wouldn't be facing any more hospital bills.

The interior of the temple looked like something out of a horror B-trid. A total of twelve bodies lay in a tangled heap where the cultists had dumped them. Each had a gaping hole in the chest where the heart had been removed. The stones underfoot were slippery with blood, and the metallic tang of it assaulted my nostrils. My eyes began to sting as I looked at the corpses. Judging by their cheap, grubby clothing, they were all either street kids or poor *campesinos* from some tiny country town. One was an elderly man—his gray hair and frail body brought back vivid memories of how helpless Mama G had been. As I stared at the bodies, a tear trickling down my cheek, I felt the last shred of guilt at having gunned down the cultists disappear. Those bloodthirsty fraggers had deserved what they got. Every last bullet.

It took us some time to get back to the village—Rafael wasn't able to duplicate his trick of starting the scooter without a magkey, and so we had to search for the cultist's van. When we found it, Teresa shifted back into human form. She picked up her dress and brushed it off, then began getting dressed. I'd have thought she would be demure, that she would step behind the van. But Teresa seemed perfectly comfortable with her nudity. Rafael tried not to stare, but couldn't help himself. The girl was beautiful, with a body that was perfect in every way. Slender waist, full hips and breasts . . . I fought back a twinge of jealousy and reminded myself that Teresa wasn't deliberately showing off—shapeshifters are animals, born in that form, and only gradually learn human ways as they spend increasing amounts of time in human form. Nudity probably felt totally natural to the girl.

We drove the van back to the outskirts of town, then ditched it in a side street. Since some of the cultists had escaped, I worried that they might recognize it. I'd insisted on bringing the scooter back with us—it was a stolen vehicle, after all, and should be returned to the village so that its owner could find it again.

We reached the town as dawn broke. The streets were empty and littered with the debris of the *fiesta*—streamers, broken bits of *piñata,* and plastic cups were everywhere underfoot. One or two celebrants lay in doorways or on benches, sleeping off the effects of the night's party. Obviously, curfews were not as strictly enforced here as they were in Izampan. Or if they were, they'd been relaxed for the *fiesta.*

The events of the night before had left me weary to the bone, and all I wanted to do was put my head down. But it was a sure bet that every hotel and *posada* would be full to overflowing with those who had come to town for the *fiesta.*

Teresa came through for us, once again. "I have friends in town who have spare beds in their homes," she said, as if reading my thoughts. "Christian friends." She placed extra emphasis on the first word, tipping me off to the fact that these "friends" were probably fellow Cristeros—or at least were sympathetic to the cause.

Rafael broke into a wide grin. I thought he was going to make a none-too-subtle suggestion about sleeping arrangements, but he surprised me by being a perfect gentleman. "Great," he rumbled. "I feel drek-kicked. And Leni and I have missed our bus connection, anyway. We might as well doss down. And then I'd like to hear more about the Cristeros. Can a lapsed Catholic join?"

Rafael sounded so sincere, he almost had me fooled. Then I realized that he was just handing the girl a line. I felt sorry for Teresa—she was young, and not entirely human. She didn't know bulldrek when she heard it.

Once again, I was underestimating the girl. She was tougher—and more cunning—than she looked.

18

The events of the night before had been too frantic for me to be able to assimilate everything I'd seen and heard out there in the ruins. The horror of seeing a human being sacrificed had numbed me, and the sheer physical exhaustion I'd felt after the spirit had blasted us with magical backwash in its surge toward freedom had left me aching, tired, and unable to think clearly. But now, after a deep and dreamless sleep of several hours, I was fresh enough to start putting the pieces together.

I sat on the rooftop of the home of Teresa's friends, enjoying the Sunday afternoon sunshine. It felt so good I'd almost forgotten the Seattle rain that I'd left behind. I sipped a cool *cerveza* and poked with a fork at the remains of my *chilaquiles*—a spicy combination of eggs, chiles, chicken, and leftover tortillas. Rafael and Teresa had gone to watch the fourth game in the *ollamaliztli* finals at a local cantina, and the woman who had agreed to let us sleep at her home was downstairs serving dinner to her husband and a horde of noisy children. She'd left me alone on the rooftop, lost in my thoughts.

I had some solid information—and a number of guesses. The whirlpool of blood that had coalesced into human form had to have been another example of the blood magic for which Aztlan was starting to gain a whispered reputation. There was no doubt in my mind that the man leading the ritual had been an Azzie priest—his black-painted face and the shieldlike obsidian "mirror" on his forearm were symbols of Tezcatlipoca, god of the smoking mirror. More and more, it was looking as if the cultists had the official sanction of the Aztlan state religion.

Yet appearances can be deceiving. The priest we'd seen in the village had been escorted by some of the most hard-hooped security fraggers I'd ever seen, yet the one who had summoned and bound the spirit on top of the ruined *teocalli* had no security escort whatsoever—Rafael and I would have been the ones waiting for MedíCarro body bags, if he had. It suggested that the priest had not been on official business that night.

I suspected that Vargas had been in league with the cultists who had come as missionaries to Mama G's door. In his capacity as an Azzie diplomat, he could have facilitated their travel visas to Seattle. And it was just a little too coincidental that he had been posted as a consular official to the same city, two weeks before the pair's arrival. It would also explain how he had known where to find them—he may even have set up a meeting with them at Charles Royer Station. Whatever they had learned from Mama G, only Vargas had taken it back to Aztlan with him.

I took a sip of my beer. Okay, so the apocalyptic cult and the Azzie priesthood—or two members of its clergy, at least—were working together, possibly in secret. They'd come north to Seattle to track down Mama G and unearth a memory that was buried after her encounter with the fovea. The memory of a place . . .

What had the leader of the ritual been asking the spirit? He wanted to know the location of something called an *itzompan*—something that was connected with their crazy goal of bringing about the end of the world and the beginning of a new age. Could that have been the secret that Mama G fled Aztlan to protect?

They'd called the spirit by the honorific title of "king." The Azzies hadn't had kings for six centuries, since the time of Montezuma—I knew that much local history. And the date the spirit had used—Four Motion—sounded as if it came from the ancient calendar.

I needed the advice of an expert. Someone I could trust—who had no links to Aztlan or its priesthood. If the cultists tracked me down through any contacts I made, they'd retaliate with lethal force. Of that I could be certain. And I had no way of recognizing the cultists before they struck—they could be anyone. All they had to do was hide the brand marks on their arms, casually stroll up to me in a crowd, and . . .

Then it struck me. The professor of Native American Studies in the Sioux Nation—the one who had answered my query about the cross on the simsense chip cover. He'd been helpful—garrulous even—spouting off all kinds of supplemental information about the "tree of life." Obviously passionate about his field of study, he'd answered my posting within minutes. What was his name and Matrix LTG address again? I called it up from my headware memory: Silas Ironfeather at the Chief Joseph University at NA/SIO-SW/TEM.

I set down my beer bottle on the low glass table beside me and started to rise from my chair. Then I paused as I heard the bottle start rattling on the table. The arms of the chair trembled under my fingertips, and my cyberear picked up a low-pitched rumble that was more of a vibration within the Earth itself than a sound. Earthquake! My heart began to race and a film of sweat broke out on my brow. This house was built of cement blocks, mortared together. The kind of construction that collapses into a heap of rubble the moment an earthquake hits . . .

The tremor was over almost as soon as it began. The rumbling faded and my beer bottle stopped dancing on the table. As soon as the earthquake was over, dogs began furiously barking and I heard a baby crying next door. But otherwise, everyone remained glued to their telecom sets, watching the *ollamaliztli* game. No one even ventured outside to see whether any damage had been done. Life in Aztlan continued, earthquake or no earthquake. People just held their collective breath a moment, then carried on.

How they could live like this, I'd never know. I could never get used to it.

I didn't want to put Teresa's friends at risk by using their telecom, and so I headed down to the bus station to use the public telecoms. It meant a slightly increased risk—I'd heard that the Azzies randomly monitored data channels, searching for "subversive" uploads and downloads. But I was betting that they couldn't monitor every one of the country's million-odd datalines twenty-four hours a day.

The bus station itself was grubby, a relic of the last century. But the telecom booths were clean and modern-looking. I slotted my credstick and direct-accessed Professor Ironfeather's number at the university. I left the telecom's optical recorder on, since the Azzies were likely to pay closer attention to any calls that didn't include an optical component—they'd naturally conclude that anyone who shut it off must have something to hide. I tapped my foot nervously as the call connected, looking over my shoulder for ACS guards. No doubt about it, I was getting paranoid. Aztlan will do that to you.

As the call connected, a head and shoulders appeared on the telecom's flatscreen display. The man staring back at me was both elven and Amerind, with ears tapering to delicate points and traditional braided hair. He wore what looked like an honest to gods fringed buckskin jacket and had the stem of a long, small-bowled pipe between his teeth. He blew a thin stream of white smoke out the side of his mouth as he spoke. "Good day. Professor Ironfeather speaking."

He sounded formal, stuffy—par for the course, when you're dealing with elves. I had already decided to play to his vanity—his answer to my previous question had held a slightly pompous note when he referred to my query as "child's play." He'd even asked for something more challenging next time. I hoped I was going to oblige him.

"Professor Ironfeather, I'm in need of your expertise on Native American studies. I'm researching a number of obscure topics to do with the ancient history of Aztlan and haven't found anyone else who can assist me. The professors at the Ciudad Universitaria in Tenochtitlán haven't been any help, and yet you'd think they'd be the experts. I know it's a long shot, contacting a professor in the Sioux Nation about Aztlaner history, but a classmate of mine once heard you speak at a symposium and she thought that—"

He cut me off before I could finish, and for that I was thankful. I didn't want to have to get too specific as to who had recommended him—or where they'd heard him speak.

"I am an expert in the history of that nation," he said, taking a draw from his pipe. "Tell me what you wish to know."

"Well, first of all, I'm looking for more information on

King Nezahualpilli. He was supposed to be a prophet, but I can't find any references to—"

"Then you haven't been looking very hard," the professor chided. "Nezahualpilli's _ollamaliztli_ match with Montezuma II is infamous. In 1516, this king of Texcoco prophesied that strangers would soon rule the Aztec kingdom. Montezuma refused to believe him, and challenged Nezahualpilli to a ball game—and to predict who would win it. Nezahualpilli boasted that he would win, and wagered his kingdom against Montezuma's rather pathetic bet of three turkeys. Needless to say, Nezahualpilli did win—although Montezuma beat him in the first two games. Three years later, in 1519, Cortés sacked and plundered Tenochtitlán, and the prophecy was proved correct."

Yet another tale of prophecy and fate. Aztlan history seemed to be riddled with stories like this one. No wonder its religious fanatics leaned toward the apocalyptic. Prophecies of impending doom seemed as popular, even in this modern century, as . . .

Wait a minute. The rulers of Tenochtitlán and Texcoco, playing _ollamaliztli_ together? Weren't those the two cities that were squaring off in this year's national finals? Could there be some significance to the fact that . . .

I shook my head, surprised at myself. I was starting to think like an Azzie.

Professor Ironfeather's history lesson hadn't enlightened me any further—it had just perplexed me. I'd thought the cultists had summoned a spirit last night in the ruins. Instead, it seemed, they had used blood magic to conjure up a ghost from the Azzie past. An actual historical figure, if the professor was correct. And Professor Ironfeather's attitude suggested that he was. As he took another draw on his pipe, I jumped in with another question.

"The references to Nezahualpilli that I did manage to find mentioned something called an _itzompan_. What is that?" I was taking a gamble—I had no idea if the two were actually connected. To my relief, they were.

"An _itzompan_ . . ." Professor Ironfeather murmured. His eyes glanced up and to the left, as he searched his memory for the answer. As his head turned I saw the datasoft links behind his right ear—he had an entire array of them, all filled with chips that I assumed to be knowsofts. No wonder the guy was a walking encyclopedia.

"Ah yes," he said, nodding to himself. "The *itzompan*. The 'place of the skull.' An alleged feature of the traditional *ollamaliztli* court—a sacrificial altar, set into the floor of the playing field, intended to receive the severed head of the victorious team's captain. The winner's head was offered up as a sacrifice to the sun god—just one of many ancient sacrifices designed to keep the sun in motion. It involved a form of what used to be called 'sympathetic magic' in the pre-Awakened world. The severed head represented the sun. The ball itself was also symbolic of the sun—its passage through the ball court's hoop represented the descent of the sun into the underworld and its re-emergence. The Aztecs believed that—"

"Excuse me," I interrupted. "The *winner* was sacrificed?"

Professor Ironfeather's eyebrows drew together in a scolding frown. I could just hear him *tsk-tsking* at my ignorance under his breath.

"It was a great honor," he said. "Even before the game began, the team captains dedicated themselves to the sun god Huitzilopochtli. When it came time to be sacrificed, the victor would . . ."

I mentally tuned Professor Ironfeather out as I searched my wetware for a piece of data that was tugging at my memory. Huitzilopochtli—that was the god that Hector, the cab driver, had been going on about. Huitzilopochtli's curse. Every year, the captain of the team that won the national *ollamaliztli* finals had died. I'd dismissed the deaths as accidents or coincidences. But what if the court ball players were being sacrificed?

Then I remembered that the team captains had died of natural causes—or what passed for natural causes in this modern world. Heart attacks, car and plane crashes, and gunshots, if I remembered correctly. None had been beheaded. I sighed. If you looked hard enough, it was possible to find a conspiracy in anything.

"Is the *itzompan* found in modern ball courts, as well?" I asked.

"Hardly." The professor shook his head. "It was said to have been located at the center of the court. That positioning would not only interfere with the game as it is currently played, but is also superfluous. The Aztlaners no longer sacrifice their team captains." He drew from his pipe once more. "And the *itzompan* itself may be strictly fictional. Surprisingly enough, although the *itzompan* is mentioned several times in the ancient codices, archaeologists have yet to uncover a ball court with this feature. It's probably the stuff of legend, since the codices refer to it being used only at the dawning of a new era."

I wanted to pursue that topic further. But then I saw an Azzie police officer out the corner of my eye. She wasn't looking at me—but she was walking my way. The combined threat of her heavy weapons and obvious cyberware made me decide to cut the call short.

"Two last questions, Professor," I said hurriedly. "First, what is the 'precious twin?' I'd guess that it's a star, since ancient Aztec ah . . . texts . . . mention it as rising in the east."

"That would be Venus. Erroneously named the 'morning star,' it is in fact a planet, and is associated with both morning and evening."

Morning then, if it was rising in the east. Whatever the cultists were planning, it would take place at first light.

"And the day Four Motion? What would that correspond to in the modern calendar?"

He told me. I did some quick mental arithmetic. It was one day after the fifth and final game of the *ollamaliztli* nationals.

Then the pieces fell together in my mind. I knew what the cultists planned to do. Grab the winning court ball team captain, sacrifice him the morning after the final game as Venus rose in the dawn sky, place his severed head in an *itzompan*, and welcome the "demons of twilight" that Rafael's friend Alberto had told us about. But where was the *itzompan* where all of this would take place?

Mama G had known its location. I knew that instinctively, in my gut. That was what the missionaries—and Domingo Vargas—had been after. The reason why Mama G had been killed. According to Parminder's description of the simsense chip, it must be located somewhere in the Yucatán. If only . . .

I glanced over my shoulder. The *policía* officer was getting closer. And she was looking directly at me, now.

"Thank you, Professor Ironfeather, but I must go now. I've run up an enormous long distance bill already, talking live like this, and I won't be able to afford much more on a student's budget. I'm afraid I'll have to chat with you again another time. But I'm appreciative of all your help. You really were a font of knowledge."

The professor tipped his head in a gracious nod, and acknowledged my gushing praise. "Any time," he said. "I am pleased to have been of service."

I stabbed the Disconnect icon, then took a moment to compose myself before leaving the telecom booth. Just in case the officer wasn't really interested in me, I'd take it slow and casual.

She wasn't. She passed me by without so much as a blink of her cybereye. Heaving a sigh of relief, I strode through the bus terminal. It looked as though Rafael and I were going to the final game of the *ollamaliztli* nationals, after all. That was where everything would come together. If the cultists really were going to try to kidnap the winning team's captain that night, it just might prove enough of a distraction for Rafael and I to get to the priest Domingo Vargas and haul him off somewhere, where we could question him.

As I stepped out of the bus terminal into the street, car drivers all around me started honking their horns. I heard cheering from a cantina up the street, and a trumpet blared out a triumphant tune.

"What's happened?" I asked a man standing next to me. He had a micro-receiver in his ear—it was a safe bet that he was plugged into whatever earth-shattering event had just occurred.

"The Texcoco Serpents!" he chortled. "They've won the fourth game of the nationals. It's a tied series—and I've just won a bet of one million pesos!" He smiled benevolently at me—and for good reason, since the win was equivalent to two thousand nuyen. "May good fortune also come your way, *señorita*."

"Thanks," I told him. I knew I was going to need all the luck I could get.

19

If we were going to get back to Tenochtitlán in time for the fifth game of the finals, Rafael and I had to move quickly. I ducked back into the bus terminal and purchased two tickets for a bus that left for Mérida later than evening. Fortunately, the capital city of the state of Yucatán wasn't under curfew—Air Montezuma flights still operated regularly between Mérida and Tenochtitlán. And so I was able to telecom a travel agent in the city and get the last two seats on the "red eye"—the midnight flight to Tenochtitlán.

As I passed the town's central plaza, I spotted Rafael and Teresa. They were participating in the time-honored tradition of the Aztlan *paseo*. The Sunday evening promenade is a curious tradition, in which single men stroll around the plaza in one direction while single women and couples circle it in the other direction. Everyone is decked out in their finest clothes and the object seems to be to flirt, rather than to make any serious connections—although being caught by the curfew could provide a handy excuse for having to stay overnight at the home of a suitor. Tonight the *paseo* participants were especially jubilant, celebrating the Serpents' victory in the *ollamaliztli* finals.

I watched Rafael and Teresa as they strolled around the whole plaza, arm in arm. They were talking in low whispers with their heads close together. I found myself growing angry at the fact that Rafael was spending so much time courting Teresa, when he should have been helping me plan how we might get to Vargas. It irked me to the point where I used my cyberear to filter out the teasing catcalls of the teenage boys strolling the plaza and listen in on their conversation.

". . . have to catch a bus back to Izamal tonight," Teresa was saying. "My employers only gave me one day off—it will look suspicious if I stay away longer. And besides, I have to prepare. The Cristeros are holding an important meeting in three days' time—"

"On the same night as the *ollamaliztli* finals?" Rafael asked.

"*Sí*. It is the perfect excuse for us to slip away from our families and gather together. We each say we are going to a friend's place to watch the game on trideo." She smiled shyly up at Rafael, enjoying the ruse.

I could see that the girl had fallen for Rafael, after all. I never could understand why women became so smitten with him—although I could admit that his muscular body was very appealing and that he could lay on the charm when it suited him.

I felt sorry for Teresa. If Rafael held true to form, he'd flirt with her while we were here in Aztlan, then forget all about her as soon as he got back to Seattle. And here she was, sharing her confidences with him. She'd already entrusted us with the knowledge that she was a courier for the Cristeros, and now she was telling Rafael about some secret meeting the group was about to hold. I could only suppose that the girl—who had started her life as a jaguar—wasn't used to human deception. Otherwise she'd have known to keep things like that to herself.

"Were you serious when you said you wanted to join the Cristeros?" Teresa asked. "Perhaps you could come to the meeting . . ."

Rafael grinned and shook his head. "If there was any way I could, I would," he said. Then his face grew serious. "But there's something that Leni and I have to do that evening. Afterward, though, I promise to come back to Izamal to see you."

I listened just long enough to make sure that Rafael wasn't going to spill any of our plans, then turned and headed back to the home of Teresa's friends. Along the way, I kept a wary eye out for the *policía*. I told myself that it was unlikely that anyone had heard our gunfire last night—the ruins lay many kilometers from town. But I couldn't help wondering how long it would be before someone stumbled across the bodies. The *policía* might not be quite so diligent in investigating the deaths of the cultists, and the sacrificial victims might have all been street kids and *campesinos* who would not be missed. But the shooting death of a priest would certainly make the *policía* sit up and take notice.

My other concern was the three cultists who had escaped. None of them had gotten a good look at Rafael or me, and they had probably scurried back to whatever hole they'd crawled out of. But I couldn't be certain that they hadn't gone back to the ruins or found the abandoned van and somehow used magic to pick up our trail . . .

The sooner we headed back to Tenochtitlán, the better.

So intent was I on watching my back that I turned a corner and nearly walked into someone who was coming the other way along the sidewalk. Then I saw who it was and gasped in surprise.

"Gus! What are you doing here?"

"I need to find Teresa. Is she all right?" Gus looked harried, watchful. He kept glancing around as if he too were afraid of the *policía*. His hair hung in rumpled curls as though he had not combed it since waking up that morning, and his clothes were wrinkled. Lines of strain etched his handsome face.

"She's fine," I assured him. "She's in the plaza, walking the *paseo* with Rafael."

The priest's eyes closed with relief. *"Bueno,"* he sighed. "Then they didn't get to her."

"Who didn't get to her? What's going on, Gus?"

He paused, as if deciding what to say. "We were . . . betrayed," he said in a low whisper. "Someone told the *policía* about the package Teresa was carrying in her bag. The man who was to have taken delivery of it was found dead along the roadside last night—a military-style execution, a bullet to the back of the head. I was worried that Teresa might have suffered the same fate."

I shook my head. "She's alive. But she had a rough time of it last night. We all did."

I quickly told Gus about Teresa being kidnapped by the cultists, and about the confrontation at the *teocalli* in the ruins. I skimmed over the details of what the cultists had been up to, however, simple saying that they had been conjuring up a blood spirit and leaving out the reasons why. I assumed that he already knew Teresa was a shapeshifter—his lack of surprise when I told him of her transformation confirmed this guess. He did seem dismayed when I told him of her part in killing the cultists—but then, killing is a mortal sin, even when done in self-defense.

Gus' face was white when I finished. "The cultists took Teresa? But Carlos promised . . ."

He looked as though he was about to faint. I took his arm and steered him toward a low wall and urged him to sit. I brushed away the paper streamers and foam cups that had been left there after last night's *fiesta*, then sat down beside him. I could see that something was gnawing at Gus, that he was being tortured by conflicting emotions. My police training screamed at me to pepper him with questions, to grill him while he was most vulnerable. But this was a man who had aided us, helping us to hide from the Azzie military and then candidly telling us the story of Mama G's past. I decided to let him tell his story in his own time.

"I am not a good priest," he said. Tears coursed down his cheeks and his hands were balled into fists. "I am not a good man."

I waited, then asked the only question necessary. "What have you done?"

Gus looked at me with grief-filled eyes. "I am the one who is responsible for the death of the man Teresa was supposed to pass the package to. I am the Judas who gave the *policía* his name. But it was the only way to protect Teresa. They would have arrested her instead . . ."

He didn't have to tell me the rest. "The *policía* knew Teresa was associated with the rebels and that she was your friend," I suggested.

Gus nodded.

"They cut a deal with you, offering to spare her if you gave them another rebel's name."

Another nod.

"But why? Why would the Azzies do you any favors?"

"Mi hermano," Gus answered slowly. "My brother Carlos is a lieutenant with Aztechnology Corporate Security—the *policía*. He was the one who made the deal with me. I thought that he would respect the fact that we are brothers, that he would honor his promise not to kill the man who was taking delivery of the package. He said he would simply

confiscate it and look the other way while the man fled. But he lied. When I heard of the death, I thought that Carlos must have lied to me about Teresa, as well."

"Teresa hasn't been arrested," I pointed out.

"No. That would be too obvious a betrayal. But Carlos knew of the cultists—the *policía* keep information on all fringe groups. He must have given the cultists her description and hoped that they would do his dirty work for him by kidnapping and sacrificing her. Then he could claim that his hands were free of blood." He slammed a palm down on the concrete. "Ah, *por que*? Why did you betray me, *hermano mío*?"

I didn't know what to say. Gus was in a tough spot, no doubt about it. He'd had to choose between the certain death of someone he cared about and the possible death of a stranger, and had made the only possible choice. Now that the Azzies—his own brother, no less—had used Teresa as a lever, it would be only a matter of time before they did it again, and before Gus betrayed still more Cristeros. Or betrayed us.

"There must be some way out of this," I said. "Some way to protect Teresa, at least until the AFL can smuggle her out of the country. You could hide her in the church until then."

Gus shook his head. "I could," he said. "But the Cristeros will be using it for their . . . It won't be safe."

As he paused, I made the connection. The meeting that Teresa had mentioned—it would be held in the boarded-up church.

Gus shrugged. "Besides, my brother knows that I am a *sacerdote*. He'll guess that I've hidden her there. It is too dangerous.

"But couldn't you hide Teresa with your . . . magic?"

It had taken me some time to realize that Gus had magical talent. That night in the church, when the soldiers had broken into it to search for us, I'd dismissed the "angel" that I'd seen hovering above us as a trick of the light. I later realized that it must have been some sort of spirit that Gus summoned up through his prayers.

When I'd first realized this—first admitted that I actually did see an "angel" shielding and hiding us from the soldiers—I'd assumed Gus to be one of those rare adepts whose magical abilities come to them via the sheer power of their religious convictions. Magic as miracle had been the subject of several trideo talk shows of late—it was currently a matter of much debate whether or not pre-Awakening Christian "miracles" and neo-pagan "faith healings" had actually been early manifestations of magic.

It made me wonder if I should have been going to church all these years. Maybe there was something to the "power of prayer," after all . . .

"I have sinned," Gus said in a low voice, refusing to meet my eyes. "How can I work miracles when I am not in a state of grace?"

"I guess you'll have to do penance."

It was a flippant remark. I'd been about to sarcastically add that a year's worth of Hail Marys and Our Fathers ought to be enough, but stopped myself before my anger at his defeatist attitude got the better of me. I decided that encouragement was more in order.

"You did what they forced you to do," I reassured him. "You thought you could trust your brother, but you couldn't. Next time, you'll know better. And you'll do the right thing."

Gus wiped the tears away from his cheeks and clenched his jaw. "I will," he said. "I swear it. May the devil take my soul if I do not."

I shivered at the passion with which he delivered his vow. He sounded like a man who was looking his own doom in the eye—who was willing to die, rather than fail his friends a second time.

It made me feel a little bit better—made me feel that I could trust Gus not to betray Rafael and I. But it wouldn't be long before I'd have cause to wonder whether I'd misplaced my trust.

20

I'd known all along that we'd need help if we were to have any hope at all of getting to Vargas in the *ollamaliztli* stadium. But that didn't mean I had to like it. Trusting a complete stranger was hard enough. Trusting a would-be shadowrunner was another thing entirely. So even though I knew it was inevitable, I only reluctantly let Rafael talk me into meeting with Fede, the scalper who'd sold him the tickets for the final game and who claimed to know Tenochtitlán's court ball stadium inside and out.

We met Fede on Tuesday, the day before the final game, in the "Thieves Market"—a sprawling, open-air marketplace that lies just east of the traffic-circle intersection of Paseo de la Reforma and Lázaro Cárdenas, two of Tenochtitlán's major thoroughfares. For decades this sprawling collection of stalls, tables, and closet-sized shops has offered everything from cheap tourist trinkets to sophisticated electronics parts, all at bargain-basement prices. We passed tables on which ultra-modern micro-camcorders and simsense units sat next to gigantic, old-fashioned video cameras the size of a loaf of bread. Clothing racks held everything from armored jackets and vests to Armanté and Mortimer of London knock-offs, complete with fake labels. Innocuous items like breathers or children's toys sat side by side with tasers, flechette rounds, and high-powered pistols.

I had to remind myself that anything less than a fully automatic submachine gun could be bought and sold legally in Aztlan, without a permit, even though there was a war on. The Azzie police didn't even consider pistols a threat—not when they patrolled the street in the equivalent of armored personnel carriers and carried enough personal body armor to stop anything short of a depleted-uranium shell.

One vendor sold garishly colored portable phones shaped like holo-toon characters whose speakers transposed the voice of the caller into the cartoonish voice of the character. All had their demonstration programs activated, and a collection of squeaky mouse voices and deep, breathy villain voices blared out at us in an unintelligible cacophony as we passed. For the do-it-yourselfer, there were bits and pieces of telecom units and everything you'd need to build your own personal computer, including monitors, peripherals, voice synthesizer and recognition chips, datastore cartridges, printers, and processors. There were also boxes and boxes of simsense chips—many of them pornographic—and skillsofts, knowsofts, and other optical chips. I shook my head. Only a fool would slot a used chip sold on the street. I'd once met a street kid who'd done just that, and then wound up suffering epileptic seizures as a result. But I suppose some people found the prices too good to resist.

Even more frightening were the stalls that sold medtech supplies. According to the hucksters who stood behind them, the auto-inject vials they offered for sale held everything from tailored pheromones guaranteed to enhance your sex life, to mnemonic enhancers for university students needing to cram, to toxin binders, to nanite symbiotes guaranteed to cure whatever ailed you. Other vendors hawked bits and pieces of used cyberware, from softlinks to entire limbs. I didn't want to know where these had come from—or why their original owners no longer required them.

The Aztlan *policía* did not patrol the marketplace in person, or even in vehicles. They probably felt it more important to maintain a presence at more upscale locations— especially since yet another rebel bomb had gone off in the capital last week, exploding outside the Cero Cero, a posh nightclub. And so the Thieves' Market was monitored only by remote-operated airborne surveillance drones. But all were mounted with nasty looking rapid-fire light machine guns and gas canister tubes. Given the Azzies' penchant for overkill, I suspected that these weapons weren't equipped merely with stun rounds or tear gas, but with something much more lethal.

The locals ignored the drones, going about the fast-paced and very vocal business of buying and selling. Everything was done on the barter system and many of the transactions were in hard cash, either metal-coated peso coins or plasti-weave bills.

We found Fede in the same spot where Rafael had contacted him earlier—inside the storefront office of the Pronósticos Deportivos Para La Asistencia Pública. The title translated roughly as Sports Predictions for the Public Welfare. It was Aztlan's only legalized gambling operation, a subsidiary of the all-powerful ORO Corporation.

The office itself consisted of a battery of automated gambling wickets. Long lines of sports fans lined up to slot their credsticks, place their bets and receive a "ticket"—an electronic notation of the bet, recorded on the credstick itself. A battery of monitor screens, located over the betting wickets, were broadcasting both live tridcasts of various sporting and racing events in progress around the world, and long listings of the odds for the various teams and competitors in upcoming matches.

The entire system was automated, but provision had been made for those who wanted to place bets using peso coins or bills. These had to be verified as authentic and then converted into temporary credsticks. The employee who performed this task sat in a bulletproof glass cubicle, off to one side of the betting machines.

Fede worked the nine a.m. to noon shift and supplemented his meager income by scalping tickets to upcoming sporting events throughout Aztlan. How he obtained the tickets was a mystery—Rafael said that Fede claimed to be able to get his "customers" a ticket to any event in any stadium at any time. His prices, however, reflected this ability.

Although Fede wore a breather, I could see why he'd gotten his nickname. His face was indeed ugly—a puckered mass of pink and white scar tissue that looked like the result of a severe burn. His hair grew in wispy patches on his head and his eyebrows were missing. His ears were twisted ruins, and I didn't want to imagine what his nose and lips looked like. The breather that hid them was as plain as our own—a basic Fellini-Med model, decorated with an overlapping collection of frayed sports team logo stickers.

As we made our way up to the booth, Rafael raised a hand

in greeting. "*Hola,* Fede," he said. "Remember me? You sold me two tickets to—"

Fede finished the sentence for him. "To game five of the *ollamaliztli* national finals." He shook his head. "I should have charged you more. Now that the series is tied, I could have gotten ten times the price for them. Would you like me to sell them for you on consignment? Or are you still planning to go to the game? If so, my offer of accompanying you and explaining the ah . . . game to you still stands."

Rafael glanced back at me. He probably thought I was still angry at him for telling Fede about our plans. But there was no time for second thoughts now. The game was tomorrow. Still, I wanted some assurance that Fede would actually be an asset.

"The price you named for helping us was pretty steep," I told him. "How well do you know the layout of the *tla* . . ."

I'd been about to ask him how well he knew the stadium, but his gesture silenced me. He touched a finger to his eye tooth and glanced behind him. The knowsoft I'd slotted on Aztlaner Spanish included a pictionary of gestures, and the one Fede was using referred to the presence of a third party. I couldn't see any surveillance cameras, but it was a logical conclusion that the ORO Corporation would be watching over its money-changers to keep them honest. Since Fede scalped tickets from the booth, I'd assumed that he could talk freely. But I supposed that he sold the tickets with the tacit approval of ORO—and probably gave them a healthy *mordida,* in return.

"My shift ends in twenty minutes," Fede said. "We'll talk then. Meet me outside, in the market."

Fede was good to his word. Twenty-one minutes later he approached us in the marketplace, then motioned us to follow him into a nearby herbalist's shop. Inside the tiny store, octagonal plastiglass jars held everything from dried mescal worms to peyote buttons, from wormseed to loco-weed sleeping teas. Nodding to the dwarf who stood behind a thigh-high counter, Fede led us through a curtain and into a back room that smelled of musty herbs and sweet ointments. Even through my breather, the aromas were a poignant reminder of Mama G—her kitchen had smelled a lot like this. Had it already been ten days since I'd last seen her alive?

The bittersweet memories that flooded my mind strengthened my resolve. We'd go through with this, dangerous and *loco* though it might be. Mama G deserved our best effort to at least find her killer, confront him, and find some means of bringing him to justice.

Fede nodded to us to sit down on packing crates, lifted the curtain to take a quick glance back into the shop, then sat down himself. Now that he wasn't hidden inside a booth, I realized what an impressive sight he was. He was only ugly from the neck up. From the neck down, he had the sculpted body of an athlete, so perfect that it must have been the result of muscle augmentation. His elbows and wrists bent and rotated with a fluidity that suggested enhanced articulation, and his legs were cybernetic—my cyberear could pick up the faint whine of hydraulic implants. I'd once had to chase a suspect with similar hydraulics and had been left in his dust when he'd jumped three meters straight up onto the roof of a building—from a standing start, no less. Fede must have made good money at scalping to have been able to afford all of those mods. And that posed a puzzle. Why hadn't he hired a plastic surgeon to reconstruct his face? Maybe he liked being ugly—or maybe he carried the facial scars like a badge, a visible reminder of some event in his past.

Time to get down to biz. I focused my cyberear's amplification systems on the beating of Fede's heart and his breathing. Even if he was able to keep a poker face, an increase in heart rate and respiration would give away any agitation that accompanied a lie.

"We're willing to pay you half the fee you requested up front, and half upon successful contact with the . . . ah . . . asset," I told Fede. Even as I spoke, I laughed silently at myself. I was beginning to talk like a shadowrunner. "But we want to be assured that you know the *tlachtli* inside and out—that you're able to guide us around the stadium's security and into the *teocalli*. And that means knowing your credentials. Every peso we have it going toward your fee. We want to make sure our credit is well spent."

Fede nodded. "I see."

He paused for a moment, thinking. I wondered if he was making up a story—weighing us to see how much we'd swallow. But his heart rate and breathing remained steady.

"I used to play on an *ollamaliztli* team, a few years ago," Fede said. "Several of our matches were held in the *tlachtli* in Teotihuacán. I got to know the areas of the stadium that the public does not see, the sections used by the teams and their support staff. The key to getting into the adjoining temple is to access the first-aid rooms—the area where MedíCarro staff stabilize injured players before their transport to hospital. Because the priests sometimes come in to pray over the injured players, there is a connecting passage between the *tlachtli* and the *teocalli*."

"Isn't it under tight security?" I asked.

"*Sí*. It is. But the *corazón* runners are allowed through without having to stop for a security check."

"Heart runners?" Rafael asked. "What the frag are they?"

Fede's breather hissed for a moment as he took a deep breath before answering. My cyberear picked up that his heart began to beat more rapidly. "When an *ollamaliztli* player is seriously injured and cannot continue the game, he is rushed into the stadium's first-aid rooms, where the team doctors and MedíCarro attendants tend to him. If he dies before he can be stabilized for transfer to a hospital, the MedíCarros remove his heart. They send it by runner to the *teocalli*, where it is offered up to Huitzilopochtli by the attending priests in ceremonial sacrifice. The wound in the chest of the player is sealed with a layer of synthetic skin, his body is sent off to the hospital morgue as usual, and no one is the wiser."

My mouth gaped open behind my breather. "How do you know all this?"

"It happened to a teammate of mine—a very good friend whom I had known since we were both boys, playing *ollamaliztli* together in the streets," Fede said. "I broke both legs in a game at the Tenochtitlán stadium and had passed out from the pain. But I regained consciousness just in time to see and hear what happened to Lorenzo down in the first-aid room. The MedíCarros let him die. One of the paramedics wanted to try to revive him, but the other said that the priests had insisted on a heart that day, that the game was almost over, and that my friend was already near death and was the best candidate. And so they waited until Lorenzo's heart had stopped beating, then cut it out and ran it up to the temple. I was shocked, but pretended I was still unconscious. I knew that what I had seen and heard would cost me my life."

Fede leaned forward, eyes glittering with intensity. "I am just one man, and cannot stop the killings. Until now I have only been able to use the pesos I make on tickets to anonymously help the families of those who were killed. But now you are giving me a chance to pay back those who were responsible for Lorenzo's death. I don't care which of the priests is your target. I want to help. And not just for the nuyen."

I could see, in Fede's eyes, something of what I was feeling. He had watched a friend die and now felt guilty that he had not been able to summon up the courage to try to prevent that death. At the time, he'd had every reason not to act—it would have been impossible for Fede to rescue his friend while he himself was lying in shock on the verge of unconsciousness, with two broken legs. But the debt weighed heavily upon his soul, nonetheless. Now, years later, he wanted a chance to make good.

I realized, in that moment, that was driving me to chase down Domingo Vargas. I felt the same sort of guilt over Mama G's death. Even though I'd taken reasonable precautions and had no way of realizing the danger she was in, I still felt responsible for her murder. I knew that it was all tied up with my guilt over not having visited my own grandmother years earlier on the night she lay dying in hospital. I'd had a good reason at the time—an impossibly heavy workload at Lone Star—but had tortured myself with guilt over not going to her bedside to bid her farewell ever since. Somehow, illogical though it might be, bringing Domingo Vargas to justice would lay the ghosts of both my grandmothers to rest.

Rafael had also been sitting in silence, listening to Fede's story. His brow creased in a frown, and his eyes narrowed. Then he nodded slowly to himself.

"I know who you are," he told Fede in an awed voice. "You played pro court ball with the Tampico Voladores. The game you're talking about was the exhibition match that kicked off the 2051 season, the one in which Lorenzo Nanchez died of a ruptured spleen. You won that game by forcing Juan Toro to touch the ball with his hand and forfeit a point, then drove the ball into his end zone. Toro was so slotted off at you that he slammed you against the wall, breaking both of your legs. We thought you were out for the season, but you came back two months later with cybernetic limbs—the ones that enabled you to leap up and slam the ball through the hoop in the third game of the semi-finals in 2055, winning the game with just ten minutes and thirty-six seconds on the clock. That was a fragging brilliant move—although I agree with the officials' decision not to let you play in the *ollamaliztli* finals, on account of your enhancements. But at least they let you remain the honorary captain of the team, even if you were benched for all five—"

"Whoa, Raf," I said, cutting off the flow of sports trivia. "Slow down. What are you trying to say?"

Rafael waved a hand at Fede. "This is Emilio Ibanez, the captain who led the Tampico Voladores into the *ollamaliztli* finals of 2055. If it wasn't for his scars I'd have recognized him right away. He was on all the sports tridcasts for years."

Fede's cheeks rose behind his breather and I realized that he was smiling. His former popularity explained why Fede hadn't had his scar tissue removed. It was indeed a mask.

Rafael continued: "Ibanez was the only captain of a winning national finals *ollamaliztli* team to escape the curse of Huitzilopochtli. He disappeared in—"

Fede's laugh startled us both. "Curse? Oh *carnal,* do you believe everything you hear? That's just a story, told to explain away the murders of the *ollamaliztli* players."

My professional curiosity was immediately piqued. "Murders?" I asked. I took a wild guess as to motive. "Is someone killing ball players to influence the outcome of future games? With the amount of nuyen that's wagered on *ollamaliztli,* I can see why."

"Betting? Oh no," Fede answered. "What do a few pesos matter, compared to magical power—mana from the gods themselves? The national finals are all part of an ancient magical ritual—one that predates even the Aztec empire. That's why they try to duplicate the ancient game as much as possible, with no metahumans and no cybernetics permitted.

That usually leaves only physical adepts as competitors. And they make the best sacrificial offerings. They're juiced with mana."

He sighed and looked down at his legs. "I didn't escape Huitzilopochtli's curse—I was unworthy of the god. The cybernetics had depleted my life force. And my presence as honorary team captain meant that another captain—one who could be consecrated to the sun god by the priests—could not be named in my place. Even so, when our team won the nationals, I knew the priests wouldn't let me live. And so I fled from the *tlachtli*, rather than attending the victory celebrations. I nearly died at the hands of the fire elemental they sent after me."

He paused to slide a finger under his breather and scratch his scarred cheek. I shuddered as I imagined the pain he must have suffered from the elemental's attack, and wondered how Fede had managed to escape being roasted. But that part of the story could be saved for another time.

"I'm alive today, but at the cost of the thing I loved most," Fede continued. "I'll never play *ollamaliztli* again. Instead I hide behind this mask of scars the elemental gave me, selling tickets to games that are still nothing more than a means of supplying the priests with sacrificial victims for their foul magic.

"I can't prove what I know, nor do I understand what is behind it all, but I can tell you this. None of the national team captains died by accident, or from natural causes. They were either killed by priests of the Path of the Sun, or by people who wanted to prevent these candidates for sacrifice from falling into the hands of the priests. In either case, the official reports on their deaths were lies.

"I started to put all of this together after Chucho Chamac died in 2051. He was a natural athlete and a strong swimmer. Even if it was true that he had fallen off the yacht during the victory celebrations, there was no way he would have drowned. And then when the *policía* report blamed the deep wounds in his chest to an eagle that fed on his corpse, it just didn't scan.

"I knew what had happened to my teammate Lorenzo Nanchez during that exhibition match—how the paramedics had let him die and then cut out his heart—and knew that someone must have wanted Chucho's heart in the same way. The drowning was all a cover-up. When I started asking questions, I found more and more to disturb me. That's why I knew I had to escape after our team won the 2051 national finals."

Rafael let out a slow whistle. I must admit that I, too, was surprised at Fede's story—although it fit with what we'd learned so far. This year, it seemed, the cultists were the ones who were interested in sacrificing the winning court ball team captain. They didn't want his heart—they wanted his head, which they believed would trigger the end of the current era if it were severed from his body and placed in an *itzompan* on the day Four Motion. Judging by what we'd heard the blood spirit Nezahualpilli say, only the priest Domingo Vargas knew the location of the *itzompan*. My guess was that he had double-crossed the cultists, and planned to make the sacrifice solo. But if all went well for us tomorrow, he'd never be able to use that information.

I was surprised at Fede's candor. By telling us about his past, he was showing us that we could trust him. A person doesn't share that kind of confidence—doesn't break cover after two years of hiding—with someone he is planning to betray. But I had to be sure. And so I asked the obvious question.

"Why are you telling us all this?" I asked.

Fede shrugged. "*No sé.* Maybe it was just time for me to tell someone—and you are the first people who were in a position to believe my story. Maybe I'm tired of being nothing more than Fede, the ticket scalper."

He stared at us, his intense gaze shifting between Rafael and I. "I would like to go with you when you leave Aztlan. To have entered the country undetected, you must have connections that I do not. I want to make use of them, to travel with you when you return to El Norte. It if comes to a fight, I can prove myself useful."

I glanced at Fede's powerful muscles and hydraulic-enhanced cyberlegs. He looked even stronger and quicker than Rafael—and I'd thought my burly ork friend was tough. It would be nice to have a little extra backup . . .

"All right," I told Fede. "You've convinced me. You're in."

Rafael broke into a wide grin. "Chill," he said, the reverence of a true sports fan evident in his voice. "Domingo Vargas had better watch out. With Emilio Ibanez of the Tampico Flyers on our team, there's no way we can lose."

I wished I could share Rafael's certainty. But I was still very, very nervous about what was to come. Anything could happen tomorrow. We had to be prepared for every eventuality.

Even for the end of the world.

21

The crowd that filed into the *ollamaliztli* stadium on Wednesday evening was well dressed and obviously able to afford the outrageous ticket prices for seeing the game live. We'd had to pay out yet more pesos to outfit ourselves so that we wouldn't stand out. Both Rafael and I had picked up high fashion knock-offs in the Thieves' Market, as well as designer breathers. Rafael looked quite handsome in his mock Vashon Island double-breasted suit, and I wore the female equivalent—a pants suit in sea-green "silk." Fede had also dressed the part, and had changed to a gilded, wide-masked breather that hid much of his face. A stylish, floppy-brimmed hat hid the rest of his scars.

Under our clothes, each of us wore short-sleeved white shirts emblazoned with a passable imitation of the Medí-Carro crest, as well as plain black trousers. Fake ID badges hung from the front pockets of the shirts. The "uniforms" wouldn't stand up to careful scrutiny, and the magnetic datastrip on the ID badges didn't hold any information and wouldn't pass a scanner check. But if Fede succeeded in getting us into the first-aid rooms of the *tlachtli*, we wouldn't have to worry about that.

I had an anxious moment as we had passed through the stadium's security gates. There were four guards at each entrance, heavily armored and armed with lethal-looking combat rifles and stun batons. They watched with narrowed eyes as the crowd filed through a series of weapon detectors, chemical detectors, and cyberware scanners whose sonic and magnetic imagers sought out subdermal cyberweapons. At least one of the guards must have been magically capable—a stocky, dog-headed spirit stood beside him, its nose quivering as it sniffed the crowd. I guessed that it was somehow monitoring astral space—although I couldn't imagine what it was looking for.

None of the guards spotted the fake uniforms we wore under our dress clothes or questioned the bottle of sweet-smelling "perfume" in my cosmetics bag when they opened my purse for a manual search—even though its nozzle had been modified to squirt a stream of liquid rather than a fine spray. One of them raised an eyebrow at the Masked Matador cartoon-character phone in Fede's suit pocket, but readily accepted his explanation that he'd been forced to use his children's phone to call in his bets after his own cell phone had broken down earlier that day. The guard popped open the back of the plastic figure but saw nothing suspicious about it and handed it back to Fede with a shrug.

So far, so good. Now all we had to do was find our seats and wait. We didn't want to enter any of the restricted areas too soon—the longer we hung about there, the more chance there was of us being discovered. But as soon as any of the *ollamaliztli* players was seriously injured we could make our move.

Our seats were high above the playing field on bleachers so steep that I felt a mild vertigo until I sat down. Rafael and I sat and watched as a group of three priests consecrated the field—I used the binoculars I'd bought to confirm that Domingo Vargas wasn't among them. Fede arrived just as the game began—he'd had a chore to carry out first—and sat three rows up and to my left.

The playing field lay far below us and was shaped like the letter I, with a long, narrow alley and end zones that jutted out at right angles like the base and cap of that letter. The walls of the alley were close to ten meters high, sloped at the bottom so the ball wouldn't get stuck in an angle of the wall. A green line at the midpoint of the alley divided the court in two, and the field itself was further divided into quarters, each painted a different color: red, blue, black, and white, the four colors of the Aztlaner "tree of life."

Play surged back and forth along this alley as the three-man teams battled it out. *Ollamaliztli* was an odd-looking game—the players could hit the ball only with their hips, elbows, and knees. They had heavy leather pads strapped over each of these areas, but otherwise wore only a loincloth and a few decorative feathers—most of which lay strewn about the court by now. Aside from having to be careful not to touch the ball with a hand or foot—which resulted in the loss of one point—they had to watch out that the heavy rubber ball didn't hit them in a vital spot. And the wildly bouncing ball wasn't easy to evade. Just five minutes into the game, one of the Jaguar players was knocked out when the ball crashed into his temple. As his unconscious form was carried back to the bench for team doctors to revive him with a stimulant patch, one of the Tenochtitlán team's three replacement players took his place, leaving only two more spares to draw from.

The game was fast and furious, with each team working to keep the ball in motion. According to Fede, a point was scored whenever a team succeeded in bouncing the ball into the opposing team's end zone, or whenever the opposing team failed to return or pass the ball after one bounce. Since the game was over as soon as one team scored seven points, I'd thought it would be relatively short. But I'd under-estimated the skill of the players. They seemed to have unlimited stamina, to be able to keep running at breakneck pace without pause. Since cybernetic enhancements were prohibited at the national finals level, I guessed that they were all physical adepts—or that they'd been pumped full of adrenal boosters and pain inhibitors prior to the game.

Above the corporate logos that festooned the walls of the *tlachtli,* carved stone rings were set into the stonework on either side of the center line. The rings had a diameter about that of a basketball hoop, but were mounted vertically, rather than horizontally, near the top of the wall. The ball—which seemed barely small enough to fit through the ring—had to pass through a ring to score.

I could see why Rafael had sounded so impressed when he recounted the story of Fede having won a game by making a ring shot. The ball that the teams below us were chasing after was made of solid rubber and bounced off the stone walls like a ricocheting bullet. Its trajectory would have to be exactly right for it to ever pass through the ring—the slightest miscalculation and the ball careered wildly off the ring in another direction. No wonder driving a ball through the ring instantly won the game—it was an almost impossible shot to make.

As the game unfolded the crowd around us roared and cheered, leaping to their feet each time a player succeeded in bouncing the ball past the center line and groaning whenever an end-zone player threw his body in front of the ball to block a point. The spectators seemed evenly divided between local Jaguar fans and supporters of the Texcoco Serpents. And tensions were running high. Three rows below us, a fight broke out between two rival fans. I winced as ACS guards in tan uniforms waded in, using stun batons to zap the unruly fans into submission. One of the men collapsed under the baton's sting—there was no way to tell whether he'd had a heart attack or had simply fainted. The security guards dragged him away, disappearing with him down one of the corridors that led to the concourse of the *tlachtli*. The other combatant looked shaken, and meekly sat down again.

Despite our mission, Rafael was intent upon the game. He leaped, cheered, and punched the air whenever a point was scored, or groaned along with crowd whenever a point was taken away as a penalty. He'd jammed a micro-receiver into his ear—the button-sized radio gave him a play-by-play broadcast of the unfolding game.

When he'd first insisted on buying the micro-receiver, I'd protested at the expense. As if he needed to be updated on what he could see with his own two eyes. But the micro-receiver would be playing a part in our plans—at the very least it would enable us to keep track of the progress of the game once we'd left our seats.

I was glad that Rafael didn't have a datajack—if so, he would probably have been as oblivious to his surroundings as the glassy-eyed businessman next to me who was plugged into the stadium's instant-replay system. The fellow zoned in and out, his eyes glazing over each time he uploaded a simsense replay of a critical moment in the game. Oblivious to everything around him, he didn't even blink or move his foot away when I accidentally stepped on it.

For me, the game was only a partial distraction. I was more concerned with finding out whether Domingo Vargas really was in attendance this evening. I'd tried to contact Caco to see if the information he'd supplied us earlier was still valid, but had met with no success. The *esquincles* with whom I'd left messages assured me that they would pass along my queries to Caco, but I'd heard nothing back in return.

At the rate this game was going, I didn't think we'd have to wait long for a serious injury to occur. At the lower levels of play, both cybernetic and hand-held, zero-range weapons are permitted on the *ollamaliztli* court. According to Fede, it's common for players to divide their time equally between chasing the ball and taking each other out with monoknives, stun batons, cyberspurs, electroprods, and hand blades. Some games turn into a battle of attrition, with victory going to the team that can eliminate all of the opposing team's three regular players and three spares from play. There aren't any penalties and ferocity is encouraged—even if an attack results in permanent injury or death. The only check is that, if a team ignores the ball completely, concentrating instead on attacking opposing players, it's easy for the opposing team to quickly rack up points and win the game. Assuming they survive long enough to do so, of course.

The national finals, however, stick to the "original" rules of the game. Besides restricting the game to non-enhanced, human male players, the *ollamaliztli* officials ban all weapons from the field. Players can still elbow, kick, punch, or gouge out each other's eyes, but are limited to doing this with their bare hands—or bare feet.

I kept my eyes on the security guards who patrolled the stands and tried not to glance up too many times at the *teocalli* that towered above the stadium. The temple, dedicated to the sun god Huitzilopochtli, rose in a series of stepped levels just beyond the eastern end zone of the playing field— the end zone that was defended by the Tenochtitlán Jaguars. The late-evening sun shone through the sprawl's smog cover, painting the temple's stonework a lurid red. I could occasionally see movement on one of the temple's upper balconies—the flash of a turquoise-feathered cape or the glint of gold as sunlight reflected off the huge golden ear plugs of one of the priests who stood in attendance there. I raised my binoculars and pointed them at the temple as yet another priest emerged from the darkened interior of the *teocalli* . . .

And there he was. I had spotted our objective for the first time since our arrival in Aztlan.

Domingo Vargas wore a similar costume to the one I'd seen him wearing in the documentary tridcast that Angie had uploaded to me. It looked like a jumpsuit of soft leather that had been dusted with a layer of powdered gold. Form-fitting and presumably laced up the back where Vargas' jaguar-pelt cape covered it, the suit included hands that dangled from his wrists. Each time he moved his arms, the hands bobbed about like balloons. I fought back my gagging reflex as I wondered whether the hands might be real—whether the suit had been made of flayed human skin.

I shifted my binoculars to look at Vargas' face. His head was bare and his face was painted with broad bands of red. More gold dust highlighted his forehead, heavy cheeks, and pouting lips. His hair was longer than it had been in the tridcast, slicked back and hanging in loose gray curls behind his ears. But his eyes were the same flat black, glittering like chips of hard obsidian.

Just below his double chin and above the gold pectoral that hung down his chest, I noticed a bulge. Stepping up the power of the binoculars, I zoomed in for a closer look. There, over his jugular—an intravenous catheter similar to the one I'd seen on the chest of the priest who had tried to sacrifice Teresa, out in the ruins. What had the blood spirit told him? To ask his "blood brother" for the location of the *itzompan.* Had the two priests each undergone some sort of blood transfusion as part of a past ritual or medical procedure?

I flinched back as Vargas looked directly at me. I hurriedly lowered my binoculars and pretended to be watching the game, instead. There was no way he could have picked me out across all that distance, lost as I was in the sea of people that filled the stands of the *tlachtli.* But then I thought about his magical abilities and shuddered. For all I knew, some sort of enemy detection spell might be alerting him to my presence. Even now, ACS guards or a malevolent blood spirit might be headed my way . . .

I shook off my fears, telling myself that they were no more than simple paranoia. To pull this off, we needed to maintain our self-confidence. Otherwise we'd be defeated before we began.

I must have been developing some sort of sixth sense myself, because just at that moment my eyes were drawn to one of the vendors who was climbing the steps between the rows of seats, hawking *pepitas*—roasted squash and melon seeds, flavored with salt and chili powder—and cold *cervezas*. As the wiry teenager reached our row of seats, he met my eye and called out his wares: "*Pepitas! Cerveza fría!* Chiclets!"

Chiclets?

The vendor winked when he saw that he had my attention. Excusing myself, I squeezed my way past the jacked-in fan next to me and the two cheering men closest to the aisle, then reached the vendor. "Chiclets, please," I said.

"A wise choice, *señorita*," he said in a low voice. "And only one million pesos."

I reached into the pocket of my suit jacket, pulling out the last of my plastiweave bills. "I've only got eight hundred thousand pesos," I said. "Will that be enough?"

"Hmm—nine hundred thousand then."

"I'm not trying to barter," I said angrily. "Unless you want to slot my credstick and leave an electronic trail, eight hundred thousand is all I've got."

The teenager shook his head, clucking his tongue. "Good thing my boss has a soft heart," he said teasingly. "All right. Eight hundred thousand pesos."

He pressed a foil-wrapped package of *pepitas* into my hand, winking and telling me to make sure I didn't break my teeth on any "uncooked seeds" that might be inside. I gently squeezed the foil between my fingers and could feel the now-familiar rectangular shape of a Chiclets box inside. I slipped the vendor the pesos. Pocketing them swiftly, he turned and continued climbing the stairs, calling out his wares as before.

As I returned to my seat, Rafael gave me a quizzical look. I tore open the foil bag and showed him the bright yellow box it contained. "Looks like our friend Caco has some more information for us," I said. I passed the seeds to Rafael and opened the Chiclets box. "I just hope it's worth . . ."

An optical memory chip slid out of the box and into my

hand. It looked like a datasoft—small and square, with a tab at one end. I stared at it, wondering whether I should slot it. If Caco could be trusted, the chip probably contained additional information on Vargas. If Caco had sold us out to Aztechnology, the datasoft might be contaminated with a virus or brainkiller program that would flatline me. There was no way to know. But then I thought back to the kid who had confronted us with a snapblade outside our hotel, after the earthquake. As he'd said, if the "Chiclets lady" wanted us dead, there were other, less complicated ways to kill us. And frag it, I'd just paid the last of our hard currency for the chip. Whispering a silent prayer, I slotted it into the chipjack behind my left ear. Then I accessed its memory—and sat down as the transducer converted the information the chip held into thoughts that reverberated in my mind like spoken words. The *ollamaliztli* game and cheering crowd faded around me as I concentrated on the data being fed into my mind.

Your target has altered his travel arrangements for this evening, the chip informed me in a voice I couldn't slot as either male or female—Caco's voice. *Instead of returning via government VTOL to the Aztechnology castillo, he will be traveling by private charter plane to Izamal, a small town in the Yucatán. Despite the prohibition against civilian aircraft using local airports in this region after curfew, your target has obtained permission for his charter plane to land. He insisted that his flight could not depart Tenochtitlán until after 2000 hours—the time the* ollamaliztli *game is anticipated to end.*

I have not been able to establish the reason for this journey, nor do I know if Izamal is your target's final destination. But I wonder if his journey has anything to do with the recent death of the priest of Tezcatlipoca. The body of this bacab, *who served with your target at the Temple of the Sun, was found yesterday in some ruins about forty-five kilometers southwest of Izamal. Your target may be flying there to investigate this death.*

My mouth dropped open as I realized who Caco was referring to: the priest who had summoned the blood spirit that called itself King Nezahualpilli. The priest whom Teresa had torn to pieces on top of the *teocalli* in the desert.

Caco's genderless voice continued: *Your target will be one of two passengers on board the flight. Name of the second passenger was not specified. I am able to supply you with the registration number of the VTOL plane that your target chartered, the name of its pilot, and its ETD and ETA as filed in the flight plan that was registered earlier today. This information follows.*

I paused the upload, shaking my head. Part of the story was easy to guess. The second passenger on the plane would be the captain of whatever team won the nationals here today. The one whose severed head needed to be placed in the *itzompan* to trigger the coming of the new age. But Izamal? That was the town where we'd met Father Gustavo Silvio—where Mama G had hidden out once, before losing her memories, and where Gus had sheltered her after her time in the fovea. If Caco was right about Vargas going there to investigate the death of his fellow *bacab,* he should have gone to Izamal yesterday, when the body was found. Or later in the week, after the ball game—and the sacrifice of the winning captain—were over. No, it didn't make sense. If he was going to participate in the cultists' sacrifice of the winning *ollamaliztli* team captain, he had to be at the site of the *itzompan* by first light . . .

I stared at the ball court below me, watching the players charging back and forth along the playing field. The ball slammed off a wall, bounced high into the air, and was knocked against the opposite wall and almost into the ring by a blow from a Jaguar player's elbow. Then it rolled down the slope of one wall, across the floor of the playing field, and up the slope opposite . . .

Suddenly I made the connection. The sloping walls of the ball court that lay below me were identical, in their angle and method of construction, to the walls in the sub-basement of the Sanctuary of the Virgin in Izamal. According to Gus, the church had been built on top of an ancient Mayan building of some kind. I now knew what that building had been: a ball court, older and much more unique than the one below. I remembered the flat, round stone on which Gus had sat while we were resting in our flight from the Azzie soldiers—the one with the skulls and glyphs carved around its edge and the hole at its center. Someone who didn't know its history might take it to be goal ring, broken free of its mount on the wall and left where it lay when the base of the *tlachtli* was turned into the sub-basement of the church. But this stone was unbroken and had been set into the floor of the ball court itself. Positioned dead center, at the spot where the four quarters of the playing field met.

It had to be the *itzompan.*

What was it that Mama G had said, the day before she was killed? "Where the priest walks, the ground shakes." I'd dismissed it as meaningless babble at the time—she'd also talked about trees, and bloody crosses, and serpents . . .

And severed heads. Which, if dropped into the *itzompan* at the appointed hour, would bring about the end of the world.

Or perhaps just one fragger of an earthquake.

I shivered, despite the heat of the evening sunshine and the press of excited sports fans around me. I knew where Domingo Vargas was headed. To the church in Izamal. To the very spot where the Cristeros were holding their meeting . . .

I scanned the rest of the information on the chip. Caco had been thorough—had assumed that we might try to grab Vargas during his visit to Izamal instead. And so he had provided us with a warning. One that sent chills through me.

If you're thinking of confronting your target in Izamal, I have just one word for you: don't. Word has it that the Aztlan military has been tipped to the hiding place of a bunch of rebels based there—some religious group that is gathering there this evening—and is going to be mopping them up in a raid tonight. Curfew in that town will be even more strictly enforced than usual—the soldiers there are under orders to shoot on sight.

Things were even worse than I thought. The rebels that Caco was referring to could only be the Cristeros. And that meant that both Teresa and Gus were in grave danger. Someone in their group had betrayed them.

I thought back to the other cryptic phrase that Mama G had uttered that day: "Beware the priest whose magic . . ." Certainly we had to be wary of Domingo Vargas. But had Mama G been referring to him in her warning—or to someone else? To Gus, for example. Also a *sacerdote,* but of another religion. Also quite capable of working magic. And also, by his own admission, quite capable of betrayal.

I didn't get a chance to think about it further. The fans around me leaped to their feet and cheered—and then the stadium was filled with angry shouts and groans.

Rafael crouched beside my seat and shook my shoulder.

"Leni!" he said. "It's happened. One of the Jaguar players has been critically injured. They'll have called MedíCarro for this one. It's time to move!"

I scrambled to my feet and followed Rafael as he elbowed his way down the steps, checking my watch as we joined Fede on the concourse. It was 7:23 p.m.—exactly twenty-one minutes into the game. MedíCarro prided itself on its response time—here in the heart of the city it was said to be four to five minutes. Right now, every second counted.

I didn't have time to worry about getting word to the Cristeros. We had a temple to infiltrate and a priest to confront.

The clock had begun ticking for Mama G's killer. It was time for Vargas to be brought to justice.

22

Fede's word had been good. He did know the stadium as well as he'd claimed. He led us briskly along the concourse to a locked door beside one of the washrooms, then punched a combination on its keypad. We passed through a janitorial storage area and into a corridor whose ceiling echoed with the thumping feet of spectators in the seats overhead. We descended a flight of ferrocrete steps at a run, passed through another locked door to which Fede also had the combination, and entered a carpeted corridor whose walls were lined with faded holos of *ollamaliztli* players.

As we jogged along, Rafael suddenly exclaimed and punched a fist in the air. "Yes!" he hissed. "The Jaguars just scored. It's two to one."

I wondered if he'd suddenly become omniscient—and then I remembered the micro-receiver in his ear. "Let me know if another player is injured," I told him.

The corridor led to a former meeting room that now served as a storage space. Chairs were upended on a massive table, and a layer of dust covered everything. Old posters, broken sports equipment, and other junk was piled everywhere. A gigantic jaguar head—a vinyl balloon that had long since deflated—lay draped over a stack of plastic boxes in one corner. Its eyes glared out at us, as if challenging intruders onto its turf. Under its watchful glare we stripped off our street clothes and hid them inside one of the boxes. We also took off our breathers—there was no need for them inside the climate-controlled interior of the stadium.

Now came the critical part. According to Fede, the hallway beyond this room connected the hangarlike area where MediCarro emergency response vans pulled into the stadium with the actual first-aid rooms where injured players were treated. Despite the fact that it was used only by MedíCarro staff—who were cleared by Aztechnology Corporate Security personnel before they entered the stadium—the corridor was monitored by closed-circuit surveillance cameras.

I checked the timepiece set into my wrist. A total of five minutes had passed since the Texcoco player had been injured on the field. By now at least one team of MedíCarro attendants should already be on the scene, working to stabilize the injured player. But I had to make sure. It would look odd, indeed, if the ambulance attendants entered the stadium ahead of the emergency response vehicle . . .

I lay down on the floor and pressed my cyberear to the crack between the door and the carpet. I filtered out the hiss of the stadium's air conditioning and the hum of its electrical systems, and heard voices that must have been the ambulance attendants working on the injured player. A reference to a stabilization unit and synthetic Fluosol universal blood confirmed it. So far, so good.

I knew from my days with the Star that, in a medical emergency, it wasn't uncommon for more than one vehicle to respond. The first team of MedíCarros wouldn't be surprised by our arrival on the scene—they would be too busy working on their patient to stop and ask us any questions. All we had to do was get into the first-aid rooms . . .

But first we had to make sure that any security guards who might be watching the closed-circuit imaging system would be focusing on another monitor screen, instead.

"Time for our distraction," I said, first pulling on one of the thin plastic protective gloves I'd hidden inside my pants pocket and then readying my perfume bottle. "Make the call, Rafael."

Rafael grinned and pulled a cell phone from his pocket. Flipping it open, he dialed the number that would normally activate the ringer of the Masked Matador—the cartoon-character phone that Fede had carried into the stadium and then left where it could do us some good. Except that we'd cross-wired the phone so that the call would activate its voice-demonstration chip, rather than its buzzer and vibration-alert system. Even now, the Masked Matador would be blaring out his warning in a low, menacing voice.

I grinned along with Rafael as I imagined the effect of its

words: *I am a bomb. Do not attempt to touch me or disarm me. I am filled with enough plastic explosive to kill everyone within fifty meters. I am a bomb. I am going to explode in twenty seconds. Nineteen . . . eighteen . . . seventeen . . . Just fifteen seconds now until I explode. Thirteen . . . twelve . . . eleven . . .*

"Where did you put it?" I asked Fede.

"Behind the counter of the most popular taco stall on the concourse," he answered. "The vendor who runs it is a very nervous man who already imagines rebels everywhere. Right now he should be scrambling over the counter, screaming about a bomb. It's certain to cause all of his customers to flee in panic."

"Good job," I said. Then I took a deep breath. It was now or never. Either our distraction was working—or it wasn't. It was time to find out.

"Let's go," I said.

Fede opened the door and we entered the corridor at a brisk walk, passing the surveillance camera and moving toward the first-aid rooms. As we entered them, I saw two attendants in MedíCarro uniforms, sealing the hatch of a medical stabilization capsule. The injured *ollamaliztli* player lay braced inside it, oxygen mask over his face and his arms studded with intravenous tubes. Quick-setting sterile plasti-foam fixative had been sprayed over his left leg and hip—I guessed he'd broken his femur and thigh. His knee and hip pads had been removed, but his leather elbow pads were still in place. I was glad to see that his chest still rose and fell—I hadn't relished the thought of having to carry an actual human heart into the temple.

The MedíCarro attendants barely glanced at us, instead concentrating on raising the stabilization capsule on its articulating, wheeled legs.

"Too late!" one called to us over his shoulder. "This one's ours. You'll have to move more quickly next time if you want to earn your response-time bonuses!"

Then they hurried away, pushing the stabilization container before them and leaving us alone in a room filled with stretchers, cabinets of medical supplies, and rehab machines. Fede immediately began opening the storage lockers at one end of the room, searching for the organ-transplant cases that were used by the *corazón* runners to carry hearts. Just then, a woman pushed open a side door and entered the room. I assumed she was a "jock doc"—a team physician. She wore a track suit in the official Tenochtitlán colors of black and gold and carried a medkit in one hand. In the other she held a string of jade beads with a tuft of turquoise feathers at one end that I guessed was some sort of spell fetish. She'd probably used magic to help stabilize the injured player. I hoped she'd used enough to drain her, or else we might be in trouble.

Time for another distraction. Rafael knew just what to do. Smiling, shrugging at having come "too late" to pick up the injured player, he moved toward the doctor, turning on all his charm and chatting non-stop about how we'd have been the first MedíCarro team on the scene, except for the inefficiency of the security guards outside, who were supposed to keep the roads to the stadium clear . . .

I pulled the perfume bottle out of my pocket with my gloved hand and edged forward at the same time. Making sure the nozzle was pointed in the right direction, I raised the bottle suddenly and squirted the mage in the face. She immediately began staggering as the drug hit her. Within three seconds, she was down on her knees—within ten she lay slumped on the floor, fully conscious but unable to move.

Rafael raised his hand, palm outward, in the team player's triumphant salute. I was feeling just cocky enough to peel off the surgical glove and give his hand a high-five slap in return. Then I pulled a fresh glove out of my pocket, made sure the perfume bottle wasn't leaking, and stowed it in a pocket where I could reach it easily. There was no telling who would come through that door next.

"Whatever that stuff is, it sure works," Rafael said in an awed voice, looking down at the mage. He reached down to grab her by the arms.

"Careful!" I warned him. "Don't touch her throat or face, or any gamma scopolamine remaining on her skin and clothes will get you too. It's mixed with DMSO—one touch and your skin will instantly absorb it."

"Right." He picked the magician up carefully and eased her rigid form inside a storage cupboard. I was pleased to see that he set her down gently in what would be a comfortable position once the muscle-paralyzing properties of the gamma scopolamine wore off. I breathed a sigh of relief at the fact that she wasn't one of those unfortunates who went into respiratory shock at the synthetic toxin. When I purchased it in the Thieves' Market I'd intended to use it only on Vargas— if he died from it, that was only justice being served. But I didn't want to see an innocent person harmed by the chemical compound.

"Found them!" Fede called out. He held up a white case, about thirty centimeters wide, stenciled with red crosses. It was old tech, designed to keep human tissue viable as it was rushed from donor to recipient, back in the days when heart patients received actual organ transplants instead of modern cybernetic hearts made of polyurethane, dacron, and vat-grown myocardium. The Azzies had found a new use for the organ-transfer case—keeping hearts as fresh as possible until they could be offered up to their bloodthirsty gods.

Rafael was busy listening to the game over the micro-receiver in his ear. "Two more injuries," he told us. "And they sound serious. One of the Texcoco players took a ball to the chest and got his jaw broken after being kicked when he was down, and in retaliation his teammates gutter-stomped the captain of the Jaguars. They say he has a broken neck, massive chest and head injuries, and a collapsed lung."

"Good!" I said grimly. "Three injuries—three heart-runners. This just might work."

Had there been no other serious injuries, only one of us could have gotten into the *teocalli* as a *corazón* runner. And that someone would have been me. As a former police officer, I stood the best chance of impersonating an ambulance attendant. I'd dealt with enough emergency cases in my time with the Star. But it looked as though the gods and the spirits were smiling upon us. Three injuries, back-to-back, were exactly what we needed. At the same time I felt a pang of guilt. Our plan depended on the pain and suffering of others. But then I told myself that the injuries would have occurred anyhow, whether or not we'd been present at the *ollamaliztli* finals.

My cyberear picked up the roar of the crowd in the stadium above as a door opened somewhere in a room beyond ours. I heard the sound of people moving toward us.

"Grab the transfer cases," I told Rafael and Fede. "This place is going to be full of people in the next few minutes. It sounds like it's time to make our run."

Just as Fede and Rafael picked up the cases, a wave of people crashed into the room. Two players were carried in on gyro-stabilized stretchers, their bodies cradled by the stretchers' lining of form-fit polyfoam. Jock docs hovered over them, working with trauma patches and applying "spray skin"—a mixture of silicone and natural polymers—to seal off the bleeding around fractured bones that had broken the skin. A doctor similar to the one we'd immobilized a few minutes ago moved along with one of the stretchers, his hands placed one on top of the other, palms down, on the Texcoco player's forehead. His lips moved as he whispered the words of a healing spell.

The Jaguar player looked especially bad. A large, bloody dent creased the side of his head, and red foam frothed at his lips as he struggled to breathe. One of the physicians barked: "María! We need your magic. Now!" He looked wildly around. "*Chingada!*" he snapped. "Where is that mage?"

Fede gave the injured captain a pitying look as he passed the stretcher. Then he jerked his head and pushed his way out of the room. Rafael was close on his heels. They would go on ahead of me, trying to get to Vargas. They would have to rely on surprise, raw muscle—and the few drops of gamma scopolamine I'd sprayed onto the surgical glove each had in his pocket. The gloves were turned inside out. The trickiest part would be reversing them so that the gamma scopolamine was on the outside without getting any of it on their hands.

I bent to pick up an organ-transfer case and follow Fede and Rafael, but just at that moment the Jaguar captain went into convulsions. The team doctor who had been shouting for the mage grabbed me by the wrist, dragging me over to the stretcher.

"We're losing him!" he shouted. "Both lungs have collapsed. We need a respiratory assist. Where's your medkit?" He shook his head in exasperation and pressed my hands against the injured player's head. "Hold him steady—I want that neck immobilized. If there's any further spinal cord damage . . ."

From the stadium above came a roar that sounded like distant thunder. A moment later, a man in a black and gold track suit burst through the door into the first-aid room, waving his arms excitedly.

"We've won!" he screamed. "Pancho scored a ring goal! The Jaguars have won the national finals! The crowd is going mad!" He skidded to a halt and looked at the injured team captain. "Ah. Poor Rico. Too bad he can't savor his team's victory."

I looked down at the man whose head I held in my hands. He lay still, his fight for life over. His eyes were closed and his jaw was slack. Bloody foam still coated his lips and chin. I jerked my hands back and wiped them on my pants.

At that moment, another team of MedíCarro attendants burst into the room. The Texcoco team doctors shouted at them to take away the other player, that the injured Jaguar was already beyond help. In the resulting commotion, I bent down to pick up the organ-transfer case, thinking to slip out of the room. But then I realized what had just happened. The Jaguars had won the national finals. The man who lay on the stretcher in front of me was the team captain whose head the cultists—and Vargas—wanted to place in the *itzompan* at dawn. Did it matter that he had died at the stadium, instead of being sacrificed at the site itself?

The answer came quickly enough.

As the legitimate MedíCarro paramedics bustled the injured Texcoco player out of the room, one of the Jaguar doctors gestured at the organ-transplant case I was holding. "Bring that with you," he ordered curtly. "And follow me." The other physicians and attendants fell into a hush, as if they knew what was about to happen. All their joy at the victory seemed to have fled.

Waving the others away, the jock doc—an elf with narrow, delicate fingers and a widow's-peak hairline—pushed the stretcher into an adjoining room. Forced to play my part, I picked up the case and followed. He shut the door behind us and motioned for me to stand to one side of the stretcher. As I did, he velcroed an apron over his track suit and carefully lifted a monofilament blade out of the medical bag he carried. He pulled the micro-thin line taut between its two plastic handles, then raised it above the dead man's neck. Knowing what was coming, I fought down the bile in my throat.

I averted my eyes while he sliced swiftly into the neck of the dead captain with the monofilament blade, trying to ignore the smell of blood and the hiss of the line cutting flesh. I glanced up as I heard a squeaking noise, and saw that the blade was cutting through the blue polyfoam of the stretcher with equal ease.

"Open the case," the elf said curtly.

I did as I was told, feeling lightheaded as the jock doc curled his long fingers in the dead player's hair and lifted the head away from its body. A rush of blood spilled from the cleanly sliced neck, and a large lump of flesh—probably part of the tongue—fell back onto the stretcher. I tasted vomit at the back of my throat, swallowed hard, and closed my eyes. The case in my hands grew heavier as he placed the head inside it. He sealed the protective gel pack that lined the interior of the case over the head, then closed the lid.

I thought I felt the ground under my feet tremble slightly just then. It might have been the excited crowd in the stadium above, stomping their feet, or it might have been another minor earthquake. Or it may just have been my nerves.

"You're awfully squeamish for a MedíCarro," the elf said coldly. "You haven't been a *corazón* runner before, have you?"

I opened my eyes and met his gaze. His eyes bored into mine. Was there a hint of suspicion there? Had he looked closely at my uniform and seen that it was a fake? If I dropped the case quickly enough, I could reach the bottle of "perfume" in my pocket and blast him with a squirt . . .

"Have you been briefed on this transfer?" he asked. "Do you know where to go and who to run this to?"

I nodded. Then I realized he was waiting for me to answer. I spoke the only possible name that fit. "To the priest in the *teocalli*. Domingo Vargas."

The suspicion fled from his eyes. "Correct. Now go!"

I didn't need any more urging. When he opened the door, I rushed through it, past the cluster of people who still filled the first-aid room and down the corridor that Fede had briefed me about. I'd converted the map he'd drawn of this area to a datafile and stored it on my headware memory, and that was how I was able to follow it without giving conscious thought to where I was going. I passed a pair of Aztechnology Corporate Security guards, held up the organ-transfer case in my arms as if it were a passcard, and sighed with relief as they cracked a door to let me through. As the door closed behind me, I heard one of them speaking into the microphone at his throat.

"She's on her way up."

Now the run began in earnest. I raced along a short corridor and found myself at the foot of a steep flight of stairs that Fede had told me led into the *teocalli* itself. The walls here were not ferrocrete but stone, narrow and pitted with age like those of the pyramids in the Yucatán. I smelled incense drifting down from the temple above.

I shifted the case into my left arm and pulled the perfume bottle out of my pocket. I paused to make one last preparation, then held the bottle so that it was hidden between my palm and the case itself. When I handed Vargas the case, I'd blast him with a squirt of gamma scopolamine. Then it would be just be a matter of playing the part of a concerned MedíCarro attendant as we hustled him up to the landing pad and into the private VTOL he'd chartered. If that way was blocked, we'd take Vargas back the way we'd come, into the stadium, and load him aboard one of the MedíCarro vans. If there was still one on site.

I shook my head. Too many ifs. I started to climb.

I used my cyberear to pick up sounds from the temple above. I heard the faint sound of voices chanting—priests in a distant room, I guessed—and the surflike roar that was the crowd celebrating in the adjoining stadium. I didn't hear any gunfire or shouts of alarm. So far, so good. It didn't seem that we had been found out.

I wondered how Rafael and Fede were doing. They couldn't have been more than a few minutes ahead of me. They must have made it past the Azzies on guard at the door below—I hadn't seen any signs of a struggle as I passed. We'd decided that, in the case of them getting into the temple before me, they were to try and track down Vargas on their own. If they were able to touch him, the amount of gamma scopolamine on their plastic gloves might not be enough to immobilize the priest completely. Instead, they would have to get an improvised mage mask on him before he could cast any spells.

I'd gotten the idea from the mage masks we used at the Star to neutralize magically capable detainees. The police-issue masks were a combination plastic hood and breathing tube that prevented the magician from seeing or speaking— easily duplicated by an old-fashioned cloth blindfold and gag. A white-noise generator, built into the hood and designed to prevent the magician from concentrating, was trickier to duplicate. But then I'd hit upon the idea of using the micro-receiver that Rafael wore in his ear to monitor the *ollamaliztli* game broadcasts. If set between channels and cranked up loud, the resulting static would do the trick.

I reached the top of the stairs, puffing a little from the rapid climb. I emerged into a long, narrow room whose stone walls and ceiling were intricately carved with boxy Aztec glyphs and painted with scenes of frowning gods and sacrificial victims dripping blood from severed fingers, hands, and throats. Modern track lighting provided illumination, but the air was filled with the sweet smoke of incense that burned in ancient-looking stone bowls, held in the hands of statues of skeletal, grinning gods that squatted in each of the four corners. Against the far wall hung a neon-tube sculpture of the stylized jaguar head that was the logo of Aztechnology Corporation. Its baleful red glow lent an eerie light to the room. Beside it, on a granite pedestal, was a bronze statue of an eagle sitting on a cactus and eating a snake—the national symbol of Aztlan and of the sun god Huitzilopochtli, patron of the *ollamaliztli* games.

From Fede's briefing, I knew that the rectangular archway in the wall to my left led up to the area where the victory celebrations would be held—and to the balcony from which the priests watched the *ollamaliztli* games. Since I'd seen Vargas on the balcony earlier, it seemed logical to assume that I'd find him in that direction. And that was the way that Rafael and Fede would have gone. It was the part of the *teocalli* that Fede knew best—the part where he'd attended semi-final victory celebrations as captain of the Tampico Voladores in 2055.

I jogged through the archway, with its ornately carved

wooden lintel and frame, and into the room beyond. And nearly dropped the case in my surprise as I skidded to a halt.

Vargas stood at the far end of room, arms folded across the golden pectoral that hung over his chest. The balloonlike hands of the flayed skin he wore dangled like obscene mittens, and gigantic gold ear plugs stretched his earlobes nearly down to his shoulders. He stood about four meters away, but even at that distance and even over the incense, my nostrils were overwhelmed by the reek of decay that clung to his costume. It smelled like a corpse that had lain in the sun for a week or more. But it wasn't the smell that had brought me up short.

It was the sight of Fede and Rafael lying prone at Vargas' feet. The organ-transfer cases they'd been carrying lay on the floor beside them, lids open. One of Rafael's arms was stretched toward Vargas, the surgical glove pulled halfway down over his hand. He'd probably been trying to touch the priest when he collapsed. I couldn't tell if my friend was breathing or not—his body lay in a contorted heap and his head was turned away from me. Fede was equally still.

I stared at Mama G's killer, hoping that the hatred I felt wasn't burning in my eyes. There was still a chance. The guards had radioed that I was on my way up and the case that I carried actually contained something—something Vargas wanted. He might not know that I was in league with the two who lay at his feet, injured or . . .

I struggled to breathe. If Rafael was dead, I could do nothing for him now. If he was still alive, I was the only one who could save him.

It was all up to me. And I was scared drekless.

23

I tried not to look at Rafael and Fede, but it was impossible. And then I realized that, had I really been a MedíCarro attendant, I would naturally be wondering why my fellow paramedics were down and whether they were in need of medical attention.

"What happened to them?" I asked. "Are they hurt?"

"They came to the *teocalli* empty-handed," Vargas answered. His voice had a slightly nasal tone to it—something I hadn't expected in a portly priest. "Is your case empty, also?"

"No. It's full. I'm to deliver it to Domingo Vargas. Is that you?"

"What took you so long?"

"I was . . . delayed." I swallowed. Maybe he really was buying this. "The physician had trouble with his monofilament blade." Slowly, carefully, I began to close the distance between us. I held the case out, as if presenting it to him. My hands began to sweat and I hoped I wouldn't drop the perfume bottle—that its nozzle would be pointing in the right direction when I made my move.

"That's close enough." Vargas held up a hand, motioning for me to stop. At this distance, the sickly sweet smell of the rotting suit of flesh that he wore nearly overwhelmed me. I wondered if I was close enough to hit him with the spray— I'd tested the accuracy of the adapted nozzle and it was approximately one meter. Slightly more than one meter lay between us. I slid my thumb onto the nozzle, preparing to depress it . . .

Then I noticed the hand that hung from the wrist of Vargas' costume. As it turned slowly, I saw the tattoo on the back of it—a horse on motorcycle wheels, the logo of the

Houston Mustangs. It was the hand of the AFL member who had guided us into Aztlan—José's hand. José's flesh that Vargas wore.

If José had been playing at double agent, working for both the Azzie government and the AFL at once, his game had ended. The Azzies' final payment to him had been death. But perhaps he had been innocent of malice. Perhaps he had been exactly what he'd seemed—an AFL member who'd had the misfortune to get captured at the border. The border patrol might have forced information about Rafael and me out of him under torture or by magical spell—and then turned him over to Vargas for vengeance after learning that the people he's smuggled in were targeting a member of the priesthood.

It really didn't matter, either way. José was dead. I wished his spirit peace.

Seeing the tattoo confirmed my guess that Vargas had known that Rafael and I were in Tenochtitlán, and that he had sent the blood spirit against us. And that probably meant that he knew who I was, and was just playing games with me. I had to move—now.

"Here!" I shouted. "You wanted the head. Take it!"

I heaved the organ-transfer case at Vargas as hard as I could. At the same time I jumped forward, jamming my thumb down on the nozzle and thrusting the perfume bottle at his face. A thin stream of gamma scopolamine and DMSO shot toward Vargas . . .

And splashed against an invisible barrier. Drek! He was ready for me—ready and waiting with some sort of barrier spell in place. I'd expected one that could stop bullets after what Águila had told me about the Azzie soldiers, but not one that could stop molecules of liquid. I tried to jam my hand through the magical barrier, but my fist smashed into something that felt like a metal wall. My fingers went numb and I dropped the perfume bottle. I cursed, scrambling for it. The drug was the only weapon I had.

A bolt of electricity streaked toward me, striking me on the shoulder. Liquid fire seared through my chest and down into my legs as the spell hit, and flashes of light danced before my eyes. My legs buckled under me and it was all I could do to prevent myself from sprawling prone on the floor. My arms trembled as I fought to hold myself up. I heard Vargas chanting . . .

And then an invisible wall of force fell onto me, slamming me into the ground. The breath was knocked out of my body and my nose flared with pain. A dull ache spread through my chest. The cut in my chin had torn open again, and my blood smeared the stone beneath me.

From where I lay, I could see Rafael. His eyes fluttered, as if he were reviving from whatever had knocked him down. And his fingers were beginning to twitch. A wave of relief washed through me. But it was short-lived. Unless a miracle happened, I was still very much at the priest's mercy.

Vargas stood over me, his dark eyes gleaming in triumph. He adjusted the jaguar-skin cape on his shoulders with a vain shrug. "You came to Tenochtitlán to try to capture or kill me," he said, laughter overlying his nasal voice. "I expected your attack to be clumsy. But I didn't expect that, at the same time, you would be delivering into my hands the one thing that I most desire."

Vargas knelt down beside me and held his hands over me, cupping them together. I watched in horror as the blood that flowed from my chin stretched into a thin stream that trickled upward into his hands. I felt a part of my strength going with it. He lifted his hands to his lips, as if about to drink deeply of my soul.

Somehow, I found the strength to speak. "How do you know . . . the case contains . . . the head? I may have . . . emptied it."

Doubt flickered in his eyes. Then they became as hard as obsidian once more.

"Very clever," he said sarcastically. "You've earned yourself a few more seconds of life."

He stood, letting blood fall from his hands, then took two quick steps to where the organ-transfer case lay and set it upright. Popping the clasps that held the lid, he opened it. I could hear the scrunch of plastic as he pulled back the protective gel pack to reveal the head that lay beneath it. And as I heard that heaven-sent sound, I prayed that Vargas had wanted to keep his magical abilities honed and pure, that he hadn't ever had any cyberware implanted in his body. Like a toxin filtration system, for example . . .

"What—?"

Vargas' cry of surprise and alarm told me all I needed to know. My hold-out weapon had worked! When I'd paused at the bottom of the stairs that led to the *teocalli*, I had cracked the lid of the organ-transfer case and poured half of the contents of the perfume bottle inside. The lining of the case was soaked with gamma scopolamine—which had mixed with the blood that was smeared on the gel pack and thus become invisible. Vargas had touched it as he tore open the plastic lining to see if the head was really inside . . .

And then was hit—hard—by the drug.

Vargas tried to stand, but fell to his knees. He lifted an arm, and a glow of magical energy formed around his hand, then fizzled out with a loud *pop!* as he fell over onto his side. His eyes still glared at me, though, with all of the menace of a jungle cat that was unable to strike.

I rose to my knees, still shaking, and wiped the blood from my chin. I was familiar with gamma scopolamine—it had been developed by Ares Arms and used by security forces such as the one I'd worked for briefly after leaving the Star. I knew that Vargas should be immobilized for up to an hour. I scrambled over to where Rafael lay.

He groaned and tried to sit up. His entire body trembled with the strain, even with all the power of his ork blood. Slowly, with difficulty, he reached over and peeled the surgical glove from his hand, then flung it away. Then he wrapped his heavy arms around me, crushing me against him.

"Leni," he gasped in a tight voice. "I'm glad . . . I thought . . . I love you. I'd be all fragged up if you . . ."

"Shh," I told him. At the same time, I tried not to smile. One of the side effects of gamma scopolamine is that it is also a "truth serum." I'd known that Rafael cared about me, but love? I'd tease him about it later, when he was able to defend himself.

Rafael seemed to be regaining control over his muscles. He fought to bring a shaking hand up to his eye and swiped clumsily at it. Was he actually crying?

"Frag it," he said. "I nearly got him. I came this close." He held a thick thumb and forefinger a centimeter apart. Then he looked over my shoulder. "How's Fede? Is he . . ."

I climbed to my feet, crossed to where Fede lay, and

touched two fingers to his throat. I breathed a sigh of thanks as I felt a pulse. "He's alive."

Rafael nodded. He stood above the priest, glaring down at him. Rafael's hands still trembled slightly, but they had balled into fists and he seemed steadier on his feet with each passing moment. Once again, I marveled at his physical stamina. Anyone else would still have been paralyzed by the drug.

Rafael lifted one foot, drew it back—then kicked as hard as he could at Vargas' lower back. The priest was unable to move or retreat from the kidney kick, but made a small, squealing noise in response.

"I know one fragger who *isn't* going to be alive, soon." Rafael walked around to the front of Vargas, then lifted his foot again. "But first I'm going to make him pay for what he did to my Mama Grande."

His heel slammed down into the priest's groin. The squeal of pain was louder this time.

"Why did you have to kill her, you *bastard*!"

Another kick—this one to Vargas' face. Despite the rigidity of his muscles, the priest's head was forced back by the blow. Slowly, the paralyzed muscles pulled it back into place. Blood flowed from Vargas' smashed nose.

"You heartless, drek-eating Azzie fragger!" Rafael's voice had risen to a shout.

I just stood and held my arms against my chest, watching. It felt as though I'd cracked a rib when I hit the floor—the pain under my right breast was excruciating. But that wasn't the only reason I held back. Something in me was at war with itself. Ever since we'd come to Aztlan, I'd been kidding myself, telling myself that Vargas was just another criminal, secretly hoping that there was still a chance I could gather enough evidence that somehow he would be brought to justice—diplomatic immunity be damned. I hadn't allowed myself to consider any other options seriously—not even cashing in on the bounty offered in Dunkelzahn's will. I just kept telling myself I'd make sure Vargas got what was coming to him. But now, as I watched Rafael kicking the priest, I felt exultation—a fierce anger that had no place in someone who prided herself on staying on the right side of the law. I wanted this fragger dead as much as Rafael did.

And that scared me. When I'd gunned down the cultists to prevent them from conducting their bloody sacrifices on top of the pyramid, it had been like firing a weapon at a criminal in the line of duty. I'd been protecting innocent people. But this was something different. It didn't matter that it was personal.

Did it?

I was saved any further soul-searching by the sounds of people moving toward us. I heard loud, jubilant voices and numerous footsteps growing ever louder as a crowd of people approached. It was probably the *ollamaliztli* players, coming to make their victory sacrifices in the temple.

"Rafael!" I called. "Quiet! People are coming. Lots of them. We've got to move!"

Rafael stood over Vargas, panting with exertion. His eyes were wild, his hair loose from its usual pony tail. For a moment, I didn't think he'd heard me—that he would continue shouting and kicking and would give us away. But then he grunted.

"Fine. I'll finish this fragger later." He stooped, picked up the priest, and slung him over one shoulder. Wrinkling his nose at the stench of the skin the priest wore, he used his other arm to lift a groaning Fede to his feet. "Which way?"

I did a quick scan of the map I'd uploaded to my memory. The staircase behind us led back to the first-aid rooms, but that meant dealing with the Azzie security guards below— who probably knew who we were, since they had radioed Vargas that I was on the way up. And we had no guarantee that a MedíCarro emergency vehicle would be there for us to use. The landing pad on the roof of the temple—and the private VTOL that Vargas had chartered—seemed the better option.

By the speed with which the voices and footsteps were approaching, we had only a few seconds left to make our escape. Even the muscular Rafael wouldn't be able to carry both Vargas and Fede at once, and so I grabbed one of Fede's arms and wrapped it around my shoulder, while Rafael took his other arm. Fede was still groggy, but seemed able to shuffle one foot in front of the other. Together, Rafael and I would get him out.

I glanced at the organ-transfer case that lay on the floor.

The plastic packing was open and the severed head was turned so that one eye stared dully out at us. For a moment, I contemplated taking the thing along with us. If the prophecy about the end of the world and the dawning of a new age was true, we'd be doing the world a favor by making sure that the head was somewhere the cultists couldn't reach it. But with Vargas out of the picture, I didn't see how the cultists could gain access to it. And if we stuck with the chartered VTOL's flight plan and flew to Izamal, we'd be carrying the head closer to the *itzompan*. It seemed more prudent to leave it here. The head might even serve as a distraction that would allow us extra time to escape. Besides, it seemed the respectful thing to do. Let the Jaguar captain be buried in his entirety.

We hurried through the temple, climbing two flights of stone steps and always managing to keep just out of eyesight of the ACS guards who prowled the temple like roving jungle cats. They didn't seem to be armed with anything other than *macauitls*—but Mama G's death had taught me how deadly a weapon an obsidian-studded wooden sword could be. And I was wary of any magical backup they might have. But by some miracle we managed to avoid both human and spirit patrols.

Fede's recollection of the temple interior—and the map he had drawn for me—was most accurate. We emerged a minute or two later onto a floodlit rooftop where a number of VTOLs were parked. I spotted the one that Vargas had chartered immediately by the registration number on its tail. It was an Azzie-built knock-off of the Ares TR55, with a set of tilting rotor blades at the tip of each wing. They were turning with a gentle whine, and although I couldn't see into the cabin, I assumed the pilot must be there. A door just aft of the cabin and forward of the wing was open, and a three-rung stepladder sat below it. The plane looked ready for immediate takeoff. I suspected that Vargas had told its pilot to keep the rotors warm. He had to be ready to flee the *teocalli* at a moment's notice, should his highly unorthodox treatment of the team captain's body be brought to light and questioned.

We hurried toward the charter VTOL, flashing our fake ID badges at the Azzie security guard who stepped out of the night to block our way. This one was a beefy ork female, armed with a modern assault rifle smartlinked into her wrist, rather than a *macauitl*—a rifle she looked both ready and willing to use.

"Medical emergency!" I called out, doing my best to appear unperturbed by the rifle that was aimed at my center of mass. "*Bacab* Domingo Vargas has been poisoned. We've got to get him to a medical facility, fast, and we're commandeering this VTOL to do it."

The guard shifted to block our way, a suspicious look in her eyes. But our uniforms seemed to be commanding her respect—so far. "*Por favor,* you must wait while I radio for—"

"Gods curse it, woman!" I shouted. "Do you want to be responsible for the death of a *bacab* of the Temple of the Sun? Let us by!"

Rafael tried to edge around the guard toward the VTOL. But the ork was no fool. She shifted the barrel of her weapon so that it pointed at him. Now it practically touched his broad chest. "Where's your stabilization container and medkit?" she asked with a growl. "And what's wrong with this man?"

She tipped her head in Fede's direction. He had been walking under his own power since we reached the rooftop, but was still shaky on his feet. A nasty bruise was just beginning to bloom on one cheek and he wavered back and forth like a tranq junkie.

"He's . . . We . . . The stretcher . . ." Rafael struggled, unable to lie due to the after-effects of the gamma scopolamine. In another moment, he'd blurt out the truth about who we were.

Fede's knees suddenly buckled under him. He collapsed, dragging at my arm as he fell. I still don't know whether he'd planned it, but it proved a beautiful distraction. Startled by the sudden movement, the guard swung around to bring her weapon to bear—then realized her mistake, but too late. Rafael's fist connected solidly with her temple. She fell, rifle slipping from limp fingers as she collapsed. In one smooth motion Rafael yanked its smartlink cable free as it fell. Then he kicked the rifle across the rooftop and sprinted for the VTOL with Vargas bouncing on his shoulder. As I hauled

Fede to his feet, Rafael tore open the door and tossed the paralyzed body of the priest inside. Then he helped me boost Fede into the plane.

We climbed inside and slammed the door shut after ourselves. Outside on the rooftop, the ork guard stopped blinking away stars and scrambled for her weapon on her hands and knees. Through the porthole in the closed door, I could see her mouth working, and prayed that the backup she was radioing for wouldn't arrive before we could take off.

As Rafael settled Fede into one of the dozen plush seats that filled the back of the VTOL, I scrambled through a hatch into the cabin. The tiny compartment had no windows of any kind—all piloting and navigation was done cybernetically. The pilot was a crewcut human rigger in a padded bomber jacket. He was jacked into the VTOL by means of twin fiber optic cables that disappeared into chromed datajacks at either temple. He turned to look at me with two eyes that were obviously cyber. Instead of irises and pupils, the centers of each eye gleamed a dull red.

"Who the frag are you?" he asked.

"MedíCarro," I answered, equally tersely. "Your customer suffered a . . . setback. But he wants you to know that the flight to Izamal is still on, Paulo." I glanced out the porthole in the door just aft of the cabin and managed to catch a glimpse of the ork guard, who was picking up her weapon and jacking her smartlink back into it. "Now get us the frag out of here, before that guard turns this VTOL into Swiss cheese."

My knowledge of both Vargas' destination and the pilot's own name seemed to convince the rigger that I was legit. "I scan that," he said. His cybereyes stared past me as he devoted his full attention to piloting his plane. The engines roared into a full-throttle whine and the rotors whirled into a blur. With a jolt, we left the landing pad behind—just as the ork guard opened fire with her rifle. Then the VTOL banked steeply left and I was thrown against the door. My knees trembled with the strain of standing as the floor of the plane seemed to rush up at me, and by the time I had recovered enough to look out the porthole again, the Temple of the Sun and *ollamaliztli* ball court lay far below us. The lights of

Tenochtitlán disappeared into the reddish-brown smudge of its smog.

I had a new worry now—that the Azzies would have been sufficiently disturbed by the apparent kidnapping of one of their priests to come after us in hot pursuit. I was fairly confident that they wouldn't blow us out of the sky—the ork guard had gotten a good enough look at Vargas to realize that he was still alive. But I couldn't begin to imagine the resources they might bring to bear to force us down. And the VTOL pilot owed us no loyalty. He was simply a civilian doing a job. If the Azzies ordered him to land, he'd obey, regardless of what Vargas' previous instructions to him had been.

I didn't get a chance to ponder my worries further than this, however. As I made my way back to where Fede and Rafael were sitting, I saw that Vargas was starting to stir. The effects of the gamma scopolamine would linger for some time, but his facial muscles seemed to be loosening. Rafael had already tied Vargas' outstretched hands and feet to the armrests of the seats next to him. When the last of the paralysis wore off, he'd be completely restrained. Now Rafael was just getting ready to thrust a gag into Vargas' mouth. But even as he wadded up the cloth, the priest began to croak out words in a faint voice. My heart leapt, thinking that he was casting a spell. But then my cyberear picked up the faint whisper of his voice:

"I didn't . . . kill . . . your Mama Grande," he croaked. "But I know . . . who . . . did."

24

Rafael paused, the gag still in his hands. I strode down the aisle, determined to shove the wadded-up cloth into Vargas' mouth myself if I had to.

"Don't listen to him, Raf. It's a trick. If you let him talk, he'll try to cast a spell."

The priest strained to lift his head so that he could look at me. "No . . . trick," he whispered. "Information in exchange . . . for my life."

Rafael's eyes narrowed, but he seemed to want to hear what the priest was going to say. I had to admit that I was equally curious. Due to the gamma scopolamine, Vargas just might be telling the truth. I sat down in a seat next to him and leaned back, favoring my cracked rib. It still felt as if my chest was on fire.

One of Rafael's huge hands closed around Vargas' neck. The priest's double chins squeezed out through Rafael's fingers.

"If you utter one word of a spell," Rafael rumbled, "it will be the last word you ever speak. *Comprende*?"

Vargas still couldn't nod. He spoke instead. "*Sí.*" His jaw and tongue, at least, seemed to be loosening up. His words were clearer now. Some batches of gamma scopolamine have that effect—someone recovering from it might regain control over one hand or another extremity such as a foot, but be unable to move anything else for an hour. Maybe that was why the drug had been for sale on the black market in Aztlan. I just hoped that the "truth serum" side effect really was working.

I asked the first question: "The cultists Dolores Clemente and Gabriel Montoya—the missionaries. Did you send them to Seattle to use a mind probe spell on Rosalita Ramirez?"

"Yes."

"Why?"

"To find something that was . . . lost."

"The *itzompan*," I said. My knowledge seemed to surprise Vargas. His obsidian-black eyes widened ever so slightly—and stayed that way, although they continued blinking.

"And then you met with them at Charles Royer Station, found out what they'd learned, and killed them. And then killed Rosa Ramirez," I said.

"No. I met with them, but did not kill them. I used a spell to replace their memories with false ones so they would not remember what they had learned from her. Someone else killed them and made it look as if I had done it. But the killer forgot one thing."

"And that was . . ." I prompted.

Vargas' eyes slid to the side. He seemed to be staring at his hand. Rafael tightened his grip on the priest's neck, perhaps thinking that Vargas was trying to gesture and cast a spell. The priest's eyes became pleading as his face purpled.

"Raf," I said. "Loosen your grip."

Vargas sucked in a deep, ragged breath. "Whoever flayed the bodies left the hands behind. A priest of Xipe Totec would have taken them."

I stared at the empty sacks of flesh that hung from the wrists of the portly priest's costume. Drek! How had I missed that? I must have been losing my edge. What Vargas was saying slotted into place. If he had been working with the cultists, it wasn't logical to kill two of their members and leave so obvious a signature behind. A memory-erasing spell would have been much more subtle—and smart.

"Who killed them?" I asked.

"One of Tito Guzman's acolytes."

"Guzman?" I asked. After a moment I placed the name. "The priest who died in the VTOL explosion?"

"Yes."

Then I realized how Guzman fit into the picture. Caco had said that Guzman was one of the four *bacabs* who officiated at the Temple of the Sun. Vargas was also one of those four *bacabs*, and would have worked closely with Guzman. Had all four of the temple's *bacabs* been working in league with the cultists—only to turn against one another later? Maybe

Vargas had refused to share the location of the *itzompan* with his fellow priests, prompting them to take steps to gather that information themselves.

The priest who Teresa had killed on top of the *teocalli*—whom I now knew was also a *bacab* of the Temple of the Sun—had summoned a blood spirit in an unsuccessful effort to learn where the *itzompan* lay. But Guzman had questioned a better source: the missionaries. And judging by the fact that he'd died a short time later, he must have gotten some answers from them.

I made the most logical assumption and stated it aloud. "You arranged Guzman's death, didn't you?"

Vargas clamped his lips together, trying not to speak. Then the drug got the better of him. "Yes."

Fede sat forward in his seat. He was looking a little less shaky now, and was completely engrossed in what Vargas was saying. "Amazing," he said, glancing up at me. "Vargas and Guzman were two of the most powerful *sacerdotes* in the Temple of the Sun. Imagine—one *bacab* killing another." His voice dripped with sarcasm, as if Azzie priests were known to betray one another frequently. Then I remembered his bias. Vargas—or other priests who followed the Path of the Sun—had been responsible for the death of Fede's teammate and close friend. But from what I'd seen and heard so far, Fede's impression of the Azzie priesthood was bang on.

"Who gives a frag about the cultists?" Rafael said angrily. He shook Vargas like a rat, thumping the back of the priest's head against the carpeted aisle. "I want to know one thing. Who killed my Mama Grande?"

Vargas' eyes burned with hatred as he stared up at Rafael, but the drug compelled him to answer. "It was the white *bacab*," he gasped. "Guillermo Acosta, priest of Quetzalcóatl, also sent one of his acolytes to Seattle. Like Guzman, he knew I had sent the cultists there—only Guzman did not know the name of their intended target. Acosta dug deeper and learned your grandmother's name and address. But the man he sent to question her used cruder means to try and make her talk. I can only guess that he must have become frustrated and—"

"Frustrated?" Rafael slammed the priest's head against the

floor, then jammed the wadded-up cloth fiercely into Vargas' mouth. He looked up at me, his expression sour. "He's not the only one who's frustrated. I don't want to hear any more of this drek. I say we grease this fragger, right *now*!"

Lost in thought, I didn't answer. Mentally, I ticked off what we had learned. Vargas served the god Xipe Totec, Guzman was a priest of Huitzilopochtli, and the *bacab* who'd summoned the blood spirit on the *teocalli* served Tezcatlipoca. Now Vargas was fingering a priest of Quetzalcóatl. It looked as though my guess had been correct. All four *bacabs* had been working with the cultists, at one point in time. But only one of them had killed Mama Grande.

All this time, we'd been chasing after the wrong priest.

Fede interrupted my thoughts. "I agree with Rafael," he said grimly. "Vargas should die. Even if he didn't kill your Mama Grande, he's killed plenty of others." He flicked disdainfully at the balloonlike hand that hung from Vargas' wrist, setting it rocking gently back and forth. It spun slowly, revealing the Houston Mustangs tattoo on the back of it.

"Frag me!" Rafael exploded. "That's José's hand!" His face drained of color, and for a moment I thought he was going to be violently ill. Then his hand tightened, slowly and remorselessly, on Vargas' throat.

Fear returned to the priest's eyes. He looked up at me pleadingly. But it was hard to feel sorry for someone who wore the stinking, flayed skin of a human being. Even so, I called Rafael to heel. But not out of pity.

"Wait, Raf," I said. "I want to ask him one more question."

Rafael shook his head and refused to look at me. His eyes were locked on Vargas' face, watching him start to die by degrees. I still had several questions for the priest, but I knew of only one that would loosen Rafael's grip. He was frustrated and wanted someone to pay—now—for Mama G's death. Even if it was the wrong person.

"I want to ask him about José," I said. "I want to know if he betrayed us."

Rafael's jaw clenched. Unclenched. "All right." His hand loosened.

This time, Vargas' intake of breath shuddered even more than it had before. His breathing had developed a wheeze.

"Was the man whose skin you're wearing working for Az-technology?" I asked.

"No."

"You see?" Rafael asked. "José was a good chummer."

"He was an acolyte of the *bacab* of Quetzalcóatl."

"No!" Rafael said explosively.

I thought I saw a gloating gleam in Vargas' eyes as he saw the effect of his words on Rafael, but couldn't be sure.

"He's on gamma scopolamine, Raf," I said gently. "He must be telling the truth."

Rafael shook his head, still not willing to believe. "But why would José . . . What did he hope to . . ."

"It follows a twisted kind of logic, Raf," I said, thinking out loud. "José was probably working for both the AFL and the priest of Quetzalcóatl. If he was ever a member of the AFL at all, that is. The priest probably figured we'd be a thorn in the side of Vargas, and instructed him to get us into Aztlan. Later José fell into Vargas' hands, and paid the price for being an acolyte of a rival *bacab*.

"José knew how to play people," I added. "Look at how fresh that tattoo is—he probably knew you were a combat biker fan and psyched you out by pretending to be one, too. He . . ."

Rafael's knobby forehead puckered into a frown. I thought he was going to rebut what I was saying, but instead he picked out the one fact that I'd missed.

"José had to have been a member of the AFL," he said. "He knew that Mama Grande liked snakes. Or else . . . " He paused, lost in thought. "Or else he was someone who had been healed by her, who knew she was a snake shaman . . ."

I stared at Rafael in amazement. For once, the big guy was really using his wetware. And now my own was starting to work, as well. I hadn't questioned it at the time, when the feathered serpent Soñador had said that it was helping us because Rafael was the grandson of a woman who had healed it, long ago. But now the reasoning sounded thin.

It was time to focus our sights on our true target—the man who had killed Mama G. I turned to Vargas. "Is Soñador the *bacab* of Quetzalcóatl?"

"Who?"

"He also goes by the name of Kukulcán."

"Who?"

Either the drug was wearing off and Vargas had started to lie, or he really didn't know. I tried another tack. "Is the *bacab* of Quetzalcóatl a feathered serpent?"

Vargas looked genuinely confused. "The *god* Quetzalcóatl is the feathered serpent. His priest is metahuman."

"Describe him."

"He's an elf. Tall, thin, with light skin. Dark hair and a mustache—"

"No beard?" Rafael asked.

"No."

Not it was my turn to frown. The description was close to that of Soñador in metahuman form—but not quite. Soñador appeared more human—although he did have the slight build of an elf. He had red hair been a dye job? Or had Soñador been using some sort of masking spell when he met with us?

If Soñador was the *bacab* of Quetzalcóatl and in league with Vargas and the cultists, why had he given us Father Gustavo Silvio's name? Did he think that Gus knew the location of the *itzompan*—and think that we might be able to sweet-talk this information out of him?

I shook my head. Too many questions. I was starting to lose the data trail on this one. The most serious consideration was that we had no way of knowing whether Soñador—our ticket out of Aztlan—was our enemy or ally. No way of knowing whether we could trust him or any "AFL" members the feathered serpent might put us in touch with. Except . . .

My eyes fell on the catheter that was implanted in Vargas' throat. I suddenly remembered the catheter I'd seen implanted in the chest of the priest of Tezcatlipoca. If Soñador had a similar device, we'd nail him. The only trouble would be spotting it under the feathers of his dracoform or the clothes that covered his metahuman form.

I thought back to the simsense chip case I'd found in the pocket of the priest of Tezcatlipoca. It looked as though all three of Vargas' fellow *bacabs* had sent agents to Seattle—whichever one served the priest of Tezcatlipoca had found the dead missionaries long after they were murdered and removed the only part of the puzzle he could find—the simsense chip covers. Which explains why the blood that stained the floor of the missionaries' rental car had a chance to partially dry before the cases were lifted out of its sticky embrace.

I seemed to have all the pieces now, but I still couldn't see the larger picture. I hoped that enough of the gamma scopolamine remained in Vargas' system to give me the answers I needed.

"The *bacab* of Tezcatlipoca called you 'blood brother,' " I said. "Why?"

Vargas' eyes widened further. "Please," he said. "Don't make me—"

"Tell her," Rafael thumped the priest's head against the aisle once more for emphasis.

Vargas bit into his lip until it bled. But the drug proved stronger than his will. As if forced open by an unseen hand, his lips parted.

"We are Gestalt," he said in a voice that croaked like that of death itself. "The four of us worked together to awaken the ancient *teocalli* and—"

My cyberear caught the explosion. It was small and muffled, a mere popping noise that was difficult to hear against the drone of the VTOL engines. Suddenly Vargas' eyes rolled back and a trickle of red began to leak from the back of his head. Fede gasped and Rafael jerked his hand back, in the process inadvertently turning Vargas' head to the side. A wisp of smoke escaped from a hole in the back of the priest's skull. A small, steaming puddle of brains lay on the carpeted aisle of the VTOL.

"Frag me," Rafael said. "What happened?"

I hadn't seen it before, but I could guess. "Cranial bomb," I said with a shudder. "Just a small one, so it wouldn't frag up the priest's magic. Looks like Aztechnology plays for keeps—and anticipates that its employees won't always be loyal. Vargas must have used some phrase—some keyword that triggered the explosion. I guess that's why he was so reluctant to talk."

"Whew," Rafael stood and wiped his hands on his pants even though the miniature explosion hadn't gotten any brains or blood on him.

Fede just stared at the corpse. "He deserved it," he said softly.

The VTOL lurched as it hit a pocket of turbulence. With a

musical *ping!* the fasten seat belts sign came on. A voice urged us in Spanish to take our seats.

Rafael stared at me, one hand holding onto a seat back to keep himself steady. "Well, Leni. What now?"

I glanced out a window. We had already left Tenochtitlán far behind. Below us, the lights of smaller cities were sliding by. If the Azzies were interested in forcing us to land, they would have taken some action by now. Wouldn't they?

I looked back and forth between Rafael and Fede.

"Your part in this is done," I told Fede. "You did what you agreed to do—got us into the *teocalli* and out again." I pulled a credstick from my pocket and tossed it to him. "If you want to bug out when we land, that's fine. But I should warn you— we may be landing in a war zone."

Fede caught the credstick, but shook his scarred head. *"Gracías.* I appreciate the payment. But I think I'll stick with you. You're my best chance at getting out of Aztlan."

I bit back my reply. Now that I could no longer be sure of Soñador, I wasn't certain that there was a way out. For any of us.

I turned to Rafael. "We'll continue on to Izamal," I answered. "I didn't have a chance to tell you before, but there's going to be an attack on the Sanctuary of the Virgin tonight—the church where the Cristeros are holding their meeting. The Azzies want to mop up the rebels once and for all. It seems that someone betrayed the Cristeros and . . ."

I had to stop when I saw the look on Rafael's face.

"Teresa," he said in a choked voice, barely able to get the word out. "We've got to . . ."

"We'll try," I answered, laying a hand on my friend's arm. I glanced out the window once more. "Gods willing, we'll get there in time to warn them."

25

The flight to Izamal took a little over three hours. During the journey, I filled Fede in on where we were going and why. Rafael spent much of the trip pacing the aisle, fretting that we wouldn't reach Teresa and the Cristeros in time to warn them of the impending attack. For all we knew, the Azzies were storming into the church, even now.

For perhaps the dozenth time, Rafael stabbed at the telecom that was built into the wall at the front of the passenger cabin, trying to reach Teresa's employers. But there was no answer. All he got was the automatic message system. And that was odd. In a household that size, someone should have been answering the telecom, if only a maid or servant. What was happening in Izamal?

Our pilot was completely occupied in flying the plane, and so we didn't have to deal with any questions from him. But I wondered what we were going to do with the dead priest. We couldn't very well toss his body out of a door—the VTOL was zipping along through the night skies at nearly three hundred fifty klicks per hour and we were likely to get sucked out along with the corpse. Besides, there was no way we could open an emergency exit without the rigger becoming alerted to the fact. He was jacked into the plane and would feel any change in its status immediately.

Fede came up with part of the solution. He'd been rummaging in the compartments at the front of the cabin after Rafael opened them to use the telecom, and found a fully stocked bar. He held up a bottle of synthscotch and a first aid kit.

"That's a good idea," Rafael said. "I could use a drink."

"Or a tranq patch," I said sarcastically. My friend's anxious pacing was getting on my nerves.

But Fede shook his head. "The priest chartered this plane and made arrangements for it to land in Izamal, no? Someone is probably expecting to meet him when we land. If he is dead, so are we. But if he is merely drunk . . ."

Rafael caught on. "So we douse him with liquor—"

Fede completed the thought. "And use the spray skin in this first aid kit to hide the hole in the back of his head. We leave him propped up in a seat—"

"Not good enough," I said. "Izamal is under curfew and there's an Azzie military operation going down tonight. There's no way we'd be allowed to move around freely on our own. But Vargas obviously expected to be able to do so. He needed to reach the Sanctuary of the Virgin before dawn. He must have made arrangements to get there. If he were alive, he'd be our ticket through town. But he's dead. And that means that one of us has got to play the part of the priest. One of us has to . . ."

I glanced at the corpse in its putrid, flayed-skin costume. Just thinking of the crusted blood that lined it and its foul smell made my skin itch and my stomach churn. But it was a foregone conclusion who would have to wear it. Being female, I'd never be able to pass as Vargas, and although the priest was on the heavy side, Rafael was simply too big and broad across the shoulders.

"I see," Fede said. "I'll wear it."

"Thank you," I said. "If there was any other way . . ."

"Está bien," Fede answered. But I could see that it would take everything he had to psych himself into pulling the obscene costume on.

It was nearly midnight by the time the VTOL touched down. When it did, a "drunk" MedíCarro attendant sat slumped in one of the rear seats, and an uncomfortable-looking Fede wore the flayed skin costume of Xipe Totec. We'd used some of the synthetic spray skin from the first aid kit to create loops of flesh under Fede's ears to hold the priest's ear plugs, and had hung the golden pectoral around his neck. The former *ollamaliztli* player now was wearing a fortune in gold. We used more spray skin to smooth out some of the scars on his face, then painted it with bands of red using cinnamon-flavored mints from a cupboard that held snacks.

Rafael and I had each pulled on the complementary plastic overcoats we found in a closet at the front of the cabin—they were part of the airline's executive service package for passengers who might have to deplane on a rain-swept landing pad. Hopefully, with the uniform-style pants and shirts underneath—but with the MedíCarro patches covered—we'd be able to play the part of bodyguards to the priest.

The VTOL sank vertically to a stop at Izamal's tiny civilian airport. As the rotors wound down and the engine noise faded to a soft hum, a holo of the pilot's head and shoulders appeared above the telecom unit. "Has Mr. Vargas regained consciousness?" the holo head asked.

Fede was quick on the uptake. "I have," he answered.

"Your ground transport is arriving now. Please exit through the door in the rear of the cabin."

"Very good, Paulo," Fede answered. "One more thing. One of my attendants will be returning to Tenochtitlán. Please add the return flight to my tab."

"Destination?"

"The MedíCarro clinic on the Paseo de la Reforma."

"Affirmative."

The holo blinked out. I crossed my fingers. With luck, Domingo Vargas' death wouldn't be discovered for three hours—not until the VTOL touched down back in Tenochtitlán. I hoped that would give us enough time.

"Now or never," I said.

Rafael and I exited first through the rear door, playing the part of cautious bodyguards making a sweep before their employer deplaned. Our pilot had extended folding steps from the VTOL to the tarmac and I descended these cautiously, one eye on the tiny ferrocrete-and-glass structure that was a hangar and control tower in one. Rafael motioned for the "priest" to stay in the plane as a military jeep approached. Its driver—an Azzie soldier in full combat gear with a heavy pistol holstered at his belt—stepped out of the armored jeep and opened the rear door. If the Azzies used the same rank insignia as our own UCAS forces, he was a lieutenant—a junior officer, but an officer nonetheless.

I beckoned Fede down the steps and onto the tarmac, and Rafael and I flanked him like bodyguards as he made his way to the jeep. The lieutenant gave Fede a crisp salute as we passed, then closed the door after us as we settled into the back of the jeep. Behind us, the VTOL's rotors began to turn more swiftly and its engines rose to a sharp whine. The door through which we'd exited closed automatically, and the VTOL rose gracefully, disappearing into the night sky.

The lieutenant climbed behind the wheel and stared straight ahead, out through the bulletproof windshield. In the rear-view mirror, I could see him wrinkling his nose at the smell of the flayed skin that Fede wore. But he had enough savvy to keep his face neutral. "Where to, Bacab Vargas?" he asked.

"Head toward the Sanctuary of the Virgin," Fede instructed. "I'll give you further directions as we go."

"Yes, sir." The response was automatic. The lieutenant began to drive. Then he spoke again, articulating slowly and obviously choosing his words carefully.

"Bacab Vargas?"

"Yes?" Fede answered.

"Are you certain you want to drive to the church? We're securing a perimeter around it, even now. I thought you had told us it was essential to keep a low profile to surprise the rebels. And that you did not wish to enter the church until just before dawn."

My cyberear picked up Rafael's quiet sigh of relief. So the attack was still to come. That meant Teresa and the other Cristeros were safe—for the moment.

Interesting. From what the lieutenant had just said, Vargas had been the one to order the attack on the Cristeros. I could only guess that he wanted the rebels cleared away so that he and the cultists could enter the church. But why not simply wait until the rebels had finished their meeting and gone? That would draw less attention.

Fede also picked up on the fact that Vargas must have been behind the upcoming raid. "Call off the attack," he said.

The lieutenant shook his head. "It is too late, Bacab Vargas. Troops are already being deployed by Major Moreno. This is a matter for the military now. And I am certain that the major would respectfully advise that you stay clear of the operation until it is over."

Fede played the part of a pompous priest beautifully, responding to the driver in a sharp tone. "I did not say to drive to the church itself," he snapped. "Merely to head in that direction. I will be passing the night at a nearby hacienda and going in just before dawn, as originally arranged. Major Moreno had best make sure that the church is clear by then."

"Ah." The lieutenant nodded briskly. "I see. Yes, *bacab*. I'm sure it will be."

The rest of the ride passed in silence. Through the tiny, bulletproof windows of the armored jeep, I could see other military patrols passing by. The curfew was in effect—not a single civilian was on the streets. Most of the homes we passed were dark, their windows shuttered against the night.

The jeep pulled up at a hacienda just down the block from the residence where Teresa worked. We climbed out and Fede dismissed the driver. We waited until the jeep pulled away—then immediately made for the hacienda of Teresa's employers. Rafael knocked on the door that Teresa had answered during our last visit, but there was no response. The house was entirely dark, and my cyberear could detect no sounds of motion inside. It did, however, pick up the sound of an engine on a nearby street. Since the military controlled the streets, I concluded that a patrol was nearby—and approaching swiftly. Time to move.

"Let's try the church," I said. "We can get to it through the 'back door'—the passage that leads to its sub-basement from the convent. If we're lucky, the Azzies may not have secured it yet."

They hadn't. Under cover of darkness, we crept through the streets to the convent, then slipped inside through a door whose padlock and chain were just for show. I eased the creaking door shut behind us . . .

And as I turned around, was blinded by the glare of a heavy-duty halogen flashlight.

My cyberear caught the sharp intake of breath and the click of safeties being flicked. *"Chingada!"* a male voice whispered. *"A sacerdote!"*

Praying that Rafael and Fede had the good sense to remain still, I turned slowly, keeping my hands in sight. "Don't shoot! We're friends of Teresa Perales. We've come here to warn you to get out of the church. The military knows that the Cristeros are meeting here tonight. There isn't any time to lose."

"Prove that you are a friend," a young voice answered, "or die." The tone was melodramatic—he'd probably seen too many action trids.

"Bring Teresa here," Rafael said. "She'll vouch for us."

I overheard a whispered consultation—two male voices. Then someone left the room. The other rebel kept us pinned in the light of his flash. By its backlight I could see the barrel of a rifle.

"Stay frosty," I told Rafael and Fede. I was relieved to see that they took the advice to heart. Like me, they remained still, keeping their hands well away from their torsos.

After a few minutes I heard someone returning.

"Rafael! Lenora! What are you doing here? And who is—"

I recognized Teresa's voice. "This is our friend Fede," I explained. "The costume is authentic, but he's only posing as a priest. He had to wear it to get us through the town after curfew. The streets are crawling with soldiers. They know the Cristeros are meeting here tonight. And they plan to attack. Soon. We've got to get you out of—"

A burst of automatic weapons fire outside drowned me out. It sounded like someone had opened up a block or two away with a heavy machine gun. The *whumf* of an exploding grenade split the silence that followed, and we all jumped as a spray of shrapnel pattered against the door behind me. The rebel who held the halogen flashlight had the sense to immediately dim its light to a faint glow. I hoped that the door was firmly shut, and that light hadn't shone through its cracks and given us away.

"Frag it!" Rafael's whisper seemed to echo in the dimly lit room. "That was close. We'd better rev it outta here."

The two Cristeros guarding this entrance—a teenage elf in a black track suit and an older man whose bulk suggested he had some troll in his blood—looked at each other, then at Teresa.

"They're friends!" she hissed urgently. "We can trust them."

"*Bueno*," the older man said. "Let's go! *Pronto!*"

We hurried down the hall to a closet whose floor contained a trap door that led to the sub-basement. The teenage rebel descended through it with a clatter of feet on wooden steps and was followed by Teresa. But the older Cristero stood outside the closet, rifle at the ready, while Rafael, Fede, and I clambered down. I could see that he still didn't trust us completely.

We wound our way through the rubble that lay heaped on the floor of what used to be the *ollamaliztli* ball court and made our way to a spot where roughly a dozen individuals were grouped around an old-fashioned electric lantern. I immediately recognized Father Gustavo Silvio among the rebels—he was hunkered over what looked like a map. A man in a straw cowboy hat and the clothing favored by *campesinos* sat cross-legged beside him, his back to us and his arms outstretched and fingers extended in a curious posture.

The rebels had set the lantern and map on the altar-like stone that was the *itzompan* itself. The lantern's harsh white glow illuminated dozens of crates, piled in some places to the ceiling. Some of them had been opened. Inside, nested on foam padding, were a number of anti-vehicle and high-explosive rockets, as well as the collapsible launchers needed to fire them. Many of the rockets bore the Ares Arms logo.

Other cases held gel-pack armored jackets, target designators, and thermographic vision goggles. I whistled softly to myself.

"Looks like the Cristeros are planning something big," Rafael whispered. "I wonder where they got the nuyen for all this hardware."

"I've heard rumors that the dragon Dunkelzahn left three million nuyen to the 'provisional government' of the Yucatán in its will," I whispered back. "I wonder if some of that was used to purchase this."

Rafael's attention was riveted on the group of rebels who had turned to see who was approaching. "Speaking of dragons . . ."

My heart did a flip-flop as I recognized the pale white skin, red hair, and beard of Soñador in his metahuman form. At first I wondered what the feathered serpent was doing here. Then I realized that, if he was in league with the cultists and knew that the *itzompan* was in this sub-basement, his rebel membership gave him the perfect excuse to come to the church on the night before Four Motion, the day on which the current era was supposed to end.

My only ace in the hole was that Soñador didn't know that Vargas had blown his cover. I decided to play it cool. "Hello, Kukulcán," I said.

The pale-skinned man smiled and nodded. In that same moment Gus, who had been busy rolling up the map, turned and spotted us.

"Leni! Rafael! What are—" His face fell as he saw the costume that Fede wore. Now that we were inside the church, Fede was happily stripping the putrid-smelling skin from his body. After peeling it back and tossing it aside in disgust, he stood in his underwear, scratching at his muscular chest and flicking away clumps of dried blood. He'd torn out the ear plugs and held them and the pectoral in one hand. I noticed that more than one of the Cristeros glanced at the gold greedily. So much for following Christ's example of poverty.

"Anybody got soap and water?" Fede asked.

Just then I heard the sound of gunfire. It was muffled somewhat by the thick ceiling over our heads, but I hadn't even needed my cyberear to hear it.

The man who sat cross-legged on the floor—whom I recognized now as Águila—began to flutter his fingers. He gave a sharp, piercing cry, then jerked out of his trance. "Soldiers in the church," he said. "And in the convent."

Knowing he was a shaman, I guessed that he had been assensing astral space.

Soñador looked sharply at his aide. "Have they found the entrances?"

The other rebels looked warily around. One or two drew and readied handguns, while another crossed to the crates, pulled out a rocket launcher, and began grimly to assemble it.

"No. They seem to be intent on preventing people from getting into the church."

"Our people?" Gus asked sharply.

"No. Others. Strangers. The soldiers are tearing off their shirts and inspecting their arms—then shooting them. I don't know what it means." He closed his eyes and his body slumped as he re-entered astral space.

I knew what the soldiers were doing—but I kept quiet.

They were searching for cultists—looking for the brands on their arms. It seemed that Vargas had ordered an attack on his own allies—he obviously had meant to betray the cultists and place the team captain's severed head in the *itzompan* all on his own. And then when the ground was torn in two by earthquakes and the "demons of twilight" emerged, he would be the one to welcome them. Presumably, he thought he could handle any *tzitzimine* all by himself. Arrogant fragger.

I glanced at my watch. It was almost one a.m. Venus was set to rise in a little over four and a half hours.

And that made me think of something. If Soñador was a priest of Quetzalcóatl, he must have been waiting for Vargas to bring the head to Izamal And now that he'd seen Fede wearing the costume of Xipe Totec, he would know that we'd gotten to Vargas. He'd take out his vengeance on us . . .

Realizing that I didn't have a single weapon on me, I suddenly felt naked. More exposed even than Fede, who stood beside me clad only in his underwear.

The gunfire above us intensified for a minute or two, then suddenly stopped. After a moment, I heard a single pistol shot

Águila emerged again from his trance to update his report. "Something odd is happening," he said in a tense voice. "A man has arrived in the company of a dozen armed guards. They're not regular military—their uniforms look more like those of security guards. The man challenged the soldiers, and shot an officer who tried to impede him. Now he's the one who's giving the orders. He's telling them to search the church and the convent for a way into the sub-basement . . .'

"Blessed Virgin!" Gus cried out in a choked voice. "Who is it? A military officer? Not my—"

"It's a *sacerdote*," Águila answered. "I recognize him by his ear plugs and feathered headdress. His face is painted white—the color of Quetzalcóatl."

"What the frag?" I said out loud. The rebels looked at me. "That sounds like the *bacab* of Quetzalcóatl. But I thought he was already . . ." I bit back what I was about to say and tried not to look at Soñador. I'd been wrong—he was the genuine article. A rebel leader, a dragon—but no more than that. But that was a small mercy, now.

Águila's next words stunned us all.

"Get ready," he said. "They've found the way in. They're descending from both the church and the convent. We're surrounded."

One of the rebels had the presence of mind to start clawing thermographic vision goggles out of a nearby case, while another dimmed the electric lantern to a dull glow that barely illuminated the cavernous sub-basement. I pulled a pair of the goggles over my eyes and hunkered down with the rebels behind the cases. The crates made a rather dubious cover—a shelter of high explosives. I knew enough about explosives to realize that only a "lucky" hit—a bullet that struck the shaped charge in the tail of a rocket—could cause its warhead to explode. But that didn't make me feel any safer. Especially when those attacking us might start tossing grenades around. If one of those landed among the rockets, it would be game over.

I looked around through my thermal-imaging goggles. The rebels nearest me were human-shaped blobs of orange, red, and blue, their own goggles a ghostly gray mask across their eyes. Soñador was the only one not wearing goggles—his natural thermal-sensing capabilities precluded this. I spotted Rafael—his arm was draped protectively around Teresa. Fede squatted beside them, his cybernetic legs a cool blue that contrasted sharply with his warmer torso.

My cyberear picked up the cautious footsteps of people approaching from either end of the sub-basement—the sounds of professional guards, creeping along at a careful crouch. Then gunfire erupted around me. Streaks of orange heat emerged from the rebels' pistols as they popped up from behind the crates to shoot at the approaching guards. I heard a grunt of pain from somewhere in the direction of the guards—and then a roar of gunfire drowned it out as the Azzies shot back at us. Bullets sang a deadly song as they ricocheted off the stone walls around us or thudded heavily into the crates, striking the rockets with dull metal *clinks*. One of the Cristeros cried out and collapsed in a limp heap a meter away from me, blood leaking from his chest. I kept my head down and prayed—to which god I wasn't sure—that none of the rockets would explode. If they did, I'd never know it—we'd all be incinerated or torn to pieces in a hail-storm of shrapnel before we realized we were dead.

I heard a *whoosh!* as one of the rebels fired a rocket. But then came the dull *clunk* of the rocket striking stone—without exploding. The rebel might as well have saved the effort. A rocket's smart circuits are designed to prevent it from exploding unless it has traveled a minimum distance from the launcher—typically twenty meters. The *tlachtli* that formed the sub-basement of the church and convent was simply too short—or too cluttered with rubble—to allow the rocket to travel that far. Our most powerful weapon was useless.

After a hellish minute, the gunfire stopped. A male voice called out to us. I guessed that it was the priest.

"Surrender, and we will allow you to leave the church," he said.

I didn't believe it for one minute. Neither did the rebels. They didn't even dignify the offer with an answer—although one of them began softly praying in a tear-choked voice.

My cyberear allowed me to pick up the soft command of the priest. "Kill them," he told his guards. And in that moment, I knew we were well and truly fragged. I steeled myself to die . . .

And then realized that there might be a way to buy us time. "Wait!" I called out. "There are crates of high-explosive rockets surrounding the *itzompan*. I am touching the barrel of my gun to the shaped charge in the back of one of them right now. Before I let you kill me, I will shoot it and cause an explosion that will tear this place apart. The *itzompan* will be lost to you forever."

Through my thermo-vision goggles, I saw a number of the rebels turn toward me, surprise evident in their open mouths. They obviously realized that I had come up with a powerful bluff—and it was equally obvious that they didn't have a clue to what I was talking about. But one of them had the presence of mind to actually touch the barrel of his pistol to the end of one of the rockets, just in case the *bacab* used his astral-sensing capabilities to spy on us.

The soft curse that my cyberear picked up let me know that the priest understood my threat very well.

"Hold your fire!" he ordered his guards.

I heaved a sigh of relief. We'd brought ourselves a few minutes' grace. But I knew that it wouldn't last long. If this Guillermo Acosta was anything like his fellow *bacabs,* he would be a powerful magician, fully capable of hurling spells that would disable us long before we could carry out our threat to explode the rockets.

Our deaths had merely been delayed.

26

In the tense silence that followed, I heard Gus praying. It sounded as if he were confessing—but to whom, I did not know. Perhaps directly to his god.

"I am sorry for these and all the sins of my past life, especially for . . ."

I tuned out the rest as he began a long list of sins, real and perceived. Some—such as having betrayed the Cristeros to whom Teresa was to have made her courier delivery—made the rebels next to him turn and look upon him with shock and horror. Others seemed trivial in the extreme—unless you were a devout Catholic. Like deliberately failing to observe Sunday Mass once, a month ago, when he was ill with a headache.

Then he began quoting the Bible.

"Then Jesus said unto them, whoso eateth my flesh and drinketh my blood hath eternal life and I will raise him up at the last day. He that eateth my flesh and drinketh my blood dwelleth in me, and I in him . . ."

I shivered. Gus was starting to sound like the cultists. I turned to look at him and noticed something odd through my thermographic goggles. Gus was kneeling on the floor, and had cast off his own goggles. His arms were outstretched, his hands together in prayer. Most of his body appeared normal—with glowing yellow hot spots at the groin and head, typically the warmest portions of the human body. But bright patches of white had appeared between the palms of his hands, as well as over his chest at a spot a little left of center—over the heart.

Now Gus switched to the Lord's Prayer. The rebels—all except Soñador, I noticed, followed his lead, joining their voices to his. I heard Teresa's voice—and then Rafael's.

And Fede's. Compelled perhaps by fear of my impending death or by a simple need to join in spirit with those who were about to be butchered with me, I too began to recite the prayer.

As it ended, Gus continued praying on his own—a prayer that apparently no one else recognized, for none of the others joined in. As he spoke, I saw him draw a cold blue object—a knife—from a sheath on his belt. He held it clenched in one trembling hand, then plunged its blade deep into his left palm. Drawing it free, he held it in the hand that now dripped with blood and repeated the process—stabbing his right hand so hard that several centimeters of the blade protruded from the back of it.

"Father Silvio—no!" Teresa cried. But her voice was drowned out by the startled shouts of her fellow Cristeros. She lunged forward, trying to reach Gus, but Rafael drew her back. She turned, snarled at him with a sound reminiscent of the jungle cat that she really was—and then quieted as Gus began to quote from the Bible once more. Like the rest of us, she stared at him in gape-mouthed wonder.

"And I saw heaven opened, and beheld a white horse, and he that sat upon it had eyes as a flame of fire, and on his head was a crown of fire, and he was clothed with a vesture dipped in blood, and his name is called the Word of God . . ."

The heat spot in Gus' chest dimmed through yellow to orange to red as the spots of white light on his hands grew brighter. My cyberear caught the sound of blood dripping onto the stone floor—a steady *plink, plink* that seemed to occur with the regularity of the beating of a heart. And then my breath caught as I saw the thing that was forming in the air above the priest

The apparition looked like a horse ridden by a gaunt human with glowing red eyes and hair of flame. The rider wore a robe that blazed white-hot in my thermographic goggles—a robe that seemed to be melting and sliding from his body in long, steaming drips. I felt a splash of hot liquid on my arm, raised it to my nose, and sniffed. Blood. More drops fell upon my hair and shoulders. Then the spectral horse threw back its head and whinnied—a sound that shivered through my soul like ice.

Now a crown of fire appeared around the head of the mounted man. It seemed to be forming from the blood of Gus, which rose from the priest's outstretched hands in long, snaking spirals. The crown grew brighter and expanded, extending outward in a wide circle that encompassed the Cristeros. It spread into the sub-basement beyond, toward the Azzie guards . . .

Gunfire erupted from one end of the sub-basement as the guards lost their nerve and started shooting wildly. I ducked, hiding as much from the spirit that Gus had conjured above our heads as from the bullets that whizzed harmlessly through it. As the creature's eyes brushed past me, they seemed to be judging me, finding me wanting . . .

Over the uproar, I heard the priest of Quetzalcóatl chanting. He was casting his own spell—raising his own demons, I saw, when I poked my head above the cases for a quick look. I could see the man clearly—he wasn't bothering to keep under cover any more. He stood with one hand clenched on the jacket collar of the guard closest to him. The other hand held a *macauitl*. It was clear that he'd just used the obsidian-tipped sword—a warm river of orange-red gushed from the throat of the guard he held.

Above the priest, a sinuous, serpentine creature was forming in the air. It writhed and shimmered, slowly becoming more distinct. Its eyes glared with a malevolent light as it opened its jaws wide, revealing fangs that dripped with what I imagined to be venomous blood.

The ring of fire that had sprung from the crown of the spirit that Gus had conjured up continued expanding. Azzie security guards scurried away from it in panic, abandoning Guillermo Acosta. In seconds it would reach the serpent that writhed above the priest's head . . .

I swore softly to myself. Rafael, Fede, Teresa, and I—and the Cristeros—were about to be caught in a magical cross-fire. I didn't want to see what would happen when the two spirits collided.

"Raf!" I cried above the din of screams and spatters of random gunfire. "We've got to get out of here!"

Fede heard me, too, and nodded grimly. I looked around for Soñador and Águila, but the pair seemed to have already bolted. A number of the Cristeros had also taken advantage of the cover that Gus' spirit provided, and were scurrying away.

Rafael rose to a crouch, preparing to run . . .

And was yanked back by Teresa, who clung to his arm. She was already undergoing transformation into her jaguar form—her nails had turned into claws that dug into his arm.

"We can't leave Father Silvio!" she cried.

I glanced over at him. Gus' body was a uniform blue now, cold and dying. Except for his hands, which retained their vivid white glow.

"Father, into thy hands I commend my spirit . . ."

He fell forward, face down. He landed with his arms outstretched and feet together, the image of a man who had crucified himself to save his friends. Slowly his body heat-signature faded from blue to black.

"He's gone," I shouted back. "He sacrificed himself for us . . . for you. Do you want his death to be in vain?"

Angrily, the girl tore the thermographic goggles from her face. I saw cold spots sliding down her cheeks—tears. "No," she said in a voice so soft that only my cyberear picked it up. "I do not." And with that she completed her transformation, dropping to all fours and flowing into the shape of a jungle cat.

Overhead the two spirits met, merged in a fierce tussle of flame and fang—and then split apart, staggering back like two battlefield combatants who had taken the wind out of each other.

Then they turned, seeking easier prey . . .

We ran for all we were worth as the blood spirits descended upon us. Their first victim was the Cristero next to me. I would have thought a good Christian would be immune to the spirit that Gus had conjured, but the horse reared up, striking the rebel down with hooves of fire. I nearly lost it then, knowing that the thing had judged me and found me steeped in sin. I crossed myself as I ran and began to pray in a mindless babble—snatches of every prayer I'd ever forgotten since my childhood church-going days.

Miraculously, the spirit did not reach me.

I heard the priest Acosta scream then—a wordless howl of rage and agony. Glancing back over my shoulder, I saw him stagger forward into the ring of crates, a cool, boxlike object clasped in his arms. I recognized it as the organ-transfer case. He must have found it after I left it on the floor of the *teocalli*. He reached into it and pulled out the severed head of the captain of the team that had won the *ollamaliztli* finals. Then he dropped the head into the hole at the center of the *itzompan*.

Too soon, I thought to myself. *Venus will not rise for several hours yet.*

I barely remember the rest of our scramble through the dimly lit sub-basement. The ground began to tremble underneath our feet, making it difficult to run. Rafael was ahead of me, racing along after Teresa and trying to keep up with her sleek, swift-footed jaguar form. After what seemed an eternity, we reached the staircase that led up into the convent. Teresa flowed up it like a dark shadow, and Rafael scrambled up behind her. He turned at the top to offer me a hand . . .

And then the earthquake began in earnest and the rickety wooden steps leading to safety collapsed into a heap of splinters at my feet.

I cried in my frustration, seeing the trap door that led to safety so far overhead. But then Fede was beside me. Wrapping his arms around my waist he crouched low—and sprang upward, using all the power contained in the hydraulic implants in his cyberlegs. Pain flared in my chest as his arms squeezed against my cracked rib, and stars sparkled before my eyes. As we sailed upward I had a giddy moment, imagining myself a ball that Fede was about to slam through an *ollamaliztli* ring . . .

And then Rafael caught my outstretched arms and hauled me up through the trap door. My chest burned like fire once again as he continued to pull, yanking Fede—who still clung to my waist—through the trap door along with me.

We staggered along a floor that danced under our feet with the shock waves of the earthquake, ducking falling chunks of masonry as we ran. It wouldn't be long, I knew, before the entire convent crashed down upon us. I had a vision of being crushed under heavy wooden beams and chunks of stone . . .

And then I was out the door and running through the darkened streets of Izamal. And not a moment too soon. Behind me the convent creaked, groaned—and collapsed in upon itself with a roar and a cloud of dust.

As the ground suddenly stopped shaking underfoot, I slowed to a jog and turned around for a look. Then I stopped to stare, hugging my arms to my aching chest. Both the convent and the church of Izamal were no more than piles of rubble—grave markers for Gus, the *bacab* of Quetzalcóatl, and any rebels and Azzie troops who hadn't been fortunate enough to get out in time.

Mama G's killer had at last come to justice.

I thought that was the end of it, but then I heard a dull *whumph* of an explosion, deep under the rubble. And then another, louder one. I grabbed Rafael's arm.

"The rockets!" I said. "They're exploding. We'd better get away from here."

"We sure as frag better," Rafael said uneasily. He pointed up the darkened street at a pair of approaching headlights. "There's an Azzie patrol on the way."

I heard the roaring *yeowl* of a jaguar. Teresa stood a few meters away, her tail lashing. She jerked her head in a motion that was easy to interpret: *follow me*.

Summoning up the last of our strength, we ran behind her, back to the hacienda of her employers. The tile-faced building was still intact, despite the fact that other houses nearby had collapsed. We reached it just in time to see Teresa transform back and use her human fingers to tap a code into the door's keypad. And then the door opened and she, Rafael, and Fede ran inside.

Something made me pause in the doorway and look up into the night sky. Overhead, silhouetted against the moon, I saw the sinuous body and outstretched wings of a feathered serpent. Soñador! The dragon too had made a clean escape.

I touched my fingers to my temple in salute, then turned and followed the others into the darkened house.

27

I fastened the seals of my wetsuit and pulled on the rubber-soled boots that would keep my feet warm. After tucking the last few unruly strands of hair under my hood, I paused before putting on my gloves and face mask. Beside me, Fede had suited up also—in a wetsuit that ended at the thighs, since his cyberlegs needed no thermal protection.

I turned to where Rafael stood on a sandy Yucatán beach that was bleached white by the moonlight.

"Are you really going to stay?" I asked him. "Are you certain it's what you want?"

My friend nodded. He'd come to see Fede and I off—Teresa was waiting for him in Mérida.

"I'm sure," he said slowly. "I always wanted to belong to something. To fight the good fight. Back in Seattle, I thought it would be the chillest thing in the world to make it onto a combat biker team. To kick some hoop with the pros. But now I want to stay here in Aztlan and be part of the rebel 'team.' This is where I came from, after all. Where I was born. These people are my blood."

He stared out across the ocean, his eyes hard. "The Azzie government was responsible for my father's death, for me never knowing my relatives, and for Mama G's death. And for the death of a lot of other innocent people. If I can help to make a difference in this fragging world . . ."

He shrugged and shoved his hands in his pockets. I was going to chide him about entering another "discovering my roots" phase, or else tease him that his passion for the rebels would ebb as his ardor for Teresa cooled, but thought better of it. It wasn't like my friend to have made such a lengthy speech—he must have thought this out long and hard. I didn't want to belittle his decision.

Especially since his motivation was so close to my own. Except that I would carry on the fight for justice back home in Seattle. Cleaning up my own back yard, one piece of trash at a time, made more sense to me than traveling thousands of klicks to fight someone else's fight.

I had come to understand the Azzie rebels and sympathize with the cause they fought for. But their enemy was too big, too amorphous. I needed a tighter focus. A single client to fight for, rather than a whole fragging nation. A single bad guy to face down, a single wrong to put right. The rebels could fight for decades without making any significant gains. I'm the type of person who needs concrete results.

I wrapped my arms around Rafael's broad shoulders, standing on tiptoe to plant a kiss on his cheek. "Remember what you said in the *teocalli*?" I said in a whisper. "I love you too. Be careful."

After a moment of surprise, he hugged me back. My wet-suit made a scrunching sound as his muscular arms squeezed me tight.

"Ouch!" I said, only half-jokingly. "My rib."

Fede discreetly nudged my arm. "We'd better get going," he said. "If we don't move soon, we'll miss our boat."

I grinned at that one. Then I let Rafael go.

"Stay frosty," I told him, punching him on the shoulder. "And kick some Azzie butt for me."

He grinned fiercely back at me. "I will," he promised. "I sure as frag will."

I pulled on my gloves and mask, made sure the plexiglass wasn't fogging, and then walked out into the gently lapping waves. I towed a surfboard behind me. Supplied by the AFL, it was no ordinary board but one equipped with a high-thrust engine that would push me through the water at close to twenty klicks. A fuel tank served as its keel. If we were picked up by radar, our low profile, lying flat against the ocean's surface, would fool the Azzies into thinking we were some sort of marine mammal. The thrusters that powered the surfboards wouldn't leave much of a heat signature, either.

Set into the nose of the board was a palm-sized, water-proof device—a global positioning system that would give my precise longitude and latitude. It would help me to locate the ship that lay in wait for us in international waters, just outside the eighty-kilometer strip of ocean that Aztlan claimed.

Beside me, Fede towed a similar surfboard. Reaching waist-deep water, he jumped onto it and lay prone, shoving his feet through straps that would hold him in place. I was about to do the same, but turned around for one last look at Rafael.

Behind me was nothing but empty beach. The big guy had done a quick fade.

I threw myself forward onto my own surfboard, and together with Fede paddled by hand through the surf.

We had a long, cold journey ahead of us—and only a promise from Soñador that the ship that would carry us back to UCAS would be waiting for us when we arrived.

28

I sat on the sofa in my basement suite, watching the latest tridcasts out of Aztlan. I'd set my telecom's Sort 'n' Save program to key in on anything to do with the Yucatán or with the ongoing civil war. But the news bites it had downloaded contained null data—they were just government-whitewashed stories of how the Azzies were dealing harshly and effectively with the "insurgents."

The only hard data I could get was that the rebels had blown up an oil refinery off the coast near Veracruz—although the Azzies hastened to assure the viewing public that no lives were lost and that the rig would be back on line in three days' time, at most. I smiled at that one—footage from UCAS newscasts showed the oil rig to be a twisted ruin, blazing fiercely and spreading a stain of oil over the surrounding ocean. I wondered if Rafael had played a part in its destruction.

My cat Pinkerton, out of sorts at having been intermittently fed by a neighbor while I was away, sat with his back to me, retaliating by refusing to let me pet him. Upstairs, the tenants who had moved into the floor previously occupied by Rafael and Mama G were throwing a noisy party. I turned up the volume of the telecom slightly and used my cyberear to filter out the worst of the laughter and music from upstairs. In response to the increased noise, Pinkerton leaped off the couch and disappeared through his cat door.

Outside, the rain pelted down on a cold, wet Seattle night. I'd been back from Aztlan for a week, but I had yet to acclimatize and was still shivering. I had a pile of telecom messages from angry clients, demanding to know what was happening with their cases, but I left then unanswered. I still wasn't back into work mode. But I'd better be, and soon. The trip to Aztlan had left me virtually penniless.

As Rafael had instructed, I'd pawned anything of his that was of value—not a frag of a lot—and cleared out the rest. I'd kept the sentimental stuff—a holo of Rafael and me from our security guard days, a few of his oversized shirts and one of Mama G's favorite sweaters, and the sad-eyed holo of Christ that had hung above the kitchen door. And Rafael's Harley Scorpion, which I couldn't bear to part with, even though I couldn't ride the thing.

I'd also kept the fragments of the pottery jar in which Mama G had kept her snake. Glued back together, the jar served as a vase for the feather we'd picked up in the cave near Monterrey, after our first encounter with Soñador. The red, green, and turquoise plume helped to reassure me that the crazy and impossible things I'd experienced in Aztlan had been real.

Despite all that had happened, I felt empty. I figured that we'd been successful in bringing Mama G's killer to justice—or at least, in bringing payback to the man who'd ordered her death, if not the actual person who'd killed her on his behalf. All four of the *bacabs* of the Temple of the Sun were dead. But the justice felt incomplete, somehow. Perhaps it would have been more satisfying if I'd put a bullet into the brain of the *bacab* of Quetzalcóatl, rather than watching as he was crushed by tons of falling masonry. Perhaps . . .

I shook my head. Justice was my goal, I reminded myself sternly. Not vengeance. In my line of work, I'd do well to remember that.

I also wondered if we'd really saved the world. Had the Azzie "prophecy" of the end of the current age been just so much bulldrek, or had the world really been on the verge of a catastrophe of biblical proportions? I'd never know for sure. The earthquakes that hit Aztlan while we were there may have been mere coincidence, rather than preludes to the apocalypse.

I was certain of one thing, however. The *iztompan* was gone. If the convent and church collapsing on it hadn't shattered the altar stone, the exploding rockets would have. The secret Mama G had died to keep lay buried forever.

I debated giving Fede a call in Houston, to see how he was recovering from his reconstructive surgery. He'd used Vargas' gold earplugs and pectoral to pay for it—and to set himself up in business as a scalper. But I decided to wait and see the finished product after it had healed. I wondered what sort of look he'd go for and whether it would be as handsome as . . .

Just then my telecom chimed with a soft *ping,* alerting me to an incoming message. I nearly ignored it, thinking it would be just one more irate client. But then, out of some urging I could not explain, I brushed a finger against the Receive icon.

Rafael's voice boomed out at me. The message was voice only, no video.

"*Hola,* Leni. It's me, Rafael. Don't bother trying to send back—I'm routing this through a whole series of LTGs in a single pulse of data so that it can't be traced back to me. I just wanted to let you know that I'm fine—Teresa's fine, too. And the Cristeros are really kicking hoop. Fire and brimstone, and all that jazz. Maybe you saw the results on the evening trids. Well, I'd better go now. Places to go, things to blow . . ."

His voice paused for a heartbeat. Then, "Oh, one last thing, Leni. If you do figure out a way to get a message to me through Angie, there's something I'd like you to include. I want to know who won the conference finals. Did the Seattle Timber Wolves make it into the nationals? We don't get the scores down here. The Azzies don't seem to be interested in the game—silly fraggers. So send me any game highlights you've got."

I laughed out lout at that one. Same old Rafael.

"Oh, and thanks, Leni, for helping me. Mama Grande would have been proud of you. Now, stop moping around and get out there and put some other murdering fragger where he belongs, O.K.?"

As the message ended, I stared out the window at the rain. And smiled. Rafael was down in Aztlan, doing what he did best. Kicking hoop. And here I was, sitting around sulking when I could be out saving my corner of the world from the bad guys.

I sighed, and began listening to the first of my clients'

calls. As the messages played, Pinkerton poked his head in through the cat door, a dead rat hanging limp in his mouth.

I took it for the omen that it was.

My next case, I was certain, would have a successful conclusion.

ABOUT THE AUTHOR

Lisa Smedman's first novel was **The Lucifer Deck**, a Shadowrun® novel published by Roc Books. She has also had a number of short science fiction and fantasy stories published in various magazines and anthologies. Formerly a newspaper reporter, she now works full time as a freelance game designer. She has written a number of adventures for TSR's Ravenloft® line, as well as adventures for several other game systems. She is one of the founding members of Bootstrap Press, publishers of *Adventures Unlimited* magazine. When not writing, she spends her time organizing literary conventions, hiking and playing sports with a local women's outdoors club, and (of course) gaming. She lives in Vancouver, B.C.

An exciting preview from
Beyond the Pale
Book 3 of the Dragon Heart Saga
by Jak Koke

His name was Billy Madson, and he was a boy in the body of a machine.

A boy with a guardian angel hovering around him. Protecting him. Calming him when the vicious memories came rushing back, the violence and the killing. Memories of his previous incarnation—a cyberzombie who was called Burnout.

The angel surrounded and buoyed Billy. The angel was the only reason Billy still lived. The angel's name was Lethe, and he had saved Billy's life. He had shown Billy the images of terrible beauty, blinding light and a song that brought tears to the boy's eyes. A voice of such power and purity that even Lethe's memory of it, filtered through Billy's mechanical body and into the recesses of Billy's mind, had moved him back from the edge of death.

Back among the living.

Now, Billy lay on his back, shackled unceremoniously to a metal operating table. Technicians and doctors had probed and studied him, apparently interested in the technology of his body. A few hours ago, they had left the room, leaving him attached to machines that monitored his brain patterns and the electrical activity of his cyberware.

The room was quite secure, he knew. His mind had automatically analyzed it for avenues of escape. He had done this without thinking, the possible scenarios running like a subroutine in the back of his mind, and he had marveled at himself for it.

I am trained to kill and to destroy. A combat machine.

"Someone's coming," Lethe said, his soothing voice dropping into Billy's mind through a device in his cybernetics called the IMS—Invoked Memory Stimulator.

Billy opened his eyes to the darkened room. It was night and moonlight shone through the barred and fenced-over windows, the crisscrossed shadows rippling over the floor and table next to him. Like hatch-marked silver.

"Not the same as before," Lethe said. "I sense stealth and barely contained aggression in those who approach."

Billy yanked at the heavy bands that anchored his legs, arms, chest, and head to the table, but he couldn't even turn his head, and much of his connection to his cybernetics had been disrupted by the doctors. "Can you tell if they're coming to kill us?"

Billy sensed laughter through the IMS. "No, my friend, I can't read minds. I can only sense auras. Here they come."

The door to the room opened and someone entered, perhaps several people. Billy could hear them only when he cranked up the sensitivity on his cybernetic ears to their maximum. He could sense the slight pressure shift in the room as well.

"Señor, aquí!" The words were barely audible, subvocalized into a throat mic or headware, but Billy understood what they meant. "Over here, sir."

The Azzies have found me, finally.

Several people surrounded him. Billy couldn't see them and suspected that they had hidden themselves magically. He felt pressure against his chest and a compartment popped open. Then something was jacked into him, running stics.

Billy knew that in his past life as the cyberzombie Burnout this had happened to him on a regular basis. Just a routine systems check. The portable deck was speaking to his brain, telling him exactly what parts were malfunctioning, what parts worked and how much damage he had sustained in his quest to destroy Ryan Mercury.

A quest that now seemed so distant, so remote as to be unimportant. In fact it had been Ryan Mercury who had brought Burnout so close to death that he had lost his identity. Or rediscovered it. His previous incarnation died in the massive fire in Dunkelzahn's arboretum, and Billy was not sad about it.

Perhaps Ryan Mercury did me a favor by almost killing me.
The irony did not escape Billy.

The diagnostic program indicated that his homing signal had been destroyed, probably when he had fallen into Hells Canyon. Another confrontation with Mercury that seemed like eons ago even though it had only been a week or so.

"Remarkable," whispered one of the invisible people standing over him. "He has sustained a huge amount of abuse, but he lives on. I think we should abort termination and take him back with us."

"*Sí,*" came the response

The paralysis started in his toes and moved up rapidly, system by system through his knees, legs, waist. Up through his torso and chest it traveled, the sheer absence of feeling. No tingling numbness, just a digital erasure of his sensory perception.

His taste turned off with a click, then his sight, hearing, until finally he was alone inside a vast ocean of darkness. A brain in a sensory depravation tank.

Lethe, he thought.

Yes, Billy?

Could you show me Thayla again?

Billy felt the spirit smile inside and suddenly the darkness gave way to a brilliant light. The silence yielded to the glorious song of the goddess Thayla who stood on a cracked plane of rock. The light shone from her like a beacon against the darkness, a wondrous sun in the blackest firmament. The song and the light were one and the same. Her voice rang out, rising and falling in beautiful melodious waves, washing over him like warm surf. Until he cared not who he was and why he was there.

He merely wanted to stay forever.

Lethe's memory of Thayla was flawless, the sensation of the experience overwhelming Billy until he knew that he must join his guardian angel in his quest to help Thayla. The beauty must not be destroyed.

But we're in no position to help, he thought. *When we wake, we will be in Aztlan.*

If *we* wake.

MORE EXCITING ADVENTURES FROM
SHADOWRUN®